Praise for the national bestselling Merry Muffin Mysteries

"Start with a spunky protagonist named Merry, mix in some delicious muffins, add a mysterious castle in upstate New York, and you've got the ingredients for a wonderful cozy mystery series."

—Paige Shelton, *New York Times* bestselling author of *To Helvetica and Back*

"Another fun read . . . There were plenty of twists to keep me turning those pages. The story is well-plotted and had me guessing whodunit right until the very end. The author has thoughtfully provided some yummy recipes."

—MyShelf.com

"Mix the crazy cast of characters with humor, mystery, and romance and you have a delightful story that will keep you captivated for hours. It's a page turner!"

—Socrates' Book Reviews

"[A] great cozy with varied and interesting characters, a nice plot with a few twists, and a good main character who has some baggage to work through . . . Excellent—loved it! Buy it now and put this author on your watch list."

—Mysteries and My Musings

"Victoria Hamilton proves herself again as [a] master plotter . . . Merry Wynter is a delightful protagonist . . . [Hamilton's] characters are complex and most are likable . . . The plot had enough twists and curves to keep me challenged and entertained."

—Open Book Society

"Another engaging mystery with a fascinating locked-room angle, and an intriguing cast."

Muffin to Fear

VICTORIA HAMILTON

BERKLEY PRIME CRIME
New York

BERKLEY PRIME CRIME
Published by Berkley
An imprint of Penguin Random House LLC
375 Hudson Street, New York, New York 10014

ISBN: 9780425282595

First Edition: August 2017

Printed in the United States of America
1   3   5   7   9   10   8   6   4   2

Cover art by Ben Perini
Book design by Kristin del Rosario

Thank you to librarians everywhere. In a world where knowledge is not always respected or prized, you consistently do the important work of making sure every man, woman, and child with curiosity and a love for the truth can read what the great thinkers and writers in history have handed down. Intellectual curiosity and open hearts and minds will save the world, if we let them.

ACKNOWLEDGMENTS

Copyeditors are the unsung heroes of fiction writing. They keep authors from committing terrible errors in judgment, as well as in spelling and grammar. I'd like to extend a huge "Thank You" to Randie Lipkin, who, by pointing out one glaring flaw in *Muffin To Fear* (as well as many other smaller errors), kept my favorite fictional librarian, Hannah Moore, from making an ethical faux pas that would horrify any librarian.

Prologue

READER, I MARRIED him.

That is certainly the most famous line of all from romantic fiction, is it not? In Charlotte Brontë's masterwork *Jane Eyre*, it goes: "Reader, I married him. A quiet wedding we had . . ." And so I start with that, as it was true for me. What was there to wait for? About three weeks after Virgil Grace asked for my hand in marriage, we stood by the fireplace in the parlor, and with Pish presiding—he has the legal right to perform weddings and has done the honors before—Gogi, Hannah, Lizzie, Emerald, Binny, Doc, and a few others stood with us as we quietly wed. I said, "I do," Virgil said, "I do," and we all cried, even Virgil. It was the best moment of my life, facing him, our hands joined, and watching one tear well in each of his gorgeous brown eyes and trickle down his cheek.

We then left town the morning after a raucous reception, driving to New York City to stay at Pish's condo for a two-week honeymoon. Pish had returned from there to Wynter

Castle in time for the wedding after taking Roma Toscano, the opera singer, back and visiting his mother, who was now off with Pish's aunt Lush on a cruise. His apartment is luxurious; I know it well because my friend is a masterful party giver. I have spent many an evening in his New York home as he played show tunes while various entertainment types lounged singing, chatting, or getting quietly blotto. He was an investment counselor for years, with many wealthy clients from the various arms of the entertainment industry and still retains a few, but since he took his own financial advice he doesn't *need* to work. One of his best investments was property, he has always said, and his condo, in a lovely building overlooking Central Park, has more than doubled in value since he first bought it.

It's also superbly comfortable, with a housekeeper who comes in every morning for three hours except on the weekend. Virgil and I stayed in bed the first two days, fortunately on a weekend so I didn't have to deal with Mrs. MacGregor, a dour Scotswoman who gets along well with Pish's mother, and that's saying a lot. They have what I call a Sourpuss Alliance. I was finally forced to get out of bed Monday morning for food and a shower, and to be decently dressed by the time Mrs. MacGregor arrived. Being married to Virgil is the best combination workout regimen and diet I've ever been on, and that's all I'll say about *that*.

After the weekend in bed we did *other* stuff; we watched old movies, *Barefoot in the Park* and *The Out of Towners*, since we were in New York. We ate out, attended the theater, shopped, walked hand in hand in Central Park—autumn in New York is the best—visited friends (it was a *lot* of fun introducing him to my old friends) and went to an ice hockey game between the Rangers and the Islanders. I thought I'd loathe it, but it was fun! It was thrilling hanging on to Virgil while he fist pumped at every goal and jumped up and down . . . cheering for the Rangers, of course. Why it's "of course," I don't know, but that's all he said when I asked who we were rooting for. He bought an oversize Rangers T-shirt, which I wore to bed at his request.

Kinky!

After two glorious weeks, I awoke on the last day and lay on my side, watching him sleep. He's the kind of guy who grows a beard moment by moment, and dark stubble clothed his steely jaw, dark lashes resting on his tanned cheeks. In repose his face isn't quite as strong-looking, his cheeks softer, throat skin slack, dark unruly hair mussed. His shoulders are broad and sturdy. He sleeps with one arm flung up over his head, and he has a dark swirl of hair across his upper chest that narrows and points down intriguingly under the covers.

"Are you done watching me sleep?" he growled.

I chuckled and ducked under the covers. "I guess I am," I said, my voice muffled.

Chapter One

❋ ❋ ❋

WE STARTED OUR drive back to Autumn Vale in a fog of happy weariness. It's a long way and takes seven or eight hours, at least, but Virgil likes driving, so I got us out of the city and then he took over. I let him pick the tunes. He's not fond of opera or show tunes, preferring old Motown, the lingering tutelage of his buddy and now partner in detective work, Dewayne Lester. I like all kinds of music, so I bopped along with the Temptations, the Supremes, Smokey Robinson, and both the Queen and the Godfather of Soul.

At a certain point, though, he decided to take his own route. We hit a construction zone that wasn't indicated anywhere, and he got impatient. He's the kind of driver who taps his thumbs on the steering wheel while he gets more and more agitated. We then got backed up in traffic, and in no time we were quarreling, finally lapsing into sullen silence when he refused to go where I wanted. That lasted until we arrived in Geneseo (not far from Autumn Vale), got out to stretch our legs, and started kissing; we quickly discovered a nature preserve and used the gorgeous, quiet, lush grassland for what I assume officials meant by the allowed activities including "low-impact recreation." As chilly as the air was on my skin, Virgil kept me warm. Afterward, we shimmied back into our clothes—luckily, I was wearing mid-rise boyfriend jeans, a T-shirt, and cotton cardigan, instead of the jeggings I had considered—picked the dead grass out of our hair, got back on the highway, and were on the best of terms again. Late in the afternoon, as the sun began to sink toward the treetops and the air got chillier, we pulled up to the castle exhausted and utterly blissful.

Which lasted about thirty seconds until I registered the array of vans, cars, and a cube van parked willy-nilly over my flagstone parking area. Several guys and a few gals in jeans and golf shirts emblazoned with the letters *HHN* bustled around carrying orange reels of black wire, lights on tripod stands, black suitcases rimmed in steel, steel suitcases rimmed in steel, tripods with screw mounts, and assorted other kinds of electrical and electronic equipment.

"What's going on?" I said, slamming Virgil's car door as he circled and popped open the trunk.

"You expecting company?"

"No. Why do I have a feeling this is Pish's doing?" Pish, my best and one of my oldest friends, had gotten me into numerous scrapes over the last year, from a murder among his aunt's group of friends I had labeled the Legion of Horrible Ladies, to Roma Toscano, a histrionic and hysterical opera diva who was detained by the FBI and almost arrested for murder. I have to admit, though, that he was not responsible for problems previous to those, including the body I found just days after arriving at my inherited castle near Autumn Vale, New York, more than a year ago now.

But this most definitely spelled trouble, with a capital

Pish. It appeared to be some sort of television or movie shoot. Had he booked a commercial? A movie of the week?

"You talk to Pish," Virgil said. "I'll get our stuff organized and start taking it in and upstairs." Virgil had moved into the castle with me while putting his house on the market to sell. Jack McGill, our real estate agent and my best friend Shilo's new husband, had sold it quickly to a couple from out of town, but closing was still a few weeks away. We had plans for how and where we were actually going to live and had started the process with the help of Turner Construction, but hadn't shared the full plans with anyone but Pish and a couple of select others.

As Virgil started toting his first load into the castle—I had, of course, shopped while in New York, and bought presents for friends, as well as myself—I approached one of the men, a slim guy in his thirties, olive complexion, and with jet-black hair and black eyes framed by black glasses. "Pardon me, but who *are* you?" I asked.

He looked up from the silver metal case he was rummaging in and frowned. "Who's asking?"

"I don't mean you in particular, I mean all of you, all of *this*," I said, pointing toward the trucks and stacks of equipment. "*All* of you!"

"Chi-Won Zhu. But just call me Chi."

"And what do you do, Chi?"

"I'm an effects creator."

"Effects, as in special?" My nerves frayed just a skosh.

Just then Pish came trotting out the door, waving his hands in the air. "Merry! My *darling*. I just spoke with Virgil. How *is* the blissful bride? You are *glowing*; it must be happiness."

Uh-oh. He was speaking in italics, which meant he was hiding something or feeling scattered. "Right now it's confusion with a hint of panic, Pish," I said. "What is all this? These vehicles, HHN, an *effects creator*?"

"Ah well, yes." He clapped his hands together and rubbed them. "You're home early! I *told* you when we talked on Monday to stay through the weekend, and here it is, just Thursday."

"We have to talk to the construction company. You *know* that, Pish!"

"Yes, yes. Of *course*! Anyway, come inside, tell me all about your honeymoon, then I'll tell you what *fun* we're having."

I took his arm and we entered. Inside was worse than outside . . . *much* worse. The great hall, normally a calm, echoey oasis, the heart of my real American castle, was filled with people consulting one another in loud tones, more cases of equipment, wires and cords snaking up the stairs, draped on the banisters and hanging from the gallery railing. There was even a burly fellow with a camera on a body mount. He was filming a guy with sandy hair who mounted a small camera on a tall tripod. Why was someone filming a guy setting up a camera? It made no sense.

Virgil, who had gone back outside, followed us in with my second suitcase and dropped it, chuckling. I turned and glared at him. "Don't you start."

He cast a sympathetic look at Pish. "You've stepped in it now, pal."

"If Merry will just hear me out—"

"Don't even." I stepped over some wires, dodged a boom mic that was headed my way, ignored the sandy-haired guy who was glaring at me for ruining his shot, and said, over my shoulder, "Pish, *kitchen*!"

In my sanctuary, the commercially outfitted kitchen my weird old great-uncle Melvyn Wynter had designed before he was murdered and I inherited the pile of stone called Wynter Castle, I sat down at the long trestle table with a cup of tea from McNulty's, a specialty tea and coffee shop in New York. Away from the mysterious hordes in the great hall, I felt the calm of my two-century-old castle seep into my bones. Pish was my saving grace, my guardian angel for many years, the friend who saved me from self-immolation after the death of my beloved first husband, Miguel Paradiso, almost nine years ago. He deserved much more than I could ever repay, and his wild ideas always had a way of turning out. Pretty much.

Okay, *usually*.

"So what's going on?" I asked, and took a long sip of tea, rolling my eyes back at the wonder of the taste. Good black tea is like honey: warm, delicious, full of flavor.

He took a long breath and sighed. "It all started when you were in Spain—"

"Pish, I mean what's happening *now*!"

"I know, I know, but I have to go back to the summer to tell you."

I had gone, in June, to visit my former mother-in-law, Miguel's mother, Maria, who was dying and wanted to make peace with me before she did. She had never liked me, and had demanded, after Miguel's death, that I change my last name back to Wynter. We made our peace, but I stayed on weeks after her death, cocooned in the protection of the Paradiso wealth. I realize now I was just figuring things out, but I had happily made the right decision, to come home where I needed to be, at Wynter Castle and in Virgil's arms.

"Okay, so tell me your way," I said.

He composed himself as I watched. Pish is a lovely man, slim, exquisitely dressed in slacks and a polo-neck sweater with the sleeves pushed up, long-fingered hands with just a signet ring on one finger. His longish hair, just touching his collar, is a natural (or natural-*looking*; I *know* his secrets, as does a certain hairdresser in Autumn Vale) light brown despite his being somewhere north of sixty. He is cultured and wise, talented and deep, and I love him like the father I've never had, combined with the wittiest New York friend a girl could ask for.

"While you were gone to Spain this summer I had a few odd experiences in the castle."

Odd experiences? *Every* experience in Autumn Vale and its environs tends to end up odd, mostly because the people are odd. Endearing, likable, but odd. "Like what?"

"Things being moved from one room to another, voices whispering, shadows moving. . . . I didn't know what to think."

"How does that relate to all of this?" I said, waving my hand out toward the great hall area.

"I'm getting to it," he said with a frown, faint lines of worry and exasperation bracketing his mouth and underlining his eyes. "I called a friend, Chuck Sandberg, who is in charge of programming for HHN."

"Ah," I said, recognizing now the symbol on the trucks, shirts, and jackets of the busy bodies. "That's Helping Hands Network. They started out as a craft and gardening channel a few years back, now they're kind of an anything-goes channel."

"They have a show called *Haunt Hunt*. Lush is obsessed with it; *swears* she has seen spirits all her life."

I remained silent with just a lift of my eyebrow, not surprised in the slightest by Pish's flighty and charming aunt's ghostly visions.

Pish ignored my expression. "I spoke briefly with the producer, Hugh Langley. He was perfectly lovely. We talked about Wynter Castle, and I told him too much, probably, about what had happened in the last year here. I was rattled."

That seldom happens. "I'm sorry, Pish," I said, covering his hand with my own. "You've never said anything to me."

This time *he* gave the look, and I felt a moment of vexation at myself. Maybe I'm not as open as I like to think. And maybe the murders that have happened had left him feeling more shaken than I knew.

"Anyway, I then talked to one of their experts, Todd

Halsey, a paranormal investigator, and he gave me some tips to understand what was going on. Did you know there are different types of hauntings? Two types are intelligent and residual. *Residual* is like an echo of things that have happened in the past, and *intelligent* is when a spirit is still stuck in one place, interacting with the living."

I was silent, wondering where this was going.

"Todd was *very* helpful, spent a good hour on the phone with me. He's had the most amazing experiences."

Why did it sound like he was trying to convince me? "And . . . ?" I was starting to understand what this all was about, and I didn't like it.

Pish had poured himself tea from the pot, and now moved his cup in a circle, sloshing a little over the edge. "I thought that was the end of it, but about two weeks ago—just after you kids left for New York—Todd called and said, would it be okay if we moved the shoot up a little, since they had a sudden cancellation." He shrugged. "I didn't know what to say."

"But . . . you hadn't arranged for the show to come here?"

"No, I honestly don't believe I did, but Todd was under the impression I had. We got muddled, I'm not sure how. Todd sounded *so* disappointed when I said I didn't think we could do it."

Ah, now I was beginning to see a glimmer of light. In his business dealings as an investment counselor and even as a writer of nonfiction to do with scam artists and their cons, Pish is cool, reflective, and unflappable, but in his interpersonal relationships he is a people pleaser. "And so . . . ?"

"He had been so kind and had spent so much time with me on the phone. I said if he and his people could come right then, I supposed it would be okay."

Pish hates to disappoint, especially when someone has done him a favor. Just what I needed, some wackadoodle crew of paranormal wonks peeping around looking for ghosts in my unhaunted castle. "Pish, I hope . . ." I paused, not knowing what to say.

"I know, my darling, I know, but he said they only take three or four days to shoot an episode." He cast me a guilty look. "I truly thought they'd be here and done and long gone before you and Virgil got home." I was about to protest, but he jumped back into speech rapidly, hands splayed out in a beseeching gesture. "I didn't want to disturb you about it, not on your honeymoon!"

"In other words, you thought you'd present it to me fait accompli."

He shrugged, tacitly admitting that. "But then they were at a paranormal convention and had to put off coming here until they were all available, so . . . they arrived this afternoon."

All I wanted was a nap. However, with the amount he has done for me, and with the love I hold in my heart for him, Pish could ask me to make the castle into a rocket launching pad and I'd probably say yes. Eventually. And Virgil's and my honeymoon in New York was perfect mostly thanks to Pish; the loan of his condo, his theater tickets, his housekeeper, and numerous other treats he arranged. Life's too short to sweat the small stuff, and this was *definitely* small stuff. "How does this work?" I asked, giving in.

"Well, they film at night."

"*All* night? Starting *tonight*?"

He winced. "We could put them off for tonight, I suppose, but that would only prolong the shoot."

I considered my options. Virgil had entered the kitchen but stood by the door, lounging against the doorframe, arms crossed over his chest, grinning. I was distracted, as always, by my handsome husband—how weird to say *that* again— and muttered, "Okay, all right. Did you hear that, Virgil? We have a haunted castle on our hands."

He crossed the room, took my face in his big hands, and kissed me. "Dewayne left me a message," he said, looking into my eyes. "We've got something starting tomorrow that'll take me to Rochester for a day or two. Duty calls."

I melted into a puddle of slush, and my day turned mellow yellow. "Okay. But I'll miss you. We still have tonight. . . . Oh, wait." I was snapped out of my happy, sensual dream by reality. "No, we don't." I glanced over at my friend. "They start filming tonight, right?"

Pish shrugged. "Sorry, lovers. But yes."

"Come for a walk with me now," Virgil said, holding out his hand. "I want to see how far along they are with the foundation work near the Fairy Tale Woods."

"Okay."

So . . . what are the Fairy Tale Woods? They are a part of my past. Wynter Castle and its environs is the huge property I inherited from my great-uncle Melvyn Wynter. It has taken me a while to explore and discover it all. In the spring I found some odd structures in the far woods, strange little broken-down buildings, one of stone and one that appeared to be a wooden gingerbread house, among others. Then with my teenage friend Lizzie's help, I found a picture, the only one I know of, that shows me as a toddler, my father, my great-uncle Melvyn, and my grandfather Murgatroyd Wynter. In it I am being held by my father, all of us posed near those odd buildings, only half-built.

It turns out that my paternal relatives were building these structures for *me*, a fairy-tale forest of magical hand-built stone and wood houses. Unfortunately, their work was interrupted by my grandfather's death and an estrangement between my father and great-uncle Melvyn.

As for that foundation being constructed near what we now call the Fairy Tale Woods . . . that is Virgil's and my semi-secret project. More about that later.

I ignored Pish's salacious chuckle as I agreed to the walk.

"We're just going to see how far along Turner Construction is on the foundation, and if they've located a spot to drill the well," I said with a virtuous sniff.

Virgil dropped Pish a wink and made an okay sign with his thumb and forefinger. "Yup, that's all. We're just going to see about some drilling."

Chapter Two

❈ ❈ ❈

TOGETHER, WE WALKED away from the hubbub around the castle, past the garage, a few other outbuildings and back across the wide-open expanse of my land, which is bounded on all sides by forest. The forest between my land and the road is a planned arboretum, planted by my uncle and grandfather, of a whole series of native tree species. I love it. It connects me to my forebears, none of whom I knew, unless you count some vague impressions of my great-uncle Melvyn Wynter from a visit when I was a child, before my mother had a huge argument with him that lasted the rest of her life. That explains why my inheritance of Wynter Castle and the Wynter lands came as such a surprise to me almost two years ago, when I first learned about it.

It was late autumn, already November. The trees had shed most of their leaves, except for a few stubborn oak and beech youngsters along the far tree line, who hold their brown leaves until the new leaves start growing in spring. I like that as a symbol of stubborn survival against all odds. It was a lovely walk, in silence, just holding hands and tromping through long, dead yellow grass. I like that Virgil and I can be silent together, with neither thinking anything is wrong.

Turner Construction had indeed dug the foundation, poured the footings, and had already built a concrete block foundation, strengthened it with reinforcing steel bars, and poured the fill, which now needed to cure before more work could be done. It was a gaping hole in the landscape, but soon it would be our home. We were moving out of the castle at some point in the near future, but we hadn't told anyone other than Pish, Rusty Turner, and his crew (who were sworn to secrecy) *exactly* what we were doing. Unbelievable how fast this was going since we had made the decision in October. This was our future, and I was unbearably excited to show everyone, and yet oddly hesitant to jinx it. I leaned against Virgil, and we stared at what was literally the foundation of our future. It was chilly, but my husband warmed me up.

I was singing by the time we got back to the castle from our walk, little bits and pieces of Gladys Knight's ridiculously sexy "If I Were Your Woman." When we got to his car, I kissed Virgil good-bye in a lingering manner. I noted that I was being watched as he drove away to meet Dewayne in town to talk about their latest case. I strolled across the flagstone toward one of the vans.

"You're the newlywed, right?" a young woman said as she stacked orange reels of black electrical cord by the open back doors of the van. She was tall and slim, narrow hips, no chest, spiky purple-dyed hair, gamine face, but with biceps and deltoids that appeared impressively developed under her skintight T-shirt.

"I'm the owner of the castle, Merry Wynter. Merry *Grace* Wynter now, I guess." We were both going to take the other's name. He would be Virgil Anthony Wynter Grace and I'd be Merry Louise Grace Wynter.

"So that's a yes. I could tell just by the look on your faces. You two are still in the loco period of marriage."

"I beg your pardon?"

"Hey, I get it. I know exactly what that feels like, that sense of only wanting to stare into the guy's eyes and missing him whenever you're apart." She grinned and strode forward, hand outstretched. "I should introduce myself. I'm Serina Rogers."

"And what do you do on this show?"

"Sound. Have you ever seen *Haunt Hunt*?"

I shook my head.

"Okay. Well, on-screen they'd have you believe the *Haunt Hunt* talent does all the wiring, sound, filming, everything, but there's a whole bunch of us tech crew types."

"I met Chi-Won Zhu when I first arrived. I guess he's part of the tech crew, special effects, or something?"

She smiled, a mischievous grin turning up her thin lips. "Don't say that too loud, at least not when Todd or Stu are nearby. It's not *special effects*, it's either 'mechanical operations' or 'technical operations manager' in the IMDb listing."

"Hmm. Okay. So what does he actually *do* on the show?"

"Whatever needs doing," she said, vaguely. "He's talented at stunts and effects, from what I understand, though we don't do that kind of thing on our show. He's worked in the movies before and has loads of experience. I don't know why he's working on *Haunt Hunt*."

"So why do you work on the show?"

"Why not? It's close to home, and there aren't that many good jobs in television in western New York. I like it."

I was curious about how it would all go down, and this gal seemed affable, so I decided to make a friend of her. "I'm a little lost here, I'll admit," I said, rubbing my arms. I found it too chilly for my sweater, though Serina had bare arms. "I just got back from my honeymoon this afternoon and find all of this going on. I'd appreciate an introduction to the . . . what do you call them all?"

Serina eyed me for a moment, then tossed the last reel of electrical wire into a duffel at her feet. "Mostly, we're sorted into cast and crew. I'm crew—sound engineering manager—and I have an intern who flunked out of Seneca College in Canada. He's not too smart, but he does what he's told to the letter and he understands the equipment. He takes care of sound on the second unit. We have camera operators, sound, tech assistants, and then there's the cast." After a pause, the light autumn breeze riffling her funky, choppy hair, she nodded and slammed the van doors shut. "Okay, look, I'll introduce you around and explain what's going on. You have a right to know what's going to happen in your home."

"I'd appreciate that," I said. I helped her carry a couple of duffel bags in, though she got impatient over my difficulty in lugging the heavier one and grabbed it from me, hoisting it up to her shoulder along with its twin with no more trouble than lifting an infant. We trudged past the other HHN vehicles into the castle, reentering the bustle and noise. I set down my burden.

Two young fellows were working in the great hall. One kicked out a tripod and set it near the base of the grand staircase while another fell with glad cries on the duffel I had toted in. He grabbed a reel of electrical wire out of it and began to snake the wire across the floor toward an electrical outlet, taping it down as he went. A young woman was up in the gallery doing much the same thing, the ripping sound of tape and the chatter as they talked among themselves echoing into the upper reaches of my thirty-foot ceilings.

If this was any indication of the bustle going on everywhere . . . Overwhelmed, I muttered, "Why do I have the feeling this is going to be a nightmare?"

Serina smiled and grabbed me, her bony fingers digging into my fleshier arm. "It'll be okay. We'll do our job and be out of your hair in no time. Come on; I'll introduce you around."

She dragged me back to the kitchen and showed me their main storage area, the butler's pantry along the back hallway, where boxes and cases of equipment were stored. They had a mobile viewing and editing booth in one of the vans, she said, though most of the postproduction editing would be done back at their studio. The trail back to the great hall seemed a flurry of wires and electronics, cameras, sound equipment, and *more* wires. They had a central setup, but were prepping other rooms all at the same time with wires and cameras. She explained that they were taping wires down to the floor to keep them from being a tripping hazard.

I swallowed hard. "These floors . . . this castle is two hundred years old."

"Relax," she said. "We do this all the time, mostly in historic homes. We're careful."

We returned to the great hall, and I noticed a long folding table near the staircase. It held a disorganized jumble of odd devices. "What are all of these things?" I asked, picking up one slim box just bigger than my hand. It had a digital screen, blank at the moment. There were three of the devices, among others.

"That's an EMF meter . . . electromagnetic field meter," she said. "Ghost hunters use all kinds of equipment, some specifically for ghost hunting and other stuff that has been modified for the purpose. EMFs come as single-axis, or tri-axis models; this one, a tri-axis, is pricier. We have several of those. They're usually used to find problems in electrical wiring, but the hunters use it to find spikes in the EMF, which they say indicates the presence of a spirit."

"Why?" I asked.

She shook her head and smiled. "You'll have to ask them."

"But you probably know about it. Can't you explain it?"

"Talk to the talent," she said. "The rest of this stuff is

interesting, too," she said, picking things up, turning them over, showing them to me. "There are K2 meters, digital thermometers to measure cold spots, infrared cameras, night-vision goggles, EVP recorders—"

"EVP?" I said, seizing on the acronym. "What's that?"

"Electronic voice phenomena. It's a recorder that is supposed to take in disembodied voices, even things the hunters don't hear."

I rolled my eyes.

Serina chuckled. "Uh, Merry? Your skepticism is showing. Contain it when you're around the cast or you'll end up with an argument. They can be a vindictive bunch if they suspect you're laughing at them." It sounded like she spoke from experience. Her tone was more serious when she added, "You do want them on your side."

A tall gentleman ducked his head out of the dining room and glanced around the entry hall. "What the hell did someone put the equipment table out here for?" he roared. "You!" he shouted, pointing at one of the young guys taping down electrical wire. "Get your buddy and move this into the dining room. Now!" He retreated.

I'd have to find the show online and watch a few episodes so I'd know what to expect. The young fellows squeezed past us with the table, sending me staggering sideways, and we followed. They marched the table across the dining room and set it down near the arched windows. A cluster of crew members broke up and some scattered. Serina led me to the gentleman who had commanded the crew to move the table of equipment.

"This is Hugh Langley," Serina said.

He was a tall, distinguished-looking man with a fringe of gray hair surrounding a polished pate. He held a clipboard, a smartphone, and his nerves on a tether, it appeared, from his icy demeanor.

"He's the producer," Serina muttered. "He doesn't always

join us on our shoots, but this time he's acting as field producer." To the gentleman, she said, "Hugh, this is Merry Wynter, who actually owns this pile."

"Hello, Merry," he said, with a smile that tugged on the corners of his lips. "Thank you so much for allowing us to go on with our schedule. I understand from Mr. Lincoln that you didn't know about this until you arrived home from your honeymoon. You're extraordinarily gracious to allow this motley crew to invade." His voice had an intangible accent, *almost* English, but not quite, posh, but not exactly pretentious. It was pleasant, well modulated. "I had to come myself when I heard we were shooting at a castle. Your home is lovely."

"Thank you so much." I extended my hand and we shook. "Welcome to Wynter Castle."

Everything about him screamed money, from his Savile Row shooting jacket (olive green with a maroon plaid) to his Berluti shoes, old but very classy and expensive, polished to a high sheen, with gleaming gold buckles. His feet were pretty big; there were likely not a lot of shoes that fit him well unless he had them made. He had very pale blue eyes and big horsey teeth, slightly yellowing and very much his own. In fact, he looked kind of like Prince Philip only younger, with the slight stoop in his posture of someone who had to bend over to speak to people quite a bit.

"I hope we don't inconvenience you too much."

"As long as I can go on with my life in the meantime and have access to my kitchen during the day, I'm good." Autumn Vale needs my constant supply of muffins. I had left two weeks' worth frozen for Golden Acres (Gogi Grace's retirement residence) and the Vale Variety and Lunch, but fresh was far better!

"I'll keep that in mind."

"You should meet the others, now that you've paid homage to the head guy," Serina said. "Todd and Rishelle are in here somewhere."

We moved away, and Hugh shouted to his crew, "I need someone to sort out this equipment. Let's get organized."

As I followed, Serina explained that Todd, whom Pish had talked to originally, was the lead investigator with his partner, Stu Jardine. Rishelle was Todd's wife. According to Serina, she had shoehorned herself into the team, insisting on becoming a part of the show once it became popular. It sounded like Rishelle was resented for hopping on the bandwagon as it was almost to the top of the hill while the rest of them had been pushing steadily from the bottom.

"Todd started out doing this part-time with Stu, just two guys pursuing their passion for paranormal investigation."

There was admiration in her voice, and it hinted that I was right about her feelings concerning Rishelle's recent addition to the team. "Did they have a job before this?"

"They were media consultants originally and kept doing it, investigating the paranormal stuff part-time. They first had a short-lived series on paranormal investigation. When it died they started *Haunt Hunt*, and in the last three years it's taken off like crazy. Hugh was new at HHN, and I give him a lot of credit for its success. He's made key decisions that have panned out well."

"Like . . . ?"

"Much as I hate to admit it, like bringing psychics on board. That was all Hugh. Every time Hugh makes a change we all hold our breath, but every single time he's been right."

"That's probably why he's a producer." I followed Serina.

My real honest-to-goodness American castle is big, with the library, dining room, and parlor lined up on one side of the great hall, and the breakfast room and ballroom along the other, and the huge kitchen at the back, with a long butler's pantry hallway, off of which was the only main floor half bath, and a side door. The dining room is large and can easily seat thirty or forty people. There is a big stone fireplace at one end with a piano by it, and a full wall of Gothic arched windows. The equipment table was now set up by them right next to a bank of laptop computers on tables with a few of my dining room chairs hauled over to provide seating.

A late-thirtyish guy sat in front of one of the laptops tapping at a keyboard and grunting at the screen, while another guy, a little older, watched over his shoulder.

"So that's Ian Mackenzie—the guy at the computer—and Arnie Ball looking on," Serina said. "Arnie is lead camera and Ian is second camera. Right now they're checking angles for the DVR camera shots. They set up a lot of unmanned digital video recording cameras around the site, as you may have noticed. They're sometimes set to run constantly while a hunt is on, or just motion activated." She turned and muttered behind her hand, "Ian's okay as a camera operator, but his real genius is editing, which takes a lot of skill when you're dealing with some questionable occurrences. He can make a door creaking into a major moment. Arnie's the better cameraman."

Arnie was the guy operating the Steadicam when I first arrived.

She strolled over to the table. "Guys, this is Merry Wynter, the castle owner."

"Hey, Merry," they chorused, both looking up only momentarily before bending back to the screen.

A young man and woman approached with technical questions, and I was able to get no more than a visual impression of the two fellows. Ian Mackenzie, the younger of the two and sitting at the computer, was fair and plump with a red complexion and thinning, frizzy, fading reddish hair, squinting and blinking through wire-framed glasses. He was slightly disheveled, wearing a Windbreaker with *Haunt Hunt* emblazoned in yellow over the HHN symbol, two hands clasped in a prayerful manner.

Arnie Ball, a more substantial and imposing man, was heavyset, broad shouldered, with dark, wavy, unruly hair held down by a gray knitted toque. He was a good-looking guy in the same way Virgil is, only forty pounds or so heavier. He must have been at least six-four, though he was slouching. His feet were clad in multicolored high-top sneakers adorned with the trademark swoosh along the side. It was an untidy look, because his khaki cargos sagged down his butt, the hem half tucked into his shoes and half dragging on the floor.

When I see a guy like that I want to style him, or at least tidy him up. That *hair* . . . and the knitted *toque*. It set my teeth to clenching in dismay. Any man that big should know he stands out, and look after himself, at least in public.

We wove around tables and entered the library, one of my favorite rooms. It is a turret room, so shaped as a half hexagon, but squared off on the other sides and lined with bookshelves. The walls are wood paneled, and there is a big old Eastlake desk near the front windows, some comfortable sofas and club chairs in the center, and a couple of leather-topped library tables with folios and hardbacks stacked haphazardly. It feels warm and homey. There we found a couple, Todd and Rishelle Halsey, apparently, sitting on one of the sofas, and a fellow who I assumed was Stuart Jardine in a club chair, staring at his cell phone and playing with something that looked like a pack of cigarettes in his other hand. Serina introduced me, then melted away, saying she had a lot of work to do before they started taping.

"This place is amazing," Todd said after we had exchanged pleasantries. He was tall, lean, with the wide-mouthed grin of a joker and well-cut sandy hair. His voice was mellow, nicely baritone, but with a gritty quality that would sound good on TV. "We've filmed in castles before, but usually they're tourist traps. This is pristine!"

"Pristine," echoed Stu Jardine, looking up from his phone.

He was what I'd call a faux nerd with a soupçon of hipster. He had the requisite dark-framed glasses, a long, narrow face with short spiky dark hair topped by a black fedora that had a plaid band. A goatee scruffed his chin, a small mustache perched on his upper lip, and he wore a long-sleeved yellow-and-black plaid shirt with slacks, suspenders, and a contrasting bow tie. He wore dark, skinny slacks too short, with plain white Converse sneakers. But tattoos peeked out from the cuffs of his shirt, and he sported a neck tattoo as well, of a dove with an olive branch in its beak. His ears were pierced all the way up to his upper lobes. At least it was a styling, even if I thought he was on the caboose end of a fashion train that was headed off the rails. A man bun would have finished his unhip-hipster look.

He still clutched his cell phone in one hand, and it was indeed a cigarette pack in the other, but it appeared to be clove cigarettes, not regular tobacco. I'd have to remind everyone . . . *no smoking in the castle*.

Rishelle Halsey smiled over at me, exposing white even teeth and a dimple winking in one cheek. Her hair was black and lustrous, her lips full and coated in red matte lipstick, a good color for her skin, which was pale and lightly freckled. It was an attractive look on an attractive woman. "You're probably wondering what the heck you've gotten into with us here," she said with a self-deprecating smile. "We do kind of overwhelm." She was slim but bosomy, with freckled cleavage displayed to advantage by a push-up bra under a V-neck T-shirt. Said cleavage was adorned with an eye-catching tattoo; it appeared to be two halves of a heart that were only together making one heart because her breasts were hoisted together.

I wondered if she got the tattoos before or after the implants, and what they would look like as she aged. Maybe that sounds mean, but I don't intend it that way. It's what I wonder all the time about unusual tattoos and piercings. This was a little distracting because the eye was constantly drawn to that darn heart. It almost looked like it was beating as she breathed.

"I'm a little out of my comfort zone, for sure. I've been on a movie set before," I said, and explained having been a stylist for a time. I sat down beside her on the leather sofa. "But this is different. I guess since it's my home."

Rishelle put one slim hand on my sleeve, showing off a giant diamond and eternity wedding set. "We'll do our best to stay out of your hair. You might even find it fun to watch filming, if you stay quiet as a mousie!"

Stu and Todd exchanged irritated looks, and I guessed that her offer was not one they would have extended. "I wouldn't want to get in the way," I said, but I'll admit, I used a tone that was calculated to make them capitulate, because I did want to keep an eye on what they did in my house.

"You can watch, if you want," Todd said, his tone grudging. "But it'll be boring as hell."

I arched one brow. "Boring to watch ghosts flit through my castle? How could *that* be dull?"

Both the men's attention had shifted as I spoke. We were not alone, a fact I had only had time to vaguely notice. An argument between two oddly dressed people flared on the other side of the room by a bookcase. Assorted crew members were gathering, and we all twisted on the sofa and watched. At first the quarrel was just a mishmash of voices, one high and fluting, one low and rumbling, but as I watched and listened I eventually sorted it out enough to get the drift.

"Millie, darling, sweet *idiot*, you're off your rocker, as usual," said the man. He was tall and had long, black, curling hair. He wore a black canvas duster coat over black jeans, but it appeared a considerable paunch was concealed under the voluminous duster coat. "You cannot possibly be sensing a Revolutionary soldier within these walls. This heap was probably built in the Victorian era by some vainglorious robber baron steel manufacturer."

"I tell you, Dirk, I *know* what I felt the moment I walked into this desolate structure! It was *horrible*. I was all atremble, quivering with the imminent threat of something *awful*, simply terrible, about to happen!"

The speaker was dressed colorfully, to put it mildly. She wore a long, floaty skirt, a multiplicity of scarves, and a colorful tunic embroidered with butterflies. She had long sandy brown kinky curly hair that was restrained by yet another scarf wrapped around her head a few times to make a bulky headband. She positively jingled with jewelry, too much to take in at one glance.

Actually, the clothes were similar to Shilo's attire, but my friend was a model, now married to local real estate agent Jack McGill, and she could pull off the hippie chic look that this girl was probably aiming for. I itched to get my hands on her, to restrain her sartorial overkill and find the elegant swan underneath the layers of fluffy feathers. *If* there was a swan and not a quacking duckling. Hard to tell with all that going on.

"You are so full of crap, your eyes should be brown," the man said.

"Who are they?" I asked Rishelle, who was watching, spellbound, a delighted smile on her pretty face.

"Those are our pet psychics," Rishelle muttered as Todd and Stu got to their feet and started across the room to the pair. "Dirk Phillipe, apparently his real name, though I've never seen his birth certificate, and Millicent Vayne, also supposedly her real name. Sounds like the pseudonym a romance writer would choose. She's one of those vague wilting-flower types."

I glanced over at Rishelle, aware of the deliberately insulting language and descriptions. "You don't like her," I said as she jumped up to follow her husband and I rose to follow.

"It's not that. She's just too, *too* precious."

"What about *him*?" I asked. "Dirk Phillipe? He looks—"

"Like a big fat phony with an arrogant attitude and zero people skills?"

"All righty, then," I muttered, following her. She didn't like either of them.

Todd had his hand on Dirk's arm, while Stu had taken Millicent aside, arm over her shoulders, and was murmuring to her in a soothing undertone. I don't like seeing women bullied—I don't like to see anyone bullied, as a matter of fact—and thought Mr. Dirk Phillipe should be told a thing or two.

"I couldn't help overhearing your discussion, Mr. Phillipe," I said loudly, over the chatter of the tech crew who had entered the library to set up cameras. I waited until Dirk Phillipe slowly swiveled and eyed me with incomprehension. He was a very tall fellow, head to toe in black (was that black guyliner rimming his eyes?) *and* with enormous black cowboy boots for footwear. Interesting choice.

"You were saying this is a Victorian copy of an old castle," I continued, now that I had his attention. "But it's not. It may not be Revolutionary period *quite*, and it likely *is* a copy of European castles, but it's just slightly post–Revolutionary era. It was constructed in the late seventeen hundreds by my paternal ancestors, who were from England. They made their fortune in lumber mills."

Dirk looked over to me, his glance lingering, his pale eyes blank. "Oh, I don't think so."

I was startled. "I beg your pardon?" Maybe I misheard him.

"You've been misinformed. This heap was built in the late eighteen hundreds at *best*. Nineteen ten or twenty at worst. With too much money and too little taste, I might add. Just *look* at the furnishings!" he said with a negligent wave of one large hand. "It's all faux medieval crap."

Holding on to my temper, I said, "You're wrong. Wynter Castle was built in the late seventeen hundreds. I've looked it up."

"You've looked it up." He smirked and snorted through a big, beaky nose. "Why does everyone say that, and with such finality, that air of confidence? *I looked it up.* Probably on the Internet. This castle is a prototypical example of the neoclassicism of the late Victorian, early Edwardian period."

What a load of garbage! I opened my mouth to argue, then shut it without saying a word. He apparently didn't know neoclassical from neo-Gothic. My castle is sturdy and in some ways graceless, with the turreted solidity of a Norman castle, not the refined neoclassical structures that copied Greek ideals. I know because Pish has done all the research. And I could *prove* it was built in the late seventeen hundreds, not eighteen hundreds—I have copies of the original land deeds and building specs for the castle built by my some number of great-grandfather, Jacob Lazarus Wynter—but . . . why should I prove anything to a stranger? Even if I offered proof, he was the kind to dismiss it. Rishelle watched me, eyes wide, and smothered a laugh as I turned away.

A plain, dark-haired young woman trotted into the library just then. "Stu, we've got a problem," she said, ignoring the rest of us. "A big, freaking, loud problem. Or rather *two* problems."

Chapter Three

THE WOMAN HUDDLED with the men, including Hugh, who had just entered the library behind her. She was probably in her thirties, no makeup, blunt dark hair straight to her shoulders, and a bosomy but graceless figure clothed in a formless sweatshirt and baggy jeans. She had a Windbreaker tied around her waist as if she were a middle schooler afraid to lose her jacket. It's hard to describe what I mean by *graceless*, but she held herself as though she disliked her body. There was nothing wrong with her figure—there is nothing wrong with *any* shape of body, in my estimation, big or small, tall or short—but she appeared to dislike her physical being.

"Who is that?" I asked Rishelle as we watched the consultation taking place in ferocious whispers and gesticulations.

"That's Felice Broadbent; she's another of the talent." She rolled her eyes as she said "talent." "She's one of *those* women, the kind who thinks that everything is a big freaking problem."

"I wonder what's wrong?"

"She probably saw a spider."

I could hear some of her complaint.

"When were you going to tell us you'd hired them?" she demanded.

"It was an agreement with Mr. Lincoln, and a condition of our being allowed to film here. It was a small concession, that's all." Hugh Langley seemed bemused but not particularly alarmed by the woman's ire.

"Not good enough, Hugh," she exclaimed. "Last thing we need is a bunch of amateurs stumbling around, getting into shots, taking up valuable time."

"I'm no amateur, I'm a freakin' photographer!"

I knew that voice and turned, overjoyed. "Lizzie! And Janice!" I cried. My young teenage friend, Lizzie, grinned and whooped, fist pumping joyously, while Janice plowed through the confusion and mess like a schooner through rough waters, stepping daintily over wires and evading furniture with a sway of her hips. Janice and her husband are both big people, but they wear it well, especially Janice, who seems queenly despite her at times strange choices in clothing.

"Merry, you're back from your honeymoon," she said as she sailed past me toward the group of men and Felice. She wore a black swing dress with a leopard print Peter Pan collar and jaunty chiffon bow, not something I would have put her in as a sixty-something plus-size lady, but taste is highly individual. Actually, she carried it off well, proving there is no age limit on style.

Lizzie, frizzy haired and unformed in her mid-teenage years, but with an enthusiastic intelligence and caustic manner I find engaging, jumped at me like a puppy, leaping up and down and hugging me. "Gawd, you have to stop going away, Merry. I'm tired of welcoming you home."

I was touched; Lizzie is often dour and moody, a condition common in the teen years, if memory serves me, so this abandoned display of joy was a miracle of sorts. "Twice. I've gone away *twice* in the last year," I said, my voice jittering as she leaped and gamboled, holding on to me.

"Yeah, but once was for months!" she complained, releasing me. "All freaking summer!"

"You'll be happier about me going away after you get the wee giftie I bought you in New York."

"Now, please!" she crowed, her eyes lighting up and widening. She likely surmised it was something camera-related, since I am a fan of her photography.

"Not now, later. How are you and your mom doing?" I asked, holding her away from me and gazing into her eyes, sweeping back the mop of frizzy hair that she tries, and fails, to contain. "Have you moved back with her yet?" Lizzie and her mom, Emerald, had gone through another rough patch recently when Em had gotten mixed up in a con artist's scheme. I hoped they'd work things out.

She made a face. "Kinda. I'm spending weekends helping her paint and fix up the house and the shop. She's decided she wants to do massage therapy now, properly, but she needs a course. There's one in Rochester and one in Buffalo, so she has to figure out which one to take and when to start. Right now she's still working at the bar. I'm staying at Grandma's during the week and with her on weekends."

I heard a screech right then, and whirled. Janice had collapsed. "Oh no!" I yelped, and trotted across the room to her, where she lay in a heap by the bookcase closest to the window.

The others, stunned, looked on as I bent over her. "Janice, are you all right?" I said, unbuttoning the top button of her Peter Pan collar, which seemed ready to choke her double chins. "Someone call 911!" I cried, but then felt Janice grip my arm in a steely grasp.

"Mmmm, I'm okay," she muttered, struggling to sit up. Half a dozen people had whipped out their cell phones. "Please, no fuss," she said, flapping one beringed hand. "Don't call 911!"

Millicent Vayne was the only one of my interlopers who had deigned to actually come over. She knelt by Janice. "Are you all right?" she asked, her voice gentle and quavering. "Whatever happened?"

I saw Janice's shrewd gaze, quickly veiled by a look of bewilderment.

"I . . . I'm not sure," she said, touching her forehead. "I felt woozy all of a sudden. I was overcome by a vision of . . ." One eye opened, watching Millicent. "Of men, in military dress."

"Ah!" the psychic cried. "Me too! I swear, I saw them at the same moment as you, a whole troop, out on the lawn near—"

"In here by the dining room windows," Janice said.

"Yes, in here by the dining room windows," Millicent agreed.

I looked back and forth between the two. What was going on? Felice was still huddled with the others, but kept shooting glances over at Janice and Millicent. Meanwhile, with Millicent on one side and Lizzie on the other, Janice heaved herself to her feet by stages and toddled over to sink into a club chair.

"Are you a medium?" Millicent asked, sitting down on the coffee table in front of my friend and leaning toward Janice.

Janice eyed her speculatively. "I often have visions. It's frightening at times. I sense that from you, too, that you see things you can't explain, and it upsets you. You're so perceptive, so *intuitive*. How do you deal with all of this muddle?" She looked around the room and shuddered. Lizzie was watching, fascinated.

Hugh had detached himself from the hissing and whispering group and strolled over to us, a look of some amusement on his face. "Mrs. Grover?" he said.

She nodded, regally, and stuck out her hand, which he took, bowed over, and released.

"Our agreement with Mr. Lincoln did include the aid of two locals, besides his own contributions."

Aha, so this was Pish's doing! He was always looking out for his friends. He knew Janice's hammy traits and Lizzie's obsession with all things photography.

"Felice tells me that you say you are attending our shoots as a medium clairvoyant, and that some teenage girl is supposed to act as an intern on the crew?" He raised one eyebrow.

"That's me!" Lizzie cried. "I'm Lizzie Turner, sir," she said, sticking her hand out toward him. "I'm a photography major. I did principal photography for a film shoot for the Roma Toscano video 'Sola Perduta Abbandonata.'"

She stumbled slightly over the title of the opera aria, but otherwise I was impressed with her go-getting attitude. Lizzie is, indeed, a deeply talented photographer, but it was stretching it a little for her to call herself a photography major, since she is just a junior in high school.

Hugh grimaced. "God save me from arts majors. All we need is someone to carry cords, fetch coffee, and tidy up after the crew."

"I can do that! I'm strong." She flexed invisible biceps under a ratty gray Autumn Vale sweatshirt.

I watched her, fascinated by how quickly she could shift gears. "I can attest to her abilities," I offered, shifting my gaze to the producer, who appeared skeptical as he examined the teenager. "Lizzie is very steady for her age. She volunteers at a senior retirement community serving coffee and tea."

She made a face, but in this case I knew what I was doing; they wanted quiet subservience, not active, curious engagement.

Intellectual curiosity, if expressed vociferously, would be seen as interference. I'd have to talk to Lizzie about it if they let her stay. She could observe, think, and notice all she wanted, but she must stay quiet and do what she was told the moment she was told it.

Hugh nodded. "Okay, I never turn down free labor. Stay out of the tech crew's way, but do whatever they want." He turned to walk away, but then stopped and swiveled, watching Janice, over whom Millicent still bent. "Mrs. Grover, could we do a video test with you at some point today?"

Janice nodded, but as I watched the cast I could see varying degrees of alarm. This was not a popular decision.

"Good. Your faint was lovely and convincing, even better than Millicent's."

He walked away, and Millicent made a face at his back. "I *hate* him. He can be such a jerk sometimes," she muttered.

"What do you mean?"

"You never know what he's going to do. Sometimes I feel like he's trying to sabotage us."

"Explain," I said, intrigued.

But she refused. I was left to infer that Millicent meant he made decisions with only the bottom line in mind, as most producers do. That didn't always go over well with cast members.

Janice and Lizzie were hustled over to meet with Todd and Stu. I retreated to my kitchen and puttered, then went to the back door, which opened onto the side terrace facing the woods. I called loudly, "Be-cket!" I saw the orange flash near the woods, and a streak rocketing across the open expanse. "Come on, sweetie! I'm home!" My cat hurtled into the hall, skidded to a halt, and stood at my feet, glaring up at me. I've gone away too much, as Lizzie noted, and I had to stay home for a while. It was nice to be missed.

It took a half hour of tinned chicken, cooing, and kitty milk—milk with the lactose removed—but he eventually appeared to forgive me and wandered off on his own. I got ingredients out of the cupboard and started baking. The chill in the air made me think of winter, and winter made me think of hot cocoa, and that made me think of a Hot Cocoa muffin! I had mini marshmallows and chocolate chips somewhere.

That's where Pish found me a while later. He seemed tentative, but I smiled as I pulled on an oven glove and grabbed a pan of muffins out of the oven. "My darling Pish, stop worrying. I'm not angry. This just happened; I get that. Heaven knows enough has happened on my watch."

"It's not just that," he said, eyeing me, then turning toward the pantry. "I promised to cook for the main members of the talent and crew. Dinner at least, for up to ten. I'll take care of it *all*, Merry, I promise." He paused as I took in what he had just said. "It's only three dinners. I'll do *every*thing. I have tonight's meal planned."

And I knew what that would be. For a group that large it would be spaghetti Bolognese. I laughed and shook my head. "Between the two of us we do get into some fixes." I hugged him and he hugged me.

"This is some welcome for you to come home to from your honeymoon."

"But, Pish, the honeymoon was glorious, and after that, I can handle anything." I released him and kissed him soundly on his cheek, smooth and soft as a baby's. He takes excellent care of his skin. "Besides, Virgil is jumping right into a job and may have to leave for a couple of days."

Pish opened the huge commercial-size fridge and took out a giant package of fresh pasta. "It's a good thing I went to Costco with Janice yesterday."

I got out some cans of tomatoes. As we chopped and sautéed, cooked and drank wine, we chatted about food. After planning meals for the next three days, I asked, "What exactly made you call the *Haunt Hunt* guy? Which one did you speak with? I forget."

"My friend at HHN, Chuck Sandberg, got me in touch first with Hugh Langley. I spoke to him briefly, but then he set me up with Todd Halsey. He seemed like a nice fellow on the phone." He paused, in the process of sweating onions, celery, and carrots and frowned down at the pan. "It's hard to explain. None of the weird things happened until after you left for Spain, and it hasn't happened since you've been back." He started moving onions around in the pan again and dumped in some chopped garlic. The delicious scent of mirepoix and garlic filled the air. "But there were too many incidents of shadows flitting past me, and unexplained noises, like whispering voices. I would hear my name said softly and smell perfume, or sometimes lamp oil."

"That's weird." I set the huge pasta pot on the back burner and took a long gulp of wine. I have never known Pish to imagine things, but the skeptic in me revolted. "There *has* to be a logical explanation."

"You know me, Merry; I'm a pragmatist. But a couple of times things even flew off shelves." He shook his head and bent back to his task, breaking up a clump of lean chopped sirloin and adding it to the pan. "I just don't understand."

JANICE DROVE LIZZIE TO HER GRANDMOTHER'S IN Autumn Vale. Hugh promised one of the production assistants would call and tell the two when they were needed. Lizzie darkly prophesied that meant never, but I told her I'd be sure they called. I didn't want her to be disappointed.

Pish and I ate dinner in the breakfast room with Hugh, Todd, Stu, Rishelle, Felice, and Millicent. The breakfast room, unlike the dining room, is human-size, with just enough room for twelve or so to sit and eat. I love the warmth of the Eastlake sideboard filled with my teapot collection, as well as china platters, silver candelabrum, et cetera. The crew, some of the lesser members billeted at a motel on the highway, had opted to go to Ridley Ridge for food, to the bar where Emerald works. They'd likely dine on one of their infamous mystery meat burgers; they're supposedly a blend of three meats, but they never tell you what the three meats are. I got the distinct impression that Stu, at least, from among the cast, would have liked to go with them, but some odd fraternal glue kept him with the other paranormal investigators eating my and Pish's excellent pasta and drinking one of my uncle Melvyn's newer wines, a Castel Boglione red sparkling wine. Serina, Ian, Arnie, and Chi would be returning later to stay in the castle.

All of the cast were there except for Dirk, who had announced he had something to take care of and headed off on his own mysterious mission with one of the *Haunt Hunt* vans. No one at the table mentioned him. There appeared to be something of a rift between him and the rest of the cast. I've met his type before; he was an egoist. Show business and the modeling world are full of them. They exist in their own world, with their own priorities at the fore. Nothing wrong with that, except they generally expect everyone else to have their success as a priority, too.

"So how does this go?" I asked, looking around at my guests, who were in various stages of finishing their meal. I sipped my wine, feeling mellower for the alcohol, if I'm being honest. "How do you start? You're beginning filming tonight, right?" If that was the case, I would have to go fetch Lizzie; I was *not* going to see her cheated of an experience she was so looking forward to.

Todd shrugged. "We got here too late and the setup took longer than expected. This is a big place. Everyone's tired."

He seemed grumpy, and kept glancing at his wife, and then his partner, Stu, who was staring at his cell phone and playing with his fork, tapping it against his plate. Rishelle ate, but eyed the others with a watchful gaze. Felice kept her head down and shoveled her second helping of pasta, but Millicent picked the meat out of her sauce and ate very little.

With an apologetic shrug, Hugh added, "We'd like to be fresh when we do this, especially since everyone is on camera and should sound chipper and coherent."

"Will that extend your time here?" I asked. "You're going to be here just over the weekend, right?"

"We hope to leave by Monday evening or Tuesday morning, at the latest."

I took in a deep breath. "What can we do to hasten . . . uh, help make things work more smoothly for you?"

"Just leave it up to us," Stu Jardine said. "We've been doing this for years and have a system down pat."

"Yeah, we know what we're doing," Todd said. "I built this into the hit it is, and you can trust us to do it again." He sat back. "I'm glad I chose Wynter Castle. Interesting place. It's going to look great on camera."

Pish smiled. "You're welcome here, of course, but this has been quite the surprise for poor Merry. I just want it to go smoothly."

"Don't worry about that," Todd said. "We know what we're doing. I've honed this team into a well-oiled machine." He shot Hugh a look, and someone snorted, I think it was Stu. "And that's *despite* everyone's efforts, not because of them. We'll spend tomorrow on some interviews with Pish, you, Janice, and anyone else who seems interesting. Tomorrow evening we'll begin the hunt."

Chapter Four

AFTER DINNER SOME of us moved to the parlor, a smallish but comfortable room tucked in by the dining room. I love it, like the breakfast room, for its more human size. There is a low, rosewood table, with a settee and two wing chairs near the fireplace. A large window is hung with Victorian-style wine-colored draperies, excellent for keeping out the blustery evening winds of November.

I had recently added a couple of slipper chairs in the corner near an Eastlake étagère I had rescued from the attic. Hugh discovered that Pish was a serious opera buff, and they sat there discussing the Lexington Opera Company—Pish's pet artistic project—and listening to Scarlatti sonatas over the excellent sound system my friend had installed in the castle. The lively piano music trilled and threaded through the quiet chatter of voices.

Todd and Rishelle had headed out for a walk. Through dinner they seemed tense and appeared to be having some kind of argument. Perhaps they wanted to fight in private.

During dinner whispered accusations had been flung between them. Felice, Stu, and Dirk—who had come back in time to reheat leftovers in the microwave—played a card game by the window at a dusty card table I dug out of the cellar.

Millicent was curled up in a wing chair by the fireplace reading a paperback, one I recognized from my stash in the library. It was an old copy of *The Lion, the Witch, and the Wardrobe* by C. S. Lewis, one of the few series of books I liked as a kid. As I sat down near her she looked up and stuck her thumb in to hold her spot. I got the feeling she didn't mind the company. Becket wandered in and stood, regarding us both with his intelligent gold eyes. Millicent lit up at the sight of my ginger buddy, set her book aside, and patted her lap. "Is he friendly? What's his name?"

"This is Becket, my late uncle's cat. He is friendly, though he's also pretty independent." As she bent over and picked him up, I told her about coming to Wynter Castle a year ago and how Becket, alone since my uncle's death, had drifted in and out of the woods, just on the edge, until I found him and coaxed him into coming home to the castle.

"This is a cool place," she said, flapping one hand as she stroked Becket with the other. "Your castle, but the town, too. I love small towns."

"I like it. I've made friends here, and I didn't expect that. I thought I was going to just fix the castle up, sell it, and return to New York City. Instead I've found my home here." We chatted for a while, and I found her to be more down-to-earth than I expected. I wondered what it was that made me think she'd be an airhead. Her clothing, or her belief in her own psychic ability? That was narrow-minded of me, and after over a year in Autumn Vale I should know better. "So, what's the deal between you and that Dirk guy?" I asked, glancing across the room at the trio playing cards. "I sensed a lot of animosity coming from him, if you don't mind my saying so."

She shrugged and stroked Becket, who was purring, stretching, and kneading the air. "I don't know. I think we just have different ways of seeing our abilities."

She was holding back, I could tell. Rishelle had claimed Dirk was a blowhard phony, while Millicent was a pretentious twit. Or words to that effect. "I've heard that he's a phony. What do *you* think?"

She slid a glance at me. "I would never be one to accuse someone of being a phony. That's the most hurtful thing you can say, in our industry."

There was more coming, I just knew it. "But . . . ?"

"*But* he does play fast and loose with the truth. Like what he did to you earlier, claiming you didn't know what you were talking about with the history of this castle."

"I've known enough people like him to know when it's pointless to protest. I'm interested in your . . . gift, though."

She smiled, a secretive quirk of her lips. "I can tell you don't believe. That's okay. I can't explain what happens—I just know what I see and feel."

I considered Janice's earlier interference and guidance of her vision. "Millicent, earlier you were *about* to say you saw soldiers out on the lawn, but when Janice Grover redirected, you agreed that it was inside by the window."

"I didn't want to embarrass her."

"Trust me, you cannot embarrass Janice." At least, not after the Queen of the Night fiasco, I thought, remembering her disastrous attempt at one of the most iconic soprano arias of all time, which she had flubbed so masterfully in front of a fairly large audience that people in Autumn Vale are *still* talking about it. If you're going to fail, she told me, fail magnificently.

"It didn't matter too much. I really *did* see Revolutionary soldiers, though. You ought to look that up; there may be more to this property than you even know."

I stood, stretching out the kinks in my muscles. It had

been a long—very, *very* long—and tiring day. I wandered over to the table where the three were playing cards. The psychic was still wearing his heavy trench coat. The castle was chilly, but not *that* chilly, I didn't think. He held his hand of cards oddly, and fidgeted a lot. Felice eyed him and frowned, then looked up at me with a frown. "I'm sorry about the state of that card table," I said, noting it was a little wobbly and not big enough for them. The psychic was leaning on it fairly heavily, and I worried it would collapse.

She was about to say something, when her attention returned to Dirk. "For crying out loud, I *saw* you palm that ace, Dirk! Really, if you're going to cheat at least be a little more subtle."

"I didn't cheat!" he said, watching her through heavy-lidded eyes. "You're seeing things, Felice, and that's *my* job."

I couldn't help it, I chuckled. He smiled up at me, and that expression lit his face with a charm I did not expect.

Stu threw down his hand. "I don't know what *you* saw, Felice, but Dirk did *not* cheat."

"Typical. You guys stick together and I'm always the outsider. I'm fed up."

I left them behind to squabble and toddled off to the kitchen, followed by Becket, who then yowled to go outside for his evening perambulation. I let him out, returned to the kitchen, and made a pot of coffee and one of tea. Dirk Phillipe surprised me by strolling into the kitchen and offering his help.

"Sure. Can you get the big wood tray down from the top shelf?" I asked, pointing to the shelves over the fridge where I keep trays and other serving dishes.

He was so tall he easily grabbed my large Indian carved wood tray. I have an array of trays, including a Sevres porcelain and a couple of silver trays that I found up in the attic, but the wooden tray was still the most serviceable, and in this case, largest. He set it down on the trestle table and I moved the thermal urn of coffee to it.

"You have an amazing place here." He leaned on the counter and stared out the window to the darkening woods. He had shed his trench coat and seemed more normal.

"Despite it being Gilded Age at best?"

He shrugged, and didn't take the bait.

"It *is* amazing. It came as a complete surprise to me when I saw what I'd inherited." I filled my largest teapot, a monstrous Brown Betty, and put it on a big serving tray beside the coffee. Over the last year I had become accustomed to serving groups.

He turned from the window and watched me. With his long dark hair pulled back in a ponytail, and wearing a shawl collar tweed sweater with suede elbow patches, he looked more like a philosophy professor than a TV psychic.

"So, I'm genuinely curious about one thing." I got out a container of mini cinnamon muffins, tumbling them into a pretty Royal Doulton bowl to add to the tray. "How did you get started as a TV psychic?"

"What, you don't believe in my gift?" He swayed back, hand over his heart, a mocking lift to his brow.

"I'm asking seriously." I was intrigued, and wondered about the man as opposed to the manufactured façade with which he appeared to cloak himself.

He looked down at the tray, rearranging things randomly, finding a balance spot for the coffee urn, the teapot, and the platters I was adding of cookies, bars, and mini muffins. "In college I got involved in a randomized experiment trying to find out if people could predict what cards would be shown behind a barricade. I scored high, much higher than the average. No matter how many times they did the test, I kept testing high, but only with certain people on the other side. It was like some people were open to me, and some closed."

He paused, and changed the balance on the tray. "Since then I've done a lot of research, and that's how I ended up on *Haunt Hunt*. Is it all real?" He met my gaze and smiled. "Of course not. How much reality TV is real?"

"I asked Serina why you all have a special effects guy on the set if you're supposed to be discovering genuine haunted locations."

He nodded and smiled. "Chi doesn't do a whole lot of effects. I don't even know why he's stuck on this show when he's worked on the most amazing movies." He named a couple of big-budget movies on which Chi was the special effects tech. "He's really talented!"

"But why employ him at all?"

He shrugged. "Chi was on the crew before I was hired. Beats me why he's here. Anyway, you may think it's all fake, but Todd and Stu are onto something. They do catch voices, noises, knocks, whispers, movement, shadows, and other things. I'm interested in how much is genuinely from the spirit world."

"Why *Haunt Hunt*, though? Why not strike out on your own? Isn't the 'psychic medium' thing big right now?"

He looked me directly in the eye and said, "You may think I'm a fraud, but I believe in what I do. However, it isn't one hundred percent accurate, and if you're a medium in it to make money, you have to at least pretend you're sure of a lot more than I am."

I wasn't sure how much I believed of what he said. "So what's your end plan?"

"You mean for me?"

I nodded.

He smiled and waggled his eyebrows. "I have plans. *Big* plans. If everything goes right in the next little while I'll have my own HHN show, *Dirk Phillipe's Psychic World*. I'll travel all over and talk to other psychics about their abilities and tape their successful sessions."

"You've already got that in the works?" It actually sounded like a good idea, if you like that kind of thing.

He put one finger to his lips. "Shhh! I don't want to jinx anything. I have a plan, but plans are delicate things."

He carried the huge and heavy tray into the parlor for me, then took Hugh aside for a talk while I organized the coffee, tea, and food. The two men were in some intense conversation. Hugh ended it by patting the psychic on the shoulder with a kindly smile. I would bet that Dirk required quite a bit of handling. I retreated to the kitchen and came back with more, adding to the trays a wedge of Brie and some fig preserves, along with some water biscuits. "Coffee, tea, and snacks, everyone!" I said, gathering them all in my gaze.

"You're too kind," Hugh said, unfolding himself from the slipper chair. He made himself a cup of tea and returned to my good friend to chat some more. It was nice for Pish to have someone around who could match him in talking about opera, classical music, and art museums.

Dirk took his coffee and plate of goodies outside to sit on the flagstone terrace and stargaze, he said. I saw him grab his cell phone, though, and would bet he was doing some business or calling someone. Felice and Stu both got coffee and returned to the card table, bending their heads together in a strident conversation. It didn't seem secret, so I ambled over and took Dirk's empty chair.

"You know I'm right, Stu," Felice said. "It's all her. Not *my* fault."

"What can we do? She's Todd's wife. No chance he's going to tell her to take a hike."

"Everything okay?" I asked, brightly.

"Yeah. No, but yeah," Felice said, grimacing. "That witch Rishelle . . . since she arrived on the scene it's funny how little screen time I'm getting. She's a jealous cat, that's what she is."

Someone was jealous, all right, but I wasn't sure it was Rishelle. I don't attribute jealousy to women lightly, but in this case it was clearly true. Nor did I think it was Rishelle's physical attributes that had Felice green. "So she's new at paranormal investigation?"

"Just in the last six months. She used to be a paralegal or something," Felice said, flapping her hand dismissively, as if paralegal work was nothing.

"You feel pushed aside, and that she's responsible?"

"I *know* she is."

"You don't know anything, Felice," Stu protested. He always appeared to be the voice of reason in a crowd of hysterical overreactors. *Or*, he was the kind of guy who hated conflict and would do anything to minimize legitimate anger.

She gave him a troubled look, her mouth drawn down in a dour expression. "You're as bad as the rest," she snarled. "Held hostage by cleavage and a boob tattoo."

"I am *not*! Felice, you have got to quit—"

The knocker in the hall startled me; it is loud and echoes through the whole place, which was a good thing. I jumped up, threaded my way through to the great hall, opened the door, and found that Serina Rogers, Chi-Won Zhu, Arnie Ball, and Ian Mackenzie had returned from Ridley Ridge. All except for Serina, who was sober and driving, were a little worse for wear with half-price shots. Dirk followed them in, and I guided them up the stairs, Dirk to his room and the others to their two rooms, which they shared.

I have seventeen bedrooms in the castle, but not all of them were habitable yet, so some of the cast and crew members were sharing. Dirk had absolutely insisted on having a room to himself, so I gave him the smallest of those I had ready. Todd and Rishelle had a room to themselves. Chi, Arnie, Ian, and Stu bunked together and Millicent, Felice, and Serina shared a room. The rest of the crew stayed at a motel on the highway.

Todd and Rishelle returned home from their walk while I was upstairs; Pish led them up and showed them to their room, guiding Hugh, who also had a room to himself as befit the head honcho, to his.

I descended to the main floor and sat on the bottom step, thinking about how often my castle had been invaded by barbarian hordes, from movie crews to a legion of miserable little old ladies to tea-swilling locals; it was like a fortress, and I the forlorn maiden in desperate need of saving. Just then my very own knight came home, striding into the castle with a grin on his face that changed to tender concern when he saw how tired I looked. He pulled me to my feet, wrapped me in his arms, and held me for a long minute in the quietude of the great hall. "I'm taking you to bed," he murmured. "This whole thing is Pish's idea; you should be letting *him* deal with it."

"I'll meet you upstairs," I said. "I have to make sure Becket comes in. I don't like him out this late with coyotes around."

"He survived for a year on his own; I think he knows to avoid coyotes."

"Go! I'll be up in a minute."

While I was in the kitchen, Millicent crept in and asked if I minded if she got a little warm milk to take back up to help her sleep. She never slept well on the first night of a shoot, she said. I led her to the kitchen, got out the milk and pan, and went to open the butler's pantry door. I called Becket and waited.

"Merry, how do I turn the burner on?" Millicent called out.

I left the door open so Becket could come in, and showed her what to do. I then went to the half bath in the hallway and was washing my hands when I heard a shrieking and wailing.

Crap, what now!

Chapter Five

I BOLTED FROM the bathroom to the kitchen to find Millicent up on the trestle table, crouching and crying. "What's wrong?" I cried.

"That . . . that *thing*!" She pointed.

There was something dark, furry, and wet on the floor near the fridge. Becket sat a ways away, licking his paw. He paused and looked up at me. If a cat could, he would have shrugged as he swiveled to look up at Millicent, who was still whimpering.

I was dismayed, but not frightened. I got out a dustpan and whisk. "Millicent, as unpleasant as this is, it's just a rabbit. A *dead* rabbit," I said, moving the poor creature onto the dustpan with a shudder of distaste. "Becket has brought me a welcome home present. It's not something he does often, but that's what it is."

"That's disgusting!" she said, and fled upstairs, leaving me to not only dispose of my cat's catch, but also to clean up after her, scalded milk and all.

I scolded Becket, which did absolutely no good, but didn't

know what else to do. He had his habits and had been an indoor/outdoor cat his whole life. He had survived in the wild for a year by eating only his own kills, so I hardly thought I could—or should—stop him now. By his standards humans are unreliable at best, and it behooved him to keep his hunting skills sharp in case he needed to fend for himself.

When I joined my husband, Virgil and I had a good laugh over Millicent's horror and screaming fit. I felt bad for laughing at her, but I had already had enough of the whole group and we'd only begun. Virgil and I showered together (a rather lovely way to get clean and dirty at the same time!) then huddled in bed, both exhausted from an extraordinarily long day, but wearily wide-awake. I looked up *Haunt Hunt* on my laptop, finding that many episodes were online to view. The first thing that interested me was an aspect I attributed to Hugh's influence, the use of spooky classical music to introduce the episodes. Berlioz's "Dream of a Witches' Sabbath" and Rachmaninoff's *Isle of the Dead*, in a couple of cases. And over some dramatic parts Mussorgsky's *Night on Bald Mountain* (or *Night on the Bare Mountain*, depending on who translates).

Awesome music, but . . . "Lipstick on a pig," I muttered.

Virgil kissed the top of my head. "What, don't you think ghost hunting is a classy profession?"

I laughed. "It's entertainment. I get that and I am not a snob!"

We sped through parts and soon found that the episodes followed a pattern. The two leads, Stu and Todd, talk about where they are going. They arrive and set up. I had noticed the filming at intervals, mostly of cast members setting up things that had already actually been set up. I had a feeling a lot more would be staged carefully and filmed the next day. There were then interviews with someone who either owned the structure, in the case of homes, or worked there, in the case of public structures and historical monuments.

In some instances they interviewed locals who had once worked there, or who had experienced phenomena while there. Most of the experiences consisted of shadows, sounds, creepy feelings, and unexplainable sensations of cold, or overly emotional responses.

"Hah. They'll have a field day with *this* town," Virgil said. "You can't go two feet in Autumn Vale without running into someone who has experienced something creepy at Wynter Castle."

Nestled against his bare chest with my laptop in front of us, I craned my neck around enough to give him a dirty look. "Ow!" I exclaimed. "Got a crick in my neck."

"Serves you right. Keep watching . . . Look—Stu feels a spiderweb and shrieks!"

Stu did indeed flail in a highly entertaining way, while Felice laughed at him. It looked like genuine camaraderie, the type you build over time with those you work with. This was an older episode, before they added Dirk, Millicent, and Rishelle. Felice certainly seemed happier. The investigative pair then did some tests; Felice opened a window in the room, then had Stu open another door down the hall, and the bedroom door slammed shut. In this case the homeowner had reported slamming doors as one of the paranormal occurrences, but Stu and Felice proved it was a matter of air pressure. One door being opened in another part of the house created an air rush or a vacuum, and another door slammed as a result.

That was the "debunking" aspect of the show. The cast made some effort to eliminate natural explanations rather than leaping to supernatural conclusions. The skeptic in me, and Virgil, too, postulated that it was actually included to give the show the aura of scientific inquiry and authenticity. Odd sounds were often debunked as plumbing, and lights the result of the headlights of passing cars outside, reflecting in mirrors or on windows.

I queued up another episode, this time with the psychics. I must admit I was fascinated with the very differing styles of Dirk and Millicent. Dirk was moody; he argued with spirits. He browbeat and confronted those he considered angry. This was especially the case in homes where the owners felt harassed. He threatened the spirits with psychic violence and talked about the hounds of hell and avenging demons as if he were familiar with the beings.

Millicent on the other hand cajoled and coaxed, feeling vibrations and sensing auras, in tune especially with lost children and fragile spirits who were confused. She wept, overcome by the pain experienced by those who had passed but remained entangled in the earthly world. In one memorable episode she held a séance and the homeowner was involved; by the end of it, he looked completely spooked by her explanation that there had been a dramatic schism in the home among two parents and an adult child that resulted in murder. He said she was right, though there was no way she could have known because he hadn't told her about it.

As if that eliminated any possibility of her having heard about it beforehand. I wondered . . . did the investigators or psychics do any advance research? Someone must, or they would have no clue what they were walking into. I had an uneasy feeling. Dirk had been in town, he said. If he asked around, I was all too aware of what he would dig up to "sense" in my castle. We had a couple of memorable bodies found, one in a hole on the lawn near the drive and one on the terrace by the ballroom windows. Oh, and one in the half bath off the butler's pantry hallway.

I closed the laptop and set it aside, then turned over, laying my cheek against Virgil's chest, playing with the dark hair that lay like a mat across his skin. "I wish Pish hadn't invited them. I was looking forward to moving ahead with our plans, no distractions. Except the pleasurable kind."

"I know."

I could feel the rumble of his voice in his chest against my cheek. He threaded his fingers through my hair, pulled my head back, and kissed me. His lips were warm and I tasted the toothpaste from his pre-bed ritual. Just before I lost my mind, he whispered that we'd soon have the place all to ourselves, that they'd all be gone in a couple of days.

Jinxed.

THE NEXT MORNING THE MALE IN MY BED WAS DECID-edly more of the ginger persuasion than when I had drifted off to sleep. I dropped a kiss on Becket's pink nose, told him I adored him as he stretched, yawned, and meowed at me, then I slipped out of bed. It was later than my usual early rising, but then, the day before had been long. The castle was blessedly quiet, the crew off doing something. I should have known then that trouble was brewing.

Had I But Known . . .

Virgil had left early and would be gone at least overnight, and perhaps for a couple of days. His partner, Dewayne Lester, needed him to surveil a worker's compensation insurance cheat who was expected to move houses in the next couple of days. If he did any of the heavy lifting himself, then the insurance company wanted proof he was malingering.

I expected I'd do on-camera interviews with the *Haunt Hunt* guys, Todd and Stu. I wasn't looking forward to it, but if I was going to be on camera, I was going to look good. So I styled my hair the way I like it, in a half updo. My makeup was perfect—smoky eye and all—and I put on something I'd bought in New York City at Monif C., a black, cold shoulder jumpsuit. Then I rethought that. It was way too fashionable for what I'd seen of the show. I chose instead an ecru lace tunic top and jeans, but left my hair and makeup.

I let Becket out for his morning constitutional, baked more

muffins, let them cool while I did dishes, then packed them in tubs. I was going to make the rounds in town, a little post-honeymoon visitation to thank everyone who had made my wedding so magical, including my dearest friend, Shilo, my fey, magical hippie darling who was, I had found out, indeed pregnant. I had suspected it first, had urged her to test for it and to start taking care of her growing baby's needs.

And I was right. Hours before my wedding, which she and Jack had come back to attend from her newly reunited family in West Virginia, she had whispered the news to me. It was my wedding present, and there could never be a better one. I don't have actual blood family; sweet Shilo is the nearest thing to a sister I've ever had, so I would be an aunt. I wanted to check in with her and see how she was doing.

And Doc English! He had given me away, representing, he told me, the men of my family, all gone now: my father, my great-uncle Melvyn, and my grandfather Murgatroyd. Pish, of course, had presided, Hannah and Lizzie had been my maids of honor, beside me at the fireplace in the great hall of my castle, while Virgil (his groomsmen were two of his brothers, whom I met for the first time on our wedding day) and I said our vows. Hannah, seated in her mobility wheel-chair, cried, tears streaming down her pale, ethereal face. Lizzie dashed tears away, too, while she grabbed her camera and snapped pictures. While in town I would visit Hannah, Gogi, and everyone else, but the gifts I had brought home would wait for a calmer opportunity. I had all the time in the world, and would wait until the ghost hunters had left so I could have all my friends to dinner.

So, sure, I was still a little peeved about the *Haunt Hunt* escapade, but even the weird specter of a ghost hunting crew at my castle could not undo the happiness I felt bone deep.

Even if my groom *had* slipped out at dawn, after kissing me awake.

Pish was in his sitting room working on the finishing

touches on his next book about the financial industry and the con artists who abuse it. I skipped in, kissed his cheek, told him where I was going, and escaped as he tried to apologize yet again for the pseudo–reality show fiasco that was about to erupt. I laughed, too happy with life to let him feel any remorse about that. "We'll get through it, my darling Pish," I said. "Back to work!"

Autumn Vale was crisp and sparkling in the autumnal sunshine. There is something so invigorating about autumn air, and our pretty town looks its best, named after its most attractive season. As I descended into town from my lofty Wynter Castle peak, driving in the old Cadillac willed to me along with the castle, joy bubbled up and overflowed. It had taken me a long time to escape the pain of mourning for my late husband, Miguel Paradiso, but Autumn Vale, my friends within it (as well as my New York friends, Pish and Shilo), and Virgil, had finally done what years in the city had not been able to accomplish. While I still remembered Miguel with love and gratitude, I had moved forward and was living for now and the future.

My first stop was brief, the Vale Variety and Lunch, to drop off muffins and be thoroughly teased by Mabel, the manageress, about my "glow." Isadore Openshaw, now working full-time at the lunch counter, offered me a rare smile. We'd never be best friends, but the woman was finally seeing that I meant her no harm. Trust me, with Isadore that is a *huge* step.

Mabel caught my arm as I was about to leave and pulled me aside. "One of those psychics was here this morning!" she said. "Sitting right at one of my tables. Large as life! I almost keeled over. Hubba hubba, what a gorgeous man!"

Gorgeous man . . . really? "You mean Dirk Phillipe, right?"

She nodded, picking a fleck of tobacco off her lip. "I watch that show *Haunt Hunt* all the time. It's gotten ten times better since he came on."

"Did you talk to him?"

She grinned. "I sure did. We chatted for half an hour." She pulled a piece of paper out of her cardigan pocket and thrust it at me. "He even signed an autograph for me!"

I read it; on a Vale Variety napkin Dirk had written, in scrawled handwriting, *To a smart lady, with much appreciation, Dirk Phillipe.* I gazed at her, nonplussed. Not in my wildest dreams would I have thought that Mabel "Tiger Lady" Thorpe, hard-nosed skeptic, would be a fan of *Haunt Hunt.* "What did you talk about?" I asked, handing the autograph back.

She stuffed it back in her pocket, leaned forward slightly, glanced around, and muttered, "I told him about when I was a teenager, and my brothers dared me to climb into the garage on the Wynter property. I saw something that night, and I'll never know what it was, but it was *not* human! I never went back."

I sighed. "I've been in there dozens of times and never had an experience."

She sniffed. "Well, so that's the final word, right, and no one else is entitled to an opinion?"

"I didn't meant that, Mabel, I . . ." But she'd walked away in a huff. I knew better than to follow her. I had to let it be, and she'd have forgotten all about it next time I saw her.

I then stopped off at Binny's Bakery. Both Binny and Patricia were there. They had helped cater my reception, a very small affair, and Patricia had done the wedding cake, a representation of the castle, with Virgil and me on the doorstep. Patricia had added a bulletin board to the bakery customer area, and a giant picture of the cake was pinned to the center. I gave them both checks for their services, thanked them, hugged them, told Binny what her niece, Lizzie, was going to be doing with the *Haunt Hunt* crew on-site, and toddled on my way.

Off to Golden Acres and a visit with my mother-in-law . . . Gosh, it is *weird* to say "mother-in-law," especially about Gogi, one of my first friends in Autumn Vale. I had a coffee with her in her office—she owns and runs Golden Acres—told her what was going on and what Mabel had told me, then found Doc.

He was sitting in the parlor, which is kind of a visiting room, with a table holding coffee and tea for clients and their guests, and shelves of books. Doc had taken up reading, sometimes with just his jam jar–bottom glasses, but often with both them and a magnifying glass. He was making his way through the classics, all the books he didn't have time to read, he tells me, as a busy general practitioner, husband, and father. His two kids, whom I had never met, lived on opposite ends of the country and visited only a couple of times a year. But both were approaching retirement age and would be able to visit more often.

Doc sat in his usual seat by a strong light, reading a newer book (for him) on Marxist philosophy. He looked up as I sat down, and laid the book aside. "Good to see ya. And a good reason to stop reading this horse pucky for a while."

"If you hate it, why are you reading it?"

He chuckled. "Same reason I eat bran; everyone needs fiber in their diet to keep things moving."

We talked for a few more minutes. He was finally scheduled for cataract surgery to fix his eyesight. He was upbeat about it, and I didn't let him know I was worried. But I had to get back to the castle before the ghost crew started filming, since I wanted to watch what they were up to.

"You know, that there ghost crew was here this morning."

I sat back down, the sofa springs squeaking alarmingly. "Really? Why?"

He shrugged. "I dunno, but the one guy, wearing a long black coat, was talkin' to Hubert."

Chapter Six

❋ ❋ ❋

OH *NO!* I felt a twinge in the pit of my stomach. A charming octogenarian with a quirky sense of humor, Hubert Dread never met a conspiracy theory he couldn't amplify. He delights in passing on—or more accurately, making up—stories about alien abduction (anal probes and all), government spying via drones (who knows; maybe he's right about that?), New World Order conspiracy fantasies, and more. He has his nephew, Gordy, who works for me sometimes taking care of the Wynter Castle grounds, completely taken in about it all. What could Hubert have told Dirk Phillipe? And how would it affect the *Haunt Hunt* shoot?

"Did you overhear anything?"

"You know Hubert; he mumbles and whispers. But that Dirk fella . . . he's got a real showy voice." Doc eyed me. "I think he was askin' Hubert about Tom Turner and those Hooper boys."

"Hubert never even met any of them."

Shrugging, Doc said, "Stop worrying. It'll be fine."

I left feeling unsettled and a little queasy. I ended my visit to town where I always do, at the library. Hannah Moore, one of my favorite people, was behind her desk, seated in her mobility wheelchair, eyes fixed on her computer screen, avidly watching something. When I greeted her and circled, I saw that it was an episode of *Haunt Hunt*, one of the ones I had seen the night before of their visit to a haunted prison.

After we hugged, she exclaimed, trembling with excitement, "Merry, the whole crew was here this morning. They filmed a sequence with me! I don't know if they'll use it or not, but I talked to one of the investigators and two others. Some guy, Dirk, and a woman, Millicent?"

The psychics? Why would they talk to a librarian researcher, other than to have stuff to "see"? "What did you all talk about?"

"They asked me about the castle. I told them some of the history, about the original builder and the area. I loaned them books on Autumn Vale. The gentleman who produces the show, Hugh Langley, made notes. He said it was for the voice-over narration."

"Is that it?"

She bit her lip and eyed me. "Well, not *exactly*."

"What is it *exactly*?" Her narrow face was screwed up into a grimace. I stared at her with sudden suspicion. "Hannah, what is it? You look nervous."

"I kind of got . . . giddy." Her slim hands fluttered and she giggled, then gave me a wide-eyed look. "Honest, Merry, I don't know what got into me. I've never been a part of anything so exciting! I'm afraid I talked too much."

Putting my hand over her slim-fingered one resting on the joystick control for her motorized wheelchair, I said, "Honey, I'm sure you didn't." I had faith in Hannah's natural reticence, as well as her innate good sense.

"They asked an awful lot of questions about . . . about Tom's murder," she said. "And the troubles with the Hoopers—stuff like that."

Good heavens . . . the murders. *Again!* First from Hubert, and now her. Poor Tom Turner, whose body I found a day or so after moving into the castle, and my trouble with the Hoopers, Dinah, Davey, and Dinty. This didn't bode well for being able to leave behind the trouble I had had over the last year. I was silent, thinking over the endless possibilities for mortification.

"I'm sorry," she said, her tone fearful.

"Don't worry about it. Hubert already told Dirk Phillipe about the deaths, so it's okay no matter what you said." I reached out and hugged her. "It's nothing I can't handle."

I released her and scanned her outfit. Her legs are small and she can't use them, which is why she has a mobility chair. She's slightly self-conscious about it, enough so that her mother, who makes all her clothes, sews gauzy skirts and dresses of pastel chiffon, things that drape nicely without being billowy enough to catch in her chair's wheels. But today she was wearing an olive green skirt suit—an unusual color for her, but flattering—in material that had a sheen. The skirt wasn't a pencil skirt, but it wasn't a true A-line, either. It was something in between, and the fabric for the skirt was soft, to drape over her knees. She had also taken to wearing more accessories, bracelets altered to fit her tininess, and a burnt orange headband swept her cotton candy hair from her high forehead.

"You look very smart today," I said. "Is this outfit new?"

She sat up a little straighter. "I'm a businesswoman and I should look like one, so Mom made this outfit. I've been asked to speak at the local library association meeting in Batavia next month about accessibility in libraries. Do you think this is appropriate?"

I eyed it and nodded. "It's perfect. Your mom's a genius;

it's tough to find skirt suit material that will lie flat when you're sitting and fall over the knee properly. She could design a whole line of wheelchair fashion."

"She'd love that!"

Fashion out of the way, we talked for a moment longer. "So, did the *Haunt Hunt* cast talk about anything else while they were here?"

"Not really. I got them out some research books. Two of them wanted to use my computer, but I couldn't let them do that; it has patron information on it!"

"Why would that matter?"

Hannah's face pinched in shock. "Merry! It's private stuff, like phone numbers and addresses! I had my personal laptop here, though, so I let them use that, while I talked to that nice man, Mr. Langley."

"Which two?"

"Todd Halsey and Dirk Phillipe."

"And they wanted to use your computer for research?"

She frowned. "I don't know. I guess they could have done other stuff. What else *would* they do?"

I shrugged. They all had devices—cell phones, laptops, tablets—and I have Wi-Fi at the castle, so e-mail or research they could do there, if they wanted. "I'm curious. . . . Can I check your laptop browser history?"

"I can't let you do that, Merry."

"But . . . why?" The expression on her face puzzled me; it was a mixture of horror and shock, as if I'd suggested she throw a nest of baby birds into traffic.

"It's private."

"I won't look at any of *your* stuff, Hannah, just whatever the *Haunt Hunt* guys were looking up."

"You don't understand. If it was just my stuff on my computer you could look at it; of course. But they were library patrons."

"But it's your computer, not the library computer."

She pressed her lips together and shook her head. "Sorry, Merry. It wouldn't be right."

I know her well enough to know when it is useless to argue. She has a finely honed sense of right and wrong, and I trusted her judgment as much as my own, or perhaps even more. I stood and stretched. "I guess I'd better get going."

"You're not angry, are you?" she asked, in a small voice.

"Honey, I could never be mad at you, and why would I be?" I leaned over and hugged her tight. "You're right, and I'm wrong. But I think I'd better go home and see what chaos the *Haunt Hunt* crew has wrought. I don't dare leave them alone for too long. Talk to you soon, Hannah!"

"Let me know how it goes!"

"I will."

As I headed toward the door I saw, on one of the long tables that filled the center of the room, a piece of paper with writing scrawled on it. I picked it up and glanced at it. It appeared to have been written by one of the guys from *Haunt Hunt*; it had their website scrawled on it, as well as the IMDb url, an NY dot gov website, and some random scribbling; FOI, SAFE, Art. 400, and other nonsense. I looked back; Hannah was frowning at her computer screen with intense concentration. I pocketed the piece of paper, curious about what the guys were using Hannah's laptop for when they all had devices of their own. Maybe some of the scribbling would give me some insight.

I had intended to visit Shilo, too, but an uneasy feeling that crept up my spine made me want to get home. Talk about haunting! I felt haunted by the troubles we had had at Wynter Castle for the last year. It was over now, I hoped. *All* over. But it wouldn't stay that way if *Haunt Hunt* didn't leave it be. I tried to imagine what the crew would put into the show; if they made it super spooky like a haunted horror house, I would yet again have carloads of oglers cruising past, trying to catch a glimpse of the murder castle, as the press called it last year. I needed to talk to Hugh Langley, because the agreement I read didn't say anything about bringing up the specter of murders past.

I called Shilo from the car, and she said she'd come out and see me at the castle in the next day or two. Next I called Elwood Fitzhugh, who was helping Virgil and me with our project out near the Fairy Tale Woods. Elwood agreed to come out and meet me by the new foundation so he could give me some advice on water. I had done a bunch of online research and was knee-deep in information on artesian wells, dousing, aquifers, and cistern systems (try saying that a few times fast), with the result being, I was more confused than ever.

I pulled up the lane, parked away from all the HHN vehicles, and stared at my gorgeous old stone castle, built, I had recently learned from Elwood, of western New York State's own Onondaga limestone, locally quarried. That's what gave it the mellow golden tones in the setting sun, though on a dull day it appeared plain gray. It is truly lovely, with a flagstone terrace along the flat front, which is edged at both corners by semi-hexagonal turrets. Over the big double oak doors is a round clear window that floods the great hall with light. Inside the great hall, over the grand staircase that splits to climb to a gallery, is a rose window, which brings glorious color flooding into the hall when the sun hits the stained glass just right.

It is a miracle to me that I own it.

I grabbed my empty muffin totes and locked the car. Becket raced to join me, thundering through the grass, and we entered, with trepidation on my part. I didn't ask Becket how he felt. It was quiet, but evidence of the TV crew's presence was everywhere. Cords snaked up the banister to the second-floor gallery and draped from there, like vines in a jungle. There were tripods set up everywhere, some with cameras already mounted. When I paused, I could hear the murmur of voices from somewhere. A soft laugh echoed, then someone whispered something from above. It was eerie, that whisper, like the sound of leaves in autumn blown along the pavement.

I threaded through my rooms, wondering what the crew was planning. The ballroom was empty, but the breakfast room had been wired for sound, and the table was bare without the tureen, which I had filled with autumn leaves and pinecones, in the center. I hoped that wherever it was, it was intact. I retreated the way I had come and headed to the dining room. It still appeared to be the hub of planning, with the table full of gadgets still there and some of the crew. I made my way to the library but was stopped at the door. They were filming, the young fellow murmured. I could listen in if I was very, very quiet.

Arnie Ball, the heavyset wavy-haired cameramen, had his camera pointed at the large Eastlake desk where Pish sat, looking elegant and relaxed, as always, fingers threaded, legs crossed, knife-sharp pleat in his trousers. He had been interviewed before by various newspapers and once by *Esquire* magazine, concerning financial scams and cons for which even the wealthy fall. Serina held an instrument in her hand, perhaps for sound levels, while one of her assistants held a boom mic over the desk. Hugh Langley stood behind the crew, taking notes and listening. Lizzie—who must have escaped early from her school day and convinced someone to drive her out to the castle—was there, too. She kept her eye on Arnie, fascinated as always by any kind of camera.

Todd Halsey had apparently interviewed Pish for several minutes and was now moving on to the meat of the piece, what Pish had actually experienced in the way of paranormal events.

Pish frowned down at his steepled fingers. "I sometimes heard whispers when I knew there was no one else in the castle. I'd hear a bang, but not be able to find the source."

"And did you *see* anything?" Todd asked, leaning forward with a look of interest on his lean face.

Cautious as always, Pish said, "I've seen shadows moving. It was more of an *impression* of something, than any visual certainty." He was holding back, I thought. There was more, but he wasn't saying it.

A faint expression of irritation flickered across Todd's face. "Mr. Lincoln, when we spoke on the phone you were upset. *Worried*, I'd even say. There *has* to be more than just shadows or impressions."

Pish cocked his head to one side. "I wouldn't say I was worried or upset." He is careful about his image. He *had* to be in his career as a financial adviser, and though retired now, he is not prone to flights of fancy. "I experienced some odd events, but there could easily be rational explanations."

Todd waved his hand and the crew stopped filming. "Hugh, I can't work with this! This is crap." He turned back to my friend. "Come on, Pish, this is not sexy, not juicy at all. I know there's something."

A mulish expression settled on Pish's lean face. If Todd continued that way, Pish would clam up and stay clammed.

"Todd, shut up for a minute," Hugh said, and approached the desk. He crouched down. "Pish, I know this may seem silly to you, but we do need to spice it up a little. You look fabulous on camera, by the way—great angles on your face—but can you just . . . Were there any human*like* shapes in the shadows? Could you make out any *words* in the whispers? You called us for *some* reason, right?"

I know my darling Pish very well; he shifted, unwound his fingers, uncrossed his legs, and sat up straight. He was conflicted. He's a people pleaser and wanted to give them what they needed. However, he has spent long enough documenting frauds and con artists to be cautious when speaking to anyone. He frowned, compressed his lips, then said, very carefully, his gaze shifting from one man to the other, "Hugh, Todd, I don't mean to be offensive, but I won't exaggerate what happened. Surely what you want is my unvarnished recollection of why I called you at *Haunt Hunt*? Won't it seem more authentic if it's . . . authentic?"

There was a snort of laughter, and I caught Serina's eye. She gave me a thumbs-up. "*Love him!*" she mouthed, pointing at Pish. "*Me too*," I mouthed back.

"We'll move on and finish this another day," Hugh said, standing and straightening.

Todd and Hugh moved away to huddle together over Hugh's notes. Todd gestured, and hissed out some expletive. Hugh appeared to try to calm him. I caught a few words. Hugh said the name Dirk, and Todd reacted badly.

"I don't want to work with that phony."

Hugh's shoulders sagged, and he turned away from his star investigator. "Everyone, cut for lunch. We'll make some adjustments, then reconvene and continue."

Lunch was "catered" (also known as, delivered by a skinny kid in sweatpants) by the closest fast-food establishment, which meant soggy, cold hamburgers all the way from glamorous downtown Ridley Ridge. I wouldn't touch them. I made Pish, Lizzie, and myself ham and cheese sandwiches, but Lizzie preferred to scarf down cold mystery meat burgers and limp fries with the crew.

Pish retreated immediately after lunch, locking himself in his sitting-room/study to work on his book to the accompaniment of a Baroque piece by composer Tomaso Albinoni, a lesser-known composer whom Pish favors for a trippingly light approach. I was in the kitchen alone washing dishes. Again. My life consists of dishes, and even though I have a good-size dishwasher it seems that the amount I won't or can't put in it grows exponentially. Nothing old, vintage, gold rimmed, china, silver, crystal: most of what I own and use, in other words.

A cheery "hello" startled me, and I whirled to see—and

gape at—Janice Grover. She was a sight to behold in one of her usual caftans, bright orange and yellow this time, but also wearing a turban with a hamsa pin right up front and center. A hamsa is the amulet with the shape of a hand, palm out, with an eye in the center, to ward off the evil eye.

"Oh, Janice, you look . . . spec-*tac*-ular," I said, wide-eyed, as I wiped soap bubbles off my fingers. I grabbed a terry towel and dried my hands.

"Do you think so?" She did an elegant gavotte across the floor, arms outstretched, caftan fluttering.

"I do. The camera is going to *love* you."

"Good! I dropped Lizzie off while you were out, and Hugh told me to come back." She clapped her hands, her eyes sparkling.

"I'm afraid to ask what you'll be doing."

"You'll see!" She chuckled, then trotted off to find Hugh.

He seemed elusive, because moments later Todd Halsey stomped in and looked around.

"You seen Hugh anywhere?"

I shook my head. "Janice went looking for him. Maybe she found him."

"Janice . . . oh, you mean that big flashy lady?" He sighed deeply and shrugged his shoulder, slumping down into a chair by the table and passing one hand over his eyes.

"Are you okay?"

"This isn't turning out like I'd hoped. And Pish isn't helping. He was nice as anything when we talked on the phone, but now . . . ?"

"He's *still* nice," I said, a brittle tone of warning in my voice. You don't criticize Pish to me, not if you want to leave my presence intact. "He won't lie. Not for you, not for anyone."

Regarding me warily, Todd said, "I don't want him to lie. I take this stuff seriously. *You* may think it's a bunch of crap, but I got into this because I've had experiences and wanted to explore the possibilities there was something out there, you know? Something beyond the world we can see."

I felt bad about snapping and sat down opposite him. "I know you're disappointed in what Pish said, and I think there's probably more to his experiences, but he doesn't like to be pushed." I was about to add that he's a people pleaser, but feared that Todd might take advantage. "You and Stu go back a long ways doing this?"

"Ten years," he said. "Longer than I've known Rishelle." His expression darkened at that.

"What's wrong?"

"Nothing. You know, you think you know someone. You *think* they're your friend, and then . . ." He shook his head. "And women . . . what the hell?" He sighed.

I didn't know what to make of his string of comments, so I stayed silent.

"Never mind." He got up quickly. "I've got to find Hugh. That woman is going to drive me mad." He stomped out.

Which woman was going to drive him mad, I wondered, Janice or Rishelle? Was I mistaken, or did he suspect that his friend Stu and his wife were having an affair? I started dinner preparations. Chi came in as I was sautéing beef chunks for a beef and mushroom dish.

"Hey. Do you have a tool kit anywhere?" he asked.

"Yes, what do you need?"

"My socket wrench kit has gone missing, and I need . . ."

He went on to give a very specific description that I couldn't repeat if I was under threat of death.

"I have no clue if I have that," I said. "But I might. How about I show you where the tools are, and you tell me if I have them."

I led him to one of the storage closets along the butler's pantry hallway and opened it up. While he crouched down and went through the tools, I made conversation.

"So, I've heard that you're a very experienced special effects guy. Why are you working on *Haunt Hunt*?"

He paused and looked up at me. "Why not?"

"It seems there would be more prestige in movies, and more of a chance for you to practice your craft."

He went back to rifling through my tool kit, tossing tools around with abandon. "I . . . I have personal reasons for sticking around."

Personal reasons . . . okay. He clearly didn't wish to speak further and I had no reason to pry. He found what he needed and took it with him, mumbling about getting it back to me when he was done. The day stumbled forward rapidly after that. I tracked Hugh Langley down in the dining room and asked, when did they want me to film my piece, as the owner of the castle?

He looked me over, twisted his mouth, and then shook his head. "You'd be great on camera. But . . . have you seen or experienced anything paranormal here?"

"Uh, no," I replied.

"Are you willing to make something up?"

"No."

"I thought not." He shrugged. "No point then, is there? Nothing for you to say."

I bit my lip to restrain a smile. "You may have something there."

At that moment, Janice wafted over. Hugh's eyes widened as he took in her getup. "Mrs. Grover, *what* are you wearing?"

"Clothing."

He sighed as some of the crew sniggered and chuckled, clustered together like schoolkids watching a scene between teachers. "Mrs. Grover, you *must* take off the turban. This is not a sideshow act; it's a serious broadcast."

Serious broadcast? Really?

She drew herself up and stared down her nose at him. Since he was much taller than her, that required her to tip her head back quite a bit. "Mr. Langley, this, *all* of it, is what Madame Grover would wear."

Just then Millicent strolled into the dining room and stopped abruptly, staring at Janice; she was followed by Dirk, who bumped into her and likewise stared.

"You are not a character, you're a . . . a psychic medium," Hugh said, eyeing her with increasing concern. I could have told him, once you unleash the Autumn Vale crazies be prepared for blowback of a gale force. "Don't you want to be taken seriously?"

"I think, Hugh, that you may have given my friend the wrong impression yesterday when you praised her swoon," I said. "Thereby approving of what you implied was playacting."

He swiveled to face me. "I'm sorry for giving that impression," he said, evenly, baring his teeth in what was intended to be a smile. He turned back to Janice. "Mrs. Grover, despite appearances, I take filming this show seriously. The turban goes, or you go."

The turban went.

Hugh retreated to a table near one of the windows and consulted his clipboard. As I approached I could see it was a shot list, a form containing the various rooms, cast, equipment, and a brief description of the shots they were going to get. He would update the list as they got the shots.

"So, what are you going to do with Janice?" I asked, sitting down opposite him.

Hugh glanced across at me. "Oh, didn't we tell you? We'll be holding and taping a séance."

Heaven help me, I thought. Words failed me.

They filmed some more bits, but I had phone calls to make, so I missed them. When I came back downstairs I was about to head to the kitchen to see how dinner was doing, but Todd Halsey trotted after me. "Merry, I'm glad you came back down. We're ready to tape your piece."

"But Hugh said you wouldn't be using me." Our voices

echoed in the great hall, and I noticed the camera mounted on a tripod; there was a faint click as we moved into its view, and a tiny red light flashed. Motion sensor?

"Hugh was wrong. I want to interview you."

He seemed tense, and I was baffled as to why. But I was game. Why not, right? By the way, never ask that question of yourself, because if you do, there is bound to be a "why not."

Chapter Seven

"OKAY. WHERE?"

He led me to the parlor, where I sat down on a low slipper chair. Arnie Ball set up a stationary camera, and one of the assistants handled the sound. It was a very intimate setting, and I relaxed. The parlor is one of my favorite rooms, smaller and more homey than the great hall, dining room, or even the library. Todd sat across from me and as the camera rolled, we talked about the history of the castle and how my great-uncle Melvyn Wynter had willed it to me as the last surviving Wynter.

"Quite the string of tragedies your family has suffered," Todd said.

"What do you mean?"

"Your uncle was murdered, wasn't he?"

I noticed for the first time that he had small, mean-looking eyes. Disconcerted, I said, "Well, yes, though nobody realized it was murder at first."

"And then when you moved here you found a dead guy within days?"

"Yes, but, it's not—"

"And then you found a guy dead in a coffin, of all things, at a Halloween party?"

"What does that have to do with anything?" I blurted out, sitting up straighter, all illusion of comfort vanished.

"That's bad luck." Todd looked around toward the camera. "A whole *lot* of bad luck. So *many* dead bodies."

I was silent.

"Don't you think that's why your castle is haunted? So many brutal murders in such a short time?"

"That's enough," I said, trembling with anger.

Todd smiled. When I looked around, after the bright filming lights were shut down, I saw that we had company. The crew congratulated Todd on a great interview, and Arnie Ball, knitted cap slightly askew, high-fived him. I was shaking and furious, but I wasn't sure what to say, how to handle it without whining about misuse. I had liked Todd. I had *sympathized* with him. Shaking, feeling ambushed by my difficult Wynter Castle history, I stood up, turned, and saw Lizzie standing there near the door, foam cup in hand, her face white. This was awful. Tom Turner, Lizzie's father, was the first body I found at Wynter Castle, and it was just a year ago.

In that moment, I realized I damn well *did* know how to handle it. I was not going to let Lizzie see me take it and not say anything. Not that she needed me as a role model, but it was important to *me*. I whirled and strode over to Todd, grabbed his sleeve, and said, "What did you mean with all that crap?"

He looked blank. "What crap?"

"That crap about murder. You are *not* going to use that interview, or so help me God I will sue your whole—"

"Whoa, hey, folks, what's going on?" Hugh Langley entered the parlor and approached, hands outstretched in a pacifying gesture, seemingly attracted instantly by the word *sue*.

I glanced over at Lizzie, who was watching intently. I calmly told Hugh what had happened. The producer appeared weary, and I wondered how often he had to wrangle this crew. He turned to his lead paranormal investigator. "We're not using that, Todd. This is her home, and she has to live among these people when we're done and long gone."

I breathed a sigh of relief; he understood.

Todd's wide mouth was set in a mulish frown. He shook his head, watched his producer for a moment, then said, "But, Hugh, this stuff is dynamite. People love murder! Murder is ratings gold."

Hugh shook his head. "Murder from a hundred years ago is one thing, but murder from last year is something else. Leave it alone."

"But, Hugh—"

"Leave it *alone*," Hugh said, his voice steely, his expression imperious. "Last warning, Todd."

"I appreciate the support, Hugh," I said as Todd stalked out of the room, throwing a dirty look over his shoulder.

Hugh touched my arm and smiled, resignedly, wrinkles seaming his forehead. "Despite what it may seem, we're not here to make you uncomfortable, and I won't let them do it. In fact, I didn't even know about the murders when we planned this hunt, or I may have nixed it."

I crossed the room and put my arm around Lizzie's shoulder, squeezing. "You okay, kiddo?"

She nodded and took a deep breath. "Yeah, I'm all right."

Hugh rounded up the crew and talent into one big group in the dining room. He stood silhouetted in one of the big Gothic arched windows. "Okay, listen up, everyone. Tonight is our first night of shooting. We're going to do a couple of things a little different. Mrs. Grover is going to hold a séance in the breakfast room, with Ms. Wynter and Mr. Lincoln present, and we're going to film it. Dirk, Millicent, Todd, Rishelle, I want you all in the séance."

"What about me and Stu?" Felice asked.

Arnie and Ian were holding a whispered conference about something technical, but Chi-Won Zhu was listening in, intently. Serina drifted close to me, arms folded over her chest, and listened in, too.

"Sorry. Too many people for that room," he said. "You and Stu will be investigating."

"Where?" she asked.

He consulted his notes. "The cellar."

"That is *bullcrap*, Hugh!" Felice exploded. "Stu and I get stuck in places you probably won't even use? I suppose Rishelle gets something sexy, like one of the bedrooms, so you can get great night-vision shots of her giant hooters?"

Stu stared at Felice in alarm and edged away from her. I had a feeling he was one to avoid drama. He understood his place in the grand scheme of things in a way Felice did not, or at least didn't accept.

Rishelle snickered. "Look, if you got it, flaunt it, right?"

"I could have a set too, but I won't buy body parts at the discount doc, like you do," Felice shot back.

Rishelle sighed, and said to Hugh, "Look, if it'll make her feel better, I can team up with Stu, and she can have Todd."

"Oh my gawd!" Felice exploded, grabbing her hair in both fists. "You *would* want that, wouldn't you?"

Todd, his gaze volleying between his wife and female colleague said, "Wait, what is this all about? Felice, why do you say that?"

I remembered my sense that he was worried his wife might be having an affair with his partner. Was that what Felice was hinting at?

"Enough!" Hugh said. He looked around the group,

which had gone silent. "Children, no fighting. I'll speak to you, Felice, in *private*. If you're not happy with your role with us anymore, perhaps something else with HHN can be arranged. You can be the mime on *Dr. DooNothing's Magical Zoo*. They're always looking for a new mime. I can't *think* why."

Lizzie laughed out loud, but Felice shuddered and stayed silent. I sidled over to Lizzie. "Why are they always looking for a new mime on that show? Sounds like some kind of kid's program?"

"One of the kids I babysit watches it," she said, chortling. "The mime always gets zapped, or slimed, or covered in mud, and can't say a *thing*!"

"Oh. Nasty."

"Hughie-boy, maybe you can get Millicent to stop sensing danger and darkness everywhere we go, now," Dirk Phillipe drawled.

"Why, 'cause that's *your* shtick?" Serina said. "Is she horning in on your personal brand of bullcrap?"

"Serina, leave it alone, please," Hugh said, giving her a stern glance.

She turned away and began rolling up a loose electrical wire, her shoulders stiff with resentment.

"No, let her speak. Whatcha want, little one?" Dirk said. He stood, stretched, and loomed over Serina, who was tall for a woman, but no match for the psychic. She dropped the wire and turned back at the psychic's intervention. "You're a *feisty* little gal, aren't you?"

"Gawd, I hate that word *feisty*!" Serina said, bunching her fists.

"I can stick up for myself, Serina," Millicent said.

I hadn't even noticed her there, but she was sitting on a low stool, listening.

"Dirk, I don't *always* see danger and darkness; you know me better than that. Normally, I keep it light. But lately . . ."

She shivered and looked down at her sandal-clad feet. "It's just harder."

Hugh clapped his hands together. "Enough, kiddies. Go have a rest, everyone, and we'll meet at eight P.M. Mrs. Grover will lead the séance."

"I'll have a cold supper ready for everyone before beginning," I said. I decided against the more elaborate feast I was planning. The less time I had to spend with this lot, the better. Cold cuts, cheese, buns, and salad were simple and enough for this crew.

Chi moved toward Millicent and knelt down, speaking gently. She smiled at him, nodded, and stood. "I'm going to go meditate," she announced.

Hmmm . . . interesting. Chi had said his reasons for sticking around were personal. Was it a crush on Millicent that kept him captive?

"I'm going to nap," Dirk said.

Both disappeared, and the rest followed suit.

Paraphrasing the inimitable Bette Davis, I muttered, "Fasten your seat belts, children. It's going to be a bumpy night."

Chapter Eight

❊ ❊ ❊

EVERYONE HAD EATEN, restlessly moving from room to room while chomping on buns stuffed with Westphalian ham and Gruyère as they discussed the night's shoot. I was beginning to get the feeling that the large crew represented an odd social dynamic; I had thought there were clear lines, cliques, groups, but it seemed more fluid than that. I've seen that before among a fashion shoot crew, how loyalties and friendships shift and change with the work. Millicent and Dirk huddled together for some time, talking in low tones, their enmity set aside. Dirk then took Hugh aside, and the two disappeared for a time. When they came back, Dirk looked quite relaxed, but Hugh seemed peeved at first, though he mellowed as he talked to Pish. It couldn't be easy wrangling this disparate group of temperamental divas.

We finally gathered in the breakfast room, which had been transformed into a highbrow version of a fortune teller's den by one of the crew. Someone had taken my collection of teapots away and had instead filled the shelves of my

Eastlake sideboard with a crystal ball, paisley scarf draped artistically, candles, incense, a crystal skull, and an ornate Ouija board. Sheesh! Janice should have kept her turban on, in my estimation, because this was just as over-the-top. She had a basketful of items that she was ready to use, including a tarot deck and a cup that was marked with tea leaf reading symbols.

Far from the eerie aura I would expect at a séance, it was bright, noisy, and confusing as they tried to get organized. Lizzie had gotten permission to stay for the overnight taping—I had forced her to lie down in my bedroom to nap during the break, but I doubt she slept—and was avidly watching all of the technical aspects.

"Okay, Janice, you're going to do your séance shtick," Hugh said. "And then you'll reveal two things; to Millicent you will say that there is a child trying to come through, but she needs help to communicate, and to Dirk you will say you're afraid there is a dark shadow that has befallen Wynter Castle and its inhabitants, and—"

"Wait, wait, *wait*," I said, holding up my hand. "Look, not to be sensitive, but can we not introduce any 'dark shadow' talk?"

Hugh, perched on a stool behind Arnie, the cameraman, eyed me with irritation. "Merry, I don't want to step on anyone's toes here, but I feel like I've bent over backward to make this work for you. We *need* some excitement."

"I've watched a few of your shows, and I don't remember any séances *or* dark shadows," I retorted. "They've mostly been random sounds and flitting apparitions. I think if Janice is going to focus on anything, why not my ancestor Jacob Lazarus Wynter? He's the one who built this place and died here."

"Look, I'm trying to be cooperative," Hugh said, his voice becoming tight with anger. "But we have a show to tape. You can't ask us to fill it with boring historical rubbish that no one cares about."

Someone lowered the lights, the crew hushed, and I fumed in silence.

"Everyone take hands around the table," Janice said, her voice modulated to a low pitch.

Serina shook her head and raised her hand. "Nope, not getting a good level on that. Come on, people, help me out here. Janice, you'll have to talk a little louder."

They made some adjustments and moved the boom mic closer over the table, but then it was in the camera shot, so they had to raise it. Then the camera blurred and Arnie Ball said, "Not working. I'm getting blur. We need to redo the lighting so I can get the swami's face." He tucked a stray lock of his wavy hair up in the knitted cap and then peered again into the viewfinder.

The talent chattered together while the technical aspects were worked out. I was getting bored and antsy.

"Come on, people, let's get our act together," Hugh said, looking down at his watch. "We have a schedule to keep. I want this done in one, and I want two or three solid hours of tape from both crews."

His rallying cry worked, and when they next started everything was a go, judging by the thumbs-up from both Arnie and Serina.

"Everyone, take hands around the table," Janice said. "Now, I need you all to concentrate. I am going to try to contact any lingering spirits. Dirk and Millicent (they were seated on either side of her), I'll need you particularly, because you already have open conduits to the spiritual forces in this old castle."

Knowing I was on camera I tried not to look surprised, but Janice's spiel was pretty good. Over the next ten minutes she spoke of swirling forces, voices calling out, and then seemed to latch on to something. If I didn't know better, I would have sworn she was an actual medium, and not just playing one on TV.

"I have a troubled spirit, a man . . . he is *deeply* upset by changes made in this place."

I held my breath and waited, not sure where Janice was going with this.

"I feel him," Millicent said, her voice faint. "Yes, he's angry! He's . . . he's gesturing at us!"

"I see him," Janice said, her deep voice throbbing with feeling. She pulled attention back to herself with her tone. "He's wearing old-fashioned clothes and speaking, but I can't make out his words."

It swiftly became apparent she was speaking of Jacob Wynter. She desperately tried to insert a little Wynter history into the séance, but it *was* dull, as Hugh had opined, and would likely end up on the cutting room floor, since it lacked any drama. "Reality" TV is all about the drama.

I was more interested, by then, in watching the interactions among the crew, Hugh, and the talent. Chi-Won Zhu moved swiftly and silently behind the scenes; at one point, as Janice spoke of a spirit who was trying to contact her, he used a small handheld device to float some fog. After editing it would probably look like some ghostly apparition hovering over the table. Lizzie looked bored and disillusioned but did whatever she was motioned to do, including moving wires and picking up obstacles. Hugh had put Todd and Rishelle together, but I noticed that the two dropped their hand-holding the moment the cameras were not on them to notice.

Dirk had a permanent sardonic smile etched on his face, but Millicent was listening to Janice so closely I wasn't sure if she was trying to debunk my friend, or if she was buying it all. Hugh motioned to Todd, who then tried to interrupt some story Janice was telling in boring detail.

"Millicent," he said. "You have an odd aura around you. Are you feeling okay?"

Chi glared at Todd and rolled his eyes; I wondered, did he think Todd was making fun of Millicent?

The psychic was breathing rapidly and deeply. She touched her forehead, staggered to her feet. "I'm . . . feeling woozy. I think . . ." And then she fainted back onto her chair, sagging limply sideways onto Janice, who supported her. It sure looked like an honest-to-goodness faint, right on camera. *And* they kept filming, even as they sounded fake-concerned and buzzed around her.

Her eyes fluttered open and she recovered nicely. Millicent babbled about some child who was trying to contact her, and how she needed to go look for the tormented little girl up in the attic. It was all so V. C. Andrews that either Millicent was extremely suggestible—possible—or as fake as I figured Dirk was—*also* possible. She had taken Hugh's "child spirit" suggestion and run with it. They went on with the séance, at that point, but by the end of the hour I was so fed up I was ready to start sticking my tongue out to make the shots unusable, except they probably would have used them and claimed I was possessed.

Janice thought that after the séance we'd be moving right along to the tea leaf reading portion of our pageant, but Hugh had other ideas. "We need to get some solid investigative stuff tonight," he said, standing and shaking the creases out of his sports jacket. "It's a good windy night, so I'm hoping for some tree branches scratching on the windows, or stuff falling on the roof."

I stared at him in disbelief. "You do realize that my castle is constructed of limestone so thick you could set off a stick of dynamite on the terrace and you wouldn't hear it in here. And, there are no trees within a hundred feet of the castle. Unless you count the four-foot-tall lilac bushes I planted, and I don't imagine they make much noise scraping against three-foot-thick limestone walls."

He glared at me in increasing irritation. "Work with me here, folks," he shouted, not taking his gaze from me, but talking to his crew. "We'll figure it out, like we always do!"

Which meant, in TV lingo, they'd add it in post. They spent another hour setting up. Chi kept disappearing with cases of instruments and things, then reappearing. I decided to shadow them as much as I could, determined not to let them do anything that would bring discredit on my house. I have enough trouble with the divided opinion about me in Autumn Vale; I didn't need *Haunt Hunt* to make it seem like my home was the castle version of *The Amityville Horror.*

The crews suited up and grabbed items from the array of ghost hunting tools available to them. Stu and Felice descended to the basement, and I followed. So far, Stu was a closed book to me, so I asked him about *Haunt Hunt.* He was noncommittal. But then, as the crew was checking sound levels—they were having some trouble in the basement—and making adjustments, I asked, "Do others in the paranormal investigation community ever give you a hard time because of the psychics angle?"

He tugged at his extended lobes, with the tunnel rings, and scruffed his goatee. "It was so cool when Todd and I first started. It was like, *Yeah, let's show those jerks what we do is legit!* You know? And now, because of Dirk and Millie, we're mocked in the scientific paranormal research community."

Felice nodded. "It's not fair," she said, pulling her ill-fitting Windbreaker down around her hips. "It's not our fault if Hugh keeps pushing the Dirk and Millicent angle. They make us look like a bunch of wackos."

"But you two and Todd, at least, are serious. Why do you think Hugh pushes Dirk and Millicent so hard?"

"Ratings!" Felice said.

Stu nodded. "I thought for sure Dirk's crap would send us into the basement, ratings-wise. When Hugh decided to bring them on, Todd and I were furious! We threatened to walk out." He scruffed his goatee again, making a scratching sound that echoed off the limestone walls, and shook his head. "But viewers love him! They're *obsessed* with him! When we do events, he's the one everyone wants their photos taken with. He's the one everyone wants to talk to! It's in*sane!*" There was a giant dollop of pure green envy in his voice.

"I don't think even Hugh figured Dirk would be so popular. Sometimes he looks at him with this expression, like he's amazed what the guy comes up with," Felice said, gloomily. "So much for serious spirit hunting."

"That must be irritating."

"You have no idea," Stu said, fiddling with the instrument in his hands. He took a pack of clove cigarettes out of his jacket pocket, but I gave him a look and he put it back. "I keep hoping something will happen, but nothing ever does."

"What do you mean, '*something will happen*'?" I asked.

He shook his head. "Nothing. I'm just over it. I'm ready to pack it all in."

I was about to ask again what he meant by that, but they were ready, and we started. I stayed behind the crew, which consisted of Ian Mackenzie, the camera operator, a sound assistant, as well as both a technical assistant who helped with cables, and a production assistant (some young guy who melted into the background most of the time) who wrote notes and referred to a shot list he held in his hands, and watched. I don't talk about the castle basement much; it's almost all storage down there, and the ceilings are pretty low. But Uncle Melvyn's wine collection is stored in a chilly room with a locked gate. Yes, a *gate*; it's perfectly barbaric-looking, a padlocked gate made of wrought iron and with spikes atop it.

The investigators weren't interested in going into the wine cellar, thank goodness. I didn't think my uncle's vintage would survive another guest like the opera singer Roma Toscano, whom I had to bar from the wine cellar, which is why the padlock was locked in the first place.

First, they did an establishing piece. Stu stared into the camera and whispered, "Stu and Felice in the basement of Wynter Castle. Pish Lincoln mentioned to us that he was down here getting a bottle of wine once when he felt a presence and saw a shadow down at the far end of the space. We're going to try to get something."

They turned off all the lights, and then Stu and Felice chatted a bit about what "the owner" had said they might expect—truly puzzling because I hadn't told them to expect anything—then crept forward. The crew was astoundingly good at being silent. The two investigators shined flashlights into corners while discussing the castle and the town with some pre-scripted comments I had seen Hugh jot down and hand to them. The comments note was now in the hands of the production assistant, and they'd refer to it if they needed it. They mentioned the age of the castle—at least they got that right, despite Dirk's assertions—and they talked about me, and how I had inherited it. They got a lot of other stuff wrong, but I couldn't exactly correct them, since they were supposed to be alone.

"Wow, Stu, this is a dramatic spike," Felice murmured, staring at the EMF meter, her plain face a study in intensity, from what I could see by the flashlight. "It went from almost nothing to three-point-two!" She turned, holding the meter out in front of her. "Let's see if we can make that happen again."

"Is anyone here?" Stu said, and waited. "Please let us know if there is anyone besides Felice and me here. You can use this device to signal us. Light it up if you are here!"

It blinked. That happened a couple of more times after much coaxing from the investigators. I noticed that several times when the EMF meter blinked to indicate a hit, Stu's cell phone, in his other hand, vibrated, as if he was receiving a text or update of some sort. Was there a correlation? I had to think it was possible.

Then their conversation turned to Autumn Vale. "I liked

that little librarian girl, Hannah, that we met in town," Stu said.

"Wasn't she the cutest?" Felice answered.

I glowed with pride; my wonderful friend was getting some much-deserved love.

"She's so *brave*," Felice went on, her voice thick with emotion.

"Isn't she, though? Wow. So much heartache she's been through, and such a courageous little soul. A tiny angel in a wheelchair."

They were treading on dangerous ground. I know how Hannah feels about the extreme worshipful "putting her up on a pedestal" crap. She says too many people either treat the disabled as if they are invisible or saintly. Like anyone in this world, all she wants is to be taken seriously for what she is, an extremely intelligent young woman with an undergrad degree in information science, now working on her master's.

"I wanted to scoop her up in my arms and hug her!" Felice said, with a tremulous tone. "Brave, *brave* little darling!"

Nothing about her library, or her ambition, or her go-getter attitude, just some poor little crippled girl. Furious and sickened by the indulgent pity party—which Hannah would loathe with every fiber of her being if it made it onto TV—I *knew* I couldn't let them air something like that. I coughed loudly, stumbled into the cameraman, and cleared my throat, ruining the shot. The next time I would make sure if they *did* talk about Hannah, they would do so with respect for her many capabilities, not her single incapability.

They admonished me to be quiet, and started again, this time focusing on other equipment, a thermal imager and some other stuff. They pointed the thermal imager down the length of the cavernlike basement.

"Nothing so far," Stu said.

"Omigod, look!" Felice shrieked. She went silent, and there were five seconds of dead air space. Were they actually leaving space for the editor to break for a commercial after her scream? That was their method; someone would see or experience something, and then the show would go to commercial. She said, in an extremely excited tone, "That was like the shape of a person, or something. It was a hit, *definitely* a hit!"

Stu pointed a flashlight into the distance, and there, his eyes glowing, was my orange cat, Becket. I put one hand over my mouth as Stu and Felice laughed and joked about it.

"Just a cat! Hah! I thought we had something there," Felice said. "Too bad."

Stu stopped and said, "Okay, let's break for a minute. I want to look ahead and see if we can figure out some better angles."

Millicent, looking huffy and indignant, joined us in a swirl of skirts and scarves. While they were resetting up the shot I whispered, "Millicent, what's wrong? I thought you wanted to be up in the attic?"

"I did, but *nooooo*, Dirk had to have the attic." She looked on the point of tears. "He only did that because I wanted the attic so badly! He's . . . he's just a *mean* man." She eyed Felice and Stu with obvious dislike. "And I get stuck down here with these two."

The shot reset, they began again. They didn't get anything else except a creak that I could have told them was the sound of the ancient boiler system cooling, since we had shut it down during taping, but if they insisted on saying it was paranormal, other than interrupting again, what could I do? I wanted them to tape what they needed and get out.

They crept into an alcove and Stu suddenly shrieked while Millicent and Felice giggled. Yet another Stu catastrophe, a

spiderweb. He apparently loathed bugs. I had seen enough
episodes to know that the results would all be rather ephem-
eral: rustles, taps, bangs, and creaks. "Voices" picked up by
the EVP. More EMF meter fluctuations in the electromagnetic
field. They got "some interesting readings," Millicent wept a
bit at the sadness she experienced—which I thought had a lot
more to do with her conflict with Dirk than any paranormal
boo-boohooing—then packed it in.

I followed them back upstairs. They were going to take
a break, and Felice loudly announced she needed a cigarette.
I made sure she knew there was no smoking inside the
castle, to which she responded that of *course* she knew that.
Hadn't she already been going outside every time she needed
a smoke? She, as a smoker, was a member of the last group
that could be discriminated against, she said, shunned and
abused. I had no comment. I wanted to see what the other
team was up to. I crept through the darkness toward the
ballroom, where I heard voices.

Dirk was in the middle, hands outspread, looking
intensely off to the ballroom windows. "I feel something
mournful, something . . . I can't explain it. There is a great
shadow of darkness in this place." He shuddered.

"What do you think it is, Dirk?" That was Todd, who
was there with his wife, Rishelle.

"I'll have to feel it more, let it vibrate through me. There's
anger. Fury, even. Bitterness." He shook his head.

Todd had a REM-POD, another of their nifty devices. It
kind of looks like a can of beans with four miniature colored
Christmas lightbulbs on top. It supposedly detects energy
disturbances and fluctuations, signaling them by lighting
up, but it wasn't doing anything tonight, so it was either
broken or sullen. I sidled closer and watched, in the semi-
darkness, as Lizzie held a boom mic for Serina, then moved
a cord when she was signaled. She was in her glory, intent

on every moment of technical maneuvering. Chi-Won Zhu was acting as the unit's director, notebook in hand, and Arnie was the camera operator, but I could also see tiny red glowing lights from DVRs mounted in corners of the ballroom. I moved out of a camera shot and tripped on a cord that wasn't taped down properly.

Todd said, "What was that?"

I was about to open my mouth and say it was me, but Serina caught my arm and shook her head.

"I don't know," Rishelle said. "I heard it, too, but there's no one here but us three. Hello? Is there someone there who'd like to speak with us? We have this device that you can talk through. If you want to practice, give it a try!" She set a device on the ballroom floor, and instantly lights began to flash.

Todd said, "You can manipulate it, and we'll get what you're trying to say!" His voice echoed in the big, dark ballroom. It's a very long room.

After a moment of silence he picked up the device and looked at it. "Wow," he said. "Oh my gawd, Rishelle, look at what it says!"

There was a pause. So . . . that was no doubt where they would insert a commercial.

Then Todd excitedly said, "It says *death*."

"Holy crap, that's creepy!" Rishelle murmured. "What do you think it means, Todd?" She paused. "Hello?" she called out. "We want to talk to you. You can trust us!"

Suddenly, Dirk groaned and collapsed, moaning, to the floor. Todd and Rishelle rushed to his side, Arnie Ball moving swiftly and silently with his Steadicam, a unit he wore on a body harness mount. He was surprisingly agile for a big man. Serina, too, with Lizzie accompanying, bolted swiftly and silently after them.

"Dirk, what's up, man? What's wrong?" Todd knelt by

the psychic, who writhed, twitched, and moaned. It was disturbing, but I could see Arnie's monitor screen, and knew that it would make for exciting reality TV. Dirk was much more proficient at riveting the attention on himself than Millicent was. Given the choice between Millicent's séance faint and Dirk's ballroom collapse, Hugh would inevitably choose Dirk's shot; they surely wouldn't have two collapses on the show, so the male psychic had outplayed his female counterpart, stealing her thunder neatly.

He moaned, then opened his eyes. "There's a spirit nearby, someone who died."

I felt my stomach squeeze with anxious trepidation. He'd better not go where I was afraid he was going to go. I glanced over at Lizzie, who was holding a cord away from Arnie's footing. She didn't appear to be paying attention to Dirk's act. Chi, standing nearby, was expressionless, his eyes dark and shadowed, faint light glinting on his glasses as he glanced down occasionally at his clipboard, which was lit with a pale book light.

"Can you give us something to go on, Dirk?" Rishelle asked. She knelt over him, and from my angle I could see Arnie's camera shot close in on her cleavage. Maybe Felice was right about why Rishelle was now featured more than her, or maybe it was just that Rishelle was Todd's wife and wanted some airtime.

"His name . . . it was Tim, or Ted or . . . no wait! It's Tom," he said, sitting up, touching his forehead. He swept his dark hair away from his face and looked up at the others. "Was there a Tom who died here at the castle? He's angry. *Furious*, in fact. He feels ripped off, like his job here on earth was interrupted. His spirit is not resting."

I was ready to interrupt the shoot again to stop them from using Tom Turner's death as some kind of drama point when I saw Lizzie out of the corner of my eye stiffen, then drop the cord, stride forward, and launch herself at the man on the floor, grabbing him by his trench coated shoulders, yelling, "Shut the hell up, you big phony! Don't you dare—" And then a string of expletives erupted from her. He smacked at her hand on his arm and it sent her over the edge. She smacked him hard, in the face, the *thwack* echoing.

The cow dung had officially hit the fan.

Chapter Nine

I DARTED FORWARD and grabbed my young friend, while the others tried to shield Dirk. "Lizzie, stop it! Stop, *now*!" I yelled as she struggled, crying.

The psychic yelped and moaned. Chi turned on the ballroom overhead, a chandelier, and as I held Lizzie clutched to me, still sobbing, I could see blood streaming from Dirk Phillipe's nose.

This shoot was most definitely over.

We retired to the library to sort things out. It was the middle of the night and we were all exhausted. I sat on the leather sofa with my arm around a huddled Lizzie, who would not speak, not even to me.

"She's a freakin' menace!" Dirk screamed, right in Hugh Langley's face. At least his nose had stopped bleeding, but there was some damage.

Pish intervened, a hand on each man's chest. "Hugh, Dirk was out of line. Especially since you had already warned everyone not to use the murders."

Hugh, looking gray, his long face lined with deep ruts, nodded. "That's true. Dirk, I did say to leave that alone."

Dirk drew himself up, all trace gone of the affable fellow who helped me carry tea trays. "I can't be expected to control spirit. Spirit comes to me, and I listen."

Lizzie tensed but I pushed her to stay seated, bolted up, strode over to the group of men, and said, shaking my finger in Dirk's face, "Now, listen here, you . . . *you*! This is *my* home, and you're here on sufferance." I glared up into his eyes, where I detected a gleam of enjoyment, as if the drama we were going through was meat to him. I stepped back from my anger, took a deep breath to calm my trembling, and continued, lowering my voice. "Dirk, I won't listen to your load of crap. You know very well *exactly* what happened; you mined every tale teller in Autumn Vale to get the dirt. I won't have you talking about poor Tom's murder. You can get out now, or you can behave. Your choice."

Pish nodded, clutching his hands together and wringing them. "This is my fault for allowing you all to come here, and I'm begging you, Hugh, *please* respect Merry's wishes. *And* Lizzie's anguish. Have you no heart?" He turned to the psychic. "Mr. Phillipe, you have gravely wounded a child we value deeply. We won't allow that."

In the ensuing silence the sound of Lizzie sobbing on the sofa behind us echoed. It was heartrending, but I couldn't go to her, not until I knew this was settled. The psychic had the grace to look ashamed. I was a little surprised by that, because I didn't think he had a conscience. "All right, okay," he muttered, pushing his mop of coal dark hair back. "It was a dramatic story and I wanted to use it."

"It's off-limits. It's *all* off-limits," I said. "If you so much as hint at any of it, I'll go on social media and tell the whole truth about your . . . your purported psychic abilities." I said it with a sneer. I was tired of his playacting, tired of the whole lot of them.

"We have a nondisclosure clause in our agreement, Ms. Wynter," Hugh reminded me.

"I don't care," I said, glaring at the producer. "As far as I'm concerned you will be breaking our contract if you bring family's and friends' personal history into this. That was *not* what we agreed to!"

"But that kid had no right to pound on me that way!" Dirk whined.

"You hit her hand, you big bully!" I said.

Some of the gathered crew, who had been remarkably silent so far, snickered. Dirk had the beginnings of a promising shiner and a puffy cheek, as well as a swollen nose, a tissue stuffed into one nostril to staunch the blood flow.

Hugh ruminated. "We could press charges, you know," he said, eyeing me. "And if you divulge any cast or set secrets, we will."

I have met his kind before. Hugh was not a bad guy, but he thinks like a business executive; he had an advantage in both the terms of our contract and the attack on his employee, and he'd not let go of it.

He was not the one to get at. "Dirk, do you want that?" I said, glaring at the lanky psychic. "Do you want to be forced, in court, to tell the whole world that you insulted a little girl's dead father, so she gave you a shiner? If I spill and you file, the court proceedings will be public knowledge, and I'll get to explain in court how you used a kid's *tragic* family story in your psychic scam and then how you, a big tough guy with all this bravado, got bested by a teenage girl. Explain *that* at the next paranormal conference. Because I'll be there, you can be sure of it." I was shaking with anger and trepidation.

Pish took my hand, raised our clenched fists, and nodded. "We *both* will."

Dirk paled and touched his cheek. "Okay, all right. Let's drop the whole thing."

I breathed a sigh of relief.

Hugh nodded, clapped Dirk on the shoulder, and turned to my friend and me. "Merry, Pish, I promise that if this happens again, I will pack up every one of these folks and drive them away from here myself." He looked at his cast and crew. "And that goes for *all* of you."

I was relieved for Lizzie's sake, though I thought I had bluffed rather well, betting that Hugh would not want to have wasted good money on a shoot he couldn't use. Producers are money-conscious. They have to be, because they answer to network brass, and the bottom dollar is the bottom line. I retreated to my young friend and comforted her, letting her sob across my lap, knowing she was tired and cranky and disillusioned by how people in the entertainment business actually behave.

I stroked her hair. "Hon, it's going to be okay. We won't let you down."

"I k-know!" she wailed, and sniffed, sitting up and wiping her nose on her sleeve. "That's why I'm crying. I love you guys so much!" She threw her arms around me and hugged.

"And we love you." And that was the truth.

It was the middle of the night, but I drove Lizzie to her grandma's place. She needed rest and the comfort of her prickly but loving grandmother. She was suitably chastened and made me promise to get them to let her keep working on the set. I said I'd try. I came home to a quiet castle and made myself a cup of tea.

I heard murmuring from somewhere and smelled something odd. I carried my tea and followed my nose and ears to the library. There was a voice, but just one.

"Look, I don't know how much more I can stand!"

It was Stu Jardine. I leaned against the partially open door, wondering whom he was talking to.

"No, I *mean* it. I'm about to go batcrap crazy. It was ugly tonight, real ugly, and I feel like getting ugly, too. I might have to do something." There was a pause. "I don't know what. Something. This has to stop, that's all I know."

I leaned too hard and the door creaked.

"Who the eff is there?"

I stepped inside as Stu, illuminated by the yellowy light of the Tiffany-style lamp on the desk, hit the Hang Up button on his phone and stubbed his clove cigarette out in an ormolu saucer. "I'd appreciate if you wouldn't smoke inside."

"They're not real cigarettes," he said, waving away the puff of smoke that lingered. "It's just herbs and spices."

"I don't *care*," I said, through gritted teeth. "It is still *real* smoke and a *real* flame in my *real* old home. Go outside if you must smoke. And clean out that saucer before you go to bed. I mean it, Stu; clean it with soap and water." I left the room, fuming that people are so inconsiderate.

I headed upstairs and was almost at my room when I heard a door creak open. Aha, I knew that sound! That was the door to the room I had put Todd and Rishelle in. I ducked into the shadows and saw Rishelle, in a short, sheer slip nightie that revealed the full voluptuousness of her figure, creep to the head of the stairs, look around, then descend. To meet up with Stu? I wondered. Maybe Todd's suspicions were correct after all.

The sooner these interlopers left my castle, the better.

Chapter Ten

✹ ✹ ✹

THERE WAS A noisy staff meeting going on in the dining room when I descended, yawning. I got my first cup of coffee and joined the cast and crew of *Haunt Hunt*. Of course I couldn't resist sneaking a look at Dirk. He had a bruised cheek and eye socket, and a scraped, swollen nose, but otherwise looked all right. I took a seat at a table alone by one of the Gothic arched windows and looked out over the lawn toward the trees, tossing in the wind, most of their leaves scattered now on the ground. It was a November sky out there, dark, clouded, with the black traceries of bare tree limbs outlined and spiky points of evergreens pointing up.

Pish entered with a cup of steaming coffee and joined me. "I'm so sorry about all this, my dear," he said, covering my hand on the table.

"Stop apologizing, Pish. You couldn't possibly have predicted this level of chaos when you agreed to it. I've been on TV shoots before. They're often hectic, but I've *never* seen this kind of bedlam." I sighed and cupped my chin in my hand, propping my tired, aching head up. "It's like the most dysfunctional family anyone has ever seen having a family reunion while trying to stage an intervention *and* hold a wake for a dearly departed."

We listened in as the crew discussed the day's business, which consisted of getting external shots, reshooting some of the "arrival" footage in the truck, and planning out the final night of shooting. *Final night*; that was music to my ears. I exchanged a smile with Pish. "It'll all be over soon."

I have to stop predicting peace and tranquillity, since it rarely happens.

Hugh, standing in front of the group, looking like a professor, clapped his hands and said, "Okay, kids, I've got the shot list of what we need and I've made copies. Todd, you take one, and Stu, you take one. Everyone outside to the vehicles so we can get morning arrival shots."

Dirk jumped to his feet. "Not so fast, Hugh! I want to know what you're going to do about that teenage menace. She'd *better* not be coming back to work." He had clearly rethought his remorse from the night before, or more likely had never actually been remorseful in the first place.

"Come on, Dirk, you were outta line and you know it," Serina said. She was sitting with Felice and Stu, who both fiddled with their packages of smokes.

Todd, Chi, Rishelle, and Millicent sat at a table next to Dirk's. Millicent (arm in arm with Rishelle, who I had thought did not like her but, oh well) chimed in, her soft voice barely audible, "You're giving psychics a bad name, Dirk. I think we should welcome that poor child back and apologize. That was her father you were talking about!"

"I *know* it was her father. You all yammered about it enough last night. But the way I heard it in town, she didn't even freakin' know him! Why should she care?"

Utter, stunned silence greeted his insensitive remark. I was flabbergasted.

"She's a menace!" Dirk hollered, looking around at the assembled cast and crew, a vein throbbing in his forehead and his eye winking like some kind of tic he couldn't control.

I stood, slowly, letting anger bubble up in me. I can't remember the last time fury was so often a part of my day. "This is *my* home," I ground out. "If you want to keep filming—"

"Taping," Arnie Ball corrected, with a half smile.

"Taping; fine. *What*ever." I made a sudden decision inspired by my care for Lizzie as well as my dislike for Dirk. "Hugh, you'll have to let Lizzie continue if she wants to," I said, turning to the producer. "And I already know she wants to." I turned back to the psychic. "I will personally vouch for her better behavior, but I do think that your deplorable pretense of contacting her father's spirit was not only in poor taste, but it was some of the worst acting I've ever seen. And that's saying a lot, since I worked on the set of the LifeLine channel original movie *She Has Her Mother's Eyes*, about a young woman who got her mother's corneas in a transplant after her mother was murdered, and subsequently started seeing what her mother saw just before her death."

Rishelle started laughing uncontrollably. Millicent, wide-eyed with wonder, gaped at me. Todd snickered, but Chi seemed oddly aloof. Dirk visibly puffed up like a threatened toad.

Hugh swiftly concealed a smile, and, holding out his hands to calm the babble that followed my announcement, said, "Dirk, you're sulking and I won't have it on my set. Behave, or sit this one out. Ms. Wynter, Lizzie can remain on the crew, but I insist that she control herself. She ruined the shot, but I agree it was something we would not have used anyway, and something I personally vetoed. Now, *enough*. Everyone, to work."

"I'm outta here. Hugh, I'll be back tonight." Dirk stormed from the room, jerking his cell phone out of his trench coat pocket as he went. Hugh watched him go with a worried frown.

I noticed Millicent and Rishelle whispering and giggling together, watching Dirk leave. Rishelle grabbed Millicent's arm with one hand while shielding her mouth with the other, whispering excitedly to the psychic. Hugh's gaze had shifted to them, and he still looked worried. There was clearly a lot on his mind. *Not* my problem to wrangle.

The meeting broke up and I left them to their own devices to make breakfast or whatever in my kitchen, telling them not to burn the place down. I said I was going out, but that I'd make sandwiches when I got back. I showered, happy to have my own private bathroom, then wandered out to my bedroom. As I stood at my window toweling my hair, I looked out. Foreshortened, I could see Dirk, who I thought was leaving, by one of the vans in a spirited conversation with Todd. Now, *that* was odd. I watched for a few moments, but Dirk suddenly whirled, got into the HHN van, and roared the engine to life, then took off.

I lay down on the bed, needing a moment to myself, and called my husband. Surveillance was boring him silly, and he was already rethinking his decision to partner with his friend Dewayne Lester. I reminded him that this was just one case, and that he liked the freedom of being his own boss. I then told him what was going on. He was a little alarmed at Lizzie's outburst, but I told him that Hugh was sympathetic and I thought we could manage. I'd pick up Lizzie later and lay down the law.

We made smooching sounds, followed by promises of what we'd do with and to each other the moment we could, and hung up. I sighed. The rest of the day promised nothing but irritation. A little deflating to know that a phone kiss was the best part of my day.

I drove to Batavia for groceries, so I was gone longer than I expected. It was Saturday, and the stores were busy. I picked up Lizzie on my way back and we had a long chat. I agreed that Dirk was a jerk, and yes, we made it into a rhyme. Lizzie rapped it to a rhythmic beat. But we came to an understanding: If she could manage to do her job and not let that a-hole upset her again, I would make sure she got a decent letter of reference from Hugh Langley to add to her college application.

"That show is weird," she said. "I looked up all about it today online."

"Yes?" I was driving back through Autumn Vale, so I took a detour and stopped along a road where there were several empty houses, many slated for demolition. I stopped in front of one in particular, a gorgeous old Craftsman that had seen better days—peeling paint and a couple of broken panes of glass and all—but was still solid. The gas company was there unhooking and capping the gas line. Good. Right on schedule.

"Are you listening to me?" Lizzie asked, twisted in the passenger seat, the shoulder belt bunching her hoodie up.

"Yes, *yes*!" I pulled away and out of town, toward the castle. "What were you saying?"

"I was saying, that *Haunt Hunt* is weird."

"Let me guess; you've spent all morning obsessively researching every single cast and crew member."

She gave me a look. "Well, if you put it that way . . . yeah, I did. Chi is a special effect genius. Why do you think he's stuck on a show like this?"

"I think he may have a little crush on Millicent. He told me he had a personal reason for hanging around."

"Really? Weird. You know those paranormal conferences? Jerk Phillipe charges ten bucks to sign something. Can you believe it?"

Hmm. So much for being in it to follow up on his paranormal studies. So Nice Guy Phillipe was the fake, and Enraged Egomaniac Phillipe was likely the real deal.

"I saw some amateur footage at the last conference. He says crappy things to the women, sexual things. And some of them giggle and seem to like it."

I took a deep breath. "Honey, some women think that attention like that, especially from someone they admire, is flattering." I hid a smile; the first time Virgil and I met, he did ogle my cleavage, but he did not do or say a thing to make me uncomfortable. It was flirtation, not manipulation. The difference was too subtle to explain.

I continued. "But some women giggle like that because they're embarrassed and don't know what to do, or they're trying not to be a Miss Priss. That's how some guys operate; if you object to being fondled or grabbed, you're an ice queen. It's a way of controlling your reaction."

She nodded. "There's a guy at school who does it." She turned back and glared out the front window. "People suck."

"Honey, not all people; not even most of them. But some, yes."

"And Jerk Phillipe is one of them."

"What else did you learn about the cast and crew of *Haunt Hunt*?" I smoothly pulled the Caddy onto the road that would take us to the castle, but bags of groceries fell over in the back anyway.

"A lot."

For the rest of the ride she regaled me with what she had learned. Stu and Todd's old show, *Ghost Groupies*, was online, and it was pure paranormal investigation, with mostly negative results and a few unexplained things happening. Some fans longed for them to go back and griped about the psychic angle of the new show, but there were far more fans of *Haunt Hunt* than the previous show. Todd and Dirk had gotten into a fistfight at the last paranormal conference, just a week or so ago. Rishelle Halsey was once a nude model, and some fans of Todd's thought she wasn't good enough for him.

"That's rude and none of their business," I said.

We were almost to the castle when I saw behind me on the road a cloud of dust. Another minute or two and Shilo's Jezebel pulled up next to me. Overjoyed, I pulled the Caddy to a stop, she stopped, too, and we both got out, raced to each other, hugged, and did a happy dance. I hadn't seen her yet since I got back from my honeymoon and had a lot to catch up on. Lizzie watched in bemusement. I held Shilo away from me, patted her tiny baby bump, and we did another happy dance.

I leaped back into the car, yelling, "Follow us back to the castle!"

Lizzie rolled her eyes.

"Keep doing that and one day they'll stick," I said, slicing a glance her way.

"You sound like Grandma."

"Your grandmother is a wise woman."

My two friends helped me unload the groceries and put them away, while I made tea to share with Shilo—herbal for her, regular for me—and sent Lizzie to photograph all of the setups of equipment and see if there was anyone she could help. Her main task was to stay out of everyone's way and be obsequious to Hugh Langley; of course I had to translate *obsequious*. I then sent her on her way. I was intent on making her cooperative and industrious toward her goal of entering a photography course in college.

"How are you feeling?" I asked my friend, who looked a little wan and pale, but otherwise fit.

"I'm good!" Shilo said, a placid smile on her face, and one hand on her abdomen. "I still throw up every morning, but the doctor says I'm doing well."

I gave her a bottle of room-temperature water to keep up her hydration, and watched her with affection while I put together a platter of sandwiches for the crew. My hippie chick boho model friend is just thirty, but she'd done a lot in those years, including escaping from an abusive home life in West Virginia, making her way to New York, becoming a model, and working her way up to some success, then following me here, to Wynter Castle.

This was followed in rapid succession by marriage to local real estate agent Jack McGill, and reconnection with the parts of her family she missed, her granny and huge numbers of brothers and sisters and nieces and nephews. She is beautiful, with long, luxurious dark hair, dark eyes, and a naturally slim build. But it is her inner beauty, a kind of tough yet fragile sweetness, that made Jack fall in love with her on first meeting. She and Jack had moved out of his staid suburban-style ranch house and were now fixing up an old Queen Anne beauty on a backstreet. My friend was letting her artistic abilities run free in decorating it, with colorful results.

I introduced her to the available members of the cast and crew as they drifted back to the castle and to work. Without exception they stared at her with admiration, even the women . . . *especially* the women. Shilo frowned at some, including Dirk, who had returned from his mysterious errands. The psychic eyed her, lowering his head, directing what I'm sure he thought was a smoldering look in her direction. He was trying one of his silly mesmerism tricks—he put on airs at times, attempting to look Aleister Crowley–esque, dark and mysterious—but she just rolled her eyes and he stalked away. Maybe it was the bruised cheek and puffy eye that made him appear simply ridiculous, but I didn't think so. If only the charming Dirk Phillipe I had experienced briefly would come out more often he'd have been bearable, but we had established one thing: Nice Dirk was a put-on. Nasty Dirk was the real deal.

Millicent slipped into the kitchen and took one of my new Hot Cocoa and Marshmallow muffins off a plate on the table. I introduced Shilo to her, and between the two young women there was some kind of immediate bond; they held each other's hands and looked into each other's eyes and were friends instantly. Millicent volunteered to show Shilo around and introduce her to the rest of the cast and crew while I worked.

I wrangled Lizzie, and we carried platters of food to the dining room, setting them on a long table by the big arched windows, along with paper plates, napkins, an urn of coffee, and mugs, which I trundled from the kitchen on a catering cart I had bought at Janice Grover's junk store, Crazy Lady Antiques. Shilo filled me in on all that had happened while I was on my honeymoon, then fell silent, watching the crew and cast while chewing on a strand of her long, dark hair. My friend does that only when she is deeply ambivalent about something, undecided as to a course of action.

Lizzie wanted to eat with the crew again—she and Arnie seemed to hit it off, since she had decked Dirk, and I trusted the cameraman to keep Lizzie out of trouble—so I led Shilo back to the kitchen and sat her down at the trestle table with a sandwich, salad, and cup of herbal tea.

"Shilo, I know you well enough to know when you're concerned about something."

She picked at her salad and drank a long draft of her herbal tea. "There's something going on," she finally said. "I don't know what it is. It worries me."

I examined her face, the lovely sloping planes of her cheeks, the dark lashes, from under which she regarded me, the slim nose and pouty lips, pink with good health and owing nothing to science nor artifice. "Honey, have you not been listening? These people are cuckoo bananas. One day two of them are enemies, and the next best friends." I explained how Rishelle had been so dismissive of Millicent. "And yet now they're best buddies. You saw them sitting together whispering. *And* hauling Chi over to whisper to him. I think he's got feelings for Millicent. I'd never have picked her as his type."

"I don't know. There's something there. On the surface someone is calm and cool, but there is kind of . . . a layer of anxiousness, you know?"

"I don't understand most of them." I remembered Todd and Dirk's conversation I had witnessed from above, still trying to decide if it was friendly or a quarrel. "There is a fluidity in this cast and crew, friendships and alliances that shift like beach sand, and I don't know what to make of it. Dirk and Millicent both pretend to hear voices and feel things, who knows what, while Hugh tries to corral a bunch of egos the size of Texas. Dirk, the dirty dog, tried to bring in the spirit of Tom Turner, and Lizzie decked him, which is why he's got those injuries. Ever since then he's been pouting, and the rest are enjoying the show."

She shook her head. "There's more to it than that. Something else is going on among them, something other than the stuff you just talked about."

"Like what?"

She shook her head. "I wish I knew. I feel . . . something."

Half Traveler, half Gypsy; that's what Shilo has always said she is. Travelers, I had recently learned, are descended from Irish immigrants and had "the sight," as do Gypsies, or Romanichal Gypsies. *She* would do well on a show like *Haunt Hunt* because her sense of things is usually spot on. "So you're sensing some psychic thing, an aura, or something?"

She touched her stomach and frowned. "Uh-uh, just a bad vibe. Tension, and not just what you see, but something else underlying it all. Something . . ." She shook her head, unable to explain.

I laughed. "Oh, honey, you don't know the half of it. All I want is for them to get done, and go. One more day."

Chapter Eleven

❈ ❈ ❈

AFTER WE ATE I walked her out to her car, which had been completely overhauled by our local genius mechanic, Ford Hayes, the fellow who had also made my old Caddy Fleetwood Brougham purr like a contented kitten. Becket joined us, Shilo cooed over him, then got in her car. As she honked and drove off, I waved good-bye, then, followed by my cat, I proceeded directly to the dining room to gather up the garbage. Becket settled down under one of the tables to feast on ham someone had dropped. What a bunch of slobs these people were! I gave them all a look almost as dirty as my dining room—which they did not notice, some clustered together over a chart of shots to be finished and others talking intently—and proceeded to stack dishes and mugs.

Rishelle and Millicent huddled in a corner, whispering. It still puzzled me that the two were now the best of buddies when two days before Rishelle had dismissed the psychic as a fruitcake. Todd and Serina were consulting about something technical, but Todd shouted over his shoulder that they had something to take care of in the attic, and they disappeared. Hugh called Millicent over and spoke with her and Dirk together; it looked like he was giving them a stern lecture. Dirk appeared sulky, arms crossed, scowl in place, and Millicent near tears, her bottom lip trembling so I could see it even from a distance. Good. Hugh was laying down the law; maybe they'd behave.

Dirk at one point yelled, "I was supposed to get that site!"

Hugh jabbed his pointed finger into Dirk's chest and gave him a dressing-down while Millicent smirked and exchanged looks with Rishelle. Maybe Dirk was being disciplined for going off script the night before. It would be good for him to not get his own way for once.

The sun descended. They started back to work. Again Pish followed one team, while I shadowed the other. Todd and Felice were paired up, with Ian as the cameraperson and a young fellow on sound. Dirk was their psychic companion.

It was boring as hell. Dirk was still sulking, claiming not to feel anything as they checked out one of the bedrooms the cast was using, staged to look unused. Their luggage and crap was all tossed into a shadowy corner of the gallery where it wouldn't be in shots. Todd did an establishing shot first, explaining that this bedroom in particular was said to be haunted. Someone in Autumn Vale had apparently told him that a person died in that bedroom. I say "apparently," because it seemed to me at this point that they weren't above making up stuff to add to the haunted aura.

Lizzie and I stayed behind the scenes, with Lizzie acting as assistant to the sound guy, who used her to hold cords and move stuff out of his way. She was anxious, I could tell, but stayed on task. Todd and Felice, who were very serious about the whole *Haunt Hunt* thing, used their EMF and K2 meters, REM-PODs, and digital cameras. They used something called a geophone, though I wasn't sure what it was or what it detected. They recorded sounds, saw shadows, felt auras. They communicated with spirits *not* of the recently dead, thank goodness, or I would have had to tag team Lizzie and deck someone. Something fell off the dresser—not surprising to me because I saw them place it fairly precariously on the edge, earlier, during the scene staging—and they made a big deal out of an "anomalous temperature drop" in the corner of the room farthest from the radiator. Big surprise in November by a north-facing window in chilly western New York. And yes, I know that's snarky.

When they took a break, I found Pish in the dining room by the technical tables and suggested we switch teams. He was more than happy to do that, since Rishelle, Stu, and crew were going to trudge out to the garage, and he had no desire to go out into the cold. Evenings were getting distinctly nippy as autumn advanced in western New York State.

"How did it go?" I asked.

He shrugged. "They heard some ghostly moaning, which I think was Stu's stomach grumbling, and caught a thermal hotspot image of a partial apparition. It was Becket wandering down the hallway, but don't tell them I told you so."

Becket, once again! Helpful little beast. The ghost of kittens past? I snickered and toddled off to follow Millicent, Rishelle, and Stu out to the old carriage house, built in the mid-nineteenth century, now a garage/workshop where the oldest car was parked until Ford Hayes could haul it away to fix up. It was frigid out, probably in the low forties. I was underdressed with just a heavy cardigan over jeans and soft-soled shoes with no socks, so I was chilled to the bone by the time they started.

Stu and Rishelle started with an establishing conversation about the carriage house, that it was built in the mid-eighteen hundreds, had been converted to a garage, and still held the previous owner's old car. It was so weird; they whispered all of this as if the spirits were listening in, or . . . something. Not sure why. They got started, creeping around a place I rarely venture into because it feels kind of cold and unwelcoming, just the thin blade of their tiny flashlights slicing through the dark. We ran into cobwebs and tripped over tools.

They scanned the car with their equipment and got nothing, but when they got closer to the tool bench that lined the far side of the space, things got better. It was a gold mine of ghostly investigation, apparently. Stu and Rishelle had strong readings on their equipment, and Millicent had powerful sensations.

It was genuinely creepy at times. I was behind unruly-haired Arnie, who had the Steadicam on a body mount, and Serina, who was holding a boom mic, as well as a production assistant and Hugh Langley, who had his shot list on a clipboard, with a book light attached, on its lowest setting. We were a veritable legion, though the hunting crew was supposed to be virtually alone. I had seen enough shows to know that it worked, in a curious sense, in the same way it does on house hunting shows where it truly feels like only the couple looking for a home and the real estate agent are present. The camera and crew become invisible by virtue of being ignored.

We all crept close to the tool bench. Millicent, visible only in a shadowy sense, quivered all over. "Oh! No, so cold, such . . . fear," she cried, and collapsed to the filthy floor, trembling and twitching.

Stu and Rishelle helped her to her feet.

"What's going on, Millie?" Stu asked, brushing her off gently.

"Tell us," Rishelle urged, supporting her over to an upturned pail, which Millicent sat down on.

Sobbing, Millicent muttered, "There is someone in this place who doesn't like us being here. There's a memory . . . sad . . . lingering . . . death! We need to get *out*!"

"Millie, we can't! We have a job to do," Stu said, earnestly. He took this all very seriously, and it was my impression that he believed in what they did. "This is important work! We're trying to help the restless spirits find their way."

"Sweetie, we need to figure this out," Rishelle said, her hushed tone soothing. To Stu, she said, "I'd love to get some levels and see if we can figure out what's going on." She turned back to Millicent. "I won't have you bullied, though, I mean that. If there is a malevolent spirit present we don't want to risk your safety."

"I can't stay, I just c-can't!"

"Why don't you go outside until we're done?" Stu said. He appeared eager to get on with the exploration.

Millicent went to huddle outside in psychic misery, but the other two spent another few minutes inside, and Arnie, the cameraman, got some great shots of the two investigators swiping cobwebs aside and examining the workbench area where Millicent had collapsed. He got some cobwebs tangled in his bushy hair, so he pulled his knitted cap down over his ears and tucked his hair up underneath it. I had to smother a laugh, he looked so idiotic, but no big deal.

Finally we exited, and Stu, Rishelle, and Millicent did some final thoughts outside of the carriage house.

"I couldn't stay, I'm sorry!" Millicent appeared distraught. "There was something in there that was trying to use me to get to you. It was terribly frightening!"

"There's definitely something there, and I think we need to meet with the rest of the crew to figure it out," Stu said.

Rishelle, looking gorgeous in a low-cut V-neck cashmere sweater, her heart tattoo rhythmically moving with her heaving breath, nodded. "I heard some things in town about this place, but I didn't believe them. Now I believe."

Mabel's story, I thought. She must have been telling it to half the town.

"Okay, kiddies, we're done for the night. Let's pack it in," Hugh said.

"What did you all hear in town about the garage?" I asked, following them.

They ignored me. We made our way back through the black night to the castle. The other team was done for the night, too. We all gathered in the dining room by the equipment table. Arnie slipped a memory card from his camera into an editing bay. He pulled off his knit cap and tossed it aside, watching something, his lips pursed. I circled and caught a glimpse; it was just Millicent doing her swoon.

"What an awesome night!" Rishelle crowed, eyeing her husband. Her tone had a distinct edge of wanting to one-up the other team. "Millicent was wonderful! She got some good stuff, didn't you, Millie?"

The psychic looked like she wanted to weep. She huddled on a chair, knees up, hugging them, swathed in her array of scarves. "I guess so," she said, faintly. "There is something there, in the garage by that workbench. I'm scared, guys. I mean, I know I always *say* I've got something, but sometimes . . ." She stopped short of confessing she pretended to feel and experience things on other occasions. "This was . . . *terrible*. Dark. *Scary*. I don't *ever* want to go out there again." She caught back a sob.

Dirk paced back and forth, his battered face twisted in anger, muttering to himself.

Chi-Won Zhu looked alarmed and knelt by Millicent, taking her hands in his. "You don't have to do anything you don't want," he said, his voice gentle.

"Aw, look at the tech guy cuddling the nutty psychic," Dirk sneered. He threw himself down in a chair and put his booted feet up on another. "Sounds like a fake-out to me."

Millicent stood, pushed past Chi, and stomped over to

face Dirk. "It was *not* fake! I defy you to go into that place and not feel what I felt! You wouldn't. You'd be too *scared*. You're a big cowardly bully, no more a psychic than . . . than Stu is!" She whirled and headed to the kitchen.

Disgusted with the lot of them, I drove a sleepy Lizzie to her grandmother's and got back just as the extra crew was leaving for their motel. It was an unsettling night, and not just because I was missing Virgil, who had called earlier grumbling about surveillance, and how much of a pain it was. The ones I was billeting started heading to bed around four in the morning.

I felt restless and ill at ease. Pish was weary and gray. I made him go to bed while I cleaned up the kitchen as the *Haunt Hunt*ers eventually made their way to their rooms. Millicent had apparently recovered her spirits, because she and Rishelle were whispering and giggling, arm in arm, as they climbed the stairs and separated, to go off to their own rooms. Millicent dashed back out, though, and grabbed Chi-Won Zhu's arm, tugging him aside and talking to him in whispers.

I was up a couple of times checking on noises. I heard whispering and slamming doors, but decided there was no ghostly origin, just the spirit of nooky and hanky-panky. As tired as we all were, you'd think they would have settled down, but no, they had to be like restless ghosts at a séance. Was that usual? I wondered

I caught Felice creeping up the stairs, a coat on over flannel pajamas; she defensively said she thought I wanted smokers to do so outside. I couldn't blame her for that. However . . .

"I thought I locked that door?" I hissed at her.

"I found the key," she said with a shrug. "On a peg by the back door."

"Hand it over!" I said, hand out, snapping my fingers. She dropped the key in it. I went down and relocked the back door, but as I was returning up the stairs, Hugh was coming down.

"I wondered what all the commotion was," he said with a frown. He had on a handsome heavy housecoat and his feet were bare.

"Hugh, you'll catch cold, with bare feet in this castle!" I told him I was just locking up, not wanting to worry him about his wandering crew, and with a sigh he nodded, turned, and climbed back up, returning to his room. I made it to bed, jammed a pillow over my ears, and slept.

The next morning around ten everyone met in the dining room, looking bleary-eyed. The day was to be dedicated to any further establishing shots they needed, final interviews, and then they were going to retreat to their offices in Buffalo to review the footage and make much out of virtually nothing. In a few weeks I would get a call, and Todd and his investigators would come and on camera tell us what they found. Or what they *said* they'd found. Whatever. Then they'd splice it all together into a half-hour segment of an hour show. I was so eager for them to leave I would have sworn to seeing a flying polka-dotted pig to give them something to talk about so they'd leave, if that's what it took.

Hugh glanced around the table and frowned. "Where's Dirk?"

Some of the cast and crew looked at one another, as if seeking answers, but most shrugged.

"Still sleeping?" Pish asked.

"With my luck he's had a heart attack," I muttered under my breath, but I was more concerned that he had some kind of hidden concussion from Lizzie's "attack" and was lying unconscious. I volunteered, since it was my abode, to check on him. But he was not in his room at all and hadn't been all night, unless he was a domestic goddess and made his bed up exactly as neatly as he found it. Unlikely. I returned to the dining room.

"He's not there, and it doesn't look like his bed's been slept in."

Some people exchanged looks. Odd looks. *Secretive* looks. My Spidey senses tingled.

Hugh appeared to catch those looks as well. "What's going on here? If anyone knows where Dirk is, he or she had better speak up now."

"I *may* know where he is." That was Chi-Won Zhu, a man of so few words I could probably repeat every one he'd said. "I mean, I hope not, but . . . maybe. Follow me," he said, and marched from the dining room and out of the castle.

Chapter Twelve

❈ ❈ ❈

W E DUTIFULLY FOLLOWED the tech specialist out of the castle, across the flagstone terrace, around the side, with cast and crew members in clusters, asking one another what was going on. More of the crew was arriving from their motel billets on the highway between Autumn Vale and Ridley Ridge, but they were too busy with their technical vans and equipment to even notice our weird troupe. Becket, who had escaped as I was closing up for the night, disturbed by the odd creatures in our midst, came bounding out of the forest and joined us, swishing through the lengthening dew-dampened grass that tossed in a turbulent wind that was picking up.

I caught up to Pish, who strode along, a worried frown on his face. "What do you think is going on?" I asked, breathless. "Why would Dirk be out here?" Doing one of those horror film classic scenes spending a night in a haunted locale? Maybe a *Blair Witch Project* kind of shoot; one man, one camera, one helluva haunted locale.

He had indeed seemed put out that we came back from the garage with lots of good stuff, as Stu and Rishelle crowed. I realized now that *that* was what he had been complaining to Hugh about the evening before when he said it was "his site"; he had marked out the garage as his once he heard Mabel's story, but Hugh had taken it away from him as punishment for his misbehavior in using Tom Turner's murder in his shtick.

He wasn't the type to take that lying down. He'd want to one-up Millicent and the others.

We got to the carriage house garage and stopped. "Who's got the key?" Chi asked.

Everyone looked around. I had my keychain and stepped up. There was the lock, looking as though it was snapped shut as it was when I left it the night before. I eyed Chi, uneasily. "Why do you think Dirk is in here?"

"Please, check. I can't . . . I mean, he likely isn't." He blinked, his eyes dark, blank pools behind his glasses. "It wouldn't be the first time he'd taken off on his own, right?" He glanced around at the others. Some nodded.

"Yeah, he sometimes goes off investigating and vlogs his findings," Todd said. "Makes me crazy," he continued, glancing at Hugh. "But he's production's pet, so he does whatever he likes."

"Did you say 'vlogs'?" I asked.

"Vlogs . . . video blogs," Lizzie said, coming up beside me. Someone had dropped her off. "Come on, Merry; get with the times. He does vlogs and posts to YouTube."

"And sometimes he takes off at the end of shoots when he knows his part is over," Stu said.

I frowned and looked around. All the vehicles, as far as I could tell, were there and accounted for. He was not gone, unless he had learned to fly. "But if he's in here, then the lock shouldn't be locked, right? I mean, that's impossible." I tugged at the padlock and it fell off the hasp; it *wasn't* locked. But I had *left* it locked at the end of the shoot, I was sure of that. I narrowed my eyes and glanced around.

Hugh strode forward. "This is ridiculous. He's not in here; he's just taken off. So let's take a look and eliminate this, then I'll call him and straighten it all out. He probably had a friend pick him up. He's a bit of a jerk, but he's the most popular jerk here, and don't any of you forget it!" Hugh yanked the door open and strode into the dim, dusty recesses.

Becket raced in after him, to my surprise, so I followed. "Becket!" I yelled. "Get out of there. I don't want you getting in trouble." The garage was dirty and had stuff like oil, chains, nails, and a workshop area of lethal-looking rusty saws. Of course Becket didn't listen; when did cats ever?

I'll admit, I was grumbling to myself as we all trooped in, but given what I've experienced in the last year, there was a frisson of nerves. Nothing could have happened. Could it?

Hugh strode around the garage. It's quite large, and in daylight fairly bright since there is a row of windows up at the roof peak. "Dirk, Dirk! Are you here?"

I noticed, though, that others were not as boisterous. Some hadn't entered at all. I looked back out the open door—someone had swung both big doors wide open to increase the amount of light in the garage—and saw Rishelle and Millicent framed in the light, huddled together, clutching on to each other. I felt an instant of worry, then heard a yelp of shock behind me. I whirled and saw, across the open space past one of the support beams, Chi-Won Zhu staggering backward and Hugh gaping in horror.

I raced over. There on the floor, his eyes horribly open and filmed with gray, was Dirk, dressed as he was when I last saw him, with his long black coat flung out, lying in a thick pool of dark, drying blood with the whole top of his head crushed by a heavy red metal toolbox that lay on its side in the blood, tools littered about him. I moaned and my stomach lurched. I shuffled backward as Todd, Stu, and some others caught up with me and saw what I saw, their voices becoming a chorus of horror and disbelief, and a wild cacophony of wailing, sobbing, hoarse croaks, and cries of dismay.

Becket, behind us, sniffed the air and headed toward the pool of blood. I grabbed him, not able to bear the thought of him getting any of that appalling liquid on his paws or in his fur. I stumbled across the floor and out the door, thrusting a struggling, yowling Becket at Lizzie, telling her to stay put outside of the garage and hold on to my cat as I bumbled around to the side of the building and emptied my stomach in the long grass.

Someone held back my hair and rubbed my shoulders. I looked up to see Virgil, who was frowning in puzzlement and staring at the garage, within which voices were still babbling. He looked dazed and tired, but a more welcome sight I don't think I've ever seen. I threw myself at him and he hugged me. I felt the scrape of his whiskers—grown in thickly while he surveilled for two days—against my cheek.

"Merry, what in God's name is going on here?" He found a tissue in my cardigan pocket, fished it out, and thrust it at me.

I wiped my mouth, then told him what we had discovered. He immediately snapped into police command mode, all traces of weariness gone. "I'll take care of this." He strode off toward the garage entrance. He may have been muttering "*Not again*," over and over; I'm not sure.

"IT'S A HORRIBLE ACCIDENT, BUT IT'S JUST AN *ACCI-dent*," Hugh Langley said to Pish as they sat together on white wrought iron chairs on the terrace, watching the sheriff's department do their job of securing the scene. The medical examiner, a local doctor I knew all too well at this point, arrived. "I don't see why I can't call Dirk's brother in Ohio," Hugh continued. "He has a right to know."

"We need to let the authorities do their job, Hugh," Pish said. "Now or an hour from now, the news will wait. It's not like his brother can do anything."

The producer shook his head in dismay. "I can't believe it. Dirk, gone? It's wildly improbable. What was he doing in that garage?"

It was now a half hour after our discovery, and I had been given permission to go to the washroom, brush my teeth, and put on the huge coffee urn. It was going to be a long day and would require copious amounts of coffee to get through. I paced back and forth, from the terrace where everyone had gathered, out to the open drive where I could watch the proceedings at the garage.

"And what are we going to do about the show?" Hugh lamented, ruffling his sparse hair, then smoothing it down again.

His lament may have seemed callous, but I couldn't blame him for thinking of the show's future, given what he had said about Dirk being its most popular cast member. And speaking of . . . there was something going on with the cast and crew. Chi looked haunted. More to the point, why were Rishelle and Millicent *still* clutching each other and whispering nonstop? The psychic appeared on the verge of a nervous breakdown. I paced away once again and turned my attention back toward the garage. Virgil stood talking to Sheriff Urquhart, at one time his deputy sheriff. My husband nodded, clapped him on the shoulder, and turned, stalking back toward us.

I stowed away my suspicions to ponder later and waited for Virgil. He motioned me aside and I followed him out to his car. It was a nondescript battered sedan, the better to blend into his surroundings, he said when first he showed

me the disreputable vehicle he bought for three hundred
dollars. He then paid Ford Hayes to soup up the guts so it
revved like a Ferrari. He leaned back against the car and
took me in his arms, holding me close. We kissed.

"I missed you, wife," he murmured in my ear. "It was a
long, long couple of nights, but we got the guy. He's being
charged with insurance fraud. You should have seen him;
he actually lifted a mini fridge on his own and carried it up
a ramp into his moving truck. And yet he couldn't do
his job."

I knew this inconsequential talk was his way of giving
me space to calm down. "I'm so glad you're home." We
kissed again, watched intently by those on the terrace. "Virgil, what happened to Dirk Phillipe?" I muttered. "It looked
like an accident, from what I saw."

"It most definitely was *not* an accident," he said, staring
over my shoulder at the group. There was a deputy with
them now, and no one talked.

"How do you know? It was a tool chest. If he tried to get
it down off the shelf, it could have fallen on his head. Right?"

"It didn't fall," Virgil said.

His tone held a certainty I rarely heard from him in the past,
when he was a police officer. Maybe as a private citizen he
felt free to express his beliefs. I looked up at his flexing jaw
and steely eyes. "How do you know . . . oh." I thought of
one way they would know it hadn't fallen. It must have been
loaded on some kind of spring or something.

I looked back at the group of people and found the one I
was looking for. Chi-Won Zhu looked miserable, his head
in his hands, staring down at the flagstone. He knew all
about special effects. His past expertise on movies, he said,
was scenes where things are made to explode and move and
fall on cue. But as far as I knew, Chi had nothing in particular against Dirk, except . . . well, there was that incident
of Dirk treating Millicent like crap, and Chi clearly had a

thing for Millicent. Dirk had made fun of the special effects wizard's crush. Hmm.

But . . . not my circus, not my monkeys, as I kept trying to tell myself. They'd have to sort this out on their own. Unless I wasn't allowed to stay out of it; there was that possibility. The drawback to Virgil no longer being sheriff in Autumn Vale is that now I must deal with Sheriff Urquhart, who does not like me and never will. I had given up thinking I could change that. It was an Urquhart thing, I guess.

The crew who were not staying at the castle had been briefly interviewed and dismissed to return to their motel rooms, or wherever else they wanted to go, I guess. The gales of November swept over us. We all shuddered and trembled at the increasing cold. I was separated from my husband and we were all shepherded inside to the dining room and guided to tables. A deputy was stationed in our midst to discourage muttering, I suppose, though it was a little late for that. If anyone needed to get a story straight I'm sure they had already done so.

I checked in with Lizzie, who was curled up in a chair with Becket on her lap. He yawned and stretched and fell asleep there after his night in the great outdoors.

"You okay?" I asked, touching her shoulder.

"Yeah, I guess," she said. "What's going on? What happened?"

"We're not sure yet."

I was called to the library, where the police had set up a kind of informal interview space. One of the newer deputies, a very competent young woman, spoke to me first. I went through our evening ghost hunting, and then the night. Yes, I had the key to Dirk's room, and no, I hadn't been in it that morning other than to check that he was not there. Yes, they could search it all they wanted, though they didn't need my permission, given that he was, presumably, the victim of a crime.

What crime, they weren't telling me. It could have been one of several: death by misadventure, reckless homicide, suicide (hard to imagine, but possible, and . . . is that even a crime? Not sure.) and, of course, straight-up homicide.

Sheriff Urquhart arrived during the interview and the young woman hastily moved from behind the desk. "Miss Wynter, we meet again," he said, grimly, as he dismissed the young woman with a flip of his hand.

"I'm Mrs. Grace Wynter now, Sheriff, if we're going to be formal."

"Right. Virge and you . . ." He shook his head in evident disbelief that the man he admired greatly would marry an outsider, and a New Yorker, at that.

I resisted the urge to choose a weapon and throw it at him, though there was a marble egg paperweight within reach. It would have been so perfect. However, giving him a concussion would not be a good first step in our détente.

He examined the notes the deputy had made in small, neat printing. Finally he looked up. "Who are these people and why are they here?"

I started to explain, and he held up one hand.

"I know some of this already. There's lots of talk in AV," he said, meaning Autumn Vale. "But I mean, why are they staying at the castle, when some of them are out at the motel?"

"It was part of the agreement, I guess. I mean, we're set up for it. We have extra space and I'm always looking for ways to make enough money to keep the castle going. They agreed to pay a set sum for room and board for the cast and a couple of the crew."

"What was this guy like, this . . ." He consulted his notes. "Dirk Phillipe." He pronounced the name with extreme care and a curled lip.

"What was he *like*?" I looked up at the ceiling, which was coffered wood paneling, elegantly perfect in my lovely library. "He insulted people. He made fun of others. He was conceited and arrogant." I looked Sheriff Urquhart in the eye. "He was a jerk."

"So, you disliked him."

"Anyone with any humanity disliked him!"

He nodded, and then took me over the same ground the deputy had. I repeated almost verbatim what I said to her, and the sheriff finally let me go. Virgil was waiting in the dining room when I emerged from the library; his expression was grim, exhaustion warring with a tightly guarded fury I recognized. A nerve jumped under the skin at the corner of his eye. My darling husband was frustrated by some aspect of the investigation.

He took me in his arms and held me close once again; I love that he always seems to know what I need, which is generally just him. I put my head to his chest and listened to his heartbeat, finding in that steady thump my center, then I looked up again into his eyes. I'm a couple of inches shorter than my stalwart hubby, and can pretty much look him in the eye.

"I'm guessing there is something going on that you would do differently," I whispered.

He let out a bark of laughter, squeezed me, then let me go. "You could say that. Why did Urquhart let the rest of the crew go? He should have talked to all of them *himself*, not just let his deputy take care of it. That's an outbuilding; there are a hundred ways to get into it, and someone could have parked on the road or on the lane near the road, snuck up, had an altercation with the vic, killed him, and then left without so much as a . . . anyway. Phillipe may have even arranged to meet someone out there, who knows? Maybe it's not that way, but Urquhart sure as hell didn't know that when he let those people drive away, back to their motel, ready to spread who knows what information to who knows who?"

I wanted to chuckle, but didn't. I wanted to remind him that Urquhart was handpicked by Virgil himself to step in as sheriff, but didn't. Discretion is the better part of marriage.

Pish joined us, looking over his shoulder at the *Haunt Hunt* cast and crew. His aesthete's face—intelligent eyes, longish nose, constantly curious expression—was lined with worry, his thin, straight light brown hair tousled in unusual disarray. "I'm sorry about this, Merry, I really am."

"So *you* killed Dirk Phillipe?" I said.

"What? No, of course not!"

"Then stop apologizing," I said with a smile.

"But I think I know who may have," he said.

Chapter Thirteen

✖ ✖ ✖

"WHO?" I ASKED, startled by his declaration.

"Hugh."

"Who?" Virgil asked.

"Hugh!"

"Hugh Langley, the producer," I said to stop the "who's on first" quality of our conversation. "That is the cultured-looking man with his legs crossed, the one looking annoyed and texting on his cell."

"He shouldn't be doing that," Virgil said with a frown. "Why didn't Urquhart ban cell phone use?"

As he had already said, my husband was concerned about what was getting out to the media. But none of this was up to him; this was Urquhart's party now. "I don't think he's going to tell the press," I said, then had second thoughts. This was TV, after all; even bad news was publicity. "Not yet anyway. He'll wait until he can issue a statement of some sort. And Urquhart may have *said* no cell phone use, but people in the business never think things apply to them." I shrugged off my worry about what that would do to our image yet again, though both Wynter Castle and Autumn Vale had taken a hit in the last year with the murders that had occurred in both places. Social media and newspapers had not been kind. But this was not about us. "Why do you say you think Hugh killed Dirk?" I asked Pish.

He sighed and frowned. "He did not like Dirk one little bit, I know that for sure. Thought he was a big phony."

That wasn't exactly what I had noticed, but Pish reads things differently than I sometimes. "Dirk was valuable to him, though, a ratings rock star. And as for disliking him, that goes for almost every single person on the cast and crew," I said.

"Why is that?" Virgil asked.

I explained about Dirk Phillipe's painfully arrogant, dismissive behavior, sharp tongue, and delight in humiliating people. "He could be nice, when it suited him, but usually he was just a *horrible* person."

"There had to be more to him, though, than his assholiness," Virgil said.

I snorted with laughter at his description, then, horrified by my own outburst, shut my mouth as all eyes turned toward me. Lizzie slunk over to me, looking more than a little frightened.

"I swear this place really is haunted," Lizzie said, eyeing the others through a narrowed gaze. "Honestly, why *does* crap keep happening here?"

I sighed and shrugged, almost in tears. My emotions were veering wildly, pinging like a pinball machine ball among irritation, overwhelming sadness for Dirk's family, and anger. I put my arm over her shoulders and hugged her to me. "Good question, to which I do not have an answer."

An hour later, everyone had been interviewed. The sheriff had taken aside Chi-Won Zhu for a second interview and set his minions to search the bedrooms, after gaining all of our permission, which was granted. I retreated to my kitchen, while Virgil left to catch a shower, a shave, and get some rest at his old house, which was still vacant, awaiting the closing date. That was *my* idea; I didn't want to chase him away, but he looked worn right out after a couple days of nonstop surveillance, and I knew darn well he'd get no rest at the castle, not with Sheriff Urquhart in charge.

Millicent, her eyes red and puffy, drifted in and sat down at the trestle table. "What are you doing?"

"I'm making muffins," I said. It gave me pause for a moment; I had just seen a man's dead body two hours ago, and now I was making muffins. Was I becoming unfeeling? I hoped not, but life did have to go on. "Do you want a cup of tea?"

"Do you have herbal?"

"Sure," I said, then named off what I had. She wanted the rest and recuperation blend, so I set the kettle to boil and continued with my muffins.

"Do you use all organics?" she asked, eyeing my pound of butter and all-purpose flour with an apprehensive look.

"No."

"You should. You're slowly poisoning people if you don't."

I kept my mouth shut.

"Do you use non-GMO flour, at least? Or better yet, fair trade, non-GMO, GF flour?"

I held my breath while I counted to ten in my head, then let it out, turning away and rinsing out the teapot to make my regular, black, no-fuss tea for myself. Instead of giving her a hard time, I decided to answer part of her question. "I've never made gluten-free muffins, but I've always wanted to try. Maybe I'll alter a recipe right now for us, if you'd like?"

"You're nice," she said, cocking her head. "Most people act like I'm a pain."

I couldn't imagine why.

I rustled around in my cupboard and came up with some

coconut flour I had bought before my honeymoon and hadn't gotten around to using. I lifted down my plastic tub of pecans from an upper shelf, then made Millicent her tea. I got myself a cup of my plain black, then set to work on a common recipe, Pecan Pie muffins, but using GF ingredients instead. We'd see how they turned out.

"So I've never asked: How did you end up working on *Haunt Hunt*?" I asked Millicent, chopping pecans as she sipped tea and thumbed through photos on her cell phone.

She shrugged. "I answered an ad online."

"What kind of ad?"

She looked up, frowning. "Well, Hugh was looking for psychics who could emote well on camera. I'd always had a feeling I was psychic—I mean, I always know what's going to happen, and I have dreams all the time that come true—so I decided to try out."

I had seen a couple of episodes with her in them, and she always seemed sweet, daffy, slightly dim, a tiny bubble off-center, but eager to connect with otherworldly sorts. How interesting that she was not a psychic before ending up on *Haunt Hunt*, though. "Have you ever worked in TV before?"

She shrugged. "I did work on a kid's show once, a few years back."

"What kid's show?"

"It was just a kid's science show on cable."

"What do you think of your coworkers and Hugh?"

"Hugh is okay, I guess. But I kinda feel like if I don't go along with what they need from a psychic, then they'll let me go, and this is the best job I've ever had."

Hmm. She had called Hugh a jerk and said she hated him. Why the change in tune? I tiptoed around the edge of what I thought she was saying, and asked, "Millicent, do you mean that you feel you have to fake it? At least sometimes?"

Her eyes widened. "No, of *course* not! Why would you say that?"

"Dirk was faking it."

"Well of course *he* was! He wasn't psychic, he was an attention hog." She sniffed and took a sip of her tea.

The texture of the batter was weird, a little like gravelly mud, but I filled the muffin tin I had sprayed lavishly with butter-flavored spray oil and popped it in the oven. Then I turned, watched her, and asked, "Is that why you set up something in the garage to scare him?"

She did a perfect spit take, tea everywhere, and then stared at me while she choked, coughed, and gasped for air.

I sat down and stared at her. "Millicent, it was obvious to me that something was going on between you and Rishelle. And it wasn't hard to figure out that one of you roped Chi in to rig something to scare Dirk. If it was a prank that went wrong, you have to tell the sheriff that. Or I will."

Tears welled up in her eyes. "Now you're just being mean to me," she whimpered, staggering to her feet and upsetting her cup of tea, which sent a pool of dark, cooling liquid spilling across my trestle table.

I grabbed a tea towel and threw it over the tea, letting it soak up the liquid while I kept my eyes on Millicent. The young woman pulled her crocheted wrap around her and tugged it into a knot, then nervously played with her bangles. She seemed riveted to the spot. "It wasn't my idea," she finally said.

"Whose was it?"

"Rishelle's. She hates him even more than I do."

Interesting. I might hunt down Rishelle when I was done with Millicent to get her side of the story. "And who roped in Chi?" If I was right, his particular expertise had been a necessary part of the plan.

She paused, and I saw her expression become more guarded. She was going to lie or evade the question, I thought.

"I'm the one who asked him," she admitted. "He was

happy to do it, because Dirk is . . . was . . . such a jerk," she continued. "To me and everyone else. We wanted to teach him a lesson."

"Yeah, I know that. So, you're going to tell Sheriff Urquhart?"

She got a stubborn look on her face and crossed her arms, swaying back and forth. "Why should I?"

"May I remind you that if you don't, I will?"

She whirled and stomped off, doing her best Lizzie impression, I must say, then stood at the door and looked back. Her expression faltered. "Give me . . . give me an hour. I want to talk to Chi first." She headed out.

I would bet that Chi had already spilled the beans. I waited two seconds and headed in the same direction. The timer on the muffins would turn the oven off, and they'd have to wait. I needed to talk to Rishelle. With any luck Dirk's death would turn out to be simply a case of misadventure, a prank gone horribly wrong, and they could all leave by the end of the day. But I wasn't counting on it. Something was off about that scenario, and I wanted to know what it was. For that I would need to talk to Virgil, Sheriff Urquhart, and Chi-Won Zhu.

I found the special effects wizard outside, winding a cord onto an orange reel. On my stroll through my castle I had noticed that many of the cords were removed, and some of the equipment. "What's up, Chi?" I asked, tugging my sweater closer around me. A wind had come up and was blowing through the drive with cold, cutting precision.

He turned, and I faltered. He looked ravaged, his face drawn, an expression of incredible pain on his face. I bolted to him and stopped, touching his arm rather than hugging him. He seemed drawn in, blinkered, like he was shut down in some way, every thought turned inward on himself.

"Chi, what's wrong?"

He shook his head.

"I know what you did," I said softly. "And I know that you didn't intend for Dirk to die."

His whole body shuddered and he collapsed cross-legged on the ground, burying his face in his hands while he wept. "I didn't! I never meant to hurt him," he said on a gut-wrenching sob. "It was supposed to scare him, not *hurt* him."

I sat down with him and watched, waiting for the tears to subside. His emotion was raw, like a ragged wound. Funny that he seemed so much more sensitive to what had happened than the "delicate" Millicent. I asked him if the psychic had talked to him yet, and he shook his head. "Look, this is not going to be easy, but you need to tell the sheriff the whole truth."

He nodded. "He asked me about it, but I . . . I lied. I was scared. I don't understand what happened."

"Hopefully, they'll figure out what exactly went wrong."

I left him tidying his equipment van, after which he promised to find the sheriff and speak to him. I hustled off to find Rishelle, hoping she hadn't already coordinated with Millicent to conceal what they had conspired to do. The police presence was tapering off. The bedrooms had been searched and cleared. I saw Rishelle coming from the library, where she had been interviewed. Millicent was hovering, and eyed me, suspiciously.

I waved to Rishelle. "I need to speak with you right away!" I said, brightly, as I trotted up to her, put my arm around her shoulders, and guided her through the dining room, watched by the female deputy, and toward the kitchen.

I looked over my shoulder. Millicent looked frustrated, but not especially upset.

"What's going on?" Rishelle asked, pulling away from me as we entered the kitchen.

In my absence the oven had turned itself off. I pulled out the still-hot muffins, used a knife to pop a couple out, and tasted one. Every bit of the Pecan Pie muffin flavor with a hint of coconutty goodness, and none of the gluten. It was pretty good, and gluten-free! The trouble was, I couldn't make this an offering to the public because I knew these particular muffins would taste good only the first day, after which they'd be hard. I took another, tossed it to Rishelle, and plucked yet another from the tin.

"What's going on is, I know you and Millicent roped Chi in to trick Dirk, and that it went badly. She says the whole thing was your idea. I want to know how and why."

She glared at me, took a bite, and her expression instantly mellowed. She slumped into a seat, ate the whole thing, then stuck her hand out. I handed her another.

"These are good. I didn't realize I was hungry." She chewed and swallowed, then sat up straight and glared at me. "This is none of your business. However, I *have* told the police everything, and that's enough."

"No, it's not enough."

"I didn't *kill* Dirk! It's Chi's fault. Something went wrong." She frowned, shook her head, and took another bite. "I don't know what," she said, her mouth full.

"At least tell me the plan." I wanted her version.

She shrugged, finished the muffin, then asked for a cup of coffee. I handed her a full mug and slid the sugar bowl and cream pitcher across the table to her.

"Dirk has been a big pain in the butt since day one. Before I joined the cast, Todd complained about him all the time. I thought he was exaggerating, but when I joined the show I found out how big a pain he was. He was toxic, you know?"

"I've watched a few of the shows. He appears to be a bit of a grandstander."

She rolled her eyes and shook her head. "*Bit of a grandstander. If only.* What you saw on-screen was only a tiny part of the ways he made it the *Dirk Phillipe Show.*"

"So you and Millicent conspired to put him in his place."

She colored and nodded. "We were so fed up with Dirk that we wanted to give him a taste of his own medicine. So we planned a little trick. I've always thought that Dirk, knowing he was a big phony himself, thought that Millicent is the real deal, with real psychic powers. So we made a big deal out of Millie experiencing something huge in the garage."

"Which he had marked off as one site he wanted to explore because of something he heard in town. I know about that. He was angry when Hugh took that away from him."

"Which is when we decided to do it there."

"So what did you do?"

She shook her head. "Look, you were there, you saw what happened. I don't understand it. It was supposed to be a practical joke. We knew if Millicent laid it on thick that there was something dark and dangerous, Dirk would be intrigued and have to investigate on his own. It was our last chance, the last night of filming. If he didn't go, then we'd dismantle the trick in the morning and there would be no harm done. It's not *our* fault if Chi did something wrong and Dirk died because of it."

"So what *was* the trick?" I pressed.

She flapped a hand, dismissively. "Just something rigged on a spring to fall and startle him, and a camera to catch him whining like a little scared baby." She stood, stretched, and rotated her shoulders. "I'm done. I hope we get out of here and go home." She left the kitchen.

A camera . . . that meant it should all be recorded.

"I hope you all go home, too," I muttered. I needed to take a walk. Maybe by the time I got back the sheriff would have reviewed the recording and solved the case.

I summoned my cat and my teen friend, and went out. Lizzie was mulish and silent. Becket was capricious, darting off through the long grass, as we passed the garage. It was still taped off, a police deputy standing watch, but he let us pass without comment. We strode on through the lengthening yellowed grass of my land and finally the view was only of trees—the forests in the distance that surrounded my open patch of land. Off to the far side, near the Fairy Tale Woods, sat the Turner Construction work equipment, which was at rest today, since it was the weekend.

I glanced to my right; Lizzie was taller now than when I met her, and today her hair was tamed, pulled back and held in a thick ponytail by a scrunchie so it didn't obscure her intelligent face. She had a more thoughtful expression, too, not the old moody, obstinate, dour look she habitually wore. She was going to be okay, I thought.

We finally reached our destination and I again looked down into the hole, now lined with a concrete foundation and rebar sticking up out of the filled concrete blocks. I don't know what I was expecting. No work had been done since Virgil and I looked at it two days before. There were mounds of dirt next to the hole, waiting to be backfilled in around the foundation when it had dried and cured and been coated with water sealant. This was going to be home, right on the very spot where Virgil and I first made love, and sealed a bond I knew was going to last for the rest of my life.

"What are you guys doing here anyway?" Lizzie said, scratching at a pimple on her chin.

I swatted her hand and told her. But I didn't tell her *everything*. That was going to be a surprise. Just focusing on this, my future, helped. We headed back, and I felt more calm. It would all work out.

I'd *make* it work out.

Chapter Fourteen

WHEN I GOT back, Sheriff Urquhart was waiting for me, watching us walk up. He sent Lizzie away with one look, but then surprised me by picking Becket up, cradling him, and scruffing behind his ears.

"Mrs. Grace, can we talk?"

I nodded.

"Away from the others," he said, eyeing my castle home with disfavor. Becket was squirming, putting both paws against Urquhart's chest and pushing away, so the sheriff set him down gently, and the cat raced after Lizzie, following her in through the big double oak doors.

We sat in his sheriff's vehicle, the very one that until recently had been Virgil's. I examined all the knobs and dials, and the laptop Urquhart had installed on a console mount. He checked his cell, then slipped it back in his pocket, a sheriff for the electronic age.

"What's up, Sheriff?"

"I wanted to talk to you away from that place, because

I'm not sure how much of their equipment is still hooked up and running."

I was startled, and looked back at the castle. Well, heck, I hadn't thought of that. "Good point," I said. How many of the digital cameras did they have mounted throughout the place, and how many were running at any given time? Were they motion-sensor activated? Were any running through the night? Something to think about later.

"We've taken the camera that was in the garage, but I don't have the authority to take the ones hooked up in the castle, and Mr. Langley has his company lawyers stalling me on that for now."

I gazed at him through narrowed eyes, surprised by the information. "Why would he do that?"

"You tell me and we'll both know."

"Well, what does he *say*?"

Urquhart frowned and tapped his fingers on the dash. "He *says* all the equipment in the castle was turned off, so it has no bearing on the murder. He *says* it is his responsibility to the production company and HHN, which own the valuable and sensitive equipment, not to let it become involved in a criminal case where it could be confiscated and tied up for months, or even longer."

I should have thought of that. "Hugh has a point, I suppose. If you *did* take the cameras, how long would it take for your lab, which I know is not in Autumn Vale, to examine it and capture the information? He's got to be wondering, what happens if no one is ever charged? And even after they looked it over and did everything they needed, isn't it possible that HHN wouldn't get it back until after a trial, if there is one?"

He looked uncomfortable, shifting and sighing. Instead of answering, he said, "Anyway, about this murder . . . I don't know how much you know, at this point."

I told him what little I did.

He nodded. "I understand you urged the three to be frank with me. I appreciate that."

"It was the right thing to do. Did Millicent tell you that it was Rishelle's idea?"

He nodded. "That's one of the points where their stories diverge. Rishelle, in turn, claims it was Millicent's idea. Chi doesn't know who thought of it first, just not him. He was brought in later."

"So . . . I suspect there's more to it than a prank gone wrong," I added, realizing how little I did know, and wondering how much Sheriff Urquhart would divulge.

"We have reason to believe," he said, carefully, his expression neutral as he stared out the window, "that while the setup was originally intended to be a practical joke by the three members of the crew, the prank was altered somehow by one of them, or by someone else."

I flashed back to the scene; Dirk was on the cement floor with a red tool chest near his head, which was bashed in. I recalled other details: There were tools scattered around, and he was crumpled, his legs underneath him at an awkward angle, so he had probably fallen from a standing position. This all took place near a set of shelves that were over the top of the workbench, which was narrow. I frowned.

I hadn't looked up, so I didn't know what had caused the tool chest to leap from its place on the shelf. It did occur to me, though, that no one would put a tool chest that heavy so high because it would be impossible to get it down safely. I shared my thoughts with the sheriff.

He nodded. "There's an outline in dust on the workbench surface where the tool chest was originally. Someone put it on the upper shelf. But here's the thing: All three involved in the prank say the original intention was for something to fall off the shelf, but it wasn't the tool chest. It was a leather tool belt with no tools in it. It wouldn't have hurt Mr. Phillipe, just startled him in the dark."

"Where is that tool belt now?"

"We don't know. Not there."

"So, this was murder?"

"This was murder. They had a camera set up to record the prank and show Mr. Phillipe as, in Rishelle Halsey's words, '*the girly coward he is.*'"

That confirmed what I had heard. "So if someone altered the joke *they* should be on camera, too, right? And Dirk's death should have been recorded? It would have been motion activated?" I wondered what all of this was leading up to. Either they had seen the footage or they hadn't.

He nodded. "It was *supposed* to be, but guess what: It doesn't show anything. We've looked at it, but after the camera recorded those three doing the setup, it goes blank. Somehow, they made a mistake and turned it off instead of leaving it on, so it's useless."

Frustrating, but also odd. "They roped Chi in for his technical expertise, and he's very efficient. I've seen him work. He leaves *nothing* undone and tends to double-check as he goes. That's quite the coincidence, that it was accidentally turned off."

Urquhart nodded. "That's what *I* thought."

One of the three of them could have found a way to turn it off remotely, possibly, intending to come back and alter the prank to ensure its lethal outcome. "Or even all three," I said. "They could have set it up to look like they had intended a prank and someone else altered it, while all along it was the *three* of them."

He nodded, his gaze steady on the castle, a thoughtful expression on his face. "I suppose that's the most likely explanation, that the three of them planned it that way from the start." He shook his head and sighed. "I know I'm supposed to follow the evidence and not hypothesize at this point, but I *don't* think they're in on this together. If one of them did it, he or she probably did it alone. Their stories match up, other than a few details that could be misremembering, like whose idea it was. That's likely Miss Vayne's flightiness."

"I'm not sure she's as flighty as she appears."

We were both silent for a time, and I thought it all over. I turned and eyed the sheriff. He's a good-looking fellow with a hard jaw and high cheekbones, probably late twenties, young to be sheriff, but Virgil has faith in him. I, on the other hand, have had a contentious, at best, relationship with him. "So what do you want from *me*?" I wasn't being difficult, though I know it sounds that way. I was asking a genuine question.

He blinked and stared out the window toward the castle. "What is your impression of these people? We can do all the investigation we want, and we may hit something—I hope we do—but I feel like I'll have a head start if I have some insider information. I'm not asking for your opinion on who did it, Merry, I want to know how they interact. Any information you can offer will help."

I was warmed by him finally calling me by my first name, then alarmed that such a simple gesture could make me warm up to him. Was that his intent? How much could I trust him, given that we'd had an adversarial relationship for quite some time? But I wanted this solved, and he was now the sheriff. Cooperation was my best shot at a solution, especially since he seemed willing to enlist my help.

"I wasn't pleased when I came home and found this lot here. It wasn't my idea," I confessed. "I gather Pish was talked into it. He had called someone at HHN network, Chuck Sandberg, who put him in touch with Hugh Langley, the producer, and he put Pish in touch with Todd Halsey, to ask questions about the strange things that were supposedly happening in the castle. Somehow wires were crossed and they thought he was volunteering the castle as an investigation site. When they called to finalize the agreement and wanted to come right away, he figured it was harmless enough, so why not? In his professional life he is matter-of-fact and businesslike, but in his day-to-day life he's kind of a pushover."

"Okay, got that." Urquhart stirred restlessly. "Mr. Lincoln already told me all of that. Let's talk about the people individually." ·

I went over what I had learned and observed of the cast and crew of *Haunt Hunt* while Urquhart made notes. Occasionally, one or another of the people inside my castle would come to the door, look out, regard me for a moment, then disappear back inside. Todd bolted out the door and stood, glaring across the open expanse at us. He looked worried. Hugh came out, grabbed him by the shoulder, and they had an intense conversation. Finally, Hugh got him calmed down, put his arm over his shoulders, and led him inside. Pish, too, popped out once, and Lizzie, who bolted out of the castle, looked our way, then strode off, head down, Becket behind her, toward the woods. As long as none of the cast and crew followed, I was okay with that.

I told the sheriff about Felice Broadbent, who was complaining about not getting enough scenes because of Rishelle. I mentioned that Dirk Phillipe had humiliated Millicent Vayne, not for the first time, while Chi, who had a thing for Millicent, had also been humiliated by Phillipe. I also made note that while Rishelle had at first seemed adversarial toward Millicent, the two appeared buddy-buddy in the last two days.

"Is that why the three were behind the prank against the vic?" Urquhart asked.

"They wanted to humiliate him."

He nodded and tapped something on his laptop keyboard. "Okay."

I didn't like how this back-and-forth was going so far, since it all seemed to be me being forthcoming and him not giving me anything back. "You don't think they were working together to kill Dirk?" I wanted some kind of definitive idea of what theory he was leaning toward.

"Maybe. Maybe not," he said, evasively.

I sighed and glared out the window toward the woods while I thought.

"Anything else?" he said.

I narrowed my eyes and examined him. "Not so fast. You're still considering Millicent, Rishelle, and Chi suspects. I see your point; one or all could have used the 'prank' as a bluff, while one or two, or all three planned a real murder." He looked at me, no expression. "And while it's true that one of them could have snuck back in and changed things up, that would be awfully risky, don't you think? I mean, the other two—if it was one of them—would know, and in any case . . ." I trailed off and sighed. I was tired and this was too taxing.

"Go on," Urquhart said.

I was beginning to remember all the reasons I dislike Sheriff Urquhart. Virgil as sheriff I had been able to work with, but this guy . . . "Okay. Possibility one is that they intended this as a bluff and that their intent all along was to kill Dirk, then claim later that someone must have co-opted their prank, turning it deadly."

He nodded and tapped away at his keyboard. I wasn't sure if that meant he had thought of that, too, or if he was madly typing my number one theory.

"Possibility two is that one or two of them snuck back to change the prank to be deadly, without the other or others knowing, thus possibly putting the blame on the innocent party."

He nodded, still madly typing.

"Possibility three is someone *else* learned or knew about their plan and, with or without one of the prankster's knowledge, went and made it deadly."

He almost smiled, but kept it to a nod. "That's what I was thinking."

It's all take, take, take with you, I thought. That, of course, is when he surprised me by giving something.

"We've examined it from every angle. It doesn't seem logical to me that the three set up the prank, then reset it to be lethal, or at least, not *together*. We've investigated their backgrounds and there is nothing to indicate they are anything but coworkers."

Something pinged in my head, some previous connection among cast or crew members . . . I'd have to think of that later, because I didn't remember who it was offhand, nor did I know if it mattered.

The sheriff continued. "Also, as far as we can tell, the crew who stayed at the motel are out of it. We've already had Sheriff Baxter in Ridley Ridge review security cam footage that shows that none of the crew left the motel until this morning, just before they arrived here. So only one of those who stayed in the castle could have known about the prank and had the opportunity to alter it," he said. "What do *you* think happened?"

"Of those three possibilities I outlined?"

He nodded.

I pondered, then shook my head. "You know what? Any one of them seems just as likely as the other. However, I can think of one way to try to narrow the list. Yesterday, I gave Hugh Langley my only spare key to the padlock. When I left the garage last night I personally snapped the padlock shut. I have two questions: One, how did the trio unlock the padlock? And two, did Hugh give them the key, or does he still have it?"

"I'll tell you what they told *me* about that," he said. "Langley told me he gave it to Todd Halsey, who says he passed it on to cameraman Arnie Ball to use for the shoot."

"And?"

He shrugged. "Ball says he doesn't know *where* it went— he seems to be generally unreliable and forgetful, according to his staff, about stuff like that—but agrees the padlock was snapped shut after the shoot. Says he saw you do it."

"So how did the pranksters open the padlock?"

"Chi-Won Zhu claims he went prepared to pick it, but it wasn't necessary. It was unlocked."

I was taken aback. Was Chi lying? Why would he? "So we have two people saying exactly the opposite. Isn't that typical?"

I got out and Urquhart drove away, after telling me that the garage was off-limits for the foreseeable future. There would be a deputy stationed there at all hours. They had taken some things from individual *Haunt Hunt* cast and crew rooms and had issued receipts, and he would now be dealing with Hugh Langley's legal obstinacy about the DVR cameras.

He implied that if I wanted to spy, he wouldn't hold it against me. Or maybe I was just imagining that part. I wanted to know who had done such a dirty deed, and in so many words told Urquhart I'd keep my eyes and ears open.

As I lingered on my fieldstone terrace, reluctant to go in to the hubbub inside, I watched Lizzie come stomping back from her walk, looking cross and much put-upon, with Becket close behind looking just as tangled and bad-tempered.

"Oh, good heavens! You're both *covered* in burrs. I thought *one* of you had better sense than to get so mired in the burdock."

"Hey, don't talk to me about it; it was Becket who went first."

"He's the one I was talking to," I said, and led them both back through the castle, sending baleful looks up at the occasional camera on a high tripod. I led them both to the kitchen so I could deburr them. In autumn everything is dried up, and nothing sticks to clothes, hair, and fur better than dried burrs. The burdock plant, responsible for most of the burrs, grows rampant along the edge of my forest. It was time to get the boys, Zeke and Gordy, out to do more work. *If* I ever got rid of the *Haunt Hunt* cast and crew, that is.

"Sit," I said, pushing Lizzie down into a chair. Becket

was about to slink away but I went and closed the door. "You, too, mister. You wait your turn."

I got my comb out of my purse and began tugging at knots. To the accompaniment of her "ouch, ow, hey!" cries, we talked. "Did Sheriff Urquhart talk to you?"

"Yeah."

"What did you tell him?"

She shrugged, then screeched as I ripped out a burr. Becket started skulking toward the door again, but I said, "Stop!" and he stopped, stuck his hind leg in the air, and licked his butt. "Lizzie, if you want this done with less pain, I'd suggest you keep me happy by telling me what the sheriff asked and what you told him. He's asked for my help, but he hasn't exactly been forthcoming."

She snorted. "Typical."

"Lizzie, stop it. I know you don't like the man, but Virgil does, and I respect my husband's opinion. After all, Virgil was right about *you*, wasn't he? Now, what did Sheriff Urquhart ask and what did you tell him?"

"If you like him so much, ask *him*," she grumbled.

I yanked a burr out of her wild hair, and she settled down.

"He asked about Rishelle, Millicent, and Chi," she said as I more gently tugged burrs from her hair, hoping I wouldn't have to cut any out. "He asked if while I was helping, I noticed anything."

"What did you say?"

"I told him what I know, that Todd hates Stu, Felice hates Rishelle, and everyone hated Dirk."

Todd feared that Stu and Rishelle were having an affair, but I wasn't going to share that with Lizzie. Felice's dislike of Rishelle was partly professional jealousy. "You've spent some time with them working. What do you think of them from that?"

She was silent for a moment. I worked on a mass of burrs and successfully got them out of her slightly frizzy hair. I gave a whoop of success and handed her the clusters, bristly with her hair.

"How come even when adults get everything they want in life, they still aren't satisfied?" Lizzie asked, turning the cluster of burrs over and over, pulling at the strands of her own hair caught in the bristles. "These guys all work on a kinda cool, popular show. I mean, *I* think it's a bunch of crap, but it's fun anyway. And yet all they do is talk smack about each other and gossip."

I let her vent while I got another mass of burrs out. "This is it," I said, and handed her the last bunch. Then I brushed her hair out and French braided it, holding on to the end of the braid while I stretched to a junk drawer, got an elastic band, and fastened it on. "Next time you decide to climb through burdock, let me do this to your hair first," I said, and handed her a mirror from my purse.

She looked at herself, rolled her eyes, crossed them, and said, "This is how my mom wants me to look."

"You should humor your mom once in a while. Help me with Becket," I said. We put him up on the counter, all seventeen chunky pounds of him, and I got a ratting comb from the junk drawer. Thank heavens for junk drawers. I tugged at a knot of burrs in Becket's soft orange fur and he squawked, hissed, and growled. I turned him around, looked him straight in the eye, and said, "No more of that, mister! You behave or you'll stay inside 'til winter." He didn't hiss again once while we evicted the burrs.

"Okay, you've been around these people a lot and know them as well as me. Let's solve a murder." When I glanced at Lizzie, she was smiling. "What are *you* grinning about?"

"I *knew* you were going to investigate."

"Yeah, well, don't tell anyone else."

Chapter Fifteen

✳ ✳ ✳

I SAID IT easily, but I was struck with doubts immediately. I did know one thing I wanted, but hesitated, since it was something I'd have to delegate to Lizzie. Was it right to drag her into it? Well, she was almost an adult; I'd leave it up to her. So I told her what I needed done.

"Is that something you can do without drawing attention *and* without being alone with any one of that band of weirdos?"

She stared at me with disgust. "You'd think I was my mother!"

"What do you mean?"

"Being a cocktail waitress and all the other crap she's gotten herself into, you'd think my mom would have learned, but I swear she meets a person, and bam! She thinks the best of them."

"Whereas you . . . ?"

"My art teacher said he's never met anyone else who was born with a nihilist attitude."

"Do you know what he means?"

"I looked it up. He may be right."

I laughed but shook my head. "He's not, kiddo. I took a philosophy course and if I recall, a nihilist believes all things, values, people, are worthless. It's impossible for an artist to be a nihilist, or they wouldn't create art. You believe in your art, and you believe in us: Pish, your mom, your aunt Binny . . . me. Right?"

She nodded, with a crooked smile.

"Then you're no nihilist."

"Okay, I guess. But Merry, I got this. I can do it. *Trust* me."

And so I did. I then called Hannah. She had recently upgraded her cell phone and used it for everything, so I no longer had to go through her parents' line.

We chatted briefly, then she told me she had heard what happened. Everyone in Autumn Vale was, of course, gossiping about it. She had gone with her parents to Golden Acres for Sunday service in the sitting room, then she headed alone to the library to catch up on some work, but everyone accosted her along the way. Knowing how close we are, they thought she'd know more than she did.

"But now you're going to tell me what's going on. And I *hope* you've called me so I can help."

She, like most librarians, is one helluva researcher, and I *had* called to ask for help. I gave her the cast list and asked her to find what she could on all of their backgrounds. I'd do it myself, but she's so much better at it than I am. She had already done research on my well water situation, zoning regulations, solving numerous problems I have with my plans, and so many other things I'm afraid to tote up all that I owe her. In return I try to put her in touch with people who can help her, influential people in public life who know how to ask for favors and how to get things done, even for a small-town librarian in western New York State. Through Pish I have connections.

As we talked, I heard her tapping away on her computer.

"Well, this is interesting," she said. "Did you say Millicent Vayne downplayed what she had done in TV up to this point?"

"Sure. She said she worked on some kind of kid's program once, but that was about it."

"There's more to it than that," Hannah said. "She started on *Kid's World of Science* in 2001, but then she got her own short-lived show, *Mandy Monday's Science Rocks*. She was Mandy Monday, the presenter, but she's listed in another place in the credits as Millie Vayne."

"For what?" I said, not sure what she meant.

"She was in charge of special effects. Looks like it was a low-budget show, and she may have had no qualifications, but still . . ."

I gave a low whistle. Hannah promised to find anything she could on the other members of the crew, and I hung up, thinking about the implications of what she had told me. Millicent was not as ditzy as she seemed, she was older than she was pretending to be, and her involvement in both science and TV was much deeper than she had told me. None of that might matter, but one thing stood out to me—given her past in special effects it was quite possible that she had rigged the booby trap that had killed Dirk. She could have used Chi to set the initial prank, knowing how he felt about her, so that he would take the blame when something went "wrong," meaning, once she had gone back and rerigged it to be lethal.

If any of that was true, she was diabolical. However, it didn't completely make sense. If she was capable of doing it on her own, then why drag anyone else into it at all? Why not go ahead and do it herself? True, their joint prank made her involvement look more innocent, and she had placed the blame for thinking of the prank in the first place on Rishelle.

I found the cast and crew in the library. Todd was sitting with Arnie Ball and complaining. He had seemed affable enough whenever I spoke to him, but sounded bitter, from what I could overhear.

"I never wanted psychics. I never freakin' *agreed* to psychics. That was all Hugh's idea. I hope this ends that for good and we can move on without them."

Arnie looked over Todd's shoulder, causing the investigator to whirl around and glare at me. His gaze mellowed. He shrugged and looked across the room at Millicent, who sat with Rishelle and Chi in a huddle of misery.

"I didn't mean Millie," he said, half to me and half to Arnie. "She's okay. But Dirk was an ass. I want to do *serious* paranormal research." Arnie mumbled something to him, and Todd nodded.

I sat down with them. "If you felt so strongly, why didn't you refuse to work with Dirk?"

"To quote Hugh, '*No one wants to see a purely investigative approach to paranormal research*,'" Todd said, his shoulders slumped in defeat. "If you don't come up with fourteen hundred paranormal events in a location, people think it's a dud. It doesn't *work* that way! I wish I could get that through people's thick skulls. Besides, Dirk was Hugh's pet. Wouldn't hear a thing against him."

I looked across the room to the Eastlake desk. Hugh was sitting behind it, his head down in his hands. "Then this solves half your problem, doesn't it?" I said, with a smile to soften the implication. "Now you just need to get rid of Millicent. Of course, that wouldn't stop him from hiring another psychic or two, would it?"

Both men looked shocked. I got up, crossed the room, and put my hand on Hugh's shoulder. "Hey, are you okay? Can I get you anything? Spot of tea? Snifter of brandy?"

He looked up, his face lined and ravaged-looking. "How about a shot of arsenic?"

I sat down on a low stool and looked up into his face. "I know your star is dead, but this wasn't your fault!"

"Are you saying it wasn't murder?"

I paused, then shook my head. "No, it has to have been murder. But it's certainly not *your* fault."

"But it is, in a sense." He sighed and squared his shoulders. "I bear responsibility for this. Dirk was an instigator. He liked to stir the pot, and we kept rewarding him for it. Every time he got more outrageous, ratings went up, so we kept pushing him further and further."

"Who is the 'we' you're talking about?"

"The owner of HHN. We talked about it many times. Fans *loved* Dirk. He was a big hit at the paranormal conventions, outrageous, larger than life! Larger than . . . life." He shook his head. "He liked to rile the others up, and it led to—"

"It led to this," I finished for him.

He nodded.

"Todd figures you'll continue the show now without Dirk. What do you think about that?"

"I haven't thought about it. It's too *early* to think about that. His colleague died, for heaven's sake; what is Todd thinking about?"

"Something important to him, which is *Haunt Hunt*."

Hugh shook his head. "I like Todd, but he's totally unrealistic. The public doesn't want two guys stumbling around in the dark with light-up instruments, not getting any hits. It wants drama, screaming investigators, fainting psychic mediums, *ghosts*! Apparitions. Goose-pimply haunting."

"You make it sound like a Halloween haunted house event."

"It has some characteristics in common. The public wants thrills and chills. If they want science they'll watch *Nova*."

I saw his point. The audience wanted results, and Todd apparently wanted to do serious paranormal research; the two aims might be mutually exclusive. "But there are other ghost hunt shows that don't have psychics, right?"

"I don't think *we* can go back to that. Once you've gone down a certain road . . ." He sighed and shook his head. "We need the viewers because viewers mean sponsors, and the viewers loved Dirk. Damn!" He pounded his fist on the desk. "Why did this have to happen now? We almost had a deal for syndication."

I knew enough about syndication to know it was a gold mine, making it so the show was on TV in perpetuity. While profitable, if you were ashamed of the show, that would not be something you wanted. I glanced across the room at Todd. He wouldn't need to worry about that now.

I turned back to the producer. "Cheer up, Hugh," I said, intending to be gently humorous. "Maybe the network will cancel the show and you'll get to produce a wine and travel program."

He shook his head. "If *Haunt Hunt* is canceled I'll retire. Write a book. Get genteelly drunk every evening on French brandy."

A piano and violin piece started over the speaker system; it was one of classical composer Clara Schumann's trio pieces for violin, cello, and piano, a favorite of Pish's. Shortly thereafter, almost as if he were reading Hugh's mind, my friend entered the library with a tray of liqueur and tiny glasses, and brought it over to Hugh. I left the two men alone. Pish would comfort him better than I, most likely. They could talk about opera and classical music and a Monet exhibit he'd like to see.

I joined Millicent, Chi, and Rishelle. I must admit I was examining Millicent with new eyes, knowing how substantially she had downplayed her past experience in TV and how she had put on a front of ditziness that was likely not legitimate. Stu sat slightly apart from them with a book on his lap, a biography of Ben Franklin. I can tell when someone is really reading or not, and he was lost in it.

I turned to look at my other guests. Rishelle seemed dazed, her pretty face pallid. Chi was impassive, but his hands were shaking. Millicent, on the other hand, appeared mulish, yet close to tears. The three weren't talking or looking at one another, and I had the feeling my arrival had interrupted a disagreement.

"Have you heard anything?" Rishelle asked, her voice trembling.

"No. I don't know any more now than I did this morning."

"Poor Dirk! I can't believe he's dead."

"Are you guys okay? Can I get you anything? I'll be bringing out tea and coffee and some food shortly."

Rishelle shook her head and crossed her arms over her stomach, hunching on the stool she perched on. "I couldn't eat. I need a bottle of merlot and a Xanax." She laughed, but it was shaky and ended on a sob.

She was much more affected than the others. Was there something between her and Dirk? I didn't think so. The two seemed to actively dislike each other, and certainly that was supported by her suggesting and planning the prank to make him look foolish, if she was the leader. Rishelle stared at her husband with an expression of naked yearning. It was sweet if a little sad, and I wondered how much his obvious suspicions about her relationship with Stu had affected their marriage.

"Do you and Todd have kids?" I asked.

She shook her head. "I'm not ready for that."

"Mmm, I understand. It's a big commitment." I paused a beat, then said to the group, "I know about the prank you intended to pull on Dirk. I get it; he was a pain and you wanted to scare him."

Chi shook his head in puzzlement. "I don't know what happened. It was just a leather tool belt. It weighed maybe twelve ounces. How did that get changed out for a toolbox that weighed twenty pounds?"

"That's a good question. Chi, you rigged up the prank. Was the setup strong enough to dislodge a tool chest weighing twenty pounds or more?"

"No way! I had a spring-loaded mechanism with a sensor pad in just the right spot below the shelf so that when Dirk got close enough, it would trigger the spring and the tool belt would tumble down. But it wouldn't have budged anything heavier." He took a deep breath. "And they'll be able to prove that. The video will show everything." He looked calmer, happier.

Little did he know, if he was relying on the video to get him off the hook, he was out of luck. "Who among you hated Dirk enough to kill him?"

They exchanged glances.

"We were just talking about that," Millicent said.

"And?"

"Serina," they chorused. And explained why.

MY HEAD SWIMMING WITH QUESTIONS, I WENT IN search of the sound technician. She was nowhere to be found in the castle, so I pulled on a heavy cardigan and headed outside. I found her in the technical truck, sitting at an editing bay with headphones on, staring at a monitor where gray images of the *Haunt Hunt* cast moved about. I rapped on the door, but she didn't hear me, so I climbed in and touched her shoulder.

"Yah!" she shrieked, and her chair tilted.

I caught her, and she pulled the headphones off and glared at me.

"You scared the crap out of me! I thought I was next."

"Next?"

"Next to die," she said dryly, hanging the headphones on a hook on the sound board.

"So if you're so worried about it, why are you out here alone?"

"Because I can't stand the smell of hypocrisy in the morning," she said, her narrow face twisted in a cynical expression of disdain. "All those people with sad faces, when every single one of them despised Dirk and aren't sorry he's dead."

"Except for Hugh," I amended.

She just smiled, and I wondered why.

"Dirk was good for ratings, a producer's dream, making money for the sponsors and the network. Hugh had to like that."

"Some of that is true," she said, and smiled again.

"But *you* had a particular reason for disliking Dirk," I said, refusing to be distracted by wondering what she was implying about Hugh with that smile, or if I was reading into things.

"You seem to want to tell me why I disliked him so deeply. Go ahead."

I couldn't read her face. She stared directly into my eyes with a challenging glare, and her smile had died, her expression now unfriendly. What had I done to deserve that? "I've been told that you and Todd are having an affair, and that Dirk threatened to tell Hugh and get you fired."

She blinked. "I suppose Rishelle told you that."

"Among others." Rishelle and Millicent both had been eager to fill me in on Todd and Serina's affair. She looked down and fiddled with a slide control on the sound board. "We *were* having a bit of a fling, but it's over. Todd wants to work it out with Rishelle."

"Who he suspects of having an affair with Stu."

She raised her eyebrows. "You have been a busy gossipy little bee, haven't you?"

"*Your* point is, you had no reason to fear Dirk, because Rishelle knew and the affair was over. Why doesn't Rishelle believe that?"

"Rishelle can go kick rocks," Serina said, angrily. "I got sick and tired of being Todd's therapist and a placeholder for a wife who isn't into her wifely duties anymore."

Her voice was thick with sarcasm, and something else, perhaps pain. Maybe she didn't realize how much Rishelle still appeared to love her husband, given the look of longing I had witnessed on her face as she gazed at him. "So who ended it, you or Todd?"

"What does it matter? It's over, period, end of discussion." She turned away. "I have to get back to work."

"Work? On what? You don't think they'll air this episode, do you?"

"Are you kidding? If Todd has his way, it'll air. 'The Ghost of Murder Castle,'" she said, with a mocking arch to her sculpted brow.

"That's not funny," I said, sidling out of the van and stepping down to the drive. Her words stung. "I don't need my problems aired on TV."

She shrugged. "Not up to me. Ask the boss man."

"Todd?"

"Hugh. Todd's listed as an executive producer but Hugh is the one with brass connections. He's the one who makes all the final decisions."

I wrapped my heavy cardigan closer around me and headed across the drive to the castle, but decided against going in. I found it interesting that Serina was working on some of the first-night footage. Was that even her job? She was a sound engineer, not a video editor; shouldn't she be working with someone else?

Instead of going in I dipped around the terrace side of the castle out of the wind and got my cell out of my pocket. I checked in with Hannah, but she said she'd have to call me back because she was in the middle of something. I snuck a look around the front corner of the castle. I was thinking of calling Urquhart when I saw Todd Halsey bolt from the castle, run to the sound truck, and climb in.

Why was he cozying up with Serina in the sound truck if they had really broken up? There was so much off about this whole thing that my nerves were twitching. But I would bet that was why Serina was in the editing van; she was expecting his visit.

Chapter Sixteen

�֍ ✖ ✖

I WAS TEMPTED to sneak up on the van and peep in on Todd and Serina. I'd bet she was lying through her teeth about their affair being over. But what would I discover if they were messing around? I already assumed their affair was not over at all, and that Serina was trying to save face. Confirmation wouldn't make a bit of difference.

I headed back in. Where, in all of this, was Felice? She had been interviewed by the police, I knew that, but I hadn't seen her since. Maybe she was back in her shared room tidying up the mess the police probably made when they searched. For some reason they can't leave things neat. They have to toss everything until it looks like a teenager's room after a sleepover. Or she was outside somewhere smoking, her one passion in life other than being on *Haunt Hunt*, it seemed.

The great hall was empty. I should join my "guests," I thought, forced to stay for the time being because of the investigation into their colleague's murder. How long would

I have to play innkeeper to this bag of assorted nuts? Lizzie ducked her head out of the kitchen and motioned for me to join her. I followed, figuring I had promised people food and coffee anyway, so I may as well do that now. But I was not prepared for what I saw.

At the far end of my kitchen is a sitting area with wing chairs, a fireplace, and a low table. Lizzie had retreated there and laid out multiple small digital cameras. I gasped in horror. "Lizzie, what have you done?"

She was hovering over her hoard like an expectant chicken over a nest. "What do you mean?" she asked, her expression puzzled.

"What are you doing with all these?" I strode across the room and stared at the variety of cameras. "Where did they come from?"

"Let's see . . . these two were from tripods in the great hall," she said, about two that sat on one of the wing chairs. "These three were in cases in the dining room," she said, pointing to the ones on the low table. Her finger swung around to some lined up on the brick hearth, each on a piece of paper with writing on it. "These four were in cases in one of the vans."

Hand over my mouth, my mind—and heart—raced. I should have known better. And I couldn't even yell at her because I had set her on a task . . . not *this* task, but *a* task. She's like a ferret; give them something to do and they do it endlessly and obsessively until it is overdone, and then they find new ways to do it. That's Lizzie in a nutshell, a teenage ferret. All I had said was I'd like to know if the cameras in the great hall were on motion detection mode. I may have mumbled that I'd love to see what footage they got, but didn't think I'd ever know.

And now this . . . this *pilfering* of their equipment from the van and technical cases! My mind kept racing; what should I do?

She was still watching me warily, her expression revealing that she knew I was pissed about something, but she wasn't sure what. I don't have a lot of experience with kids, but I remember being a teenager. The things that anger adults are so often a mystery at that age.

I sighed and sat down on the free chair. "I'm afraid to ask. Have you looked at any of the video on the memory cards?"

"No."

"Good. Then we can put these cameras back where they belong."

"But you wanted me to find out if the cameras in the great hall were working last night. Don't you want to know?"

"I've changed my mind."

"Too bad," she said, mulishly, arms crossed over her stomach. "I've taken out all the memory cards and replaced them with blank ones, so I've got them *all*. We don't have to guess; we'll know by the video. It'll all be time-stamped."

"You *what*?" I screeched, then covered my mouth again, pressing my fingers to my lips. I wasn't sure if I was going to laugh, scream, or throw up.

She blinked and said it again, then added, "They're all labeled, if that's what you're worried about. I know which is which. Plus, you can tell by the—"

"That's not the point!"

"Gawd, what is *wrong*? You wanted to *know*, and now we can find *out*! I told you, the video will be time-stamped, and we can see what went on."

I took a deep breath and counted to . . . well, probably three. "Lizzie, I *said* I wanted to know if the cameras in the great hall were on motion detectors. What part of that was unclear? And what's with the rest of these?"

"I figured it would be good to know what was on the other cameras, too, and I know that doofus Urquhart won't get them."

"That's because he legally *can't*! HHN lawyers are balking. Lizzie, you've jeopardized the whole damn investigation."

For the first time I saw doubt in her eyes. Her lip trembled and she blinked. Darn! I jumped up and wrapped my arms around her, giving her a hug. "Honey, this is my fault. It is *all* my fault. I should never have set you on this task."

"But now that I've done it," she said, her voice muffled, "we may as well watch the videos, right?"

This was a sticky situation. However . . . it was murder on my property yet again, and one of those people in my library had done it. She was probably right; Urquhart was never going to be able to get these videos. If we figured out who killed Dirk Phillipe and told the police, maybe they could find some way of proving it.

"Okay, here's what we're going to do," I said, and set her on another task, asking her to wait until I had taken food to the group in the library before she did it, because I wanted to be sure she would not be discovered.

I did a swift job of throwing together a cold luncheon. Nothing relaxes people like food and drink, in my experience. Funerals and wakes make people hungry. This was neither, but it was close, so I put together sandwiches, cheese, a relish tray, fruit tray, coffee, tea, and a selection of cold meats. It was lucky I had done that gigantic shopping trip to Batavia.

I thought back to Dirk Philippe's charming behavior and thoughtfulness while he helped me carry stuff when no one else offered. If only he had always been like that! And I remembered Hugh pleading to call Dirk's brother to tell him personally what had happened. The man had a family, a life outside of *Haunt Hunt*. That was always the thing I remembered in murder cases; every person is more than his or her worst behavior. I made Lizzie help me tote things to the library, then sent her away while I guarded the *Haunt Hunt* cast and crew.

Felice had joined the others in the library, but was sitting alone in a club chair by the window overlooking the drive. Serina and Todd had rejoined the group, but a couple others were missing. Arnie was gone, and so was Rishelle. Drat! No one knew where either was when I asked, so I lined up trays on the library table on the far side of the room and stacked paper plates, napkins, mugs, and other necessities nearby, then set out to look for the two missing lambs. I went outside and circled the castle, but didn't find them. I saw Lizzie while I was out there, and she saw me, but she was busy.

I stopped for a moment and watched the garage area; the police were still there and had the whole area taped off, with one deputy standing guard. Or *sitting* guard, actually, on a chair with a laptop on his lap, ignoring everything else, fortunately for Lizzie. Another uniformed officer emerged from the garage with a paper evidence bag. She headed straight to a car and drove away. I knew that at the sheriff's department they would be doing research and investigating the backgrounds of each and every member of the *Haunt Hunt* cast and crew.

I returned inside by the back door to the butler's pantry and through my empty kitchen. Where could Rishelle and Arnie be? I trotted upstairs, checked a couple of bedrooms— what a mess!—and then moved back out to the middle of the gallery.

And heard a muffled thump and a moan.

From the cleaning closet.

My stomach dropped; was someone else in trouble? I whipped open the door and there was Arnie with his arms wrapped around Rishelle, who looked dazed at the sudden light, her cheeks and lips whisker-burned. Both blinked at me, expressions of dismay on their faces.

"Lunch is served in the library. I expect you down there in thirty seconds," I said, and slammed shut the door. I returned to the library and slumped own on the sofa, my mind again racing, this time because of this new information. Not Stu, but Arnie, the one Todd turned to, to complain about his wife. And . . . my eyes widened in sudden realization. That explained Rishelle's look of longing; she was *not* looking at her husband, but at Arnie, her lover.

"What a delightful spread you've produced in such remarkably short order," Hugh said, taking a seat beside me on the sofa.

Snapped out of my wandering thoughts, I smiled at him. He had a plate full of Genoa salami, Westphalia ham, double cream Brie with fig preserves, kalamata olives, grapes, and a roll from Binny's Bakery. "I'm happy to see that you're feeling better. Did Sheriff Urquhart say you could call Dirk's brother yet?"

He shook his head, a somber expression on his face. He set his plate down on a side table, barely touched. I was sorry I had spoken of it when it seemed he was getting his appetite back.

"No, the sheriff hasn't come back. But I think I'll call anyway. I believe that Dirk's brother has a right to know what has happened, and has a right to come here and find out for himself what investigation, if any, is going on."

"Aren't you worried about the fact that the killer has to be one of your group?" I murmured, glancing around at the crowd. Rishelle sauntered in, a new smear of concealer on her chin and cheeks, and headed for the food. Arnie did not accompany her and wouldn't for another ten minutes or so, I guessed, based on my observation of past affairs I had witnessed.

"I don't see why you think that is true."

Hugh had not seen the murder scene. Maybe he hadn't even grasped the prank setup, and how someone had altered it to kill Dirk. I wasn't about to enlighten him. "I'd hold off on notifying his brother, Hugh. I know it seems arbitrary to you, but the sheriff probably has a good reason for asking, and it is the police who will inform the next of kin."

Just then my very own former local sheriff sauntered in looking terrific, in jeans and a white shirt open at the throat. Virgil always looked good to me, and I could tell by the way Rishelle's eyes widened that she thought so, too. She stopped chewing, swallowed hastily, and tugged down her top.

Virgil crossed the room, I stood, and he hugged me, whispering, "Any news yet?"

I shook my head. "Not that I know of. I didn't expect anything. Can we talk?"

He nodded. I took his arm and we left the room. I had real food set aside for him in the kitchen, so I led him there, had him sit down by the hearth, now cleared of extraneous cameras, and let him eat in peace. I had made him roast beef on a kaiser roll with Dijon and horseradish, as he likes it, along with his favorite coffee and a bowl of salad to try to balance all the protein and carbs.

"Did you get some sleep?" I asked.

"A little." He stabbed at the salad and wolfed it down, then ate the roast beef sandwich.

I waited until he finished eating. He's always more reasonable after food. I had to talk to someone about the videos. I knew what Lizzie and I had done was wrong but not how to fix it, or whether to confess it to the sheriff.

He sat back in the wing chair and put his feet up, taking my hand in his and stroking my palm with his thumb. I wanted to surrender to the enjoyment of being with him, but dang . . . there was once again a murderer on the loose, and I couldn't relax knowing I had likely just served him or her lunch in the library.

"Virgil, I have a confession to make."

He looked over, a slight smile on his clean-shaven face. His hair was still damp from his shower, and he smelled *so* good. In a moment his eyes would turn cloudy and he'd be exasperated at me and maybe at Lizzie, too, though it was all my fault. I know the girl, and know that if you give her an inch she takes sixty-three thousand, three hundred and fifty-nine more.

I explained the theory about the digital cameras on mounts in the great hall, and how I had wondered if they were set up to start by motion detection. If they were, they might show who snuck out in the night, thereby telling us who might be guilty of altering the prank, killing Dirk. His expression became wary, and he watched my eyes.

"Hugh is never going to give Urquhart permission to take those cameras," I said. "He might be able to get a court order to seize them, but that'll take time, and HHN's lawyers will block it every way they know how."

"Okay."

I was about to explain, gently and with great diplomacy, about how Lizzie had misunderstood my request that she find out if the cameras were set on motion detector mode during the night when the girl herself stomped in, declaring, "I got it all loaded on your laptop and the memory cards back in all the cameras and—oh yeah, I wiped my fingerprints off everything."

Virgil, who had turned at her intrusion, now whirled back to glare at me, his dark thick brows raised. "Am I missing something?"

This was going to be a tedious explanation, with many husbandly recriminations. Actually, it didn't go as badly as I expected.

The first question he asked was of Lizzie. "Did Hugh Langley or the others ever specify what your duties were as an unpaid intern?"

"It was kind of informal, you know?" She shrugged. "Do what I was told and stay out of trouble, that's all I got."

Virgil nodded. "So, what did you end up doing?"

"At first I fetched water and coffee for the crew and cast. But after a while I was holding wires for them, and then I was holding cameras between shots. They take stills, too, sometimes for lots of reasons. Arnie especially. He likes to see a still image of the lighting of a spot so he can adjust angles. They use infrared cameras a lot, of course, but he likes stills with the light on, too, for later in production so other staffers at the studio can see what the room is like."

He nodded and got out his phone. I had forced him to get an up-to-date phone so we could not only call, but text and video chat. He had quickly seen the applications for his new business venture as a private detective and had turned his first phone in for one that was bigger for his big hands. It had all kinds of apps, like GPS trackers, maps, and assorted other doohickeys, the technical term for whatever I don't understand.

"What else did you do?"

"Arnie got me to fetch things all the time, and when he figured out I knew what I was doing he let me change out memory cards when one was full. He's a lazy guy."

Bingo. I saw what Virgil was getting at. It was shaky, but could save us. I sighed and leaned my head on his shoulder as he tapped at his phone screen. His cell phone is big enough that he can use it like a tablet. I looked over his shoulder and there it was, right there; a website explaining the duties of a TV intern, among the standard fetch and carry jobs, lots of technical tasks, like helping with lighting, camerawork, logging . . . oh!

"Logging!" I said, pointing at it in the description. "What is that?" Though I had a pretty good idea, having worked in TV.

"That's reviewing all the video and writing down exactly where it was taken, how long the piece is, and stuff like that," Lizzie answered.

I sighed in relief and Virgil nodded.

"Okay. Do you still have all those memory cards, Lizzie?"

"Duh, *no*. I *told* you, I put them all back into the cameras because Merry had a freakin' fit."

"Go and get them out again, exactly the same as you did last time," Virgil said. "Labeled and everything."

"What?" she shrieked. "Are you *kidding* me?"

"No, I'm not kidding. You are, after all, an overzealous and hardworking intern doing what your duties are as described on numerous websites about TV internships."

She looked dumbstruck for a moment, then a sly smile twitched at her lips. "Hey, you guys are pretty smart. And then what?"

"Then you'll come and tell me what you did, and hand them over to me," Virgil said. "I'll be surprised but understanding, and talk to Urquhart on your behalf. I hope this works. Just forget everything about Merry telling you to do anything, *and* about putting them back in the cameras and wiping your prints."

She nodded. "Oh, I can lie. I'm pretty good at that."

I rolled my eyes. "Good lord, don't tell your grandmother any of this or she'll never let me near you again. And she'll probably take you to church to get you exorcised."

"So what are you going to say, if asked?" Virgil said.

"What, *me*?" she asked, and blinked, the very picture of innocent teenagedom. "Well, like, of course, as soon as I realized the shoot was over, I, like, took all the memory cards out and labeled them because, like, I was hoping I'd get a chance to start logging them. For experience. Because that's what TV interns do. Isn't it?"

I smothered a laugh. "I think she's got this," I said to my husband. "Except lose the 'like' part, Lizzie; everyone knows you don't talk like that."

It was Virgil's turn to sigh. "What the hell have you done to this child?"

"Hey, don't look at me. She started out this way," I said.

"Yeah, I've always been awesome," Lizzie said. She trotted off to do what Virgil had asked, and came back with everything labeled perfectly, handing over the cards. "Now . . . can we look at the footage?"

Chapter Seventeen

"WHAT'S THIS 'WE' stuff?" I said as Virgil snorted in laughter. "No one said you were going to look at it."

She rolled her eyes and stomped to the fridge, hauled out a bunch of food, and started to make herself a sandwich.

"Don't you think you should be home with your mother?"

"She's the one who dropped me off this morning."

"Shouldn't you have called her cell and told her about the murder when you found out about it this morning?"

"Do you think I'm nuts? Of *course* not. Anyway, she was heading to Buffalo to stay with a girlfriend overnight. If I'd told her, she would have come back and made me go to Buffalo with her. Tomorrow morning she's visiting colleges that offer massage therapy courses," Lizzie said, over her shoulder. "She says she'll look at colleges for both of us." She cut lopsided hunks of bread and piled meat and cheese on one, along with sliced pickles and a slab of tomato, then jammed it all together and cut it in half.

"You didn't say that earlier." I didn't think Emerald was

necessarily a good person to choose Lizzie's college, since her planning is sketchy and she tends to take stabs at life that often veer wildly off course. But that was another conversation for another day.

She shrugged. "I'm staying with you, and tomorrow is a professional development day, no school."

I watched her through narrowed eyes. "Are you *sure* about that? Should I call someone and find out, since you're such an awesome liar?"

"But I wouldn't lie to *you*!"

I was skeptical about that. "Virgil and I will review the video when we have time. Meanwhile, *you* are going to do the homework I know you have. If you don't have it here, I will take you to get it. I know you have it, though, right?"

She nodded, but the look in her eyes was like a puppy that's been promised a treat, then put off.

Virgil was about to say something, but I stayed him with one hand. "Lizzie, come here."

She came over, sat down on the hearth, and looked up at the two of us.

I composed my thoughts, then met her gaze. "I'm not chastising you, but I do want you to realize that this is not entertainment. If I've given any other impression, if I've spoken with too much levity, I've been wrong. A man died, and one of those people in the library probably arranged it. Someone is dangerous," I said, and my voice quavered. "A man is dead, and it's tragedy, not comedy. Someone loved him and will miss him. Okay?"

She nodded, a sober expression on her face. I saw that she was aware of my intentions and didn't take offense. That's what I love about the kid; she's sometimes pouty or cross, and she can be snarky at times. But she does get the message if I take the time to tell her the truth in the right manner.

"Lizzie, I don't want you going anywhere alone, I don't

want you talking to them, or asking questions, and I was dead wrong to rope you in to find out about the cameras. Understand?"

"Okay, all right. I got it," she said, around her sandwich. She swallowed the bite she was chewing. "I am almost an adult myself. I can do stuff, and you know it. But I promise I won't be stupid."

While she slipped out to the great hall to get her knapsack that held her laptop and books, Virgil pulled me down into the chair with him, circled me in his arms, and we kissed. It felt so good. I love him so much it's hard to remember a time when I didn't.

"You'd be a good mom," he said.

My stomach clenched. What did *that* mean? We had never had that talk, I realized with a thumping heart.

He looked up at me with a quizzical expression. "Hey, what's going on? You jolted like you touched an electric fence."

I took in a deep, long breath and avoided his gaze. "Virgil, we've never . . . I mean, I don't know if . . ." I stole a look at his face, not able to finish.

He looked puzzled for a minute, then understanding dawned in his eyes. "Jeez, Merry, it was a comment, not a request!" he said, pulling me closer.

"*Do* you want kids?"

I love that he never answers reflexively, he always thinks things through. After a few minutes, he said, "I've never thought much about it. That's why it's taking me a minute to figure it out."

I twisted to watch his expression. "But you coach every single kid's team there is in Autumn Vale. And some in Ridley Ridge! You must *love* kids."

"I *like* kids, I *love* sports."

I laughed and relaxed. "I've never truly considered it, having kids, I mean. It's never been a priority, but if you wanted, we could discuss it."

"I have nieces and nephews, as you know from our wedding," he said dryly.

Our wedding had been the first time I met his siblings and their children. It was noisy and messy, but I was okay with that.

"Merry, if having kids isn't important to you, I'm good with us the way we are."

I thought about it. People have always said to me, *"You'd be such a good mother,"* but I've never especially felt maternal. I like teenagers better than babies.

"Know what? I'm good," I said, patting his leg. "I have everything I could want right here, right now."

He kissed me just as Lizzie came back. She gave us a look and set up her homework on the long kitchen trestle table. Virgil departed to find Urquhart and tell his former deputy what we had done. I decided to sit down with Lizzie while she did her homework and write down on paper who I suspected and why. I like notebooks rather than computers for that; the physical act of writing helps me think.

With the perfect timing she often displays, Hannah called just then. Lizzie and she connected on FaceTime and we both greeted her. She moved around, her face blurry at times, getting a piece of paper and looking at it. "I have a lot," she said. "I've e-mailed you the info, Merry, but I wanted to ask you a couple of questions, too."

"Ask away," I said. I hopped up, closed the door, and came back.

"Who do you want to hear about first?" Hannah asked.

"Let's start at the top," I said. "Hugh Langley, the producer."

She went through his professional credits. He was sixty-seven years old, and had started in the early seventies at a small TV station in his hometown of Albany. He lived in Texas for a time, worked for a network station, and from there moved to San Francisco and worked in news production.

Since then his work life had been checkered. He got the job at HHN and ended up producing *Haunt Hunt* three years before. He was responsible for bringing Dirk Phillipe and Millicent Vayne on board, which sent ratings soaring.

"His listing on IMDb is pretty long," Hannah said. "I'm impressed. He produced a TV show I liked, a crime drama set in a big-city library, but it only lasted a season."

"Why is he working on a show like *Haunt Hunt*?" I mused. "It feels like a step down after the work he's done in his career."

"Are you kidding? You think that because you're old," Lizzie said. She slewed a look in my direction. "No offense. *Haunt Hunt* is way cool, according to kids at school."

Hannah nodded. "You would not believe how many people in town are secretly excited about *Haunt Hunt* being at the castle, though they won't admit it."

"Okay," I said, grudgingly. I had seen that firsthand with Mabel Thorpe. "But Hugh does have other aspirations."

"I suppose if he did well on this, he'd have his pick of jobs, right?" Hannah said. "And it is doing well, in part because of Dirk Phillipe."

"How about the others?" I asked.

"Todd Halsey and Stuart Jardine worked together in media consulting as Halsey Jardine. They were still working in media when they had a show called *Ghost Groupies*," Hannah said. "It only lasted eight shows. They started *Haunt Hunt* three years ago, with Hugh Langley as producer. As I said, he was the force behind bringing on psychics, with Todd and Stu resisting at first. A source online says the resistance ended when the network made it clear this was an either/or proposition."

"What does that mean?" Lizzie asked.

"Either they accept the psychics or else, I guess," Hannah said.

That pretty much put the kibosh on the possibility of

Hugh setting up the murder, though I hadn't seriously suspected him anyway. Todd and Stu were definitely in the mix, either separately or together, though it seemed like shooting themselves in the foot to kill the goose that was laying golden eggs in the shape of better ratings. However, Todd had been pretty vocal about not liking Dirk's role on the show. Surely, if he planned to or had killed Dirk he wouldn't be making his disdain for the psychic so clear?

"What about Todd's wife, Rishelle Halsey? She's a recent-ish addition to the show, and there is some tension with Felice over her being preferred in shots, because of her looks and, uh, attributes, Felice says."

"She means her implants," Lizzie said to Hannah, leaning into the screen.

I elbowed her. "We don't put other women down, remember? What they choose to do with their bodies is their own decision. Always. No exceptions."

"Hey, I *wasn't* putting her down for it—you assumed that, which means *you're* the one putting her down for it," Lizzie protested. "I was just saying, that's why Felice is so bent out of shape. Millicent told me that herself. She says Rishelle is nice and has been kind to her, unlike some of the others."

Actually, Rishelle had been pretty dismissive of Millicent when I first talked to her, so was it a case of being fake-nice? And "others" had been unkind to Millicent, others like Felice? Had Felice perhaps killed Dirk as a strike against having psychics on the show, or a way of killing the show to get back at Todd for having Rishelle join them? That was a bit of a stretch, since Todd hadn't liked Dirk and wanted him gone anyway. So no, that didn't make sense.

"Okay, so, the camera guys, Arnie Ball and Ian Mackenzie," I said. "Have you learned anything about them?" I thought of Todd's suspicion of Rishelle and Stu having an affair, while it was Arnie he should have been concerned about.

"Ian Mackenzie has worked for *Haunt Hunt* since the beginning. Not much else on him. He was a tech guy on *Ghost Groupies*, though, so he's worked with Todd and Stu for a long time."

Tech guy . . . as someone may have had to be to alter Chi's supposedly harmless prank. "And Arnie?"

Hannah looked at her notes and frowned. "Well, Arnie Ball has been in the business since he was a teenager. He's received some awards for his work, but that was a few years ago." She paused, then looked at me, biting her lip. "I came across something on a subreddit about *Haunt Hunt* that said he had done something on a movie set, got fired, and ended up working on the show because no one else would have him."

"What exactly did he do?"

"According to someone on the subreddit, he punched out one of the talent, breaking his nose and causing a concussion. The guy sued and won a huge lawsuit against the studio."

That was serious. Punching the guy and hurting him was one thing, but a lawsuit was something entirely different. Still, I didn't think it had any bearing on the underhanded way Dirk was killed, which took a more devious mind. A guy who punched someone out in anger was not the same guy who would slyly change up a prank to kill someone. "How did he get hired on *Haunt Hunt* if he was blackballed?"

"He went to college with Felice Broadbent, or that's what the subredditers say. She supposedly put in a good word with Hugh Langley, and he decided to take a chance on Arnie."

There was a connection I hadn't expected . . . Felice and Arnie went to college together? But it didn't appear, on the surface, to mean anything. "Speaking of Felice, she's a bit of a puzzle to me. She doesn't appear to get along with anyone on set very well."

"A fan group I dropped in on had a poll, and Felice was the least-liked on-screen personality. Someone said she was about to be fired, but there's no real reason to think that person had insider knowledge. They said all kinds of goofy things on the fan group."

"Like?"

Hannah smiled. "There was a lot of back-and-forth about how legit the hunts were. Most seem to think they're real, but some were making fun of them for thinking that way."

The kitchen door opened and Millicent bumbled in, followed by Rishelle. I told Hannah quickly that I'd get back to her and closed the laptop, since I didn't want any of the *Haunt Hunt* people knowing what I was up to. I also turned over my notes, while Lizzie opened her textbooks and appeared to work on a calculus algorithm, though what she was really doing was doodling.

"What can I do for you?" I didn't feel very friendly toward my guests at the moment, since I knew I'd have to put up with them for a day or two more, until the sheriff dismissed them or we found the culprit.

"We're out of tea," Millicent said.

I got up to put the kettle on.

"And I was wondering, can you call your friend Janice to come back? She had a Ouija board among her things. I'd like to ask a few questions of the spirit world, and Ouija might work."

"Millie, no," Rishelle said, touching her arm. "That's messing with weird stuff. I don't like it."

I eyed the woman with interest. She did look alarmed, but then, she and Millicent and Chi had accidentally set up a murder. It must be quite unnerving to sit in that library with all the others and know that one of you was a killer, and that the killer had used your prank to murder.

"I can call Janice," I said, watching the two. "I don't know if she'll do it, but if you like, I can ask her."

"Would you?" Millicent said, genuine tears starting in her eyes. She crossed her arms over her chest and hugged herself. "I wish I knew who messed with things, who caused it." She looked over her shoulder at her friend. "We never intended this to happen."

"Even as much as you hated Dirk," I finished.

"I didn't *hate* Dirk!" she said with a gasp, her hand to her throat. Her eyes were wide, like a startled fawn. "Whatever gave you *that* idea?"

"Maybe that you appeared to dislike him and argued with him? Maybe the fact that he was a jerk to you? And belittled you? And that he was a dirtbag most of the time? I hardly knew him and I didn't like him."

"He wasn't *that* bad," Rishelle said. "Dirk had some good points. We wanted to have a laugh at his expense. He needed his ego punctured a little."

"How did you know he'd do what you wanted him to do, go out to the garage?"

Millicent exchanged a glance with the other woman. "Everyone heard that restaurant woman's story, and after that episode in the ballroom we knew Hugh wasn't going to let him have what he wanted, which was to work the garage. So after my performance, and how we emphasized that there was a spirit in the garage, we were sure Dirk wouldn't be able to resist checking it out. So we set up the tool belt to drop down from the upper shelf on his head. We had a camera set up to film him jumping around like an idiot."

"Were you planning on putting a clip of it online?" Because otherwise there was no point, and they knew that would drive a narcissist like Dirk crazy.

Rishelle shrugged. "Maybe. Maybe not."

"It depended on how he reacted. It was a little joke among coworkers," Millicent said, her tone becoming combative. "I resent that everyone is making it seem so mean-spirited."

"Everyone? Like who?"

"Hugh is mad," Rishelle said.

"Of course he's angry. It's a producer's worst nightmare; the one guy who was boosting ratings is gone."

Rishelle said nothing, glaring at me in simmering silence. She didn't dare talk back, since I had a little secret of hers, what she and Arnie were up to. I didn't intend to tell anyone, but she didn't know that.

"So will you call Janice?" Millicent said impatiently. "I want some answers. Maybe Dirk is still here and can tell us what happened."

That was a creepy notion, but I don't happen to believe in Ouija magic. I nodded. "Sure. Go back to the library for now. I'll call Janice and see if she'll come out this evening with her Ouija board." I filled a teapot and set it down for Millicent to pick up. "I'll let you know what she says."

I had a tentative plan, but needed to run it past Virgil first. I wanted to see if we could trick a trickster.

Chapter Eighteen

❋ ❋ ❋

I CALLED JANICE and she agreed to come out with her Ouija board, though I begged her not to dress up like a crystal ball swami. "Janice, one more thing. Do you believe in it, the Ouija board?"

She chuckled, a rich sound like a gurgle rather than a giggle. "I think it works great to show what people are really thinking, maybe even on a subconscious level."

My thoughts exactly. I was relieved she didn't believe in it wholeheartedly. Things were weird enough as it was.

I wanted to watch the videos Lizzie had loaded on my laptop, but we didn't have time. I needed to set up everything for the evening, and I also wanted to ask a couple of people questions. I started dinner while Lizzie did some homework, then she settled down to read a book for English lit, *The Lovely Bones*. It's an excellent novel, and one I hoped she'd enjoy.

I put a beef roast in the oven on low and slow, the easiest way to feed a large number of people. I'd do hot roast beef sandwiches with some rich dark gravy, or roast beef on a bun for those who preferred. Pish came in as I was chopping garlic and stirring beef broth for gravy.

He summoned me away from Lizzie. I followed him down to the sitting area. "These people," he said, wide-eyed. "They're snapping and sniping at each other constantly."

"What's going on?"

We sat down in the wing chairs and he explained what happened when Millicent and Rishelle came back in and announced they were having a Ouija reading that evening, with Janice Grover. "Hugh thinks it's disrespectful to Dirk."

"I never thought about that aspect." I could see how it would appear, but the idea did not come from me. It was their own cast that wanted to go ahead. "When the girls wanted to do it, I saw it as an opportunity to get at people's thoughts. The Ouija table thingie is supposed to work on micro movements, or something like that, directed from people's subconscious. If we ask the right questions, we may figure out if anyone suspects anyone, or . . . I don't know."

"Sure, I remember playing as a kid with my sister and cousins," he said. "I always tried to catch people moving, but never could. With any group of people, how do you tell who is really directing the planchette?"

"True." I could see the problem with that. We might get answers, but from whom? "Let's say I'll be watching people to see if I can detect anything. Pish, who do *you* think killed Dirk?"

He frowned, two pinched lines between his brows. "Last night was truly odd. Did you hear all the commotion?"

"I heard doors opening and closing, and could tell people were going to each other's rooms. Not my business, I figured, so I stayed out of it." I didn't say anything about who was cheating with whom, at this point.

"I couldn't sleep, so I came down to the library to find a book I left on the desk. I was headed out through the great

hall when Rishelle and Millicent came in. I asked what they
were up to. They said they were out for a walk."

"A walk? In the middle of the night? That's when they
set up the prank. Was Chi not with them?"

He shook his head. "He must have come in before them,
or more likely, *after* them. They went upstairs laughing and
talking, and I headed to the kitchen." He frowned down at
his hands, interlacing his fingers. "Now that I think of it, I
did hear the front door while I was in the kitchen. You know,
it kind of thuds when it closes. So someone must have come
in a few minutes after the girls."

"So that was likely Chi, right?"

He nodded. "It *has* to be. But, Merry, after that I wandered outside. I was hoping Becket would come in, or
thought he might be waiting." Leaning forward, he whispered, "Do you remember the surprise party you and Miguel
tried to throw for my birthday?"

I flashed back to that night, an elaborate party with all
of his friends doing a classic "hide behind the sofa" surprise.
Pish entered the room in the semidark, but had stopped dead
and said, "*Who's there? Come out!*" thus spoiling the surprise. "Sure, I remember."

"That's what I felt like outside. The hairs on the back of
my neck stood up, but I ignored it. I thought I was just cold.
I'd swear now that there was someone there. I think I heard
something, a *clank.*"

"Maybe that was Chi."

"But why would he hide from me?"

"Because of the prank setup. He wouldn't want you asking him any questions."

"But then who was it who came back in and closed the
door before that?"

I thought. "We don't know that the door you heard was
anyone coming *in*; it could just as easily have been someone

going *out*. Here's what we know: You saw Millicent and Rishelle coming in, but you didn't see Chi. You did hear the door. That may have been Chi coming in, or someone else going out. And we know that if the trio didn't set up the prank to kill Dirk, then someone else from this group did, and so had to go out to the garage between the time the trio came in and Dirk went out."

"Succinctly summarized, my dear."

"I suppose someone could have been hiding behind one of the production vans. Or . . ." I thought a moment, remembering Serina in the production van earlier. "Or maybe *in* one of the vans, doing something? Like maybe getting the tools to alter the prank?" I told him what Chi had said, about the spring he had used only being strong enough to heft a leather tool belt, but not a heavy tool chest full of tools.

Pish nodded. "That could be it, you know—someone in one of the equipment vans. That could have been the *clank*."

"Or, maybe it was just Dirk skulking around. Maybe he heard the door open and didn't want to be caught going out to the garage, so he hid until you went back in."

"I guess that's possible. If only I'd stayed outside longer, maybe I would have seen something."

"There is someone else; I heard some noise and caught Felice sneaking back in after having a smoke outside, so she says. She had the key. I took it from her and locked back up."

"That's interesting. But as far as we know, Felice had no part in the prank. And this was later, you say?"

I nodded. "Not sure how much later, though. We have no idea when Dirk went out. It could have been before Felice, it could have been after. If someone went out after I locked up, it would leave the door unlocked again. Did you tell Urquhart all this?"

"Of course."

"I'll have to tell him what else I've remembered. This

gives us something to go on. I'd bet on your feelings. What time was that?"

He frowned. "They wrapped up about four, right? And then there was some rustling around and doors closing, and then I went back downstairs, say, four forty-five or so, give or take some minutes. So . . . maybe five or five twenty?"

I rubbed my eyes. "Who do you think would do this, Pish? I'm scared, I'll admit it. One of them killed Dirk."

"I don't know. I'm so sorry, my darling, that I invited this awful group to come here."

"You didn't set this in motion, Pish. If someone is intent on doing evil, they'll find a way and place to do it. We happened to be handy." I had learned that from our springtime adventure with the group I named the Legion of Horrible Ladies. One of those horrible ladies orchestrated events to place them all together at my castle so that she could kill one who was a threat to her.

"I know you're trying to make me feel better, Merry, but I do keep getting you into messes."

I covered his hand with my own. "Pish, we didn't do anything to deserve this; it just happened."

We separated. I went on with dinner preparations. Lizzie was supposed to be reading, but she kept throwing me glances until I finally made a cup of tea and sat down across from her. "What's up, kiddo?"

She turned the corner of the page down and closed the book. She fiddled with it, stacking her stuff together, got up and got a bottle of water out of the fridge, then sat down again. "Do you believe any of that?"

"Believe any of what?"

"The Ouija board."

"No, I don't."

"But some people say you shouldn't play around with those, that it's not a game." Her eyes were clouded with doubt. "My grandma heard about me and a friend messing around with one at my friend's house, and she was upset. She said it's not right to fool with spirits. That it was toying with the other world, and that you never knew what you'd let in. Or out. Whatever."

I thought for a moment, watching her face. Lizzie is a rationalist in most things, but she's also a kid in many other ways. "Did you wonder about any of this, the ghost hunting?"

She knotted her thick brows and twisted her mouth. "I guess since those shows never find anything except for some strange noises and orbs that are clearly dust particles in front of a camera lens, I didn't think it was real. But Ouija boards . . . I've heard of some strange things happening with them."

"Honey, that's because *people* are strange. Let's do a little research," I said.

She got the laptop out and brought up some articles, several of which I closed off as they were subreddit threads of believers and occult sites with zero information and lots of woo-woo speculation. That was the trouble with Reddit; so much was just people talking. How did you know what to believe and what to dismiss? Young people aren't stupid, but they do need guidance to keep sparking the skepticism bone. Teens especially are at a dramatic point in life and can go off the rails if their worries and thoughts aren't challenged, explored, and listened to. The Internet, with its unfiltered Dumpster of misleading information, can be a dangerous place.

So I went for science-based sites, and pretty soon we were reading about the ideomotor effect, and research studies that had been done with blindfolded subjects. Essentially, they all said the same thing: A Ouija board works using humankind's deep desire for answers to questions, combined with involuntary hand movements. They pointed out how impossible it is to be truly still, using a laser pointer for an example. Any attempt to keep a laser pointer completely still will show movement no matter what. The information both settled Lizzie's mind and gave me some insight into what to watch out for.

"Can I help this evening?" she asked.

I thought about it seriously. On the one hand, she's a teenager and I don't want her spooked or being misled into dumb beliefs, like Ouija board mysticism. On the other hand, she's a rational human being and would soon be making all of her own decisions when she went off to college. Her mom, like single parents everywhere, is trying to keep her child afloat and do the best she can to raise her. She's done a great job so far; Lizzie is one of my favorite human beings. But a little input from all sides couldn't hurt. Ultimately, I decided this was too important to her future to not let her participate. I wanted to be sure she saw the absurdity firsthand.

"You can help on one condition. If you for one single minute get spooked or think it's real, I want you to tell me. I promise not to ridicule you, but I *will* tell you what I think and believe." Skepticism is a learned skill. "Do we have a deal?"

She nodded, the fun back in her eyes. "I promise not to believe a single thing I hear or see unless you tell me to."

I laughed. "Exactly!"

She took my hand and we shook. "Are they going to tape the session, do you think?" she asked.

"If I have anything to say about it, yes. I'm hoping the opportunity to guide things will be too tempting to the killer." I shivered. I pictured a master hand moving us around like game pieces, feeding information, inflaming passions, inciting quarrels. "I want to be able to document who's guiding this show."

DETECTIVE URQUHART RETURNED WITH VIRGIL AND found us in the kitchen putting supper together. My husband took Lizzie and me aside and told us what the sheriff had said. He was not thrilled with what Lizzie had done, but he had accepted the intern explanation without question. Everyone knew of Lizzie's passion for photography, her ambition, and her tendency to go overboard once given a task related to something she was interested in, so it was not a stretch to think she would remove all the SD cards to catalog.

We handed over the memory cards from the various cameras. To forestall what I knew was coming next—a request that he be able to question Lizzie about the sequence of events—I openly told Urquhart I wasn't comfortable with him interviewing the teenager again until her mother was back. Emerald would make the ultimate decision regarding the interview and whether they wanted a lawyer present, since Lizzie was still underage. He could have Emerald come back early, but I didn't think it would make a difference timewise since she was returning the next afternoon anyway.

I was not going to budge on that for any number of reasons, mostly the one stated but also because I didn't want Lizzie having to fib. Urquhart was peeved, but reluctantly understanding. I wasn't misled in the slightest; the only reason Urquhart was being semigracious to me and Lizzie was because of my husband.

"One last thing, Sheriff," I said as he turned to leave the kitchen. "Can we talk outside?"

He nodded. I linked arms with Virgil and pulled him with us, out the back door off the butler's pantry. The wind was whipping up as the sun descended. I was so tired I was practically hallucinating, and wavering on my feet, but I was going to see this through to the bitter end and get someone arrested.

Nervously, I glanced between the two tall men. "We're having a Ouija board party tonight. Millicent and Rishelle are convinced Dirk is still lingering."

Virgil sighed and rolled his eyes. Urquhart looked confused. I started to explain what a Ouija board is, but he put up one hand.

"Mrs. Grace, I know what one of those damn things is. I can't figure out why the hell you'd let that lunatic asylum bunch in there play with it." His eyes were cold, his short sleeves flapped in the stiffening wind.

I wrapped my long cardigan closer around me and felt a little better when Virgil put his arm around me and held me close to his warmth. "I'm going to make sure the whole thing is taped, even if I have to have Lizzie set up the equipment. But if I'm lucky, they'll think it's a grand idea."

The sheriff shook his head and squinted into the sunset. "I can't stop you from doing whatever fool thing you want," he finally said. "Messing with the other world is not a good idea. I go on record as saying I think this is a bad idea."

I was startled to find that he actually gave some credit to the Ouija board. It reminded me that some very intelligent people—and the sheriff is smart, no two ways about it—believe some very weird things.

Chapter Nineteen

❈ ❈ ❈

I USED PISH'S, Virgil's, and Lizzie's help with dinner, making a buffet-style meal in the dining room. Everyone was edgy, but most still ate a fair bit, except Millicent, who picked at the salad I had created and the fruit and veggie trays, and Todd, who never seemed to eat much. Once dinner was done and we had toted all the dishes into the kitchen, we moved to the little parlor. I settled on that for our Ouija board session because we needed somewhere where people could sit around a low table with their fingers on the planchette, as the small heart-shaped plank is called. It was a little crowded.

Janice arrived. I took her aside to the library and explained our hopes. I didn't want her guiding anything at all and in fact preferred that she keep her hands off the planchette. I wanted to know it was one of them doing the guiding. She nodded, a thoughtful expression on her round face. She was dressed soberly this evening, for her, which translated to a plum and orange dashiki. Her graying hair was piled on her head in a bun wrapped in a somber gray scarf, and she wore very little jewelry; just a crystal pendant that she said was her good-luck piece.

"I think I can help. Millicent seems to believe I have some abilities." She smiled and chuckled. "Poor kid. I'm going to play that up."

"What are you going to say?"

"Leave it to me."

I was a little worried, but at heart Janice is smart and levelheaded, no matter how the way she dresses or plays the loopy owner of Crazy Lady Antiques and Collectibles indicates otherwise. We joined the cast and crew in the parlor. This was Millicent, Rishelle, and Janice's party, and I, an observer. A very *intent* observer.

At dinner I had asked, in an amused voice, if they intended to film the event for posterity. There had been a gleam in Rishelle's eyes as she took up the notion and soon *demanded* that it be filmed. Her husband seemed loath to fall in, but after some badgering by the women, Hugh, with a weary wave of his hand, had given permission for them to use the company cameras, and Todd went along with it. He had been doing his utmost to curry favor with the producer, finally realizing, it appeared, that his show was in jeopardy with Dirk gone. It was interesting that he hadn't considered that until now, and left him in the running as a suspect.

Of course, neither Todd nor Hugh knew yet about Lizzie's helpfulness in taking the memory cards out of the cameras to log, and our subsequent handing of them to the sheriff . . . our civic duty, we intended to explain if confronted about it. And by "we" I mean Virgil, who had said, in a steely tone, that if anyone dared question me or Lizzie about it to refer them to him. He'd take care of any questions. It was all well within Lizzie's rights, we'd argue if pressed, since she had been given tacit permission to work on the equipment. And once she had the memory cards, she was obligated to hand them over to the police. Virgil was sitting in on the Ouija experiment because he was highly distrustful of the whole *Haunt Hunt* cast and crew.

Janice set the Ouija board on the low table around which we had arranged various chairs and settees. There was a lot of bickering over who would take part. Ultimately, the group decided on two sessions. They would start with Felice and Serina, both of whom rolled their eyes but agreed to participate, as well as Stu, Chi, and Ian. The second session would then be Arnie, Todd, Rishelle, Millicent, and Hugh, who shook his head in dismay, but when badgered agreed to go along for the sake of team unity. Janice would act as facilitator, directing the others, Lizzie would monitor the sound recording equipment when Serina was busy in her session, and Virgil, Pish, and I were going to silently observe, as would those not participating.

I was nervous, my stomach grumbling and knotting in waves of discomfort. One of the ten was a killer, and I still had very little idea which. There were subterranean tensions in this crew that I hadn't mined. I didn't know what to expect from the sessions, but I hoped there would be some revelation.

Even if nothing in particular came out of the Ouija sessions, my ultimate goal was to keep the group together and hopefully stir up some conversation that would tell us more about relationships, jealousies, conflicts; anything that may have led to Dirk's demise. I wondered, was this a dangerous game we were about to play? I didn't mean in a psychic or haunted way, but in an interpersonal dynamics way. Were we exacerbating tensions that were already stretched to the tearing point?

It was too late to turn back.

Janice's board was an antique, quite large, with the alphabet in two arcs over the top, *Yes* and *No* in script on the top two corners, and *Hello* and *Good Bye* in the bottom corners. There were black-painted images of witches on brooms flying over rooftops along the bottom. The planchette was made of different wood and appeared handmade, in Janice's expert antique appraisal. Perhaps the board's original planchette went missing. This one was a round wooden table with four legs and had a hole cut in the middle, a glass lens that looked like a crystal watch face set in the hole.

Janice cleared her throat and held her head high, then met the gaze of each of the five people who sat on low chairs around the table. Virgil was perched in the far corner with his eyes on everyone, Pish was next to me, and the five not participating in the first session sat on chairs behind to watch. Pish's delight in life is to orchestrate it, so he had cobbled together a playlist including some Saint-Saëns, Mussorgsky, and others I didn't recognize. Good spooky music played softly in the background.

"Some of you may believe in the power of the Ouija board and some may not," Janice said. Ian Mackenzie snorted, and she sent him a baleful look. "I don't mind skeptics present, but I ask you to be polite to those of us engaged in the activity, at the very least."

Millicent sniffed and glared through the dimness at him from her position sitting as an observer behind Felice. "Yes, *Ian*. Just because *you're* a cynical jerk doesn't mean some of us don't want to be a part of this."

"You'll get your turn, *Millie*," he said, his face red right up to his ginger hairline. "I have a right to express my opinion. This is crap, and you all know it."

"Ian, don't be mean to Millicent," Chi said.

Ian flashed him a puzzled look. The guy was out of the loop, it appeared, concerning Chi's affection for the psychic.

Janice shushed them. "Quiet, *please*! This is how it's going to work: You five will place your fingers lightly on the little table and calm your breathing. I am appointing one of you to ask questions. I may suggest them, or you may think of them yourself." As we had preplanned, she added, "Merry will be writing down any messages we receive." I held up my notebook and pencil and smiled. She scanned the five who watched her expectantly. Surprisingly, she lit on the sound technician. "Your name is Serina, right?"

"Yeah. But I'm not one of the cast. I'm the sound engineer."

"Would you take the lead and ask the board?"

Serina shrugged. "Okay. But I don't know what to ask."

"Well, let's decide now. What do you all want to know?"

There was a babble of voices, but Janice held up one hand. "One at a time." She pointed at each one, and they swiftly agreed on a list of questions.

I exchanged a look with Pish and gave Janice's leadership the thumbs-up. Virgil caught my eye and nodded, then he melted back into the shadows as we lowered the lights, leaving dimly lit the upside-down tulip-shaped pendant light that hung over the center of the room. *Danse macabre* drifted through the room.

Ian rolled his eyes and sighed at the intentional drama of it all, but quieted down as Janice gave him a stern look. "Begin," she said to Serina. "All of you, fingers lightly resting on the planchette, please."

They did as told, and Serina began with, "Is there anybody with us?" Nothing. She repeated it, and still there was no movement. Five minutes passed, with variations of those words, and finally the planchette began to sway, slowly. It moved to center the glass bubble over *Yes*.

"Can you tell us your name?"

No.

"But you're with us now?"

Yes.

"Do you have a message for us?"

Yes. It began to pick out letters with increasing rapidity.

I scribbled them down, trying to figure out the message as I went until—"Enough!" I said, holding up one hand.

"What's wrong?" Millicent cried from behind the Ouija players. "It was going so well. Don't stop!"

I sighed and shook my head. "Unless you think the spirit is spelling out *This is a waste of time and is a great pile of steaming cow poop*, then I think we're done with this session."

Ian Mackenzie broke out in raucous laughter.

"Ian, how could you?" Rishelle said. "What a jerk!"

"Oh, come on, Rishelle. Even *you* can't be dumb enough to think this is going to work."

"Don't talk to her that way," Todd said.

But Rishelle didn't need her husband's help. "What are you working on this show for, if you don't believe in spirits?"

"I *do* believe in spirits," Ian shot back, his cheeks flaming. He tugged at a lock of red hair. "Or I wouldn't have worked with Todd and Stu from the beginning. This is garbage! *This* isn't science," he said, waving at the Ouija board. "It's hocus-pocus sideshow magic. It's all Hugh's fault for hiring Dirk and Millie in the first place."

"Enough!" Janice said.

I was a little miffed she'd stopped them from squabbling, because this stuff is what I was hoping for, the conflict and tension. I found it interesting how irritated by the Ouija session Ian was. He seemed just as irritated by Dirk's and Millicent's inclusion as part of the show. But I let Janice order the first session finished. She had the participants change places with the others.

"I would like to lodge a protest," Hugh said, shooting his wrist out of his cuff and straightening his cuff links as he took his seat at the table. "I, like Ian, do not believe in the board. I should think I will only be a hindrance to those who do."

More than anything else, that illustrated that hiring psychics for *Haunt Hunt* was a pure ratings move on his part.

"That's why you're going to be the leader," Janice said, eyeing him sternly.

"Why can't *I* ask the questions?" Millicent pleaded.

"We can try that after, if this doesn't work," Janice said. "But right now I'd like Hugh to take the lead."

We had agreed on this in advance. I thought that Hugh asking questions would ensure that whoever was likely to be guiding the planchette could have at it in peace, rather than trying to talk *and* move the table. This was starting to seem like a waste of time. What did I think we were going to learn? My best hope was going to be in the session after, when we would talk over what had happened, or, more likely, what had *not* happened. I wanted them to talk.

"Please take your places, ladies and gentlemen."

They were seated Hugh, Millicent to his left, Arnie to *her* left, Todd to *his* left, and finally Rishelle, between her husband and the producer. This was the group I was anticipating, since it held the two women who had planned the prank, the most fervid believers in the board's powers. But still there was little at first, some faint movement, but nothing definite. Hugh drawled his questions in a bored voice. Rishelle remonstrated with him to at least try to be unbiased.

He sighed, cleared his throat, and sat up straighter. "I'll do better just for you, Rishelle." He winked at her.

They all leaned forward, fingers lightly on the planchette. Rishelle's expression was eager, and Todd's resigned. I couldn't see the other two's expressions, but Millicent appeared rigid with anticipation, while Arnie slumped in apparent boredom.

"Is there any spirit here with us tonight?" Hugh asked.

There was a faint movement, then nothing, then the planchette swayed over to *Yes*. Millicent gasped, and Rishelle focused all her energy on the board, her bottom lip caught between her teeth.

"Do we know who you are, spirit?" Hugh asked.

Yes.

"Can you spell out your name for us?"

There were a few moments of uncertainty, and nothing much was spelled out but a seemingly random string of letters. It was confusing, but Hugh simply asked again for the spirit to spell out his or her name. This time it slowly and clearly spelled out *D-I-R-K*.

Millicent was trembling so much I began to wonder if she really believed as she appeared, or if she was faking it. Todd frowned. Rishelle looked spellbound. Arnie was no longer slumping.

"This is the spirit of our friend Dirk?"

Yes.

There was a pause. Hugh looked disconcerted and glanced around at his playmates. He had to know someone was controlling the planchette, as I did, but who? And why? We'd soon know, I hoped.

"Ask him what he wants," Janice murmured.

"Dirk, we're very sorry you're gone," Hugh said. "Can you tell us . . . we want to know why you are still here."

You all know, was spelled out next. But there was more . . . *who killed me.*

Chapter Twenty

✳ ✳ ✳

M ILLICENT CRIED OUT and broke contact, starting violently back in her chair. "What does that mean?" she cried.

"People, don't quit!" Janice urged. I watched her, and she had a mischievous look on her face, her eyes dancing, but since she didn't have her fingers on the planchette, she wasn't the one speaking for Dirk. "Come back and focus. Hugh, why don't you ask who did it?"

"I *won't* take part in this jiggery pokery," Hugh said, angrily, looking around at those who were with him. In the dim light his eyes were shadowed but his mouth had a grim set to it.

I sympathized; I'd feel the same in his position. But we were close to a revelation, not perhaps of who had done it, but who someone *suspected* had done it, or who someone wanted us to *think* had done it.

"But we *have* to continue," Rishelle said, trembling. "If we leave it open, his spirit may give us trouble. I've heard of things happening before, people being haunted by ghosts upset about Ouija parties. We have to go on, and then close with *Good Bye*, or he'll never leave!" There was an edge of hysteria in her voice.

"Why didn't you say that before?" Millicent said, leaning forward.

Her voice had a panicked edge to it, too, and I wondered if we were going too far. Or if someone at the table had ulterior motives. I glanced around, but everyone seemed serious and intent on those using the board.

"We have to do this," Millicent pleaded when no one answered. "Come on, guys; let's do this. *Please*, Hugh, can we continue?"

"This is *not* Dirk," he protested, sitting back in his chair, folding his arms over his chest, and eyeing all the participants with mistrust. "This is one of you; I don't know which one, but someone's playing games. Don't you see that Millie, Rishelle? This is a silly board game, not some connection to the spirit of Dirk Phillipe."

"Come on, Hugh, humor the ladies," Todd said. "Let whoever is moving the thingie around say what they want to say. Let's get this over with so we can go to bed. I'm exhausted, and I want to sleep, then get the hell out of this monstrosity tomorrow. Rishelle and I are leaving, and I don't care what that two-bit Barney Fife has to say about it."

"Come, my friends, this is disrespectful to Dirk. Can't you see that?" Hugh glared at me. "Merry, I thought better of you."

I stayed silent and refrained from pointing out this was not my idea.

"I agree," Serina said, from the shadows. "This isn't Dirk, guys. I mean, come *on*! I didn't think you were *all* idiots."

"I won't feel comfortable unless we finish this," Rishelle said, stubbornly. "Even if you don't believe, some of us do and you should respect that. Isn't that what all you know-it-alls say, that we should respect everyone's opinion?"

"This isn't an opinion, this is antiscience mumbo jumbo crap!" Serina blasted.

I saw Todd give her a quick look and slightly shake his head. She shut up then and sighed. I don't think anyone else noticed their interchange. It struck me then that Serina had placed herself in the row behind Hugh, where she could see Todd's face.

"Please, Hugh, even if you don't believe," Millicent said, her voice quavering. "Do this for us!"

"Why don't you five involved take a vote and agree to go with the majority?" I murmured.

They seized on the idea. Rishelle, Millicent, and Todd voted to continue, and Hugh acquiesced. I found it interesting that Arnie wanted to end it. They reestablished their connection with the planchette, but Rishelle took over as speaker. "Dirk, are you still there?"

Nothing. She asked again, and a few moments later the little planchette started to move. She again asked if Dirk was there and it pointed to *Yes.*

"Dirk, we're so sorry you're gone. I hope you know that Millie, Chi, and I set up a prank, never meaning to hurt you. Someone . . ." She trailed off, her voice shaky, took a deep breath, and continued. "Someone used us to hurt you. Do you know who did that?"

Yes.

"Who? Dirk, who did that to you?"

The spelling started, with Rishelle naming the letters. *T-O-D-D.*

Gasps erupted around the room, including from me.

"Oh, come *on*," Todd said, leaping to his feet, sending the board and planchette flying. He looked at his wife and friends. "Who's doing this?"

"I *told* you this was ridiculous," Hugh said. His lean face was twisted in an expression of distaste. "Whoever thinks this is funny, or, or . . ." He shook his head, looking around at the others. "This is a disgrace. Dirk was your friend, not someone to be used in some awful joke. Todd *is* your friend, not a pawn of whoever thinks this is funny."

Rishelle was weeping. "I didn't do it! Todd, it wasn't me. It was moving on its own!"

Todd glared at his wife. "Like I believe that! You trying to get me arrested for murder? Was that the plan from the beginning?"

I raised my brows, as did Pish. Didn't see *that* one coming. But given what I knew about her affair with Arnie . . . *Arnie!* I looked over at the fellow who hadn't said a word about the accusation against his friend. The friend whose wife he was having an affair with.

"How can you *say* that?" Rishelle said, her voice thick and low.

"I think we all need to calm down," Hugh said, his hand on Todd's chest. "No one actually thinks you killed Dirk, Todd. It's an ugly practical joke. We have to stop or we'll tear each other apart."

Everyone did shut up, though looks were still passed. Darn Hugh for stopping what was proving to be a very interesting confrontation, I thought.

"It's just crap, folks," Serina said. "Let's call it a night. I don't know about the rest of you, but I'm tired. Todd, can you come out to the equipment truck for a moment? I want to show you what's wrong with that processor. And maybe you have some idea what to do with that malfunctioning control board."

He mumbled something and followed her out. People heaved a sigh of relief as tension deflated, and gathered in small, tight groups, whispering, motioning, and chattering anxiously. Hugh sank back down in his chair, head in his hands. But I eyed the door in interest. Serina and Todd . . . there was no malfunctioning equipment, of that I was sure. There could be a number of reasons why she'd want to pull him aside. She was having an affair with him and despite her protestations, I thought it was probably ongoing. So she either wanted to canoodle—unlikely, given the dramatic events that had just transpired—or she had something to tell him. Had she noticed something? She was a very perspicacious woman and didn't believe in any of the Ouija nonsense.

Lizzie grabbed my arm and hauled me out to the great hall.

"What's up?"

"I saw something. Arnie was acting weird. He ran into the library and then came back a coupla secs later. Then he handed Rishelle a piece of paper. She unfolded it, looked at it, and nodded."

"Wonder what it said?" Though I had an idea; Arnie probably wanted to talk to her about something . . . maybe their plan to pin Dirk's murder on Todd? Thus getting rid of him? But even as I formulated the idea in my brain I acknowledged that it seemed far-fetched. Who would make an accusation via Ouija board?

"Well, wonder no longer." She produced a balled-up scrap from her pocket like some teenage magician. "She dropped it in the trash and I got it."

"*Lizzie!* No one saw you, did they?" I was aghast and worried for her safety.

"No, of course not. Do you think I'm a complete doofus? But look at what it says."

I trotted over to one of the sconces that illuminate the great hall and unfolded the scrap of wadded-up paper. It simply said *Tonight?* How could I tell Lizzie the truth, that this was probably just two sneaky lovers arranging a clandestine meeting? "Thanks, Lizzie. Good work, kiddo; we'll figure out what's up, but right now you're going to your grandmother's."

"Aw! No, it's just getting interesting. I was supposed to stay the night."

"I've changed my mind. Despite what you witnessed, this is no parlor game, it's murder and I won't have you in danger. You've stretched your neck out enough. Too much! You can come back tomorrow, since you supposedly have the day off school, but I'm not letting you stay in the castle overnight with this bunch of lunatics."

Virgil emerged from the parlor. "Janice is asking where you were. She wants to head home, but I think you ought to talk to her first."

Pish followed my husband and nodded. "Let's *all* go into the library."

"I'll meet you back here, Lizzie," I said to my young friend. "Make sure you have everything. And don't stray into enemy territory!" I gave her a stern look. "Kitchen *only!*"

She stomped off to the kitchen, where her backpack and laptop were. I followed my friend and my husband back to the library, where Janice awaited us, pacing by the bookshelves.

"What's up?" I asked.

Janice gave a mysterious look and motioned for us to close the door. We gathered around a low table by the windows where it was quiet and private. My friend glanced around with great mystery while I restrained my impatience. "I was watching during that whole thing, you know," she said. "I think I know who was controlling the board while they were doing their session."

"Who?" we chanted, like a trio of owls.

"Hugh."

Not this again. I felt like it was a repeat from Pish's earlier thought that Hugh had committed the crime. But I determined to open my mind to the idea that Hugh was the controller. "Why do you think Hugh Langley was controlling the planchette?" I asked, leaning against Virgil in weariness. He put his arm around my shoulders. "I can't imagine why he would want to single out Todd."

The others were silent for a long minute. Pish cleared his throat. We all looked at him expectantly.

"I can think of one very good reason."

We waited.

"If he believes Todd killed Dirk but is afraid to point the finger of blame himself, would he do it this way, given the opportunity? I'm not saying that's it, but it *could* be. Maybe he wanted to try to get him to confess."

It was a rather good thought. "He does seem to be upset about Dirk's murder . . . I mean, we all are, of course, but this seems to be devastating him." Maybe I'd have a conversation with Mr. Langley myself to float that theory.

"I felt like there was a lot going on, a lot of simmering tensions," Pish said.

"That's what I saw," Virgil agreed. "There was definitely something wrong between Todd and his wife, for one thing, as we saw by that outburst after Todd was fingered as the killer."

I shared what I knew about the couples and their square dance partner trade-offs, Rishelle with Arnie and Todd with Serina.

Virgil gave a long, low whistle. "I didn't get any of that," he said, hugging me to him. "Maybe Dewayne ought to hire *you* as an investigator."

"No thank you," I retorted. "I have enough on my hands as it is. Besides, I just stumbled into some of that information by opening a door at the wrong time. I had it *completely* wrong. I thought Rishelle was pining for her husband, not the knitted toque–wearing hulk."

Virgil's cell buzzed, and he looked at it. "It's Dewayne; I have to take this. He was getting back to me about something." He strode away, out of the library.

The rest of our little group broke up, since no one had any other ideas. Janice was going back to town, so she would drive Lizzie to her grandmother's. When I walked them out I noticed that Todd and Serina were indeed sitting in the sound van, but it appeared they were just having a conversation, and with a morose expression he waved to me. I returned to the castle while Janice unlocked her car and piled her Ouija board inside and Lizzie petulantly kicked gravel behind the HHN van. Janice's chauffeuring the teenager home left me free to corner the producer, who was sitting in the library tapping out a text on his phone when I tracked him down.

"Mr. Langley, just the man I want to see." I took the chair opposite him.

He politely put away his cell and folded his hands together. "How may I help you?"

"I was wondering if the police have told you when you and the others can leave."

"Unfortunately, no."

"They have interviewed you all, though, some on multiple occasions. How did that go?"

"As could be expected, I suppose. I had little to add. I seem to be sadly out of the loop with my own cast and crew," he said with a shake of his head. "I had no idea of this little joke Millicent and Rishelle planned."

"Tragic, as it turns out," I said.

"They're so young. I feel the gap especially with all of their philandering and dramas. I am past that agony, thank heavens. I have had a supremely successful career doing what I love, and now my sole wish in life is to have the rest of my career go as profitably." He straightened the pleats to his slacks, smoothing the fine wool fabric.

"Has it been so profitable?" I asked, doubt creeping into my tone.

"Oh, yes indeed. I have been *very* fortunate. I've won many awards over my career: a Critics' Choice, a Dallas and Area Culture Award, many more. But I've prepared, you know. It didn't just come to me. I have a Ph.D. in media studies from the University of Texas at Austin."

"That's great."

"I do hope we'll be leaving in the morning. None of us even lives out of state, so it shouldn't be a problem. I'll put it to the sheriff." He smiled wearily. "You've had more legal experience than I, so perhaps you know more than I do."

It was a gibe, but I didn't take it amiss. "I guess we'll know soon. This is truly terrible for you all, but for *me* it feels like this recurring nightmare I'm caught in. It keeps happening! I wish I knew why."

He appeared undecided about something, but then shook his head.

"What is it?"

He still hesitated. "I'm worried. I don't like what happened earlier, at the Ouija board."

"You mean naming Todd as the killer? I had half a thought *you* were behind that, trying to out him because you suspected him."

He looked shocked. "Good grief, *no*! Todd being Dirk's killer would be a disaster for me personally—I like Todd and can't see him as the murderer—*and* it would be bad for the network if it is him or one of the other cast members. To be blunt, we'd prefer the culprit was one of the crew." He paused. "As terrible as that sounds," he added, with a shrug and resigned look.

"You're not planning to continue the show, are you? Without Dirk?"

He shook his head but more in sadness than denial. "I don't know anything at this point. It will be up to the network. On the one hand, it's already getting a lot of media attention."

I nodded. The landline had been ringing nonstop all day, but by now I knew to ignore it. It was a simple statement of fact that this was bound to stir up lots of publicity for *Haunt Hunt*.

"HHN *could* decide that this would be good for ratings,

and ratings are all-important, though advertisers are notoriously gun-shy about scandals. I have control over some things, but not whether we continue or not."

"Hugh, who *did* kill Dirk?"

"If I knew, don't you think I'd be telling the sheriff?"

"Not if it was someone you like," I said, thinking of Todd. "You've already said you don't want it to be one of the cast, that you'd prefer if it was a crew member."

"But that does *not* mean I'd throw someone under the bus, my dear." He frowned down at his cell phone. "If I had to cast someone as the villain, I don't see why it can't have been someone from Autumn Vale, maybe someone who didn't like us being here, or . . ." He hesitated and slewed a glance in my direction.

"Or someone who doesn't like *me*," I said, guessing at his thrust.

He shrugged.

"Sorry, but in this case that doesn't wash. Neither Virgil nor the sheriff thinks that's likely." I shifted in my chair and leaned forward, watching his eyes. "Hugh, I feel like when I said I wondered why this keeps happening, you had something to say."

He looked down at his hands, then up at me. "Okay, all right; I have to say this. It's weighing on me terribly. When Todd and I had the original conversation about coming here I had no idea it was a surprise to you, nor did I realize that Pish hadn't asked us to come. I leave those details up to Todd and Stu. We often have to change our schedule around when someone backs out at the last minute, or if something gets in the way of shooting somewhere, a natural disaster or some such, so we usually have a few places we can go where the owners have left it open to us when to come."

He moved slightly, rotated his shoulders, moved a book on the table in front of him. "But this time . . ." He sighed. "I've been in contact with our network boss and it's *most* unusual. I don't understand this. Someone at a historic home where we were going to be shooting this week called to complain that she was told at the last minute we wouldn't be coming. She said that Todd called to tell her we couldn't come because of some crisis. He then apparently switched up the schedule so we'd come *here*. I can't help but wonder . . . Merry, he's our resident research nut. He *always* knows more about every location than anyone else and reads up on the stuff online relentlessly. We call him Encyclopedia Todd. I wonder, had he heard of your castle's reputation? And if so, was that why he pushed so hard to come here?"

"What are you saying?" I asked. "By Wynter Castle's reputation are you saying the articles in newspapers about the murders in the past year?"

"I don't know," he said, exasperation in his voice. He passed one hand over his thinning hair. "I'm going to have a conversation with him about it. I can't have him upsetting homeowners that way."

"Hugh, who do you think pushed the planchette to indicate Todd was the killer?"

"I don't know for sure." He paused, irritation flickering over his expression. "I don't know why he'd do it, but I *think* it may have been Arnie."

Chapter Twenty-one

I **COULD THINK** of a good reason why it might be Arnie pointing the finger at Todd, given he was enthusiastically boffing Todd's wife. But I didn't comment. I wanted to talk to some of the others, in particular Todd, before they all headed to bed. Some appeared to have already gone upstairs. I couldn't find Felice, Chi, Stu, or Millicent. But as I returned to the great hall, Serina flung herself into the castle from outside, stormed past me weeping, and headed up the stairs.

"Serina, *Serina*!" I called after her, but she headed to her shared room.

That likely meant Todd was outside alone, and there was no better time to talk to him. I grabbed a sweater from the coat tree I had tucked in a corner of the great hall so I wouldn't have to go up to my room if I wanted to head outside. I exited and saw the dome light on in the van.

I strolled across the terrace, down to the drive, and stood at the edge, looked toward the woods. I cupped my hands around my mouth like a megaphone. "Be-cket! Here kitty-kitty-kitty!" I called. "Be-cket!"

I strolled over to the van. Todd was sitting in the driver's seat, smoking a cigarette. "Hey, Todd. Have you seen my orange cat?"

He glanced toward me. "No," he said dully, and flicked his cigarette into the weeds.

I strode over to it and ground it out with my shoe heel, then returned to the van. "I'd prefer if you didn't do that," I said.

"Sorry."

I got closer and leaned my folded arms on the van window. I hadn't known he was one of the smokers, but maybe he was an occasional addict who smoked when tense. "Todd, what do you make of what happened in there tonight? You seemed to blame your wife for naming you the killer."

He shook his head, staring straight out the windshield. "It doesn't matter."

"What do you mean, it doesn't matter?"

"It doesn't effing matter. None of this does."

I was worried about his demeanor. I watched his face, but he simply stared straight ahead. "Todd, I know you were having an affair with Serina, and I saw her crying just now. What's up between you?"

He swiveled his head slowly in my direction. "You are so frickin' clueless. You and your clown car of friends. None of this matters."

"What do you mean?"

"Look, you can't trust anyone. You think you've got friends, but they'll stab you in the back the minute it's turned."

I waited, but he didn't go on. Unsure what to say, I ventured, "Hey, at least you've still got *Haunt Hunt*, right?" No answer, but he lit another cigarette. "Todd, can I ask you something? Did you know about the murders here at the castle? Is that why you wanted to come?"

He glanced sideways at me, then blew out a puff of smoke, shaking his head. "Who gives a crap?" He drummed his fingers on the steering wheel.

"*I* do! I heard you canceled on another homeowner to come here. Is that why? Because you learned about the murders? Were you manipulating Pish all along?"

He gave me a cold, calculating look. "I'd be careful who I was blaming for manipulation here." He took a deep drag and blew out a long stream of smoke. "Did you ever find out that everything you thought you knew was a frickin' joke? A lie? That's what I found out tonight."

"Todd, what's going on? What's wrong?"

He shook his head, bitterness twisting his mouth. When we first met I had thought he was a lighthearted joker. I was apparently completely wrong.

"Nothing's wrong. Nothing's right. Nothing matters. I'm going for a drive." He started up the van and pulled out of his space and roared down the drive, the CD player sparking to life with "Bohemian Rhapsody" playing full blast, Freddie Mercury's high keening wail that *nothing really matters* echoing Todd's refrain.

I called for Becket again, but when he didn't come, I retreated inside. I was fed up and angry at being held hostage by this bunch of weirdos. I stomped upstairs and rapped on the women's door, feeling like the dorm mom when the chattering inside silenced.

"Yes?"

That was Millicent's voice.

"It's Merry. Can I come in?"

"Sure," she said.

I entered. The room looked like a tropical storm had hit a clothing boutique. Millicent was sitting on the big bed, cross-legged, her skirts splayed out around her and a warm stole tight around her shoulders. Felice was sitting on the floor with her back against the daybed, looking at her tablet.

Serina was standing in the middle of the room. I had a sense that the "chatter" I had heard was not friendly girlie banter, but something more confrontational, judging by Serina's stance. Her face showed the ravages of weeping, mascara rimming under her eyes, and her punky hair was plastered down on her narrow skull.

Warily, I eyed them all. "Okay, what is going on?" I finally asked.

"Why don't you ask them?" Serina sobbed, pointing at Millicent. "Her and Rishelle, so buddy-buddy all of a sudden."

Though I wanted to get around to Todd's behavior and Serina's part in it, I was unsure whether to bring that up with the others present.

"Serina, I'm sorry. I don't know what you're so upset about." Millicent had a look of concern on her face. She glanced toward me. "She's accusing us of sabotaging Todd. It's not my fault the Ouija board pointed at Todd as Dirk's killer."

"That's enough garbage, Millicent," I said. "I don't mean to squash anyone's belief system, but really . . . a stupid board as a way of talking to spirits? One of you around the board was guiding it, *that's* what Serina is talking about. One of you, or more than one, with your fingers on the planchette, were accusing Todd of murder."

Millicent looked wounded, her bottom lip trembling. "I resent that. I would *never* do that to Todd. He's my friend. It's not *my* fault the Ouija pointed at him."

"Millicent might be a little wacko, but that much is true; she and Todd are cool," Felice said. "He despised Dirk, but he doesn't have a problem with Millie."

Both Serina and Millicent glared down at her. Her statement didn't help as much as she perhaps thought it would, since it acknowledged Todd's deep dislike of Dirk, a possible motive to kill him.

"You *all* seemed to have a problem with Dirk. Isn't that so?"

"He was a jerk," Serina said. She had calmed significantly and sat down on a stool by the makeup table. "It's true!" she said as the other two women murmured protestations. "The least we can be is honest. I didn't like Dirk, but I didn't want him dead, and neither did Todd. Poor guy's worried. He's convinced that everyone is going to band together and pin it on him."

"How can they, if he didn't do it?" Felice asked.

Serina gave her a dirty look, but it was a viable question.

"Todd doesn't trust the cops," Serina said. "Not since he got in trouble a few years ago."

"In trouble?" I said.

Millicent and Felice watched Serina, too, and it appeared to be news to them as well as to me. The sound tech caught her bottom lip between her teeth. She had shared information not meant to be shared.

"Never mind," Serina said, shoving her hands in her jeans pockets. "Forget it. It's not something he talks about, but it was nothing important." She pushed past me and headed to the door.

"Todd's gone for a drive, if you're going looking for him," I said, turning to watch her in the doorway. She paused, but then stomped away. "You two, I want to talk to," I said, pointing my finger at Millicent and Felice. "I'll be back.

I raced out the door and caught Serina before she went downstairs. "Serina, what did you and Todd fight about? Did you break up? What did you say to him? He seemed distraught."

She stopped at the railing and looked down, leaning way over until I tugged on the back of her shirt to keep her from falling. She straightened and stared at me. "Have you ever been in the middle of an argument so bad, and then you hear yourself saying things, like it's an out-of-body experience? You can't stop yourself?"

I nodded. I remember arguments like that. No good ever came from them. "So what did you say to Todd?"

She took a deep breath. "I was hurt, because he called

me a name and said we were done. So . . . I told him about
Rishelle and Arnie."

I sighed. That was what I expected. "Anything else?"

She nodded, tears streaming down her cheeks. "I told
him about Stu."

"What about Stu?"

"Stu has lined up another show and he's bailing on *Haunt
Hunt*. He's had enough of Todd, Rishelle, Millicent . . . all
of them."

No wonder the guy was distraught. It was a dangerous
moment for Todd, when it appeared that everything was
being taken from him. Serina clattered down the stairs. "Serina, *Serina*!" I yelled. But she was gone, out the front door.

I returned to the room. "Do either of you know what
Serina meant when she said Todd had been in trouble? And
about him not liking cops?"

Millicent shrugged.

Felice, knees drawn up and tablet propped on them, said,
"Holy crap! So this was Todd? We live in the same city and
I heard about this, but it was before *Haunt Hunt* so I never
made the connection, or didn't remember the name. Listen:
*Local Man Pleads Guilty to Second-Degree Felony Assault:
John Halsey (also known as Todd) charged with first-degree
felony assault after a shooting in Rochester, received pro-
bation and a lifetime ban on firearm ownership after pleading to the lesser charge Tuesday in a Rochester court. The
incident occurred in October of 2013, and involved a road
rage incident, followed by pistol-whipping and a shot fired
that grazed the individual. The accused claims the gun went
off accidentally.*"

I took the tablet and read the whole piece. Though it was
supposedly a road rage incident, buried in the article was
the suggestion that Todd knew the victim, who was a friend
of his wife's, they had had an argument, and Todd had followed him in his vehicle. He then confronted the guy on the

road, which was when the pistol-whipping and shot had occurred. The accompanying mug shot confirmed it was Todd. "This doesn't prove anything, though," I said. "Really. It doesn't say a single thing about *this* case."

Felice and Millicent exchanged a look, and something secret passed between them. But Felice shook her head, and Millicent shrugged. They were hiding something. I sighed. This crew could not get out of here fast enough for me.

I was troubled by it all as I left the room, and even more troubled that Serina had so casually revealed what was formerly not known about Todd, that he had a violent incident in his past. As his lover, shouldn't she have been trying to protect him, rather than sabotage him? I wanted to talk to Rishelle, but neither she nor Arnie were anywhere to be found.

Todd's career seemed to be crumbling, his marriage was breaking down, and so was he. There was probably more I could have discovered, but it appeared that most of the *Haunt Hunt* cast and crew were headed to bed.

Pish came up the stairs, his face gray with exhaustion. "I'm heading to bed, my darling," he said, kissing my cheek. "I'm far too old for this."

I stood in the shadows of the gallery, looking down over the great hall. I was exhausted and deeply troubled about the day's events, but I had no idea how to proceed. Virgil emerged from our room. He wore pajama bottoms and nothing else, my favorite look on him. "What did Dewayne want?" I asked.

"We've got another case. This one is more interesting than insurance surveillance, but I'm going to need a couple of suits for it. Go shopping with me?"

"Oooh, I get to style you?" I teased.

"You can do anything you want. But right now, come to bed," he said, winding his arms around me and holding me pinned tightly against his chest. "Maybe I can take your mind off things for a little while," he said. He whispered some naughty nothings in my ear.

"Becket is still outside," I whispered against his lips.

"The cat will be fine. It's not that cold right now, not for Becket, anyway. You know he'll likely stay away until this crew is gone, and I aim to make sure that they are all gone tomorrow morning. I'm calling Urquhart first thing and telling him I'm throwing the whole lot out of the castle. Figuring out which one of them killed that poor guy is his job, not ours."

I acquiesced, relieved Virgil would take charge of that aspect and talk to Urquhart about getting rid of my house nuisances. He was right. It was not my job to solve this deed. Good thing, because I didn't have a clue what to do

I DON'T KNOW WHY I WOKE UP. A BAD DREAM, I THINK. But I awoke thinking about Becket. He's getting to be a lovely cat, and when I'm alone he snuggles up to me. But of course, for the last few days, with all these people and equipment cluttering our castle he's been grumpier than usual. I was worried about him.

As I slipped from bed, Virgil snored on. The hour glowed on the clock, two forty-five. I had been exhausted and so was Virgil, so we fell asleep almost immediately. I had actually intended to look through the footage from the memory cards Lizzie had loaded onto my laptop, but the task was daunting, and I didn't think I'd find anything quickly. Or maybe at all. So I had said "screw it" and gone to sleep wrapped in my husband's arms.

But now I was wide-awake and worried. Over my sleeveless nightie I pulled on Virgil's flannel shirt that was hanging from the bedpost, and shored my feet into slippers, the ones with the thick rubber soles that I use when I may need to go outside. Once I'm downstairs it's a long way back up to get shoes, so I wear them whenever I go downstairs instead of my warmer soft-soled slippers.

The gallery was thickly silent; I don't know how to describe it otherwise. I felt like I was being watched, but there was no one else there. The silence was heavy and fetid, the very air laden with menace. Something was wrong, but I didn't know what. My stomach twisted. I tried to dismiss it. Maybe it was all the crap that had happened lately catching up with me, or anxiety and poor eating habits.

I descended, slipped through the darkness to the kitchen to get kitty treats to shake to attract Becket. I took the treats to the front door, hoping I wouldn't have to go too far onto the terrace—the nights were getting pretty cold—before he'd hear me and come. I opened the door, stepped out onto the terrace, and before I even called, Becket bolted in. I shrieked and skittered sideways as he raced through the great hall toward the kitchen, carrying something dark and damp. Heaven help me, some new poor dead beastie I'd have to dustpan up and carry out.

I turned and followed, but only got as far as inside the doors when I heard a screech. Rishelle staggered toward me through the door. She fell on the floor, screaming and wailing. I flicked the switch to turn on the chandelier, and she was writhing, blood on her hands. "Rishelle!" I screamed. "Oh my gawd, Rishelle, what's wrong?" Thoughts coursed through my mind: Rishelle had fallen, or hit her head, or Becket attacked her, or . . .

Becket had returned empty-mouthed to the great hall and yowled, his howl echoing through the cavernous great hall. He stalked sideways, back arched, a big orange ball of fur; his hair was standing on end all over his body. Doors started to open upstairs. Sleepy-eyed folks stumbled partway down the stairs, and Hugh, in elegant pajamas, materialized by my side.

"What's going on?" he asked.

I pulled Rishelle up, trying to help her. She was shaking all over, and her hands were slippery, covered in blood.

"Rishelle, tell me what's wrong. Where are you hurt? How can I help?" I looked up at the faces above, blinking, sleepy, scared, and to Hugh. "Call 911! Rishelle is hurt!"

"No, *no!*" she shrieked. She grabbed me with her bloody hands, shaking me by the shoulders and staring into my eyes. "You don't understand. He's d-dead!"

"What is she talking about?" Hugh asked, hovering.

"I don't know," I said. "Rishelle, *tell* me what's going on!"

"He did it. I never believed he would, but he did it. It's Todd . . . He sh-shot himself . . . out in the van!" She sobbed and collapsed. "He's *dead!*"

Chapter Twenty-two

❋ ❋ ❋

ONE MORE TIME: Someone dies, we call the police, investigate, rinse, and repeat. It was unthinkable, the regularity with which these events occurred. I was numb with horror.

We all sat, guarded by a deputy from the sheriff's office. For once I had not been the one to find the body. Rishelle was a quivering, shaking, bloody mess from what she had witnessed, the lifeless body of her husband. No matter that they were cheating on each other, no matter that they may have broken up at some future point, Todd was her husband. The story she had babbled before the sheriff arrived was awful. She stated that Todd's body was slumped over in the driver's seat, the gun still in his right hand, the driver's side window shattered. It was *truly* deeply horrifying and I pitied her from the bottom of my heart.

I thought of Todd's last words, the message of "Bohemian Rhapsody" floating out the van window. What haunted me was the refrain that repeated that *nothing really matters*, and the gun reference. It was chilling. Todd Halsey, joyful ghost hunter, was dead. This was not the outcome I had expected, a suicide to add to the awful murders we had experienced in the last year. I was grateful I had sent Lizzie back to her grandmother's home the night before.

Virgil sat down beside me and grabbed my hand. "You okay?"

"Relatively, I guess."

"I got Urquhart to talk to me," he whispered, cradling my hand in his. "The gun wasn't registered to Todd. He couldn't get a gun because he had a—"

"Felony conviction, and had been barred from owning any firearms," I finished, then told him what I had learned the night before.

"Yeah. Well, what you may not know is, the gun in his hand was registered to Stuart Jardine."

I looked at Virgil, surprised. "Really?" I'd said that too loudly in my surprise, and glanced around, then lowered my voice. "Stu bought the gun? He is *so* not the gun type."

"He told Urquhart that he never wanted the gun; he bought it for Todd."

"Isn't that illegal?"

He nodded. "It's called a straw purchase, when you buy something—guns, cigarettes, alcohol—for someone else who either can't or doesn't want to buy it for themselves. And it is indeed illegal in New York State. Here, if you buy a gun for someone else, that person has to be eligible to purchase a firearm, and the gun *must* be passed off through a licensed gun dealer. This means that though Stu *says* the gun was Todd's, it's still registered as Stuart's."

My gut hurt; we only had, at this point, Stu's word for it that he had given the gun to his partner. What if that wasn't true? What did that mean? "But why did Todd *want* it? Did Stu say? Did he plan this suicide?"

Virgil shook his head and squinted. "I don't know. Not

necessarily. Some guys feel the need to have a gun. Maybe Todd was one of them." Virgil was bothered by something. That may sound strange, given that someone had just killed himself in our driveway, but there was something else. He was checking out the others through squinty eyes, a look I recognized as him thinking deeply.

"Virgil, what is it?" I whispered, watching his face.

He turned toward me and shielded his mouth from view of the others by scruffing his sprouting beard. The man grows whiskers in minutes, it sometimes seems. "Urquhart let me view the scene. He's out of his depth, and he knows it. I told him there's no shame in calling in the state troopers, and he's considering it, but he asked my opinion. I gave it to him straight up. This is *not* suicide."

I felt the hit like a punch to the stomach. *Not* suicide. "So the killer has struck again?" My heart thudded and I swallowed past a sickening lump.

"Maybe. Maybe not."

"Virgil, I'm scared."

He put his arm around me and hugged. "We'll get through this."

"How do you know it's not suicide?"

"Angle's *all* wrong. It's from slightly above. He *could* have shot himself that way, but I don't see it. The scene doesn't feel right. It looks like it's been staged for a TV movie of the week."

I knew Virgil's feelings on TV mystery movies of the week and the way they staged homicide or suicide scenes. He always says it looks too careful. I'm still not sure what he means; he says it's "wrong."

"A few other things that Urquhart told me, too," he continued. "I'll tell you later, but one thing is a phone found on the seat in the van beside Todd. They're trying to get phone records right now, but the server is balking, so he has a call into someone higher up in the company. A warrant is on the way, which he wants before he goes any further. Urquhart needs to talk to you about the evening, before, during, and after the Ouija session. I told him what little we learned, but that you might remember different stuff, or have noticed different stuff."

I nodded. "I want this over with. I'll do whatever I can."

Pish was watching us, his eyes filled with tragedy and tears. He was likely blaming himself. I beckoned to him. He cast a quick glance at the deputy, then scooted over to us. He grabbed my hands and kissed them. "My darling, I'm so sorry we've landed in a pickle yet again. This is terrible! Poor Todd. Did that Ouija session push him over the edge? Do you think he killed Dirk?"

I exchanged a glance with Virgil, and he gave a faint nod. I told Pish, emphasizing this was in confidence, that it likely was not suicide. He got the implication immediately, and surveyed the group.

Serina was a weeping, wilting basket case at first, but now she was narrow-eyed and glaring at Rishelle. Todd's wife was quiet, and it appeared that her thoughts were all turned inward. She wore a housecoat, since she had handed her clothes over to the police. If Virgil's training held sway over Urquhart, I assumed the sheriff would also have had her hands photographed and tested for GSR, as well as fingernails scraped. She had been questioned, and then finally allowed to wash.

At first, when she joined us, Arnie had openly tried to comfort her, but she had shrugged his arm off her shoulders and moved away from him. She was alone and appeared to prefer it that way. Even when Millicent tried to comfort her, she shook her head, refusing sympathy or comfort. Instead, she isolated herself in a high-sided club chair, hugging a cushion like a shield and curling up in her pink housecoat.

Stu was mumbling to himself and wandering, looking under seat cushions for something and patting his pockets absently. He had probably misplaced his clove cigarettes or the Ben Franklin biography he had been reading. He kept shaking his head and muttering. Was he going round the bend, too, his hipster mind irrevocably broken by his partner's death?

I watched them all. So far no one had said *murder*. I assumed that they all still thought it was suicide, given Rishelle's hysterical description of it as such. I tried to organize my thoughts and what I knew about Todd. Something Hugh had said came back to me; Todd was a thorough researcher and so very likely knew about the recent history of my castle. He had tried to corner me about that, and had intended to use the tragedies. In that attempt he had been ably assisted by Dirk, also dead.

Which meant that the others could have known about it, too, though they didn't have the power to push the production company into sending them here. Or did they? Had one of them used Todd to push Wynter Castle as a *Haunt Hunt* site and make him break his plan to go elsewhere? Who had that power of persuasion over him? And why would they convince him to come *here*? Why Wynter Castle?

I was confused and troubled. Todd's last words and that snatch of music came back to me again and again. *Nothing really matters . . . at all.* Those were the words of someone who had given up, and yet I trust Virgil's opinion over anyone else's, especially that of the new sheriff in town. My gaze slid around the room: Rishelle, Arnie, Stu. All had betrayed him. Each also had a potential motive for murder.

Urquhart looked in the door, caught my eye, and beckoned to me. I followed him to the parlor. He shut the door behind me and indicated one of the low slipper chairs near the fireplace. I took a seat. I *may* have indicated in the past that the new sheriff and I don't see eye to eye on many things, but Virgil is standing by his pick, and in general, I get why. Urquhart is smart. He never, to my knowledge, lets his emotions influence his investigative behavior. I think his dislike of me has mellowed to a general lack of understanding why Virgil— a man he deeply respects—loves me.

"This is awful, Sheriff. I don't know what to make of it, I'll be honest," I said. I had given up my husband's flannel shirt, since Rishelle had laid her bloody hands on it, and was wrapped in a heavy cardigan. It was time to start lighting fires or turning up the ancient boiler system in the castle.

"I assume Virge told you that it's not suicide, in his opinion?"

"Yes. You sound neutral about it. Are you still investigating it as a possible suicide?"

He nodded. "He might be right, but the doctor says it's completely possible to kill yourself that way. There was one gunshot, there appears to be a contact between the gun barrel and the head, and other things are consistent with suicide."

My phone vibrated in my sweater pocket, but I ignored it for the moment. "Other things?"

"Your own words about how he seemed hopeless. And Serina Rogers said they were having an affair, but they had a big fight and she told him some things about his wife and best friend that devastated him."

"Serina did tell me last night she had said those things. And Todd was devastated. He took off for a ride, like I told you, but last I saw Serina, she was headed outside. Maybe she waited for him to come back? Or maybe she phoned him. She may have come back inside, because I went to bed soon after that. I didn't lock up; I wanted Todd to be able to come back in."

He digested that, nodding. "The wife claims he has threatened to kill himself in the past. And you say that was her first assumption, when she entered?"

"Yes, that is the first thing she said, that he'd actually done it. And Todd's last words to me . . . it sounded like he was suicidal." I sighed deeply. How different this all seemed from my first impression of Todd Halsey as a happy-go-lucky sort dedicated to his mission of investigating haunting. It was a potent reminder that behind many a smile lurked desperation. "Virgil mentioned a cell phone on the van seat, and that you're trying to unlock the phone, or get phone records to see if he was talking to anyone before his death?"

He nodded. "Nothing yet. Can we go through last evening?"

I found myself organizing my thoughts as I spoke. I stuck with the facts with Urquhart, though, rather than some speculative stuff that occurred to me as I mulled over the happenings of the last three days. I made some mental notes that I hoped to jot down on paper later. I simply told him everything I had observed, and whatever had been said, including repeating my late-night conversation with Serina, Millicent, and Felice. I shared what I had heard about Todd's record. He nodded; he already knew about that.

He dismissed me and I exited to the great hall, getting my cell phone out of my pocket. Lizzie had texted me to ask if I was picking her up. I looked at my watch. Good heavens, it was after seven A.M. *Hours* had passed! She thought she was coming out today to help the *Haunt Hunt* crew pack up and get a recommendation from Hugh for her work, such as it was. I might still be able to wangle a recommendation from the producer for Lizzie, even if they never broadcast the Wynter Castle *Haunt Hunt*, and I was assuming they wouldn't, especially in light of the cohost's death.

Todd's suicide or murder had complicated things for the show, but also was going to inevitably slow down the sheriff's department's investigation of Dirk's murder. It had become exponentially more complicated. Or . . . it was possible that if the sheriff was right, and Todd had killed himself, then it would simplify things, I reflected. He quite possibly killed himself out of remorse for murdering Dirk.

In any case, life was not getting easier for the moment.

And I *still* hadn't looked at the footage Lizzie had loaded onto my laptop, the stuff the sheriff's department was probably going over even now, in reference to Dirk's death. It didn't look like I'd have time to do that, but Lizzie or even Hannah might.

Meanwhile, what to do about Lizzie?

I hustled through the kitchen and out the back door, looking out over the long grass toward the garage, rather than to the parking area with the van and Todd Halsey's body. Pacing back and forth near my dying herb garden I called Lizzie.

"You on your way?" she asked, chewing on something in my ear.

"Lizzie, no. Something has happened." I told her, as gently as possible, about Todd's death.

She was silent for a long minute. "I think I ought to come," she said. "I should talk to the sheriff. I heard something last night, and it might be important."

Chapter Twenty-three

❋ ❋ ❋

"WHAT IS IT?"

"I'll tell you when you pick me up."

"Honey, no, I can't!"

"Then I'll find my own way. See you in fifteen."

She hung up and wouldn't answer her phone. I texted Hannah to call me when she got up, and she called immediately, moments after I texted. I told her some of what happened as I paced back and forth behind the castle, and she wowed a couple of times, then told me she had more stuff she had researched, and when did I want to hear it?

Not right that moment, I said, then heard a long, low rumble. Were we having an earthquake? I whirled and there, up my drive, came a caravan of Turner Construction vehicles. It was Monday morning, and work was commencing on the foundation we were building near the forest, as well as drilling to discover a well.

Crap on a stick. The sheriff's deputy stopped them and spoke to the lead driver, then waved them on, guiding them past the garage and away from the suicide van sitting on my drive. She pointed at me, then them; I took that to mean that I was to speak with them and decide what to do. I nodded, waved, then held up one finger. I turned away.

"Hannah, we'll have to talk later, but I do have a big . . . an *enormous* . . . favor to ask of you." I explained quickly about the rough footage from the camera SD cards. I asked if I could e-mail it to her to look over, and told her what I was looking for.

"You are in luck," she said calmly. "This particular librarian happens to have the whole day free, since I'm not opening the library today, and I'd love to help. I can't imagine I'll be able to watch every minute, but if you send it now, I'll get to it right away."

"You are a rock star, Hannah. I mean that sincerely. I'll tell you the pertinent people, dates, and times in an e-mail."

I stuck my phone in my cardigan pocket and strode over to the equipment, signaling that I needed to talk to the operator. I climbed up on the doorway and asked him what they were up to, and he told me their plan. There was still a lot to do before we proceeded, and I didn't see any reason why they couldn't continue. I wanted them to be able to finish most of the work before the snow started. Unless the sheriff told me otherwise, they were continuing.

I returned to the house and slipped up to my room. I have a little desk by one of the windows on which I keep my laptop. I booted it up, attached all the video files that Lizzie had downloaded from the SD cards to an e-mail to Hannah, and told her some things I was looking for. But I also asked her to keep her eyes open for anything that seemed off to her—looks, people where they shouldn't be, conversations that seemed off—anything odd.

I scanned some of the footage myself very quickly. There was one time point in particular I was curious about, night before last, just a while after Chi, Rishelle, and Millicent set up the prank. I watched; this was from the SD card of a camera I hadn't even noticed, attached to one of the equipment vans in the parking area. Leave it to Lizzie to notice it and be sneaky enough to get the memory card without anyone noticing.

I wondered, did everyone know about what DVR cameras were going? Some were set to motion sensory activation, it seemed, from occasional bits and pieces: Becket trotting across the grass and whining and scratching at the back door, a bunny streaking across an open area, someone out for a smoke. It looked like Felice, but it could have been Stu; it was hard to tell. Both smoked, and the night-vision camera didn't always have the best resolution.

Ah! There . . . was that who I thought it was? I watched it carefully; right height, right hair, right hat. And the right loping manner of walking out toward the garage after the others had returned from their practical joke setup. He had a motive, too, especially if the long game was to get Todd accused of killing Dirk, and thus get rid of him. It was something to think about.

Virgil joined me as I shut down. He took my hand, led me to the bed, and pulled me down to him. We kissed, but then I pulled away from him. Gazing directly into his eyes inches from mine, it was difficult to keep my focus, but not so hard once the reality of the day pushed back at me. I sat up and put my feet over the edge of the bed. "Lizzie is coming in a few minutes; I didn't want her to, but she insisted. She says she has to talk to Urquhart, that she heard something that might be important."

He sighed and sat up, too, beside me. "What did she hear?"

"She hung up before I could ask. And the work guys arrived. They're finishing work on the foundation today and the well expert is coming to start drilling. They're hoping to hit water by one hundred feet. If everything goes well, the crew leader said, we can move ahead while the weather holds."

He took a deep breath, put his head back, and closed his eyes. "I can't wait until we have our own house," he murmured, and pulled me toward him, kissing my neck.

"It's difficult to think when you do that," I whispered, moving my hair aside so he could continue."

"I'll have to stop then, right?"

"Yes, you have to stop." I didn't sound too convincing.

Finally, though, he stood and pulled me up to my feet, wrapping his arms around me. "You said something about the kid coming out?"

"Oh *yes*! I have to get downstairs." The deputies would keep her away from the awful scene and guide her into the castle, I figured.

"And she has something to tell Urquhart?"

I nodded as we let go of each other. I changed into yoga pants and a thick tunic sweater.

"So why haven't you done what you usually do at this point?" he asked.

"What's that?"

"Write down everything you're thinking and wondering so you can figure out whodunit?"

I laughed. "Yes, Watson, I should do that, right?"

"I thought Hannah was your Watson," he growled.

"What does that make *you*?" I asked.

"Your distracting stud muffin," he said, nuzzling my neck again.

I smiled and pulled away from him. He always knew what I needed. I kinda liked the new more relaxed version of the Virgil with whom I had fallen in love. He had been a "by the book" sheriff, but now he was a "let's take some chances" PI. I returned to my desk and got out a notebook and pen. "I saw something a few minutes ago on the DVR recordings that has me wondering." I told what and whom

I thought I saw. "So, let's figure this out, Mr. Private Detective."

"Didn't you say Lizzie was coming?" he reminded me yet again.

"Oh cripes, yes. You got me all flustered with the kissing and nuzzling. We'll have to take this downstairs to the kitchen. You can glare at anyone who trots in unannounced."

In my kitchen I feel at home, like things are somehow normal. However, there was nothing normal about life in the last three days. "I guess we need to think about feeding this mob. Virgil, what if they're here for days and days? I don't think I can stand it." I sat down at the table, head in hands.

"We'll get through it. And don't worry about food. I'll take care of it."

Years of being on his own had forced Virgil to become self-sufficient. Even when he was married, his wife didn't enjoy cooking, so he took care of most of it. He began assembling the ingredients for his chili con carne, which had, when I first tasted it, taken my breath away, and not in a good way. He likes food spicy, while I have a more sensitive palate. He has since restrained the heat, and adds hot sauce to his own bowl at dinnertime.

The scent of garlic, onions, and peppers cooking gently in some olive oil and butter filled the kitchen, and he clattered around getting out the giant stockpot to make his huge batch of chili. Becket slunk in, chastened, so I got him some of his treats and moved him to one of the wing chairs by the fireplace. He could stay in the kitchen with us, for once. I closed the kitchen door and wrote down notes, something I had intended to do the evening before.

First, Dirk's death. Who had a motive to kill him, no matter how weird or weak the motive seemed? Virgil and I quietly chatted and I wrote notes.

1—Todd Halsey: Loathed Dirk. Felt Dirk was damaging

the Haunt Hunt *quest to prove ghosts exist. Since his wife, Rishelle, had a hand in setting up the prank, Todd may have known about it and altered the prank to be deadly. If his own death is suicide, it may indicate his guilt, but if he was murdered, it pretty much rules out his culpability.*

Virgil warned me that the last part I had just written was not necessarily true.

"The part about if he was murdered, it means he didn't kill Dirk? Why?" I asked.

Virgil turned away from the separate giant frying pan in which he was cooking lean ground beef and spicy Italian sausage. Spatula in hand, he crossed his arms and leaned back against the counter. "Okay, say Todd killed Dirk with the help or knowledge of someone else, like Stu or Rishelle, just to name the people he was closest to."

"Or his girlfriend, Serina."

"Right. So he starts to feel bad about it and wants to confess, or he threatens to tell someone else. His coconspirator might stage a suicide, killing him to get him out of the way."

That was true. I jotted down what Virgil said under Todd's entry. "Or, if he killed Dirk and someone else who liked Dirk was angry, they might kill him for revenge."

"Kind of weak, but okay." He turned back to the stove and broke up the ground beef, which sizzled and popped in the oil.

"I guess Rishelle would have similar motives," I said, writing down her name. "But it's complicated by her affair with Arnie. Was it some elaborate scheme to ultimately get rid of her husband by pinning the blame on him, then having him supposedly commit suicide, leaving her clear to get with Arnie?"

Virgil gave me a look over his shoulder.

"Yeah, kind of weak," I said.

"Unless she somehow gains by Todd being blamed and

then dying a supposed suicide, like insurance, or inheritance—always a possibility—it feels too complicated, especially for her. She's a straightforward gal, not subtle in the least."

"Why do you say that?"

He snorted, turned and eyed me, raised his eyebrows, then said, "She implied that she would be open to some hanky-panky."

I was aghast, and my mouth dropped open. "*Really?* Wow. I thought she and Arnie had a serious thing going on, but maybe it's just sex."

"There is that possibility," he said with a wry tone.

"When did this happen?"

"Before her husband died," he said, his expression sobering.

"So what did you say to her?" I asked. I didn't seriously think he'd do it, but I did wonder how he'd handled such a blatant come-on.

"What do you *think* I said?" he asked. "I told her it was a little early in our marriage and that I hadn't had time to get tired of you yet, but call me in a few months."

I rolled my eyes. "Virgil!"

He shrugged. "I told her she was barking up the wrong tree. She took it like a champ."

The butler pantry door banged open and Lizzie trudged in from the back hall. She tossed down her backpack, sniffed the air, and eyed the chili. But then she sat down at the table opposite me. Without even saying hello, she launched into her tale.

"So, last night, I was waiting for my ride, right? Waiting for Mrs. Grover to get her bus started."

"Yes, I saw you back there kicking gravel."

"I was sitting on the bumper of the HHN van, the one where Todd was sitting in the driver's seat. Serina was there, right, at that point?"

"She was when I saw them; she was sitting in the passenger seat and they were talking."

"Yeah, well, I don't like him much so I didn't say hi to him or anything. He always treats me like a pain in the butt. So anyway, I didn't talk to him and I don't think he even knew I was there. I waited. Mrs. Grover is *super* slow."

She caught my disapproving eye and waved one hand. "Gawd, don't get bent out of shape. That's *so* not a criticism of an adult. She just *is*. And her car is on its last legs . . . wheels, whatever, so it takes a while to warm up. Anyway, like I said, I don't think Todd even knew I was there. So, he's talking on the phone and smoking."

"On the *phone*? But Serina was with him, right? We established that? She came back in a while after. She said she had an argument with him."

"Yeah, they had a fight. But she didn't go right in. She stomped off around the corner of the castle, yelling something into her cell phone. *Anyway* . . . are you gonna let me tell my story?"

"Yes, go on," I said, exchanging a look with my husband.

"So anyway, I can smell the cigarette smoke, but I'm chilling and waiting for Mrs. Grover."

"And?" I said, impatient for her to get to the point.

"*And* he says in a real annoyed tone—and loud, like, cell yell, you know, how people talk real loud on cell phones and don't even realize they're doing it? Especially old people? Anyway, he says he knows something that could get someone else in trouble, and that he—whoever's on the other end of the phone—better help Todd out, or they'd pay."

I blinked, confused by the flurry of pronouns.

Virgil turned. "Let's get this straight. First, did you have the feeling that Todd was talking to the person who he thought killed Dirk?"

"I don't know."

"*Think*, Lizzie," I said. "You need to have this straight

before you talk to the sheriff. Was there anything that told you who Todd was talking to?"

"Not someone here, I guess. I mean, he was talking on the phone."

"That doesn't mean it wasn't someone here. We can't assume that," Virgil said.

I nodded in agreement. "He may not have wanted to be seen talking to someone in particular, so they spoke on the phone instead." I exchanged a look with my husband. "That doesn't even rule out Serina, considering she was on the phone, too, as weird as that seems."

"No assumptions, Lizzie," Virgil said, straddling the bench on their side of the table. "Did Todd say a name? Or anything specific about or to the person? Like indicate they weren't among the cast and crew? Or if it was one of the other crew at the motel?"

She thought for a long moment, picking at a scab on her knuckle. She was finally settling down to remember. Lizzie is like that; she can be careless about what she says at times, but when challenged she'll focus and then her excellent memory unwinds the sequence of events or words like a filmstrip.

"He said something like, '*I know what happened. I know what you're up to.*' And then he paused. I guess the other person was talking."

That immediacy sounded to me like Todd was talking to someone among the cast and crew. "Did he specifically say anything about Dirk's death?" I asked.

Lizzie shook her head.

"What next?" Virgil asked.

"He got all steamed up and told the other person to shut up. He said something like, he wasn't going to see his whole career go down the tubes because . . . and then I couldn't hear what else he said right then."

"What was the next thing you heard clearly?" I prodded.

"That was when he said something like, *'If I go to—mumble mumble—with what I know, the crap is going to hit the fan.'* Only he didn't say 'crap,' if you know what I mean. And then he said he wanted something in return for shutting up."

"And then?" Virgil prompted.

"Then Mrs. Grover got her car going and I left. Is it important?" she asked my husband, her gaze following him as he returned to the stove. "Should I tell the sheriff?"

"Yeah, it's important. You do need to tell Urquhart," Virgil said, dumping the wilted vegetables and fried ground beef into the stockpot. "And time is vital, so we can't wait until your mom is back. But I'll go with you, if you want, or Merry will."

"Okay," she said, rubbing the palms of her hands along her thighs. "You, I guess."

I leaned across the table, knowing she was anxious, given that she was wary of Urquhart. "It'll be okay." In the case of the SD cards I wanted to wait until Emerald was back, but this was too important not to share.

My husband opened some cans of diced tomatoes, tomato paste, and kidney beans and scooped, rinsed, and dumped the items into the pot. He measured some spices in as well, and some water, and put the pot on to simmer. In a while the whole kitchen would smell wonderful. I'd make corn muffins or cheese biscuits, and we'd dole out steaming bowls of chili con carne, with a dollop of sour cream and some chopped green onion, maybe a smidge of grated cheese over the top. People could spoon it up or scoop it up with corn chips. Or, if a miracle happened and they all left, we'd eat some ourselves and I'd freeze the rest for a day when Virgil and I were working on the new home. I could only hope.

Virgil accompanied Lizzie to talk to Urquhart. As I looked down at my notes, I was brought back to the problem at hand: Who killed Dirk? Did Todd do it, then kill himself in a fit of remorse, or was he murdered to cover up what he knew? I wrote down, quickly, every other person I could think of who may have killed Dirk: Rishelle, Millicent, Chi, Stu, Arnie, Felice, Hugh, and even Ian. First, I decided to go through the three who set up the prank.

Millicent Vayne: Motive . . . loathed Dirk. He made fun of her constantly. She set up the prank, with Rishelle's and Chi's help, to humiliate him. But there is every possibility she saw him as her main competitor on Haunt Hunt, *and wanted him gone. She very probably had the ability to alter the prank to be deadly, but she has significantly downplayed that past technical proficiency. That in itself is suspicious. Why play dumb? If Todd figured out she had done it, I think she's smart enough to set up a suicide.*

I paused and thought about it; could I see Millicent doing that? I wasn't sure. But playing dumb and skimming over the truth about her past on a science show was suspicious.

Rishelle: Motive? Good question. Nobody liked Dirk, but she didn't seem to have any specific reason to want him dead. Unless . . . if the real aim was to get rid of her husband, it would take a cold and calculating brain to see Dirk as a means to an end. Did Dirk die so Todd would be blamed? And then, when Todd "committed suicide" it wouldn't be any big surprise.

Unlikely, I scrawled after that section. It was too complex a scheme for Rishelle, who seemed, as my husband said, to be a straightforward woman.

Chi-Won Zhu: Motive? Dirk insulted Millicent relentlessly, and Chi is in love with Millicent. He helped set up the prank, and was probably the most likely to know how to alter it to make it deadly, as well as his technical knowledge making him the best bet to know how to turn off the motion detector camera pointed at the prank. Or . . . Millicent could have put him up to it, making the prank deadly. Could be in it together. But his motive seems so slight with Dirk, and nonexistent with Todd.

Stu Jardine: Motive?

I had . . . nothing. I knew little about Stu directly, but if what Serina had said, about him getting a new show, was true, there was something there that could make him want Todd dead, if Todd set out to sabotage him. That seemed weak, though.

Now, Arnie was a different matter. I wrote his name down on my pad of paper. I could certainly make a case against him, given what I now knew about his affair with Rishelle. The kitchen door opened and Pish slipped in. He got a cup of coffee and sat down beside me, looking over my shoulder, as Becket jumped down from the wing chair and meowed, restlessly pacing. Pish read my work so far as I got up, poured some kitty crunchies in Becket's bowl, and returned to the table.

"Good girl. We need to figure this out. They all are giving me the chills, knowing one or more of them is a killer."

"I agree wholeheartedly."

He read over my shoulder:

Arnie Ball: Motive? Unsure, with Dirk's murder. Disliked him as everyone did. But motive to kill Todd is clear; Arnie was (is?) having an affair with Rishelle.

Pish gave me a quick look. "Is that true?"

I described what I had seen of Arnie and Rishelle making out in the closet. "But my husband informs me that she came on to him, too, so the affair may be purely physical for her. Who knows how Arnie thinks?" I hesitated a moment, but then said, "I sent the DVR footage to Hannah to look over, but there is one thing I noticed. The night of the prank on Dirk?"

"Yes?"

"I saw Arnie heading out to the garage after the others came back in and before Dirk skulked out there."

"Are you sure?"

"Pretty much. He's got that knit toque and head of hair.

And he's got kind of a way of stooping. What reason could he have had for going out there other than to reset the prank to kill Dirk?"

"Interesting," he said, but didn't comment further.

"The police will see it; I'm sure they'll be looking pretty carefully at Arnie."

It might be that simple; Arnie killed Dirk with the intent of putting the blame on Todd, then killed Todd, setting it up to look like a suicide. He most definitely had the technical capability, especially to stop the DVR camera in the garage from taping his work. I did have some nagging doubts: Wouldn't he have known there was a camera pointed in that direction? Wasn't that a circuitous route to getting rid of Todd?

Anyway . . . Felice. I wrote her name down, but the amount I knew about her would fit in a thimble, with room left for a finger. I did know that she resented Dirk and didn't like the effect the psychics had on the show. I moved on, for now. So far, I needed to know more about Stu and Felice.

Ian Mackenzie . . . Well, in a way he was the same as Felice. I knew very little about him, though he had seemed miffed by the Ouija board session, and had worked with Todd and Stu on *Ghost Groupies*, where he was a tech guy. He had expressed a belief in the scientific exploration of paranormal events. Come to think of it, he was a definite possibility in redoing the prank on Dirk to be deadly. I wrote down his name and put question marks after it.

Hugh Langley, I wrote down. I tapped my cheek with the pencil. "What do you think about Hugh? Could he have done this? Kill Dirk, then set up Todd's death to look like suicide?"

Pish shook his head. "I don't know. I just don't know."

"But you're the one who told me it might be Hugh who killed Dirk, right?" I said.

"I know, but it doesn't make a whole lot of sense. Hugh, in a way, had the most to lose by Dirk dying. You've said it yourself—the show is a hit. Hugh has admitted that the show would have been canceled by now if not for Dirk's popularity."

Hugh Langley: Motive? Was Dirk too popular? I jotted down.

Pish read what I wrote. "That could be motive for a lot of them, I think, but certainly not Hugh, who only benefited from that," he said. "Any one of the cast members may have resented that."

"I don't think *everyone* cared that much about it, though. Not enough for murder. However, I have found out one thing." I told him what Lizzie had overheard from Todd. "He was threatening someone. If the police ever get the cell phone company to give up their records, they can figure out who he was talking to on his phone. That might solve it all. But we don't have access to that information, so we'll have to do it the hard way."

"By asking questions." He nodded. "If we can figure out who was physically capable of both setting the trap for Dirk *and* setting up Todd's suicide, we've got the killer, who is definitely among those people sitting in the library right now."

"Good point," I replied. I kept thinking about Arnie. It was quite possible that there was a perfectly innocent explanation for his actions, and if so, I needed to figure out what it was. "So let's try to figure it out together."

And keep hoping the sheriff got to a rational explanation before I did. That would be the best of all conclusions.

Chapter Twenty-four

✳ ✳ ✳

I STIRRED VIRGIL'S chili con carne once and put the lid back on, setting it very low so the bottom wouldn't burn. Pish and I made coffee and tea and loaded up trays. That was our excuse to talk to everyone. I was going to make sure I talked to Stu, Felice, and Ian, since I barely knew anything about them, certainly not enough to know if they were capable of murder.

Everyone was in the library and edgy, the silence deafening. I had a feeling that with the deputy sitting there with them, suspicions and grudges were simmering like the chili, not burning, but getting hotter and hotter. Pish and I set up the coffee and tea station near the fireplace. It was midmorning, and I announced I'd be making yet another luncheon—or a bruncheon, I guess—for them all . . . but not yet. I didn't want the tension to ease at this point.

"But please help yourselves to coffee and tea, and let me know if we run out of either. I'll make more." With that, I headed toward my first target.

This was something Pish and I had decided as we readied the trays; we would divide and conquer, but with a slight difference. He was clearly most comfortable with Hugh, and I got along fine with Serina and some of the others. But this time I was going to tackle Hugh and he was going to nestle with the ladies. My darling Pish is a complete charmer, as well as being cultured, courtly, and stunningly intelligent.

I took a seat by Hugh, who relaxed on a sofa with a book open on his lap. Instead of reading, though, he was simply staring out the window.

He glanced at me and smiled. "I had so hoped to be out of your way today," he said. "And then . . . this." His smile faltered and he let out a breath.

"Please, don't worry about us. This must be so difficult on you all. But more so on you. I imagine you knew Todd better than you knew any of the others, besides Stu. You started with just those two guys, right, and Ian Mackenzie?"

He nodded. "Three years ago. We had another team then, with a couple of other investigators besides Todd and Stu. I never expected it to take off like it did. But it seems to have caught the zeitgeist, if you'll pardon the term."

"I've always wondered what that means, *zeitgeist*?"

"The spirit of the times."

"So how does *Haunt Hunt* capture that, to you?"

"I think it fits in with the antiscience movement we're seeing right now: anti-vaccine, climate change as a hoax, conspiracy theories discussed as though they have factual bases. *Haunt Hunt* is one of a dozen shows that explores the 'science' of ghost hunting. These guys are serious about it." He shook his head and sighed.

I let that sink in for a moment. "So what you're saying is, all of this, the instruments, the experiments, the attempt to prove scientifically that ghosts exist, you believe it's all fake?"

"No, not at all!" he said with a charming smile. "I mean, yes, it's fake. Of *course* it is. But it's harmless, isn't it? We're not promoting quack medicine, like some shows, or selling bad investment advice, or saying the Mafia killed JFK. It's like those medium shows, where a psychic tells people what they want to hear from their loved ones who have passed on. Harmless diversion."

I thought of our struggle to keep Gordy Shute, my dear friend and sometimes lawn crew with his friend Zeke, from going off the deep end in his conspiracy theory belief. I vehemently disagreed with Hugh, actually. Every little chip off the block of reality was another step into an alternate universe for someone like Gordy. We have a moral responsibility not to promote things we know are false. That's not silencing free speech; it's an attempt not to add to the mistrust some of the public appears to have of science. The very definition of truth is under attack. I expressed my fears to Hugh.

"Ah, you're speaking of the Dunning-Kruger effect," he said.

"The what-what effect?"

"Dunning-Kruger." Explained simply, he said, it was that dumb people don't know they are dumb because the skills they need to assess their intelligence are the very ones they lack.

I shook my head. "That's not what is happening with conspiracy theories and their adherents," I said. "Lots of smart people also believe conspiracy theories. And to be completely fair, in some cases conspiracy theories are only labeled that until they're proven true. Anyway, that doesn't explain any of *this*," I continued, meaning *Haunt Hunt* and shows of its type. "Don't you think the popularity of ghost hunting is just that people *want* it to be true? They want to believe in some existence beyond the grave? I'd love to think I could talk to my grandmother or mother."

"You may have something there."

This was getting me nowhere. I could see that Pish was deep in conversation with Millicent and Rishelle, and hoped

he was getting somewhere. Rishelle appeared to have re-
gained some of her equilibrium, but was she too relaxed for
having just seen her husband's dead body?

I turned back to the producer. "What did you do before
this? Professionally."

"I've had a varied career. I was never one to stay in place
too long. I've done some public broadcast programming,
worked on a documentary series, produced news programming, did my time producing movies of the week."

I was puzzled. In my experience people in the industry
find a niche where they're comfortable and move around
within that sphere. "It's unusual to have so eclectic a career."

"I have had a great deal of success, but just when I tri-
umph over one peak, I seek another to conquer. I'm like a
mountain climber, you see . . . always looking for new chal-
lenges."

"What will you do now? You may have been able to go
on without Dirk, but not now, not without Todd, one of the
founding members of the *Haunt Hunt* show."

He looked around, his gaze shifty.

"Or *can* you?" I asked, in light of his behavior.

"As bad as this is going to sound, as difficult as it may
be, it's possible we'll be able to resurrect the show. We'll do
an episode in tribute to Dirk and Todd, featuring their best
moments. It would probably be our highest-rated show to
date. We'll do an 'in memoriam' thing. And . . . maybe we'll
move on." He waved one hand. "Anyway, I'm *way* ahead of
myself. I need to talk to the network boss and Chuck, head
of programming. She may want nothing to do with the show
after this. He may have other ideas to pursue. But we can
hope. I'll be guided by what these folks want, and what the
network will allow."

These folks, meaning the cast and crew of *Haunt Hunt*?
I was a little surprised. He had variously expressed his wish
to do a travel show, classical music programming, or alter-

natively, quit the business altogether. He appeared to openly scorn the show's audience, but maybe he saw resurrecting *Haunt Hunt* as a new challenge.

"But with no killer yet named for Dirk's death," I said, careful not to spill that my husband believed Todd's death was also murder, "how can you go on? One of you killed Dirk."

He shook his head. "I don't believe it. It was an accident. Simple as that."

Denial ain't just a river in Egypt, as I am sometimes reminded. Perhaps he had more in common with the *Haunt Hunt* audience than he would admit. "Do you think people will want to eat if I make lunch?"

He put one hand over mine. "My dear, you have been so gracious. I hate to think of what this is costing you emotionally. But yes," he said, with a sigh. "I think many of these people would love something to eat."

Now, on to Stu, Felice, and Ian.

Stu perched on an uncomfortable chair by the bookshelf reading, seemingly wanting to stay as far away from his coworkers as possible. I approached and straightened the shelf, then glanced over at him. "Oh, you're still reading the Ben Franklin bio. I thought you had lost track of it."

"I would never lose a book," he said, reading on.

I hesitated, but then said, "I'm terribly sorry about Todd. You must be devastated. I know you guys have worked together a long time."

He frowned and stuck his finger in the book, marking his place. "I'm going to miss him, though lately I think we were seeing different things."

"What do you mean, you were seeing different things? For the show?"

"Everything. He kept getting in feuds with the others. I'm more of a 'go with the flow' kind of guy."

Feuds with the others. Interesting. I hesitated, but then

said, "I understand that he thought you and Rishelle were having an affair."

He started, and his cheeks flooded with red, but I could tell it wasn't anything he hadn't already heard. "He was *wrong*. It's ridiculous. He knew better." He paused, but then, with a troubled look he said, "My betrayal was of a different sort."

I wondered if he meant his professional ambitions and intentions. I tried to formulate a question about that, but couldn't find the words. He was feeling his pockets again with a worried expression. Felice stomped into the library, looking upset. She grabbed a cup of coffee and sat down in a chair, glowering around at everyone. "Wonder what's wrong with her?" I said, distracted.

"Felice?" He smiled and his mustache twitched. He tugged at his goatee. "What isn't wrong? *Everything* upsets her."

I wandered over to her and huddled down, my arm propped on the arm of her chair. "You okay, Felice? You look upset."

She leveled a look of scorn in my direction. "And you're not? A murder and a suicide on your property and you can write it off as another day at the office? Boy, I wish I had *your* coldhearted nerve." She flung her hair back. "But then I guess this *is* just another day at the office for you, given how many dead bodies you've seen."

I bit my tongue. She was one of those people who can irritate you into unwise words, but I think she was once a happier woman, before the psychics invaded *Haunt Hunt*. "So what will you do, if the show is canceled because of these deaths?"

Felice shook her head. "I don't know." She glanced over at Stu, then lowered her voice and leaned toward me. "I might be okay. I know Stu has something in the works. If this hadn't happened, he would have had to get out of his contract somehow. The show being canceled is going to be the best thing in the world for him."

"What do you mean?" I knew about his new show, but I wasn't going to let on.

"With Dirk and Todd dying, he'll be able to walk away from this and right into another show he's got lined up. I'm hoping he'll take me along with him."

"What kind of show will it be?"

"Kind of like a true crime show, only with a ghost hunting aspect," Felice said. "Just think . . . famous or infamous murders and murderers, and the places they've lived. Are they haunted? Do the killers or victims haunt these places? Jeffrey Dahmer. John Wayne Gacy. It could be awesome!"

I was unnerved when I realized Todd had been pursuing that angle here, with the murders we had suffered through. Had he and Stu in truth been competing for the same idea? It was possible, since Todd was unhappy with the psychic angle his show was taking. And was that a motive for Stu to get rid of Todd? I shook my head, trying to clear it. I was even more confused than I had been. Once again, a new suspect. Stu needed out of his contract, and was starting a show about killers, victims, and their ghosts. "This all must be upsetting to you."

"Meaning . . . ?"

"*Meaning*, Dirk and Todd are—were—your coworkers. I suppose it's going to affect each of you differently."

"Oh."

"Felice, can you think of any reason why Todd would kill himself?"

She frowned into her cup and shook her head. "The last person on earth I would think would kill himself would be Todd. He was upset about Dirk, but still . . ." She took a sip and gave me a sly look. "Unless he killed Dirk himself."

I was taken aback that she suggested it, though I had considered the possibility. "Do you think he could have?"

"They *hated* each other."

That was not exactly news to me. "Unless someone saw

him out near the garage that night, I doubt he was Dirk's killer."

"Who knows? I saw a few people a coupla different times while I was out having a smoke: Chi, Rishelle, Millie, Arnie. It was a busy night."

"Arnie?" I was stunned. It was corroboration of what I saw. "Did you tell the police?"

"I don't *know* anything, I just saw Arnie, that's all."

I sure would tell Urquhart what she'd said. My cell phone purred in my pocket. "Excuse me." I ducked out to the great hall to answer it. It was, as I had hoped, Hannah. "Hey, how's my favorite librarian?" I paced to the doors and slipped out to my flagstone terrace. The CSI crew was still there at the van and I turned away, shuddering.

"I'm good. I'm only partway through the videos, but I've already got some things I'm wondering about."

"Shoot." I walked the length of the terrace and slipped around the far edge, to the ballroom side, and stared off at the distant woods. I'd had enough of death and horror, and enough of that whole crew. If Hannah could help us figure out who did these crimes and thus help us get rid of the *Haunt Hunt*ers, I'd be ecstatic.

She wouldn't tell me her concerns, but she asked several questions, starting with, did any of the cast and or crew wear certain pieces of clothing all the time when filming, and even when just walking about? Yes, they did, I answered. Arnie always wore a knitted stretchy toque jammed down over his thick hair; I told her I'd seen him on the tape heading out to the garage, and I thought that Felice had seen him, too. He'd become my number one suspect. Stu always wore a plaid sport jacket with suede patched elbows and often donned a fedora. Millicent was in something different every time I saw her, a new combination of scarves, skirts, and bell-sleeved tops, but Felice always wore a *Haunt Hunt*

Windbreaker with fluorescent bars on the lapels and wrist bands. Dirk always had worn that long caped duster.

"Okay, that's good to know," she said. "I kind of thought as much."

"What does it mean? Why are you asking that?" Of course, right then it occurred to me—Felice said she was out there and had seen Arnie. That meant she was out there, too, and could be the killer herself. She certainly loathed Dirk.

"Tell you in a while. Now, am I right in thinking Dirk Phillipe was generally disliked?"

"Yup. I don't know anyone who actually liked him. Some had tolerance for him, like Hugh, the producer, who thought he was good for the show. I actually found him charming once, and impossible the rest of the time."

"That explains a lot of the looks and behavior of people around him."

"Are you going to tell me what any of this means?"

"Give me another hour," she said.

"All right. We can talk later."

I went back in through the front doors but headed to the kitchen, stirred the chili, and started to make lunch. I'd let them assemble their own sandwiches from platters of cold cuts and precut cheese, and I'd set out commercially prepared salads, and some cut veggies and fruit. That was lunch. Frankly, I was tired of feeding them and even more tired of cleaning up after them.

As I loaded a tea cart with the platters I wondered about Hannah's question regarding the *Haunt Hunt* cast and crew clothing. Something like Felice's fluorescent Windbreaker might have shown up on some of the night footage, indicating she had snuck out to alter the prank to be murderous. I hadn't had time to view as much as I would have liked, so my own idea of who was out of place might be sadly erroneous. For all I knew, each and every one of the crew was out and about the night Dirk was killed.

I hustled down the hallway to the butler's pantry area, where there were cabinets holding all manner of serving dishes I had gathered over the year I had lived in the castle, as well as what had been left behind by generations of Wynters. I needed an epergne to hold bananas and apples for folks to eat, something that would sit slightly above the other trays. The cabinet was ajar. Odd. I opened it and something dark and furry leaped out at me. I shrieked, jumped back, and . . . discovered that the furry thing was whatever Becket had streaked in carrying during the night.

It lay still and damp on the stone floor. Eeuw! I kicked at it with one toe, and it flopped over to reveal an underlay of fabric holding the hair in place. It was a *wig*. A dark bushy wig. I suddenly got it, or at least one part of it. It looked like Arnie's hair. Becket must have found it somewhere and dragged it home, as he had a tendency to do lately with all manner of fuzzed and furry things. It told of a purposeful plot to implicate Arnie in Dirk's death. So whoever did it must have donned the bushy hair and a toque and mimicked Arnie's movements on their way to set the killing trap. That meant it must be one of the taller men: Todd, Chi, or possibly Stu. The camera angle was such that the figure was somewhat foreshortened, meaning there was no accurate gauge of the height, except that it was not someone exceptionally short, like Rishelle.

I wheeled the cart into the library and set up the food. Everyone looked exhausted and unnerved. There was suspicion among them; I could see how glances slid sideways, and how people were isolated in little groups, those who trusted one another together. That in itself was odd. Didn't they all believe Todd had committed suicide? Why the suspicion? Or was this still about Dirk? But that didn't make sense; they should all think it was solved, that Todd had killed Dirk, then committed suicide out of remorse.

Rishelle was still distancing herself from the others. She was huddled in her housecoat, curled up in misery and staring down at her wedding ring. She was a widow now. My heart hurt. I remember how that felt, that you were alone even when surrounded by people and that nobody in the world understood your grief. This would be even more complicated, if she believed Todd had killed himself. The guilt and pain would be amplified, repeating on a loop through her heart.

As some of the others went to the food and began assembling plates, I knelt by Rishelle's chair. "Honey, I know how you feel, and I don't say that lightly. I lost my first husband in an awful accident. It took me a long time to come back to life again."

She met my eyes. Hers were big, red-rimmed, and drowning in tears that welled and flowed down her cheeks. "No one here cares like I do; even Stu, one of his oldest friends. They all hate me. None of them understand," she whispered, reaching out to grab my hand like a lifeline.

"Do you have family you can call?" Her hands were icy, and I chafed them, feeling the wedding set still on her left hand, third finger. "Can I do anything for you?"

"They let me call my mom, but we're not very close. She's going to tell my sister. I hope she can come get me. I don't know what to do. I want out of h-here." The last word came out on a gasp and a sigh.

It was a cry for help. She looked younger, sitting there in an oversize bathrobe with her makeup off and tears streaming down her face. The very best thing I could do was help figure out who killed her husband, if he hadn't killed himself. But she also needed support, and this lot was doing what people did to me: not make eye contact, back away from turmoil, not engage when an emotional wreck of a woman is needing them most. Even Arnie was now ignoring her, since she had pushed him away. None of them liked her at all. How lonely a place that must be for her.

"I'm here for you, Rishelle," I murmured. "I'll do whatever I can do, but you'll have to suffer through the next day or so. The police won't or can't tell you much at this point. You can't even make arrangements for poor Todd yet. Hang tough and know, I'll help you every way I can."

A weak and trembling smile quavered on her lips. "Thank you," she whispered.

"Why don't you lie down for a while? Or . . . first, have something to eat and drink. I know you don't feel like it, but you won't do yourself any favors by getting sick." I glanced around. "Millicent, can you get Rishelle a cup of tea, with sugar for shock, and a sandwich?" I asked, raising my voice. "Nothing too big. Some turkey on a roll, or something like that. *Someone* needs to help this poor girl cope."

Millicent nodded. She looked frightened herself. The best thing for them all was to solve this crime. Now. I returned to the catering trays and checked to make sure I had thought of everything.

"Look at her pretending she cares," Felice muttered, glaring at Rishelle. "She didn't give a damn. All she was trying to do was get in the middle of everything, get more attention for herself."

I held my tongue when what I wanted to do was tell Felice to shut up. Instead, I asked, "Why do you say that? She loved her husband."

"Right," she said, giving me a withering look. "She didn't care about Todd, or she wouldn't have been messing around on him. She was screwing one of the other guys. Everyone knows that."

Life is so black-and-white for some people. I was pretty sure Rishelle did love Todd, even though she was cheating on him. Love and pain, when they coexist, can cause such deep turmoil that people do and say things they never thought they would. At that precise moment my phone buzzed in my cardigan pocket. That would be Hannah. The woman was a godsend, and had excellent timing. I left Felice to stew in silence and ducked out of the room, heading upstairs to talk to my friend.

Chapter Twenty-five

❈ ❈ ❈

I SAT ON my bed, phone in hand, and pondered what Hannah had just told me. She had fresh information, and a lot of it worked together. I had told her about the wig I had found that Becket had dragged in. I thought that this eliminated Arnie, essentially, but rethought that. It could easily be a red herring, I supposed. Hannah said that seemed kind of diabolical, but it still could be true. She had confirmed some things I already knew. Stu did indeed have a new deal for a show in the works; that gave him a fairly strong motive to get rid of the other guys, but surely breaking the contract would be easier than double homicide? Todd did have a physical confrontation with Dirk at the last paranormal conference a week before they came to Wynter Castle, and the video was on the Internet. It was witnessed by many fans, who related the substance of it online in breathless tones, but they didn't seem to know what started it.

But there was more. I had made many wrong assumptions, and now I had to face them. It was jumbled right at that moment, but I was actually beginning to see a glimmer of light. The intent of it all was, I thought, to irrevocably kill *Haunt Hunt*. Now I needed to get it all straight, and for that I needed to talk to my two men, Virgil and Pish.

My poor brain was holding a tangle of conflicting information, possibilities, and mistaken impressions I had believed. I made a few random observations.

Online sources are notoriously untrustworthy. I knew that, and yet I had unthinkingly accepted information from such unreliable sources. Some subreddit commenters were misinformed; Arnie Ball had never hurt anyone on set, had never caused a studio to be sued, nor had he ever been black-balled by the major studios. But someone else working on *Haunt Hunt* had.

Also . . . people can be evasive or lie without being guilty of anything heinous. I hear folks all the time asking why someone would lie if they didn't have anything to hide, but just because they don't have *one* thing to hide, doesn't mean they're not hiding something *else*. That sounds confusing, but it's true.

And finally, sometimes the best way to succeed is to not try so hard.

There was so much I had missed or mistaken, and it all worked together, if I was right. But now . . . how to expose it all?

I paced to the window and saw Virgil striding back from the construction site. I stuck the phone back in my cardigan pocket and raced down to meet him at the side door. Lizzie had done well with the sheriff, who appreciated her input, he said. He had sent her back into the castle and sternly told her to stay in the library where there were people and a deputy, before he set off to the construction site to check their progress.

At least *there* everyone was doing their job and doing it well, he groused.

I gathered Pish from the library, where he was trying to keep the *Haunt Hunt* people from devolving into a free-for-all, and asked if we could, all three of us, talk in Pish's sitting room office. Virgil asked for half an hour to shower, so as he ascended, followed by Pish, who had a phone call to make, I reentered the library.

A deputy stood off to one side, with a bemused look on her face as Felice and Rishelle quarreled, hurling insults at each other across a coffee table. Millicent was crying.

"What's going on here?" I said, loud enough to cut through the invective.

Lizzie darted over to me. "Well, Felice said Rishelle was mining Todd's suicide for sympathy and why didn't she confess that she and Stu were having a hot fling?" It was like a catfight play-by-play. "Rishelle said that Felice was a jealous hag who was green because she couldn't get a man to notice her even if she flashed him her boobs."

Millicent sank down on the sofa, head in her hands, weeping. "You're all so awful!"

"Okay, *enough*," I said, wading into the fray and looking around the room at the angry, sad, ambivalent, worried expressions. "We're all getting on each other's nerves, but none of you are going to go until they clear the scene and make some headway. Believe me, I want you all gone, but I want them to figure this out, too." The two women glared at me. "Felice, maybe it's best if you go and sit with Stu for a while. Rishelle, I know right now it feels better to be angry than sad, but this is not going to help you in the long run."

Her breath caught and she sobbed, tears streaming down her face. "I don't know what to think, how to f-feel."

"I know, but there's no shortcut through this. Millicent, come sit with her."

The psychic obediently jumped up, put her arm around the widow's shoulders, and got her to sit down.

I turned to the producer. "Hugh, normally I'd send you

all packing, but that's not an option right now. Staying busy would be good for everyone. Is there anything at all we can do?"

He shrugged, helpless. "I'm sorry, Merry, but I don't know what to say. Or do. I'm so tired." He swiped at his eyes and leaned back on the sofa.

I understood his weariness. Would this day ever end? It felt like it had been going on forever, and now, late afternoon, showed no signs of getting better. The sheriff was tight-lipped when I saw him occasionally. He wouldn't say if he had called in the state police, and they had not yet moved the body or the van. Until they did, I was not going outside again.

"Anyway, Rishelle and I are *not* having a fling, Felice," Stu said into the silence. "Whatever gave you that idea?"

Felice started to say something—probably something rude—but I interrupted. "Everybody, cool it, okay? I know you're all tired and upset." I scanned the room.

Serina, her eyes bloodshot, was curled up in a ball in a chair near a window, staring out. She had removed herself as far as she could from the others. Ian was wide-eyed, his gaze darting from one to the other of his colleagues. Stu, book still in hand, perched on a windowsill, Felice now sitting nearby, glaring around the room. Arnie was practically reclining in one of the chairs, staring off into space. He seemed separate, alone, his mouth set in a straight line. Millicent was sitting with Rishelle now, while Chi hovered nearby.

This wasn't getting us anywhere. I turned to the producer, an idea for how to proceed finally coming to me. "Hugh, these people need to do something to keep their minds occupied. I know you may never be able to use it, but can we do something for the show?" I hesitated, but looked at the widow and asked, "Rishelle, would you be okay with that?"

She nodded. "Todd would have wanted it that way."

Felice snorted, but I gave her a look that would have cut

diamond. She was being difficult and unpleasant and I was fed up. "Deputy, may we do this, just to keep these folks busy?"

She shrugged, but then nodded. "I don't see why not."

"Now, everyone, please," I said, raising my voice. "I know this is hard. You're all missing Dirk and Todd. In the little time I knew him, Todd seemed like a great guy. Do this for him." *Win one for the Gipper*, it almost sounded like, but I plowed on, amazed at my own mendacity. "You haven't had a chance to review the footage yet, but *can* we talk about the experiences on camera, perhaps? It would be cathartic for you all." I scanned the group. Some nodded, some shrugged.

Hugh roused himself, sitting up straighter. Work is the one constant in many lives, and maybe he saw it as an opportunity. "Arnie? Serina? Can we set up some sound equipment in here and a camera or two? Merry's right; we need to do *something*, work as a team again. We're getting on each other's nerves."

Serina gave him a dark look; this must be devastating for her. But surely you couldn't commiserate with the mistress and the widow, both in the same room? It was awkward, to say the least.

Arnie heaved himself up out of his chair and pushed his bushy hair behind his ears. Without his toque I could see the threads of silver in the dark matted thicket. "Yeah, sure," he said. "Give me a while to set up the shot. We'll need the lights out of the supply van, and to re-lay some wire."

"I can help," Lizzie said. "Since the rest of the crew can't be here."

"Lizzie, you stay inside, though. I don't want you going out near . . ." I couldn't finish, thinking of poor Todd in the sound truck.

"I'll make sure she stays here," Hugh said, gently.

"What would we talk about?" Felice asked.

I sighed with some relief. If work would get these media hogs thinking about something else, it would give us all a break from the tension and bickering. "You all figure that out. Lizzie, you can help set up, but you go nowhere else, okay? I've had it with this crew, and I don't trust any single one of them." I glared around at the whole lot of them. "I'll be back down soon, so maybe you can interview me and Pish about the castle."

I headed out of the library as the cast and crew of *Haunt Hunt*, or what was left of it, started to discuss where to shoot, what to shoot, who to shoot, what to say, etc. For all I knew, more quarrels would break out, but that was not my problem.

I tapped on Pish's door. Virgil emerged from our room, his hair wet, freshly shaved, white T-shirt and jeans stretched over his bulky frame, looking handsome as he always does. As Pish shouted "Come in" and I opened the door, my husband joined me, gave me a swift side hug and kiss, and we entered together. We sat down in chairs by Pish's desk in his sitting room, and I told them what I had learned from Hannah.

"Felice was outside, but apparently just to smoke. I saw a brief snippet of who I thought was Arnie heading out; he is distinct, with that bushy hair and toque jammed over it. But a short while ago I discovered a bushy wig that Becket found out there and dragged inside last night, when I opened the door on Rishelle's screaming."

"So someone dressed as Arnie to fool the cameras and set up the trap to kill Dirk," Virgil said.

"That's probably what the police will think when they see that tape, right, that Arnie did it?" Pish said.

"Until I tell them about the wig. From what I saw, it has to be one of the guys. Also, Hannah gave me some intel; originally she learned on a *Haunt Hunt* subreddit that Arnie had a troubled past, and that he was unhirable in the industry because he had almost killed someone, and that person sued and won a huge settlement from the movie studio. Hugh *apparently* gave him a chance. Except . . . the gossip was wrong. It was *not* Arnie." As I said, online information should be viewed with skepticism.

"Who is it?" Pish asked.

"Chi-Won Zhu." I faced two blank stares of incomprehension. "I know, right?" I said. "Surprising. He's the last guy I would have expected to have a short fuse. I'm not sure that he has anything to do with the murders, though. Just because he has that past, doesn't mean anything in relation to this. His involvement in the prank could be solely because Millicent asked him to help, and he has a thing for her."

"Good job, Hannah!" Virgil said. "I wonder if she'd be willing to work for Dewayne and me as a researcher?"

"She'd be thrilled! It's her superpower, ferreting out information."

"Did Hannah get anything else?"

"Yes, she did. She noted multiple examples of Felice sneaking out, but most times it was to smoke. I don't know how much Felice told Urquhart. She was oddly defiant about it."

"She's that dark-haired glary girl, right?" Virgil said.

"Yes. She's kind of sneaky and definitely confrontational. But I don't think she's involved in any of this. As far as I know, she has no motive, and if the show dies, so does her TV career. She won't find anyone else to hire her."

My phone pinged, and I fished in my cardigan pocket for it. "Something from Hannah," I said. A clip of video came up. It was hard to see on my little screen, but it was the exact image I had noticed, with the Arnie look-alike heading toward the garage, and the time stamp was the night of Dirk's murder. But it was *not* Todd; Hannah had found a way—Zeke had helped her, she said in the attached note—to enhance the video.

I have a good eye for people's stance from years working as a stylist, and there was something about the set of the shoulders that I recognized. I drew in a swift breath. "Oh.

Yes, I *do* know who that is." I turned it so Pish and Virgil could both see the screen, stopped the video, and pointed out something that told me everything I needed to know.

"I get what you're saying, and maybe you're right, but we never see his face," Virgil said. "That's not proof; the costume did its job."

"I know. It's irritating. I need to see this on a bigger screen. Pish, can I use your laptop for a moment?"

We changed places and I hooked my phone up to his computer, brought the video up, and zoomed in. I scanned the figure and what had caught my eye jumped out at me. Confirmation; it *had* to be a conspiracy between two unlikely people. When I thought about it, there was much that had pointed in that direction, even though we had been misdirected by so many other things. It was inescapable proof to me, because there was no other reason for this particular person to be out there doing what he was doing.

Pish got it immediately, though Virgil, not being a fashion guy, took a moment. He was still doubtful, but willing to be convinced. He even called Urquhart for me. They had a long discussion, during which Virgil was forced to admit I may have let someone unauthorized view the copies of the tapes I had. The sheriff was angry, from the sounds of Virgil's slightly defensive tone, but I thought he'd work with us to ensure the right person was caught with enough objective evidence to convict.

I hoped.

While Virgil was busy with Urquhart on the phone, I asked Pish if he could do me a favor. "Can you call Chuck Sandberg, at HHN? I have some questions."

It took him a few minutes, while Virgil paced behind us and talked to Urquhart. Pish did get the programming director at HHN, though, and asked the questions I jotted down. Sandberg didn't know everything, but he had someone look into it, and it all confirmed my suspicions. The shoot they were supposed to be at was canceled by Todd himself, the homeowners had complained, not them, and Todd had offered no explanation. They were angry because they had rearranged their schedule to accommodate *Haunt Hunt*. Todd had simply told them he'd get back to them to reschedule.

Except that it wasn't Todd, if I was right, and the not-Todd knew the *Haunt Hunt* paranormal investigator would never "get back to them," nor would Todd be alive to discover the lie.

Sandberg told Pish that his boss at HHN was deeply troubled by what had happened, but was cooperating with the sheriff's department in Autumn Vale. Urquhart had been in touch with them, it seemed, to review the backgrounds of each member of the cast and crew. Hugh Langley had also called his network bosses. Pish covered the receiver and told me that his friend said that Hugh was very upset by the deaths, but had confidence it would be solved swiftly.

"Pish, one more thing," I whispered, checking to make sure my reasoning was right. "How did the homeowners *know* it was Todd who phoned them?"

Pish asked Sandberg that question and shrugged. When he signed off he said, "They took his word for it that they were speaking with Todd."

"That's what I thought. So it *could* have been anyone: Todd, Dirk, Hugh, Stu, Ian . . . any guy!"

"But only one who could be sure he could change the schedule," Virgil, who had just gotten off the phone, said. I could see he was coming around to my way of thinking.

"Exactly," I replied.

Virgil was deep in thought.

"Is the sheriff going to help us?" I asked, when he didn't say anything.

"Well, yes and no."

"It can't be both," I said.

"He will, but he thinks he already knows who killed Todd, at least."

Pish and I exchanged a look. "So he does agree with you that it's not suicide?" I asked.

"He has come to that conclusion. He's not a hasty guy, Merry, but he does get there. He's solid."

"Okay, I know." Virgil keeps trying to convince me about Urquhart, but I remain unimpressed. He's solid, maybe, but slow. "So who *does* he think killed Todd? And why?"

"He finally got access to Todd Halsey's phone records. Apparently, the last person Todd talked to before he died was Stu Jardine, and it was a longish conversation. He's not sure yet why Stu would have killed him, but if he had been talking to Todd for that long shortly before he died, why wouldn't Stu have said something?"

Pish said, "Maybe Stu got scared, afraid he'd be accused?"

"Remember what Lizzie overheard? She heard Todd threaten someone that they'd better help him, or he'd tell what he knew. If that was Stu . . ." Virgil shrugged. "We can't avoid the undeniable truth that Todd was shot with a gun that Stu bought. It fits. Anyway, Urquhart told me I could share the info with both of you, but asked us to not say anything." He gave me a warning look. "*Especially* you."

I rolled my eyes. So the sheriff didn't trust me. What was new?

I reviewed the video one more time. Was I wrong about everything? Could the person in the video be Stu? Or alternately, was it possible that there were two murderers; one had killed Dirk, while Stu had killed his partner? I didn't think so, but my confidence was shaken.

THE THREE OF US DESCENDED TOGETHER. MY stomach was twisting and my gut rumbled. I felt sick inside, confused and jumbled and worried. I had thought I knew who did what, but now, with Urquhart's information, I wasn't sure.

Trouble was, I could build a compelling case for why Stu might kill Dirk, but not so much why he'd kill Todd. Stu, like Todd, was serious about ghost hunting. Dirk, with his over-the-top antics, was bringing ridicule down on their heads, in social media, anyway. Though many fans of the show loved Dirk, in the paranormal investigation society as a whole, the fathers of *Haunt Hunt*, Stu and Todd, were seen as jokes at best, traitors at worst, for allowing their show to become the *Dirk and Millicent Fake Psychics Hour*. Stu was already planning his exit. However, if he had an ironclad contract binding him to *Haunt Hunt*, it might be tricky. If Dirk died, though, given how popular the psychic was, maybe Stu felt it would kill that show. Had Todd found out and confronted him about it? With his new show at risk, had Stu killed Todd to keep him quiet?

I didn't think so, but the reasoning made a good case. Urquhart would take the information to the DA and possibly get an arrest warrant. Stu being the last to talk to Todd was definitely not a fact in his favor, especially if he had failed to admit it in his interview with Urquhart.

We needed solid evidence, the kind you can't refute. They were taping a segment as we entered the library. I motioned to Lizzie to follow me into the dining room for a moment. She did, but she wasn't happy. Hands on her hips and shooting glances back toward the library, she hissed, "What d'you want? I shouldn't leave, you know. Hugh doesn't like it when crew leaves in the middle of a shoot."

"Okay, all right, but I need you," I said, hand on her shoulder. We were by the fireplace, the farthest part of the dining room from the library, but I still whispered. "You're the only one I know who understands the equipment." I asked her to do something for me.

She looked surprised, but crossed her arms over her chest and glared at the fireplace for a minute, then nodded. "Yeah, I can do that."

"Can you do it without being caught?"

"Jeez! I've been sneaking out of my room at Grandma's for a year now. Even when she catches me sneaking in at four in the morning I can convince her I'm up getting a glass of warm milk to help sleep." She snorted. "I think I know a little something about not being caught *and* getting up to no good."

"What were you doing out at four in the morning?" I hissed, alarmed by the thought.

"What d'you think? Taking pictures! There was a meteor shower last month and I wanted to get some shots." She snorted again. "Grandma believed me. Warm milk!"

Though I was more than a little concerned by her answer, it was nothing I hadn't done at her age in a far more dangerous city and for far less savory reasons. She would never be in any actual danger; I'd make sure of that. And surprisingly, something she had just said provided one more little tiny piece of the puzzle. Distracted slightly by my thoughts, I said, "Okay. Do it, then."

We wove back through the dining room to the library and reentered. Virgil, Pish, and I took seats away from the others, as quietly as we could.

Hugh and Rishelle were sitting together on the sofa, and Arnie was manning the camera, for once not zooming in on Rishelle's cleavage, but staying steady on her ravaged face.

"We all loved Todd so much. And he was such an important part of the paranormal investigation community," Hugh said, his cultured voice gentle. He was actually very good on camera, with a lovely voice that resonated with the right tone of sorrow. "Can you tell us what his death has meant to you, his adored wife?"

As Rishelle talked about how they met, and how Todd's past led him to believe in ghosts—a touching story about a beloved grandfather who communicated with him from beyond the grave—I examined the others while trying to ignore Lizzie creeping around and surreptitiously setting up digital cameras around the room, setting them on tables and shelves, all while appearing to be watching the action from different angles. Truthfully, she had it down pat, bumbling quietly around in the background. Arnie, Chi, Serina, and the others didn't seem to notice her in the slightest, riveted as they were on the piece being filmed, Rishelle's finest moment, in a sense.

Felice, though, watched through narrowed eyes. Irritation radiated from her. I thought about how someone had used Rishelle and Millicent's prank on Dirk to kill him. Felice hated Rishelle, but not enough to kill someone to blame her nemesis for it. That was ridiculous. And yet Felice had been the one outside more than anyone else, and had actually seen more than anyone knew. She was not, however, on tape approaching the garage. She had not killed Dirk.

I was basing much of my entire assumption of the murderer on some circumstantial evidence, mostly fashion. The psychology was correct, and I've spent a lot of time with people in various areas of show business. Enough to recognize certain aspects of narcissists and their manipulation of the world to feed their own needs.

However, if someone had been a good actor, or if someone had gone out of their way to pull a double bluff, the kind of thing beloved in fiction, it was barely possible that I was being led down the garden path. I didn't think so. I was pretty sure that the killer had simply underestimated us all, thinking that we were a bunch of dummies who wouldn't notice the slipup even if we did see the footage. Footage . . . I smiled.

Then I tuned back in. Rishelle, tears on her cheeks, faced the camera and said, "If Todd was right about the paranormal, he is greeting his grandpa in heaven. I hope that's true."

Sobered, I was reminded once again that the discovery

of the killer was no academic exercise. It was a bid to find peace for the families of the victims. They *all* deserved answers. I felt responsible, to some extent, especially since I now suspected that the timing and location of this shoot at Wynter Castle, which had ostensibly been set up by Todd, was the result of manipulation on the part of the murderer. The call Pish had made to Chuck Sandberg at HHN confirmed many of my thoughts; the whole affair was a masterpiece of subterfuge, in a sense.

Wynter Castle had been chosen as a perfect location *because* of our last murder-filled year, not in *spite* of it, and that made me furious. How was I ever going to change my home's reputation if people used us like that? Pish, too, was angry, that a simple call from him to *Haunt Hunt* had been the catalyst used by a heartless killer to corner their prey.

The crew stopped tape on the touching wifely tribute to her husband, and Hugh gave Rishelle a hug. "Good girl. I hope we get to use it somehow, some way, even if only on social media. I think the community would appreciate what you've said."

I stood and approached Hugh as Rishelle walked away and Arnie disassembled his heavy Steadicam rig. "Pish and I would like to do a bit of reminiscing about strange occurrences at the castle. Would that be appropriate?"

This was something we had worked out in hushed whispers upstairs. Pish felt like he was the one who got us into the mess, though I had pointed out to him that if it hadn't happened here, it would have happened somewhere else. Virgil was not totally on board, but what I love about him is he tends to trust my judgment . . . most of the time.

Hugh looked uncertain. "Perhaps." He glanced over at the others. "Stu? Rishelle? Felice? As the remaining cast members, I'll be guided by you."

I watched Stu. His call with Todd just before his friend died and why he hadn't spoken of it still puzzled me. He *had* to know the police would ask him about it. But then, with a clearer sense of who did what and why, I remembered a small detail. *Now* it made sense. And *now* I knew what Stu was looking for earlier.

"Okay, if no one objects I don't see why not," he said. "Though I don't see why, either."

"I always figure, better to have too much than too little," Pish said. "And this *is* Merry's home, after all."

The producer nodded. "If the rest of you are all right, let's roll. What do we have in mind?"

"Let's wing it," I said, with a slight smile. I had no intention of letting anyone control the action but me.

Chapter Twenty-six

HUGH WAS GOING to resume his producer role while Pish and I talked with Stu Jardine and Felice Broadbent.

"The sheriff is supposed to release the scene anytime now, and then you can all pack up and go home," I said. "But I *would* like to get on tape some last thoughts."

"Where do you want to sit?" the producer asked. "I don't know if you've ever seen our show, but normally we'd do this, a conversation with the homeowner, at a table with the equipment, and you'd be reviewing the tape and audio with two of the investigators, but we don't have the tape reviewed yet to isolate what has gone on."

"Where you taped Rishelle, on the leather sofa with me on one side, Pish on the other, and one of the investigators in between?" I said. "It's just a chat. Informal would be best."

Hugh nodded. "Sure. Arnie, set up again across the coffee table."

Arnie grabbed his heavy camera and a sturdy tripod, moved around opposite the sofa, while Pish and I hustled over to sit, and set up the equipment. Arnie snapped his fingers without looking up. "Kid, get me another memory card for this camera."

Lizzie, startled, tripped, righted herself, and brought him a card.

"Not that one!" He tossed it back at her with a glare. "That's for those dinky DVR cameras the cast use. You *know* that! I need the professional camera card!"

She reddened and whirled, digging in an equipment bag and getting the right card, longer and thicker than the standard SD card for the DVR cameras. She mumbled an apology to the cameraman.

"Don't be such a dick, Arnie," Serina said as she returned her boom mic stand to position it over the sofa. She got out her meter for sound levels. "The kid is just trying to help."

"It's okay," Lizzie said. "I messed up. No big."

I caught her eye and smiled, and she nodded. One thing she had learned in the last year was that when you mess up, own up. Virgil, who had stood, probably thinking of taking Lizzie's side, sat back down and crossed his arms over his chest. He didn't look particularly happy, and I knew he was on edge about what we were doing.

Arnie inserted the card in the camera, put the full one in the plastic case, and tossed it to Lizzie. "Don't lose it!"

She nodded and slipped it into the equipment bag. We were ready to go.

"What do you want to do, Merry?" Hugh asked. "This is your shoot. You tell me how it's going to go."

He was being indulgent, and I appreciated that. It would hopefully let Pish and me spring a trap. "Can Felice come and talk to us first? Pish wanted a chance to better explain what he experienced in the castle."

Felice hustled right over, grateful, I think, to be called upon. "I can do whatever you want," she said, eagerly plopping down between us. "Felice Broadbent, speaking with

Pish Lincoln and Merry Wynter," she said, looking into the camera for the establishing shot. She said the date and time.

It turned out that she was surprisingly good at going along with our free-form chat. She stayed engaged and listened, asking my friend to first describe what he had experienced in the castle that led to him calling *Haunt Hunt*. "Merry was gone all summer," he said to Felice. "So for much of the time it was just me and my elderly aunt living here. Most of this occurred then."

"What happened first?" she asked.

"I was alone in the kitchen. Lush, my aunt, was upstairs taking a nap, and I was making dinner. There is a shelf over the counter with plastic bottles of spices on it. For no reason at all, one out of maybe ten bottles pushed out from the row and fell off."

"My goodness! What did you think?"

Pish looked thoughtful. "At the time, I thought that perhaps I hadn't put it back right. But that wasn't so. I *know* that bottle was in line with the others."

"If you knew Pish, you'd know that's so," I added in. "He's meticulous. He'd have noticed if it wasn't in line."

We chatted in that vein briefly. I was surprised by some of his experiences, which were odd, to say the least. He had been in the great hall when he heard whispers from the gallery, even though no one was there. He saw the shadow of a person in the library, but when he turned on a light it disappeared. In the wine cellar he saw a shadow, too, of what looked like someone creeping around. I have no explanation for the incidents.

Then Pish and I met eyes. It was time.

I sighed. "I've been thinking a lot about this castle and whether it is truly haunted, in the last few days. I *must* speak of the tragedies we've suffered." I looked up, and right into Hugh's eyes, where he sat slightly behind Arnie, a notebook on his lap. "Two people have been murdered here in the last couple of days, and certainly not by ghosts."

Hugh looked startled, and the camera joggled as Arnie jumped slightly. I heard a gasp from someone who then whispered, "What is she doing?" I *knew* what I was doing. I was outing a killer.

Felice stuttered, "W-what are you . . . I m-mean, what do you . . . ?" She gave up without finishing.

Pish said, "She means we've figured out which of the *Haunt Hunt* cast or crew killed both Dirk Phillipe and Todd Halsey."

"B-but Todd committed suicide," Felice said. The expression in her eyes was pure panic.

"He'd *never* do that!" Rishelle cried out.

"Why, Rishelle?" I asked, turning to look toward Todd's widow, off camera.

"Because he was raised Catholic! He'd *never* think of actually doing such a thing."

"Rishelle, just after you found him, you yourself thought he committed suicide," I said. "You're the one who said it *first*."

"I wasn't *thinking*," she sobbed. "He said a lot of stuff when he was depressed, like, he thought everyone would be better off without him around, and that he wasn't good enough for me, and that he was tired of living."

It showed that the public face and private face of someone often did not agree.

"And he had found out something that upset him." She looked at Arnie. "It upset him a lot." She took in a deep shaky breath and looked over at Stu. "And then he suspected you were planning on jumping ship, Stu. He *knew* you had another show lined up. But still, in my heart of hearts, I know he'd *never* have killed himself. We talked about it once when I was worried. When he got depressed he'd say things, but he told me then that he'd never actually do it because from his Catholic upbringing in the church he believed suicide was a mortal sin."

"Rishelle, what about the gun?" I asked. "Was it his or not?"

"It was *not!*"

"Who did it belong to?"

"I bought it, but not for myself," Stu said. "Rishelle, it *was* Todd's, like I told the cops. He's the one who wanted it. He was paranoid ever since Dirk had that weird accident last month while we were investigating in Kalamazoo."

Kalamazoo? Weird accident? Some of the cast were exchanging looks, and I remembered Millicent, Felice, and Serina exchanging similar looks in the bedroom and my sense that there was something they were not saying.

"What happened in Kalamazoo?" Pish asked.

"It wasn't *in* Kalamazoo," Hugh spoke up. "It was *near* Kalamazoo . . . a haunted cottage on a small lake nearby that the crew was investigating."

"It was three weeks ago. Someone took a potshot from the woods," Stu said. "It tore Todd's jacket. He made a huge fuss over it at first," he went on. "That's when he had me get him the gun. He wanted to protect himself and Rishelle if it came down to it. He thought some stalker was on the loose. Trust me, we get some weird threats online. But then for some reason he let it go."

"That's because he thought he knew what happened," Millicent said.

"What do you mean?" I asked, turning to watch the psychic.

"Todd was never the target of the gunshot; Dirk was."

"How do you know that?" I asked. This was all falling into place, and it meant I was not only right, but there would potentially be more evidence than I had even hoped.

"I heard them talking about it. Dirk said it was a shot at him, not Todd, and that he'd take care of it."

This was definitely what the women had been not talking about, this gunshot in the woods.

"When did Todd and Dirk talk about this?" Pish asked.

"Last week after the paranormal conference in Albany,"

Millicent said. "That's what the big fuss between them was about, why they got into a fistfight. Todd thought Dirk was dramatizing himself again, but later they talked it through. I think Dirk finally convinced him."

"It was shortly after that that your schedule changed, and you came here instead of where you were supposed to go," I said. "Is that right, Hugh?"

"I suppose. I knew about the gunshot, but I understood it was a wild shot by some hunter." He turned his attention to the psychic. "Millie, why didn't you tell me you were frightened?"

"You told us not to talk about it to outsiders, that you didn't want it getting out to the media," Millicent said.

Hugh tossed his notebook aside and looked back to me. "Where are we going with this, Merry? Pish? I'll not have my cast and crew misused."

I ignored him and instead watched the psychic. "So, Dirk was shot at, but said he knew what was going on and told everyone to drop it."

"Not everyone," Millicent said. "Just me. Everyone else had already let it go. They figured it was like Hugh said, some random gunshot in the woods from a hunter."

"Stu, did you know that isn't legal? To buy a gun for someone who wasn't legally allowed to have one?" Virgil said.

Stu shrank down in a club chair. I gave my husband a look and he rolled his eyes. Once a cop, always a cop.

"You had to know it was illegal, Stu," Hugh said. "*Everyone* knows that you can't buy a gun for someone not legally allowed to have one. It's like buying alcohol for a minor."

But Stu shook his head again.

"So the shot actually hit Todd?" I wanted to be clear.

"It didn't *exactly* hit Todd; I mean, it tore his jacket sleeve," Stu said. "I swear, I didn't mean any harm buying the gun, but Todd was my friend, and he was legit scared. Any of you would do the same thing!"

"Uh, no, we wouldn't," Felice said. "I wouldn't buy a gun for anyone! I *hate* the damn things."

The producer turned his attention back to Pish and me. "You still haven't told me what's going on here," Hugh said, standing and setting his notebook aside. "This is enough. We're stopping right now."

I stood, too, and looked at the producer. "Dirk spent some time in Autumn Vale the day after you all arrived and the next morning. He used a computer to look something up while you were all busy interviewing the librarian." I was about to fudge a wee bit, but I thought I was safe, given what I had found written on the piece of paper on the library table, in what I knew was Dirk's handwriting from the autograph he had given Mabel Thorpe. All of his scribbling, especially "Art. 400," short for Article 400, in this particular instance, related to one thing. "He was looking up your name."

Hugh looked puzzled. "*My* name? Concerning what?"

"A gun ownership permit." Article 400 of New York State Penal Law concerns gun ownership in the state.

He was silent.

"There's a list out there of everyone in New York who has a gun permit. The list was released online after someone got a hold of it using the Freedom of Information Act, and you're on it." The power of information!

"It is a legally owned handgun for my own protection," Hugh said, his tone tight with anger. "Can't an American own a gun anymore? It's my Second Amendment right."

"But it's not something you've shared with anyone, is it? And Dirk thought perhaps you were behind the random shot that caught Todd's jacket sleeve, since he was right there next to Todd but stepped away in the nick of time. Hugh, I may as well tell you now, we know what happened the night of Dirk's murder."

There was a wild jumble of voices, but I kept my focus on the producer. "Why don't you tell your cast how much you loathe this show? How you've been trying for two years to find another job, but that more and more in the industry you were becoming a pariah, in part because of your job with *Haunt Hunt*, but more particularly because of your past poor track record and your behavior on location."

"That's ridiculous!" he said. "A job is a job. No one in the industry takes this stuff seriously."

"That's somewhat true," I said. "It wouldn't matter in a lot of cases. If you were a stellar producer who took a job and made a success out of a silly ghost hunting show it would be no big deal. But your trouble goes back further. Your decisions and background on *five* past network shows were pinpointed as the reason they failed, even ones that had every potential of succeeding. You were becoming a liability. You only got *this* job with HHN because of connections with the network boss."

Stiffly, he said, "I don't know where you're going with this."

"I'm just saying . . . you don't have a great track record when it comes to making decisions, even though you talk a good game. You certainly had *me* fooled. I truly thought you were some kind of superstar in the industry. That's why I was so puzzled about why you were producing *Haunt Hunt*." I looked around at the cast and crew. "No offense, folks."

All eyes were on us, and no one moved a muscle. No one even blinked.

"You don't know a single thing you're talking about," Hugh said.

I ignored him. "Funny that with this show, the one you *desperately* wanted to fail so you could move on to a show you thought more befitting the image you've built up in your head of yourself, with your Savile Row bespoke suits and Berluti shoes, you *finally* succeeded." Sometimes, the best way to succeed was to stop trying so hard.

"In true form for you," I continued. "When you make decisions to improve a show, you fail, so when you make choices to try to sabotage a show, like bringing in psychics and encouraging them to act up, it only served to make it enormously popular." I turned to Millicent. "You were right, Millie; he *was* trying to sabotage the show. Thank you for that early insight."

"You'll never get that wining and dining travelogue show, Hugh," Pish interjected.

"It was all about the psychics, Hugh, right? The *psychics*. You were impatient, waiting for *Haunt Hunt* to be canceled, so you hired two wacky psychics. You thought viewers would ridicule them and the ratings would nosedive, but instead they skyrocketed. You were *finally* succeeding right where you did not want to succeed. The very few people you respect in the industry were starting to treat you not just as a failure, which you were used to despite your bragging, but as a *joke*."

His face was turning red, his nose looking like a Rudolph beacon. His fluffy eyebrows were drawn so low over his eyes they looked like they were buried in a nest. Despite that, he remained relatively impassive. He needed more prodding.

"You were becoming desperate to get out of the mess you were in so you could move on to something you actually wanted to do," I said.

"We're done here." He snatched up his notebook and whirled to leave.

But Stu stood and stepped in his path. "Hugh, what's this about? Don't leave; defend yourself, man!"

"He can't," Pish said, raising his voice over the whispers that were beginning to ripple through the room. "Merry is right. Hugh has been trying desperately to ditch this job for two years. When *Haunt Hunt* became moderately popular in its first year because of you and Todd, he thought that bringing on psychics would be the way to kill it for serious fans of paranormal investigation. I'm sure he told you and Todd that you had no choice in the matter, or some such mumbo jumbo. Dirk Phillipe was brought on board to destroy the show. So was Millicent. He encouraged every quirk they had, every silly impulse. Ratings were supposed to go down, not up. But they *did* go up, *way* up. Dirk Philippe was enormously popular, and he knew it. It was two narcissists colliding. Hugh tried to destroy *Haunt Hunt* and ended up making it more popular."

"That can't be true." Millicent, trembling, reached out and grabbed Rishelle's hand.

Felice, her face reddening, bolted to her feet and said, "*Now* it makes sense! I could not figure out why Hugh said one thing and did another."

"What do you mean, Felice?" Stu asked.

"He kept saying he wanted us to be a serious ghost hunting show, but then he didn't stop Dirk's antics. You guys know what I'm talking about," she said, her gaze sweeping the others. "Stu, you, me, and Todd went to him and *begged* him . . . we tried to get him to get rid of the psychics, but he wouldn't. Said it was the psychics or the show would be canceled."

"They were the most popular things about the show, you idiots," Hugh said. "You were on a hit, and I'm to blame? This woman doesn't know what she's talking about," he said, angrily waving his hand at me. "Do you honestly think I'd kill the goose that laid the golden egg?"

Interesting choice of words, I thought. Pandemonium broke out, recriminations were hurled, and Millicent, the only living psychic on the show, wept and collapsed in a heap on the couch, wailing that they all hated her.

"So, what are you saying, Merry?" Arnie asked, since there was no one else to do it. "What is this all about?"

"This is about who killed Dirk Philippe and Todd

Halsey." My words cut through the noise and silence fell. Everyone watched me.

Rishelle spoke first. "Who killed my husband? Do you know? Because he did *not* kill himself. I know what I said that night he died, but I was distraught. Since then I've been trying to tell everyone he wouldn't do it, including that dork of a sheriff."

Virgil snorted faintly in the background, but we all ignored him.

"Merry, Pish, if you have something serious to say, then say it," Hugh said. "Otherwise, stop right now. I won't have my cast and crew—and myself—subjected to your amateur guesswork and grandstanding. It's all innuendo and insinuation. I told Todd when he wanted to come here that I didn't like the idea that you had these murders here before."

Aha! Bunch of stuff there. I looked at him and smiled. "That's funny, Hugh. You've been messing up on that. Sometimes you say you didn't know about the murders, and sometimes you say you did know about them and so didn't want to come here. You can't have it both ways." It was true; liars usually do trip themselves up at some point. "You've been saying all along that Todd is the one who wanted to come here, and I was told that he had even lied to cancel the place where you were supposed to go this weekend."

Stu nodded. "I know for sure it was Todd who wanted to do this."

"That's because Hugh is a great manipulator, Stu. He made Todd think it was all his idea. But in truth, it was all Hugh." I turned back to the producer. "Wasn't it? *You're* the one who canceled the other shoot, calling them as Todd. And then you told Todd the homeowners had postponed, and 'encouraged' Todd to choose Wynter Castle," I said, sketching the air quotes. "Todd did what Todd always did, took credit for ideas even when they weren't his own. And you did it *because* of the murders in our past, not in *spite* of them. Just another example of Murder Castle working its magic." My tone was dripping with bitterness, which I felt down to my soul.

But Hugh was silent. And that wasn't good.

"Hugh, *say* something!" Stu cried.

"Stu, shut up! This woman has *nothing*. She's grasping at straws, fancies herself as an investigator."

Pish faced the producer. "So, if that's true, who do you think, among your cast or crew, killed Dirk?"

Calming and taking a deep breath, Hugh said, "We *know* who did it." He turned to Rishelle. "I'm sorry, sweetheart, but your husband did it; Todd killed Dirk. He found out about your little prank and went out and altered it to be deadly. He got the idea because of that accidental shot in Michigan, which really *was* just a stray bullet, despite their wild imaginings. Todd was out of control with jealousy over Dirk's popularity. *You* remember his behavior at the last paranormal conference. He sulked like a little girl and then he and Dirk had that raging argument."

"He did *not* kill Dirk! Why are you saying that, Hugh?" Rishelle was trembling, and tears started in her eyes. Despite having an affair, she did love her husband. The fling with Arnie was her effort to retaliate against his ongoing affair with Serina; Todd's affair with Serina was his attempt to self-medicate away his depression.

"So, Hugh, was it you who guided the Ouija planchette to Todd's name to put the accusation out there?" I said.

"That's ridiculous!"

"Someone did it. Todd was overheard, you know, the night he died," I continued. "Sitting in the van, talking on the phone . . . he was overheard threatening someone with exposure. Who do you think he was talking to?"

"You seem to know so much," the producer said. "Why don't you tell me?"

I had thought that Hugh, who was a classic narcissist,

would crack and brag, but instead he was so disciplined he was giving me nothing. "Well, I can tell you whose phone it was."

Hugh was silent, watching me.

"Wait," Stu said, bolting up, his hands going to his jacket pocket automatically. "Is that where my phone went? I haven't been able to find it since last night. Did someone steal it and use it to talk to Todd?" He turned and eyed everyone, but his gaze settled on Hugh.

I could almost see the penny drop. There was silence for a long minute; everyone seemed stunned, holding their breath.

"You," Stu said, glaring at Hugh. "*You* stole my phone and used it to talk to Todd so the phone call wouldn't be traced back to you."

Hugh sighed with exaggerated weariness. "Stu, *anyone* could have stolen your phone. You're continually laying it around everywhere."

"But not everyone was downstairs on the night Dirk died," I said. "I thought you were coming down when I met you on the stairs, but you pulled a classic trick." I glanced at Lizzie. "If you're trying to sneak in and are almost to the top but get caught, turn around and folks will think you're heading *down*, right?" He had been in bare feet; there was a reason for that. I would have wondered what was up if he had on his heavy housecoat and his expensive Berluti shoes. He was the kind of guy who would have Giuseppe Zanotti slippers. "And not everyone was trying to hide that they were really the one who canceled the shoot scheduled for this weekend in favor of a place where multiple murders had occurred."

"I knew nothing about that! Not . . . not *before* we came. I misspoke earlier, that's all. I meant once we got here and I found out about the murders, then I told Todd we shouldn't have come."

"That's not true, Hugh," Pish said, gently. "We talked about it the very first day we spoke on the phone. I told you far too much; you have a great deal of charm, even over the phone."

"You *knew* we had a history of recent tragic murders. And I think you knew that Todd not only had a gun, but had it with him." I paused for effect, remembering the scene of Hugh comforting Todd on the terrace, as the ghost hunter stared at me talking to Urquhart in his sheriff's car. I think Todd, worried that the cops would find the gun on him, had told his boss, who reassured him that he'd take care of it. That was guesswork, but it fit. I finished my speech with, "*And*, not everyone was in the right place at the right time to attempt to shoot Dirk at the previous incident in Michigan. Dirk had that figured out after a little investigation of his own; he *knew* it was you shooting at him in the woods in Michigan—not Todd—and was using it to blackmail you into producing his next show." Dirk couldn't have been sure that it was Hugh shooting at him, but it was clear that he had done some research and discovered Hugh's love of guns and his handgun permit.

I watched the producer and felt Virgil's tension radiating; if Hugh made a move toward me, he'd find himself on the floor with his arms pinned behind his back. The producer was giving us nothing. I was beginning to wonder if this was a mistake. "Dirk had big plans, and you were going to be tied to him for the rest of your professional life. So the narcissist psychic had to die to kill the show. And then, when Todd realized what had happened and was using it to pressure you, *Todd* had to die. Which was fine. You had prepared before Dirk's murder to make it look like Arnie was guilty, but this worked better and you adjusted. You staged Todd's death as a suicide, knowing there was a good chance he'd be blamed for Dirk's murder. You'd see to that."

I paused and it felt like the whole group was holding its

breath, silence so profound you could hear a pin drop, almost literally. But no one said a word. I scanned them; they were stunned, minds racing, breath held.

"You are out of your mind," Hugh said.

"Todd figured it out, didn't he?" I asked Hugh. "So he took over where Dirk left off, pushing you to bankroll and produce a show all of his own. He'd heard that Stu was flying the coop using an idea they had discussed together about ghosts and murder victims, and was angry. You would have *never* been free to produce the shows you want to do, for the intellectual audience you think you're aligned with. You killed Dirk to get out of one mess, only to find yourself in another with Todd. It was your last shot to escape *Haunt Hunt*, regain your reputation, and produce your wine, travel, and fine dining shows."

Hugh sighed, the much put-upon innocent. "I don't have to listen to this. I'm leaving."

Arnie strode forward and grabbed him by the arm. "You're not going anywhere until you answer. Did you kill Dirk and set me up for it, like she says?"

But Rishelle spoke instead. "*That's* why you sent me out to find Todd," she said, her voice hollow.

I gasped. "Rishelle, are you saying Hugh *sent* you to look for Todd? You didn't say that before."

She looked blank and shook her head. "Didn't I? I guess . . . I guess I was so upset . . . Hugh tapped on my door and asked if I knew where Todd was." She turned back to Hugh. Tears streamed down her face. "I got up and was worried. But you *knew* he was dead because you killed him, and that's why you sent me out to find his destroyed body. You *bastard*!" She flew at him, flailing with her fists, but hit Arnie instead, and all three went flying.

That's when Virgil stepped in.

Chapter Twenty-seven

※ ※ ※

H E SEPARATED THEM forcibly, while Pish called the sheriff and Lizzie ran outside to get one of the sheriff's deputies who were still at the scene. Chaos ensued for a few minutes, but the deputy and Virgil between them subdued the culprit, and soon Urquhart arrived. With Virgil's help, he sorted out the proceedings.

And yet . . . nothing was resolved. I was deeply troubled. Not only had my little scheme not gotten a confession out of Hugh, I may have intolerably interfered with the investigation to the point that it was contaminated. I had hoped for so much more, even a confession on tape. Urquhart had asked for my help and I had been eager to offer it, but instead, I may have bumbled things terribly. From beginning to end Hugh played me for a fool. I could remember many instances where I thought I understood what was going on because of my familiarity with the show business world, when all along I was as clueless as Millicent. Hugh schmoozed me good.

And yet he had made a lot of mistakes and taken many chances. I had to hope those cracks would reveal the truth.

Urquhart rounded them all up, the whole cast and crew of *Haunt Hunt*, confiscated the memory cards of our interview and conversation, and ferried them to the sheriff's department for formal statements. Virgil went with them, so Lizzie, Pish, and I were left alone, sitting in the kitchen awaiting news.

I felt lower than I had in ages. I made tea for Pish and me, and hot chocolate for Lizzie, then moped while Pish and Lizzie cleaned up the kitchen, shooting me worried looks. No one felt like eating Virgil's chili, but it would keep for another day. There was only one thing that would make me feel better, and that was learning that I hadn't fumbled things so badly that Hugh, who I knew darn well was a double murderer, got off.

The door knocker banged, and I ran through the great hall and threw open the door. Emerald stood there, looking over her shoulder at all the *Haunt Hunt* vans and equipment.

"I thought they'd all be gone by now! I've heard the wildest rumors in town, and I didn't know what to believe. I just got back and came to pick up my daughter, who I hear is *still* here, and who skipped school today!"

"She told me she had a PD day today. I should have known to check with someone else."

Emerald sighed in disgust. "What's this I hear about *another* death? What's going on?"

"Come on to the kitchen and we'll explain everything."

She had barely gotten seated when Janice and Shilo showed up. Hannah called, and I put her on the laptop on Skype so she could join the conversation. I was whining about what had gone on, when Emerald held up one hand.

"Wait, what? Are you saying *no one* knew what was going on behind the scenes with Todd and Dirk and Hugh?"

"Yeah," I said, looking at her in mystification. "Why?"

"That whole group . . . what a bunch of drunks! Thursday night at the bar, a couple of them said some stuff that doesn't line up with that."

"Like what?" I asked.

"Well, there was a lot. I mean, the big guy with the wild hair, the one wearing the toque . . ."

"That's Arnie Ball, the cameraman."

"Okay . . . he was teasing the girl . . ."

"Serina Rogers, who is the main sound engineer."

"Sure . . . Anyway, he was saying something to her about why did she like so-and-so and not him."

"She was having an affair with Todd. I guess it was more general knowledge than I'd thought."

"And Arnie was talking to the Asian guy . . ."

"Chi-Won Zhu . . ."

". . . and said when he was producer on Hugh's new show, maybe Chi could be the technical adviser. They'd have a chance to travel abroad, since it was going to be something international."

"Sure, okay, but that still doesn't say anything other than that Hugh was planning some other show and Arnie knew about it. It's interesting that Arnie had aspirations to produce, but Hugh made no secret of the fact that he wanted to do a fine dining and travel program."

"But then Chi made a joke. He was *so* drunk! I've never seen *anyone* that drunk. I tried to cut him off, but my boss said if I didn't keep serving, I'd be fired. He wasn't driving, so I kept serving him. *Anyway*, he was talking out loud, but with no one there, you know? He was talking to himself, mumbling and slurring. But I *think* he said, '*You and me are gonna take care of it . . . gonna take care of all of it. Dirk'll be done, gone, and I'll be the producer then, not effin' Arnie useless Ball.*' I was surprised because he had seemed so friendly with Arnie."

"*You and me . . .*" I sat up straight. "Wait, Em . . . Could he have said '*Hugh and me*,' not '*you and me*'? Is that possible?"

Emerald stared at me for a long minute. "Yeees," she said, her eyes blank for a moment as she considered. "Yes, actually that makes a whole lot more sense, doesn't it, given that he was alone at the time he was talking? That is *exactly* what he could have said."

Chi had seemed so . . . so normal, besotted with the flaky psychic, just a quiet, nice guy. Besotted with the psychic . . . wait . . . when had that happened? I hadn't noticed it at first, but there was a moment when that changed. It wasn't until I questioned why a guy like Chi, with so many skills and such a great résumé, would be working on a lowly reality ghost hunting show. He said he had *personal reasons*, and after that he started making up to Millicent, who looked surprised, but willing to go along with it.

A whole bunch of stupid random details dropped into place. As we already knew, it wasn't Arnie who had been unhirable because of a lawsuit, it was Chi. Hugh must have gone to bat for him and hired him onto *Haunt Hunt* so he'd have a willing lackey, as proved by Chi's drunken mutterings.

I called Virgil, dancing around anxiously in the kitchen, waiting for him to answer. I babbled out everything Emerald had just said and what I thought, but he was skeptical. He'd see, he told me. A half hour later he called. "Hey, Merry. How is it going there?"

"Just hunky." I waited.

"Good, good to hear."

"Come *on*, Virgil, no messing around. What's going on? Have you found anything out?"

He chuckled. "You could say that. We have a full confession. Chi-Won Zhu told Urquhart everything, how he couldn't get a job because of his problems with the studios—a giant lawsuit, I understand, that made him uninsurable—how he worked with Hugh before, how Millicent and Rishelle asked for his help to set up a prank against Dirk, and how he told the producer about it. Hugh asked him to alter the prank on Dirk. He constructed the spring mechanism to be strong enough to move something heavy, but the two women didn't know that. The three of them then set it up with the light tool belt on it. But Chi made some excuse to return to the garage, and set the heavy toolbox up on the spring."

"So *that's* why Chi wasn't with them when they came in! And the video camera . . . I'll bet Rishelle and Millicent counted on him setting it to record and he just didn't, or he turned it off when they weren't looking, most likely. I was trying to think of some fancy technical reason, but it was probably that simple. He lingered to set up the prank to kill instead of startle."

"All Hugh had to do was follow Dirk out to the garage and make sure he died. We're pretty sure the toolbox didn't kill Dirk right away, that Hugh had to bash him on the head with it. And yes, you're right about the footage, it *does* show Hugh sneaking out to the garage after Dirk, and Hugh's wearing a wig and toque, but with his shiny Berluti shoes still on."

"That was one of his few mistakes; those shoes were evident even in that night footage." And that was why, when I caught him on the stairs, he had bare feet. He was sneaking *in*, not *out*, and had his shoes clutched under his bathrobe, so I wouldn't wonder. He must have hidden the bathrobe somewhere to slip on when he came back into the house but forgotten about his shoes. I said all that to Virgil.

"Yeah, that's probably true. The shoes have now been tested, and though they have been cleaned, they do show traces of blood in the stitching. Chi still insists that Hugh was solely responsible for setting Todd's murder up to look like suicide. He apparently drew the line at up-close murder."

"But Dirk's death . . . it's premeditated murder," I said,

realizing it suddenly. "Hugh came prepared with a wig to imitate Arnie, and Chi knew about it the first night."

"Yeah, that's true. If that hasn't occurred to Urquhart, I'll be sure to mention it. They've both been arrested and charged."

It was over. Finally.

IT WAS ALREADY DECEMBER 15. WE NEVER DID FIGURE out what Pish was experiencing in the way of haunting occurrences, but he didn't seem to mind. He said if there were Wynter ghosts occupying the castle along with us, well, it was their place, too! They could toss stuff around as long as they didn't throw anything at him.

The weather was icy and had been for a week, but that was good because the ground was frozen. It meant there would be less damage. There were a lot of people crowded round looking cold and miserable, but unwilling to leave the Wynter Castle property. Shilo, bundled up in a hand-knit shawl over her winter parka—which was a little too snug across her growing belly—and a knitted Nordic-print hat with earflaps and a long tassel, stayed close to me, huddling for warmth. Lizzie and Emerald, Hannah with Zeke and her parents, Simon and Janice Grover, Gogi with Doc, who sat in a lawn chair, watching my drive, and many more were present.

Inside, the castle was decorated for Christmas. There were enormous Christmas trees in the great hall by the fire-place, in the library and the dining room. I had already set up the dining room with huge commercial coffee urns and tea urns, as well as two large slow cookers with mulled cider, and trays and trays of treats from Binny's Bakery and my own freezer. This was going to be kind of a Christmas party, though we had another purpose for gathering.

Pish, dapper in a long camel hair coat and tweed muffler—

the scarf was my gift to him from New York—came trotting up the drive. "They're coming!" he hollered. "They're coming around the bend any second!"

And then an "oh!" of surprise sounded from the crowd as his words came true.

First the truck cab, then its load, hove into view, taking the long curve of my drive. And on the flatbed was the article itself, the big Craftsman-style house Virgil and I had purchased, built a foundation for near the Fairy Tale Woods, and which was now being moved into place. I jumped up and down in excitement. I had been at the site in Autumn Vale the day before to watch them load the house on the trailer, and had driven out this morning to make sure the journey started, but it was Virgil and his partner, Dewayne, who had overseen the professional company that was moving it, with Turner Construction's assistance.

I held my breath as it came up the slope. Oh, I hoped it went all right!

"That house looks like crap," Lizzie said, snapping photos all the time. She had been with me the day before, documenting the first part, had accompanied me that very morning for the start of the journey, and had been down on the road taking photos as it lumbered along the worst stretch, hemmed in by a rock face and steep decline, along the road to my property. She paused and grabbed a different lens from her Spider holster, her gift from me from New York. It's a handy device around her waist allowing her to grab lenses and even the camera itself, all easily, rather than from a camera bag slung over her shoulder.

"You wait," I said, squeezing Shilo to me. My lovely friend's shawl was feather soft and warm as toast, my gift to her. I had bought it at a specialty shop in Manhattan. Her hubby, Jack, was in the cab of the truck moving our house, too excited to be kept out of the action. I smiled at my teen friend. "You wait, Lizzie. It's going to be beautiful. We'll be moved in by spring."

Pish, out of breath despite being in great shape for a man of his years, puffed up to me, his cheeks red and his face wreathed in a smile. "I didn't think they'd make that turn, but they're doing great."

Virgil drove up and he parked. He and Dewayne climbed out, and Virgil strode over to me, his eyes gleaming with excitement. Dewayne joined Patricia, his lady love and locally the best cake baker, and gave her a long kiss. Lizzie angled her camera over the table on which I had the plans and renderings laid out and took a photo, as a brisk breeze riffled them.

"What do you need a picture of that for?" I asked.

She shrugged. "Better too many than not enough photos. You'll want this all recorded. Plus, I may use it in my blog."

The layout, drawn up by Elwood Fitzhugh, the former and current local zoning commissioner, was the plan for Wynter Acres, our new experimental arts community. My Craftsman-style home was the first of hopefully ten to fifteen rescued homes from Autumn Vale. Months before I had noticed valuable old houses in so many different styles abandoned in Autumn Vale. Most were slated to be torn down for some revitalization that was happening. They would be replaced by the new sheriff's department, as well as a possible site for a fully functional community mall, a combination of city hall, municipal offices, local library, and a recreation center for young and old alike, all accessible for persons of every ability.

I was excited. While Autumn Vale was experiencing an unexpected revitalization, thanks to forward-thinking people like Gogi, Wynter Castle was to become, after Virgil and I finished our home and moved to it, the summer home of the Lexington Symphony Orchestra and Opera

Company, much like the Tanglewood Music Center is for the Boston Symphony Orchestra. This was all Pish's doing. When he first broached the idea I was not only skeptical but horrified by the thought of my castle being invaded, but I felt completely different now that I knew my husband and I would have a human-size home to call our own.

Elwood's plan was a tangible layout, showing the new road through the property, which was already under construction. We had started fund-raising for the performing arts building, which would be on the far side of the property near the woods directly opposite the Wynter Wood Arboretum. If it all worked out according to Pish's plan, there would be indoor and outdoor concerts in the summer. In the fall, winter, and spring there would be a series of artistic retreats, ballet camps, writing retreats, and room for conferences on the arts. Separate sketches showed Elwood and Pish's vision of the garage made over into a chic carriage house–style residence, a new facility for the orchestra and opera to perform, and the homes, some of which we had already lined up.

A few of Pish's artistic friends in New York, many patrons and contributors of the LSO and the opera company, had expressed interest in buying or leasing the houses as vacation retreats. We are a ways from New York City, true, but not out of reach, and we are close to Buffalo, Rochester, Niagara, and Niagara-on-the-Lake, where the Shaw Festival was held every year, Stratford in Ontario (and the Shakespeare festival there), and the Finger Lakes Musical Theatre Festival. It was exciting and scary, but overwhelmingly good news for the village and surrounding area. I hoped.

The whole event, moving our home to its new foundation, took an hour. There were traumatic moments but overall, with the ground frozen, it was relatively trouble-free. Once the house was parked next to the new foundation, that was it for the day. I invited everyone, including the crew of the house moving company, whom we would be working with on other moves, to come join us in the castle for coffee, tea, drinks, and treats. A House Moving Christmas Thanks to Autumn Vale party!

Using the ramp I had Turner Construction build, Hannah, in her motorized wheelchair, entered my castle through the front entrance for the very first time and laughed out loud. My castle was now truly accessible and would become even more so, with an elevator in the works for one end of the gallery. I was weak with gratitude as I stood in the dining room and watched them all, my old friends, my new friends, my new family, all drinking, talking, laughing, and chatting. Pish eventually sat down at the piano near the fireplace and began playing the opening of the Queen of the Night aria, and Janice good-naturedly went along until she got to the difficult part, when Pish switched swiftly to a show tune, "I'm Gonna Wash That Man Right Outa My Hair" from *South Pacific*. Janice saucily fluffed her husband's hair at the same time, though Simon admittedly did not have much left to fluff.

Then came Christmas songs. As they sang about carols at the spinet, Virgil grabbed my hand and my coat and we escaped; he led me on the long walk to the back of our property. We stood staring up at the big Craftsman-style house that was still sitting on the flatbed, ready to be hoisted into place on the morrow. Becket, who had followed us away from the tumultuous fray, wound around our feet and purred. He'll be happy to move with us, I think, to a home away from the artistic madness within which Pish thrived.

"Can you believe it?" I asked, held close to Virgil's chest by his tight grip.

"Not yet," he murmured into my hair. "I'll believe it when we move in."

"And you still don't mind selling your house in Autumn Vale?" I asked, twisting to look up at him. He had used the money to buy, move, and renovate this home.

"Nope. This is going to be perfect."

I shivered. "It's cold. Let's go back home." He turned with me and we walked, but then we stopped and looked at the castle. "Home for the moment, then we'll be saying the opposite."

Virgil turned us back to look at our for-the-moment mobile home. "After we move, when we're at the castle visiting Pish, we'll say, *Let's go home* and mean there."

"Mmm. I can't wait."

We stopped for one last kiss, caught exactly halfway between the castle and the construction site. Halfway between our present and our future.

Halfway to heaven.

Recipes

Gluten-Free Pecan Pie Muffins

Makes 12 muffins

1 cup brown sugar
½ cup coconut flour
2 cups finely chopped pecans (leave a few in larger chunks)
⅔ cup softened butter
2 eggs, beaten

Preheat oven to 350° F.

Grease muffin cups generously or the muffins will stick! I used butter-flavored spray oil. Don't use paper liners, since they will not peel off these muffins easily. In a medium bowl, mix brown sugar, flour, and pecans. In a larger bowl beat butter and eggs together. Combine dry ingredients into wet until just combined. This batter will be gravelly and dense. Spoon batter into muffin cups until ⅔ full.

Bake for 15–17 minutes. These will not rise much, so don't be surprised! Let cool slightly and then run a knife around the sides of the muffins to ease them out.

When these are still warm, they are awesome with vanilla ice cream and caramel sauce.

Merry's Hot Chocolate Muffins

Makes 12–18 muffins

1½ cups all-purpose flour
½ cup unsweetened cocoa powder
½ cup white sugar
1½ teaspoon baking powder
1 teaspoon baking soda
½ teaspoon salt
½ cup milk chocolate chips (optional)
¾ cup milk
⅓ cup vegetable or canola oil
1 large egg, beaten
1 teaspoon vanilla extract
⅔ cup miniature marshmallows, plus more for the top

Preheat oven to 400° F.

Line 12–18 muffin cups with paper liners, OR spray with spray oil. In a medium bowl sift flour, cocoa powder, sugar, baking powder, baking soda, and salt. Put the chocolate chips (if using) in with the dry ingredients and mix. This is so they don't sink to the bottom of the muffin cup. In a larger bowl, whisk together the milk, oil, egg, and vanilla extract. Add the dry ingredients and stir until just combined. Add the first measure of miniature marshmallows to this mixture.

Fill the muffin cups ⅔ full. Make sure mini marshmallows are not showing at the top of the muffin batter, or they'll melt too much and be sticky! Bake 18–24 minutes, or until a wooden toothpick inserted in the center comes out clean. If you want these to look like cups of hot chocolate, use a thin chocolate glaze over them and stick on more of the tiny marshmallows! These are cute served in small coffee mugs, as they look like cups of hot chocolate.

Virgil's One-Derful Chili Con Carne
Serves 6–8 people

Merry calls it "one-derful" because it takes one of each of most ingredients. It can easily be doubled or tripled.

Olive oil
1 lb. lean ground beef
1 lb. mild or hot Italian sausage meat
1 medium to large yellow onion, diced
1 pepper—green, red, whatever color you like! Diced.
1 stalk celery, diced
1–3 cloves garlic, minced, depending on how garlicky you
   like your chili
1 pound fresh cremini mushrooms, sliced, OR 1 can sliced
   mushrooms
28-ounce can tomatoes, with liquid, diced
6-ounce tin tomato paste
1 cup water (more or less to thin or thicken; add more as
   chili simmers if you want the chili thinner)
14-ounce can red kidney beans
1 teaspoon garlic powder
1 teaspoon Old Bay seasoning
1 heaping teaspoon brown sugar
1–3 heaping tablespoons chili powder
1 tablespoon chili flakes (optional)

½ teaspoon cayenne (optional)
Salt and pepper to taste, but not until near the end!

Additions to serve it with:
Hot sauce (optional)
Chopped green onion
Sour cream
Corn chips or tortilla chips.

Pour one turn of the olive oil bottle into a Dutch oven or stock pot and get the pot hot. Brown the ground beef and Italian sausage meat, adding in batches so the meat browns and doesn't just steam or boil. Remove and set the browned meat aside.

Add a little more olive oil, if necessary, and wilt the onions, pepper, and celery until onions are translucent. Then add garlic (you don't want it to burn, or it will turn bitter) and the mushrooms, cooking until the mushrooms are softened.

Add the browned meat back into the pot with the vegetables, then add: tomatoes, tomato paste, water (one cup or enough to thin the mixture appropriately) kidney beans and bring up to a simmer.

Add: garlic powder, Old Bay, brown sugar, chili powder, and if using, chili flakes and cayenne.

**Slow cooker instructions*: You can put the browned meat, wilted vegetables, and all the other ingredients in a slow cooker. Mix, and set it on high for an hour or so, and then on low for the rest of the time, a few hours at least.

Simmer on very low for at least a couple of hours, checking occasionally to be sure it is not getting too dry. Stir it to be sure it's not sticking on the bottom. Add more water, tomato sauce, or *passata* (passata is an uncooked tomato puree in a bottle) if desired, for a richer sauce. Taste just before serving and add salt, pepper, chili powder or anything else you feel it needs for flavor.

Serve in bowls topped by any one or combination of the following: sour cream, grated cheese, green onions or scallions, or set out the toppings in bowls and let your guests add whatever they wish. Accompany it with buttered bread, biscuits, or tortilla chips.

This is a delicious potluck meal in a slow cooker, and the leftovers are often even better. In fact, you can make a large batch ahead, then heat and serve in the slow cooker. It also freezes well (once cooled) for an easy meal any time!

Ready to find
your next great read?

Let us help.

Visit prh.com/nextread

Penguin
Random
House